GIRLFRIEND, INTERRUPTED

Patricia Caliskan

GIRLFRIEND, INTERRUPTED

Published by Sapere Books.

20 Windermere Drive, Leeds, England, LS17 7UZ,
United Kingdom

saperebooks.com

ISBN: 978-1-912546-51-0

Chapter One: Capital Punishment

It hadn't occurred to me that the love of my life would turn out to be somebody else's dad. If I'd thought about it long enough I'd have realised, the best thing that happened to me ended up being the worst thing that happened to Dan's kids. Well, at least since the divorce anyway. And, if it was any consolation to them, I got a second-hand romance. It wasn't exactly the kind of thing you'd look out for in a dating profile:

Brown-eyed, brunette, 25.
Enjoys walking barefoot across shards of broken home.
Likes loaded silences, festering resentment and insomnia.
Dislikes romantic weekends, sexy lie-ins and any chance of future happiness.
Former GSOH. Developing PTSD.

But, as with all great love affairs, it hadn't started out that way. Those two, very separate worlds had slowly collided. We never really talked about what that meant. I mean, how could a man love you if his children didn't even like you? You've probably already guessed, but that was exactly the question I'd been trying to avoid lately as I made my way into the office Friday morning. Only a few hours ahead of being utterly useless around the children for yet another weekend. Although, I thought, glancing over at reception, it was a far better option than falling in love with somebody else's husband…

'I am going to leave her, Karen!' Harry Collins, Head of Digital, was leaning over the reception desk. 'I promise I will, but it's not that easy. I've got three children to think —' He flinched at my footsteps. 'So, those er … those staples? We'll need at least another two boxes up there…'

Suddenly scrutinizing her to-do list, Karen-From-Reception, all blow-dry and diamante earrings, rearranged her cardigan. Scribbling everything down with a professionalism bordering on the provocative.

'And those A5 notebooks, please, like we said.' He pretended he'd only just noticed me. 'Not the A4.' He raised a hand. 'Ah, morning Ella!'

'Morning, Karen. Harry…'

The three of us exchanged polite smiles as I carried on towards the stairs, avoiding the lift in case I ended up stuck in there with him.

Steen & Heard Communications was located on the second floor of a listed building on Hanover Street. Sunlight streaked through the blinds as I fixed my jacket onto my chair and opened my first email of the day:

URGENT!
FOR IMMEDIATE ACTION.
ACCOUNT DATA FOR PREVIOUS 12 MONTHS!!!

This was a typical greeting from Heather Constantine, Public Relations Manager extraordinaire. I'd found the best way to deal with her emails was to pretend they were computer-generated by a machine too primitive to know any better. Although, the 'Read Receipt' she included on every message was particularly annoying. Especially when she sat close enough to accept my offer of a Smint without leaving her seat.

I glanced over at her, peering behind her bifocals. Her short, sharp, red hair, hinting at her short, sharp disposition. She scrutinised her screen, searching out juicy worms of commission fit for the taking. First thing in the morning, her lack of hello, eye contact, please or thank you, had the same effect as having a jug of iced water poured over your head. In fact, I'd have chosen the ice bucket challenge every time.

Heather Constantine was the reason I dreamt about being sacked the way other people dreamt about winning the lottery.

Initially, I had worked for James Steen (who was really posh and semi-retired, which is what really posh people aged around sixty seemed to do), and his partner, Audrey Heard, as a copywriter. I was initially hired to write press releases, manage website copy, oversee editorial pieces for our clients, that kind of thing. But within weeks, Heather made me into her unofficial personal assistant and psychological punch bag. Nowadays, I took care of her admin, weekly diary and, on one occasion, a furious outbreak of cystitis, rather than becoming some kind of capable business protégé to her wise mentor-figure, the way Audrey seemed to think it worked.

'Morning, Ella!'

Leah, Office Support, walked in behind Harry. Her neon-painted grin brightened the shadow of Heather, looming permanently over the rest of our day.

'Morning, Heather…'

The typing continued.

Leah hung up her coat and straightened her skirt.

'Would you like a cup of tea, Heather?'

Heather glanced at her watch.

'Ten minutes ago. I trust you'll be deducting the time from your lunch hour?'

I gave Leah a sympathetic look. Heather classed five-past-nine as unforgivably late. The only time she'd left the office for anything other than a meeting was when she gave birth to her son.

'Would you like a coffee, Ella?'

'I'd love one, please.' I was deliberately perky. I hoped Heather might pick up on more pleasant ways to interact with other human beings. 'Thanks for asking. Hey, Leah — we made it! No matter what happens, they'll *never* take Friday away from us…'

'Make sure you use my almond milk.' Heather's fingernails clawed at high-speed across her keyboard.

Almond milk? I'd never heard of it. I wondered if they made it especially for people like Heather, who must have problems with turning the regular stuff sour.

'Will do.' Leah smiled, not wasting another minute. She paused briefly at Harry's desk to take his order as he fired up multiple screens on the digital bank.

Harry headed up a team of three almost identical lads. They all wore beards, checked shirts and sprayed-on jeans. As far as I knew none of them had any interest in harvesting trees, but you'd've sworn they'd just trekked back from an Alaskan Lumberjack convention. Either that or been knitted as a matching set by someone's well-meaning grandma. I'd tried striking up conversation with them in the past, but they only communicated in instant messages. And, while the rest of us lived on the stuff, none of them drank tea or coffee, even though it was the lingua franca of our offices. Maybe there'd been some sort of technological advancement, I thought. Apple had launched the *iRefreshment* while the rest of us still stood around, boiling the kettle.

'Is almond milk good for you?'

Heather caught my eye, standing to unlock her filing cabinet.

'Well, obviously.' She inhaled a laugh, combing through an assortment of colour-coded files. 'I wouldn't be drinking it if it were bad for me, now would I?'

I wasn't sure if she was trying to make a joke or not.

I'd never learned to speak fluent Dictator.

'It's vegan friendly. Cholesterol and lactose-free. Those things are bad for you,' she explained as if talking to a three-year-old. 'So, yes. It is.'

She shut the metal drawer with a *thunk*!

Heather was vegan? I was surprised. You'd have imagined most vegans being quite nice to the people they worked with, considering they were so kind to animals.

'Good morning!'

All heads turned as Audrey Steen, lady boss and agency owner, walked in, looking chic as ever. All curled lashes and nude lip gloss. Wearing my favourite outfit of hers, the grey trilby and pastel pink trench combo.

Audrey was utterly fabulous. One of those gorgeous, older ladies who crystal and diamonds cried out for, rustling up timeless glamour every morning.

'How's everything going, Heather?' She cast a brief smile of hello my way. 'Apollo doing well?'

If we hadn't already worked out Heather had a messiah complex, she'd humbly named her first-born after a Greek god.

'He's doing brilliantly.'

'Good to hear it. Did I tell you Peter's wife's expecting in the next few weeks?'

'You must be thrilled.' Heather still managed to look glacial despite the baby talk.

I'd tried mentioning Dan's kids, Grace and Ethan, to Heather once. She'd looked at me as if I'd been clipping my toenails at my desk. I'd decided to drop the topic indefinitely.

'We are. We are.' Audrey smiled. 'Listen, we really must have that catch-up. I've been meaning to put some time aside, see where we're up to.'

'Everything's back on track.' Heather squinted at Audrey with what I think was meant to be a smile, unless the sun was in her eyes. 'I'd like to schedule in a meeting with you today if that's convenient, Audrey? Four o'clock?'

'Right-o!' Audrey said. 'Well, nothing pressing springs to mind...'

'Ella?' Heather rearranged her desk. 'Could you update my diary?'

'Of course, Heather.' I wished I could schedule her in for a routine personality transplant while I was at it.

'And, by the way.' Audrey took off her hat, running her fingers through her perfect hair. 'It's great to have you back, Heather. Oh.' She glanced at Leah's desk then looked my way. 'Have I missed the first brew of the morning?'

'Coffee?'

'Please. Do you mind? I'm always in need of a complete transfusion by the end of the week.'

I noticed a faint sneer from Heather as I walked past her desk, possibly because I wasn't taking IMMEDIATE ACTION on compiling her account data. Instead, I made my way into the staff kitchen and found Leah standing against the counter, mobile in hand.

'What's the matter?'

'I'm fine.' She put her phone inside her pocket and took a teaspoon from the drawer. Then stopped, eyes flooding. 'I split up with my boyfriend.'

'Oh. That's not good.'

'But then we got back together.'

'And that's bad?'

'He's just messaged saying he thinks we should leave it tonight. And.' She checked her reflection in the mirror. 'I just can't handle Heather today. *Urgh.*' She wiped inkblots of mascara from the corners of her eyes. 'I missed the early train, doing my makeup. Now it's ruined and I'm not even seeing him...'

'Here.' I grabbed another cup for Audrey. 'You go and get yourself fixed up. I'll finish the drinks.'

'You sure?'

The kettle clicked to a halt as I busied myself at the counter.

'Thanks, Ella. Oh.' She paused on her way to the door. 'Make sure you use her special milk, whatever you do. Heather's almond milk's in there. Bottom shelf. She's labelled it.'

Of course she has, I thought. Even though everyone else in the office shared the same two-litre carton, it obviously wasn't good enough for the Constantine constitution. *Almond milk.* I stared at the weird, peachy liquid. It didn't look all that bad, but it definitely smelled a bit funny. *Sod it.* If Heather was going to stress us all out, the least she could do was lower our Cholesterol. I gave us all a free sample.

Back at my desk I found another email lying in wait to sabotage my happiness:

URGENT: FOR IMMEDIATE ACTION.
Re: SUBJECT HEADING.
Re: Previous email: Account data for previous 12 months!!!

I couldn't help but look over again.

Not a flicker.

Working with Heather was like catching a virus. You started slightly off-colour and ended up wanting to crawl under the covers, slayed by a highly contagious case of her utter misery. I found the files on the system and opened a new document. It was so bad that the thought of meeting Mum for lunch formed an emergency raft in my mind that saw me safely through to half-past twelve.

Chapter Two: Dirty Dining

I wished I'd made more of an effort as I noticed Mum through the window of our favourite bistro. I should have at least worn my new top. Maybe a quick curl of my hair wouldn't have gone amiss. She was smiling down at her mobile, immaculately blow-dried. The collar of her shirt flicked obediently as if she was about to be interviewed for some sumptuous Sunday supplement. Knowing Mum, it wouldn't surprise me.

'I know you're on a tight schedule, so I've already ordered the lemon and asparagus linguine, for both of us.'

'Thanks, Mum.' I took a seat opposite. 'Love the hair!'

'Thank you, darling. Fancied a change. A few highlights work wonders. And, I keep trying to tell you, we should do this more often.' She took a sip from her wine glass. 'I can't remember the last time you and I had a proper catch-up. You *are* coming to the theatre?'

'Oh, yeah.' I'd forgotten all about the message she'd sent in the week. 'I dunno. I need to ask Dan.'

'*Do you?*'

Mum was a relationship therapist. This was despite the fact the only piece of dating advice she'd ever given me was to carry emergency cab fare and her mobile number inside my shoe. And the fact she'd been single (*voluntarily* single, she always clarified) for the last twenty-odd years. Nowadays, Renée Shawe, Psychologist-Turned-Journalist, and regular columnist in women's magazines, was currently heading up feminist debates loosely disguised as a 'love and relationships phone-in' every Friday night on Rising Radio.

'Anyway, since when do you like interactive rock musicals?'

The Rock 'n' Roar of Thunder, it was called.

'Your mother's very cultured, I'll have you know,' she said. 'I happen to know one of the writers, actually. I get all the best invites. You know how it is. Now I'm on air, online, in print...' She gave a playful flourish, a wiggle of her head, setting down her glass. 'Anyway, aren't you going to ask what I'm doing here?' She reigned in a smile, eyes sparkling. 'Off out in Avington in the middle of the afternoon?'

'Having lunch with your daughter?'

I sipped my water as the waitress returned with our dishes.

'I've just been for a wax. *Hollywood*,' she attempted to whisper, the word almost becoming a growl. I gave the waitress a quick, apologetic smile. 'Bare as the day I was born! Bloody tender though.' She pulled a face. 'Sunburnt, I suppose, is the best way to describe it. Looks like I've been stripped off for far too long on one of those funny, little, nudey beaches.'

'Mum, we're about to eat.' I cast a look at the other ladies lunching at surrounding tables. 'Do you have to be so crude?'

'You know —' She re-rolled her shirtsleeve — 'I can understand you not wanting to hear your mother being *crude*, as you so charmingly put it, but I'll never understand why you're so uptight. It's not how you were raised.'

'Yes, I know,' I said. 'Unfortunately...'

'Pubic hair's nothing to be ashamed of, Ella. We've all got it.'

I hoped the rest of the tables were enjoying the rough draft of my mother's latest manifesto.

'Well, at least some of us have.' She giggled. 'Up until about an hour ago.'

I unfolded my napkin and sipped some water.

'Anyway, if you must ask —' She gave me one of her looks because I hadn't — 'it's all in the name of research. I'm dedicating a show to it: *Hair or Bare: The Politics inside your Pants.*

Do you know, there are young girls out there, not much older than Dan's daughter —'

'Grace,' I reminded her.

'Grace,' she said, warming to her theme, 'who actually think pubic hair's some kind of disgusting abnormality? They've seen that much porn, taken that many selfies, they think their vulvas need to be completely exposed and ready for close-ups. And, I'm sorry, but who wants a man with a shaved penis?'

'Mum!' I was about to tuck into my linguine. 'Keep your voice down! They'll think you're offering. Please, can you eat your lunch and stop bloody talking?'

'Talking's my job. It's what separates us from the animals.' She paused to spool a bale of pasta around her fork. 'So, you and Dan? Come on. You seem a little tense.'

'I'm not tense,' I snapped.

She smirked, raised her eyebrows and tucked into her lunch.

People actually call a radio station to tell my mother how they're feeling. Share their deepest, most innermost secrets with her. We'd never been so touchy-feely. Not after I'd grown up having every thought and feeling processed with a full, psychological evaluation.

'Great. Good.' I concentrated on my food, nodding along. 'Yeah, it's good...'

'Great and good? How *exciting*...'

'Why does everything have to be exciting, Mother?'

'Because you're young and in love and you shouldn't have a choice.'

I'd worked out my mother was dating through me. She was appalled someone my age would move in with a divorced man with children. I should be swinging, wild and knicker-less, into my next big mistake. The same way she'd spent most of her

20s before I'd arrived to spoil the party. *Bad decisions make better stories.* That was one of her favourite sayings.

'Well, sometimes the simple things in life can be pretty perfect.'

'You didn't say it was perfect. You said it was *great, good,* and *simple.*'

'Oh please —' I put down my fork — 'just this once, can you stop analysing every single thing, I say?'

'I'm not analysing, Ella.' She reached for her glass. 'I'm asking. And you're avoiding the question...'

'Ok, then, the weekends.' I decided to give her what she was so desperate to hear. 'If you must know, The kids, I'm still trying...' I wasn't sure how to describe it. 'We're one way together during the week. Dan and I. Then, when Dan's on Dad Duty, it's completely different. I mean, I feel like I have to start all over again every weekend.'

'When was the last time you had sex?'

'Why does everything begin and end with sex in your world?'

'Because everything begins and ends with sex in *the* world, Ella.'

'No, it doesn't.' I wondered why she still bothered asking me those kind of questions. 'And I'm not talking to you about that.' My answer was always the same: 'You're my mother.'

'Okay, then *theoretically*, I suggest you make love, not war.' She made a peace sign. 'I'd highly recommend giving Dan a little —' She smiled over the top of her glass — '*undivided attention.* Especially at the weekends...'

'He gets my undivided attention,' I managed, tongue-tied with linguine. 'But, we're both so tired during the week. Then, it's the weekend. Then the kids are around...'

'As I was saying...'

'That's not down to me.'

'Well, think of it this way. I'm guessing you weren't too tired before you moved in, or he wouldn't've bothered suggesting you unpack.' She dabbed her perfectly lipsticked mouth with her napkin. 'You need to learn to combine your romantic and physical relationship with family life. And will you please relax? *Look at you.* You can barely eat at the mention of the word *sex*. It's quite simple. You. Him. A bed…'

'The kids. His mother…'

'Incest's never an option, Ella…'

'You're disgusting.'

'I'm your mother!'

'Yes, I know.' I glanced across the room and lowered my voice. 'But no one else's mother talks this way.'

'Of course they do!' She worked at her pasta, undeterred. 'But, maybe not with their daughters.' She smiled at the trio of elderly ladies dining at the neighbouring table. 'That reminds me,' she said. 'Got you a little present. Well, it's quite a big present actually.' She let out a slightly horrific laugh. 'I get these things sent to me occasionally. Talking points for the show. And this one's quite the centrepiece. Ten out of ten reviews. And, I have to admit —' She slid a carrier bag wrapped parcel over the table — 'It gets my vote. Don't open it!' I quickly bundled the bag back in place. 'Put it away. Open it at home…'

'Oh God…' I shoved my handbag back under the table. 'I don't want some weird sex-thing, Mother.'

'You say that now…' A shadow-smile played across her lips. 'Have a wild time in the bedroom. You'll soon develop a wonderful sense of perspective. And, I know you don't want to hear it —' Her fork hovered over her dish — 'but unless you take on a more established role… Building a relationship with his kids? You won't become part of what those children consider family, until you all form one of your own. And that takes a tremendous amount of commitment. Otherwise, it's like —' she paused, borderline irate — 'running into a brick wall and expecting to turn into mortar.'

'Take on more of an established role? It's not a stage play, Mum.'

'Well, you make it all sound very dramatic,' she said, in that knowing tone I was sure she must practice just to annoy me. 'Ella, why do you look at me like that? I'm actually on your side, believe it or not. You need to know where you stand, and so do those children.' She paused to eat more pasta. 'Clear boundaries. Understandable dynamics. That's what children respond to.'

'Like you'd know.' My mouth hit the Thought Brakes too late. 'You were hardly a hands-on mother yourself...'

'I bloody was!' she insisted. 'Forgive me if I had to work really hard as a single mother!'

'Yeah, well.' I tore off some ciabatta. 'I think you left my childhood in one of your files somewhere. Marked under *Parenthood*.'

'That's not fair!'

'Life's not fair. There's another pearl I heard from you, growing up. You know all about the theory of everything. I'm the one actually living it.'

'Well, in theory, all I'm saying is, you've not long moved in with Dan. What is it? Three months?'

'Nearly five.'

'And you're stressing yourself out, trying to placate his children. Stop making life hard for yourself.' She smirked as the thought crossed her mind. 'Instead of making *other things hard*, like —'

'Yes, Mum. I know where you're going.' I lowered my voice, gesturing towards the ladies nearby. 'Zip-first, as usual.'

'Oh, they won't mind.' She cast a smile at the elderly trio, dividing up the bill at the next table. 'It's the battery of any relationship, Ella. The *tick-tick-tock* of the cock. *Clock*!' Her eyes widened. 'Freudian slip.' She laughed.

'Mother.' I put my hand to my forehead, casually shielding my face. 'You're getting worse.'

'Oh, whatever happened to your sense of humour? I'm not suggesting anything drastic. I'm just saying, maybe a little more time together would help. *Quality time*. Maybe that's what you need. I'm not criticizing.' She held up her hands, pleading innocence. 'I just happen to know you've always been a little insecure. Maybe, Dan's sensing that. Insecurity can be a major turn-off.'

'So can over-confidence.' Mum pulled a face at me. 'There's nothing wrong with me and Dan. Thanks very much...'

'I never said there was.' She sipped at her glass. 'There's no need to take your insecurities out on me, Ella.'

'And there's no need to say it's my fault I'm miserable, just because I'm not super confident like you.'

'I'm not super confident. I just accept the things I cannot change.' That took me straight back to those wooden quotation plaques my old flat mate, Kim, hung on every naked door handle. 'But, whether you like it or not, men are turned on by women who are comfortable with themselves. I've seen those pyjamas of yours...'

'What do you mean?' I was hoping they weren't the ones I thought she meant, with the nail polish down one leg and the slightly frayed sleeves. 'You should see some of the t-shirts he wears to bed,' I told her. 'Sometimes he sleeps in the same boxers he's worn all day. At least my pyjamas are clean and ironed.'

'*Ironed?*' She winced, but you'd hardly know it, not now she'd started getting a little 'help' from her beautician.

'Yes, ironed. Not creased! And pyjamas do come off you know. The buttons still work. *I think.*' I noticed a hint of amusement at the corners of her eyes, which only made me wish I'd never said anything in the first place. 'If you want me to be really honest Mum —' I picked up her glass and took a generous gulp of wine before she had chance to protest. '— my dentist spent more time inside me the last time I had a root canal. *There.* Is that what you wanted to hear?'

'Ella!' She mock-clapped her hands. 'Who knew my daughter could be so sexually assertive!'

'Dan. That's who,' I said. 'But I'm so *tense* when the children are there. I feel like —' I struggled to think. 'I feel like a kids' TV presenter or something. Imagine trying to have sex with someone's dad while the kids are watching you on TV.'

'Well, it's no wonder you look so miserable.'

'I don't look miserable!'

'Don't get hysterical. You described yourself as miserable a moment ago, without any prompting from me.' She straightened her back, adopting professional mode. 'Don't start projecting, Ella…'

'I'm not projecting. It's just…*it's boring.* There!' I faffed with my napkin, brushing away the first stirrings of guilt. 'It's all a bit boring. Happy now?'

'Ecstatic.' She almost-frowned, folding her arms. 'Are you going to explain?'

'A few months ago I was not thinking about anything remotely serious, living with Kim. Then I met Dan. I was really happy. Now, as soon as the kids have gone back to their mum, he just sits there, scrolling through his phone. And the worst part of it is, that's when he looks happiest. Apart from when the kids arrive the next week and the whole thing starts again. I just don't know where I fit in, that's all...'

'Scrolling through his mobile, looking at what? Hardcore stuff?' Mum's eyes flashed. 'Not those Virtual Reality orgies from Japan?'

'What Virtual Reality orgies from Japan?'

I was starting to wonder if my mother was some kind of functioning Nymphomaniac, conveniently disguised as a fully-trained sex therapist.

'No, don't tell me! I don't want to know.' I closed my eyes and shook my head for a second. 'He looks at normal stuff. The news. Sport. I don't know.' I loaded up another forkful of linguine. 'Unless I make the ten o'clock bulletin or win the World Cup, I may as well be in a different time zone.'

'Ella, slow down. Now you're making *me* tense.' She looked far from it, elegantly working her pasta between fork and spoon. 'Have you tried Sexting?'

'Mum, I can't go from sending text messages about what fresh veg I've picked up for dinner, to telling Dan I'm not wearing any knickers, or whatever it is you're supposed to *sext* someone.'

'And *that*, right there, is the problem. You live together. You spend your weekends with the children. You have all these shared, *boring* responsibilities,' she said. 'So it's up to you, both of you, to keep your fantasy life alive.'

'Right now, my only fantasy's me, on a beach, wearing a straw hat and a string bikini, sipping Mojitos until sunset.'

'Then book a holiday together.'

'We can't. What about the kids?'

'What about the kids? They've got their mother. You two need time alone.'

'That's not how it works, Mum. God forbid we have a free weekend, or do anything that doesn't involve buying a family ticket and a Happy Meal on the way home.'

'*Excuse me?*'

We looked up at an elderly lady standing next to our table, shopping bag resting in the crook of her arm. Her friends were oblivious, putting away spectacles, pulling on jackets, making their way over to the counter.

'I hope you don't mind me saying so, but your mother's quite right, dear.' She offered a fragile, shell-pink smile. 'If I had my Charles back, we'd spend every last minute in bed!'

'Good for you!' Mum gave me her *I-told-you-so* nod, as the lady finished buttoning her coat, following her friends to the door.

'If it was just about Dan, I wouldn't have a problem.'

'This whole stepfamily set-up's already getting to you, isn't it, darling?'

'It isn't getting to me...' I picked up my napkin and realised I'd had a piece of linguine stuck to my chin the whole time I'd been pouring my heart out. 'It's just difficult. We spend so much time talking about the kids. And I know that's the right thing to do. Putting them first and everything, but it's hard to be so considerate when they couldn't care less about me. I feel like the live-in nanny or something.'

'You'd be having a lot more sex with their father if you were the live-in nanny...' Mum muttered, almost under her breath for once. 'Even the Hollywood lot've learned that one the hard way...'

'Then maybe I need to move to Hollywood...'

'Seriously, Ella, there're hundreds of people out there, right now, having the exact same thoughts about their partner's children.'

'I know. You try looking up stepmother online. See how long it takes before you find something without the word wicked in front of it.'

Mum laughed into her glass.

'It's not funny. It hurts! I'm not a wicked stepmother.'

'No, you're not. You're Dan's partner, and you need to forget about those kids of his for five minutes.' She folded her napkin and placed it neatly on top of her dish. 'Try remembering how to be his girlfriend instead.'

Chapter Three: Recipe for Disaster

Back in our early days together, Grace and Ethan used to ask if they'd be seeing me over the weekend and would erupt with '*cool*'s and '*yes*'s, whenever Dan said that they would. Nowadays 'cool' was the last thing Grace thought about having me there, living with her dad, while her little brother didn't seem to think too much about any of it at all.

I remembered the first time I stayed over. Stepping into last night's clothes the next morning. The faint breath of last night's perfume. Every part of me every bit as delighted in daylight. We'd sank deeper into his bed that first time, until it became an ocean of us. Cinnamon warmth against white, cotton sheets. Finding each other, losing each other, all in the same second. His body seemed to swim against, beneath, inside me, for hours. Every time I closed my eyes, I heard him sighing into my hair as if his life depended on it. His kisses fossilized against my lips. Until it was suddenly morning.

A Lego man, broken on the bedside, as I looked for my loosened earring.

A small, pink dressing gown on the handle of the bedroom next door.

At first, those early traces of his children seemed to hint at the fact that he was a good guy. A *really* good guy. It didn't seem so difficult, imagining those two worlds aligning. But now, here I was. Holding Dan's hand in an oven glove.

Dan and Ethan trundled into the kitchen as I was thinking about all this. Remembering how I got there, as I set down the last plate, finally taking a seat next to Grace.

While the kids would probably have preferred me cooking up some Disney-style mission to get their parents back together that night, I'd trundled around the supermarket after work. I'd decided maybe Mum was right. A home-cooked sit-down meal might make us feel like an actual family. Deep down, I knew that was quite a lot to ask of anyone's first attempt at Italian, but a hell of a lot to ask of mine.

I knew the basics, but not on a family-scale, with children and fresh ingredients involved. When I got to the part when you were supposed to *brown* the mince, I was tempted to prop up the sun lounger and make a Pina Colada. And how the hell did you sauté an onion? *Sort-a* cook it? Unless you had a mother like mine, who refused to pass on domestic advice in favour of administering feminist theory, grown-up girls like me were already supposed to know how to do these things. So far, I'd turned to my mother for advice and all I'd got was a stupid vibrator. That's what she'd given me over lunch. And, if that wasn't inappropriate enough, it was a glow-in-the-dark, cerise pink one, called The Pulveriser.

'This looks great.' Dan reached for the pepper mill, making me feel like the type of sophisticated woman who serves mints and decaf before the carriages arrive at midnight. My old flat mate, Kim, could vouch for the fact that my signature dish was Cheesy Beans on Toast, which I still say is perfect for every occasion. Breakfast, Lunch, Dinner. In sickness and in health. I'd somehow gone from snacking my way through being single, to attempting to cater for a family of four without so much as a well-used chopping block to my name.

'I'm really not that hungry...' Grace gave a reluctant nod as her dad offered some grated Parmesan. She'd been in a foul mood since her mum and soon-to-be stepdad, Vic, had dropped them off. First of all she didn't like the clothes her mum had packed. Then she announced my lasagne tasted funny.

'Does it?' I was well aware it was a possibility.

'Tastes fine to me.' Dan carried on making conversation about Sports Day.

'*Urgh* … what's *in* this thing?' Grace grabbed her glass, washing away the taste, making her brother roar with laughter.

Dan finally looked up and told her to stop being so ridiculous. But she wasn't being ridiculous. Ridiculous could be fun; leaving us laughing around the table while she made a wig out of her spaghetti or adopted a terrible Italian accent. Grace was actually being quite smart. Figuring out if the best way to hurt my feelings was through her own stomach. She was acting like some kind of dining room Voodoo doll. I couldn't take it to heart. My lasagne was burnt around the edges and all I could taste was my own disappointment. I'd have been quite happy to save Grace the effort. Grab us a few packets of crisps and hang up my apron for good.

Dan went back to his food, while I tried to ignore the deadweight scrape of Grace's fork. Conversation reached a chest-tightening halt. The opening cords of 'Hungry like the Wolf' lightened the atmosphere, but singing along to the '*Do-Do-Doos*' only made the whole thing seem worse. I've never been very good with silence. I always get the urge to cause a distraction, which usually involves making a complete and utter show of myself. True to form, because if nothing else, at least I was consistent, I grabbed the nearest props and stuffed my mouth full of garlic dough balls for the kids: '*I'll make him an offer he can't refuse...*'

I held up my hands, pretending to be Marlon Brando.

Dan almost smiled. The kids looked at me like I was deranged, because obviously no one their age had ever heard of *The Godfather*. Or Marlon Brando.

I started to chew, but gave up for the sake of my jawbone, discretely emptying my mouth into my napkin.

'Nice manners…' Grace muttered, as Ethan gave a snort of amusement. 'This still tastes *weird*.' She slowly, almost painfully, eyed her food. 'Doesn't it, Ethe?'

She issued a threatening glance across the table before her little brother agreed that they only really like Daddy's cooking.

'I like his cooking the best too,' I admitted. 'But your dad's been dropping major hints about my lack of culinary skills.' I gave Dan a wry smile. 'So you'll have to blame him.'

'That's not true.' Dan shook his head, wearing that deep frown that always made me want to sit on his lap. 'I just wondered why you were trying to make an egg mayonnaise sandwich with raw eggs.'

'Eggs are fattening.' Grace sneered at her plate, her chin cobbled with concern. 'I don't even want to think how many calories there are in this thing.'

'It's good for you.' I reached for a second serving of Parmesan, taking my cue from Dan. Pretending we were all having a lovely time, all the while thinking how I wouldn't have even known how to spell 'calories' at her age, let alone count them. 'Freshly made.' I smiled.

'Yeah, we all know you made it, Ella. You've only told us, like —' She rolled her eyes — 'a *thousand* times. That doesn't mean it's not fattening?'

She always did that. Turned her statement into a question whenever she was talking down to people way too old to know anything.

'*Grace*.' Dan gave her the briefest of looks and turned to Ethan with a wink.

'Well!' She fixed on her dad. 'Grandma said I've never been able to digest heavy dishes like this,' she said. 'Grandma can't eat stuff like this either. She's given up dairy now, too.'

I'd already guessed it was Pippa who Grace had been chatting to on her mobile earlier. Documenting my every move like I was on a reality TV show. Both of them conferring on this weekend's excuse to vote me out:

"Ella Shawe, you have failed this week's task. The public have spoken. You can't cook for shit. You have 30-seconds to leave The Step-family Robinson House…"

'And I've got my final bridesmaid dress fitting next week,' Grace pointed out, aligning herself to a good cause. 'Mum's practically living off Superfood Smoothies. Some of us care about our figures…'

She gave me a glance which implied I definitely wasn't one of them.

Wasn't I? Fair enough, you'd hardly have had me down as a health nut, not like the kid's mum. Bryony was into Weight Training, Yoga, Pilates. All that palaver. She could probably twist the tops off her Superfood Smoothies using only Mindfulness Meditation and her Kegels. But I wasn't being peer-pressured into a leotard by a twelve-year-old.

I sipped at my water. Dan chewed on lasagne. I was grateful at least someone was eating it. While Ethan told us all about the new *amazing* football boots Vic had got for him, I passed on the rest of the dough balls. I gave up any hope of my Jamie Oliver-inspired, family-friendly version of Friday night. I was done with the cooking. I didn't need food. I needed wine.

'I meant to say —' I noticed the chirpiness of my own voice, the way I always sounded when the kids were around — 'Mum asked if we wanted tickets to that new show she was telling me about? It's one Friday, middle of next month. I've got the date somewhere on my phone...'

'Great.' Dan nodded along. 'But we're pretty full-on for the next few weeks, you know? We're at the zoo next Saturday.' He picked up his napkin and turned to Grace. 'What date's Mum's wedding?'

'The 8th. Three weeks, Dad.'

I hadn't realised the wedding was that close.

Or that Bryony was seriously going through with marrying Vic.

'Wow, that's gone quickly.'

'It's right there,' Grace insisted. 'I put it on the calendar.'

Grace was always putting things on the calendar. Every weekend was outlined with her and Ethan's arrival, as if it might slip our minds otherwise.

'It's my birthday first!'

'I know, Ethe. That's what I meant,' Dan said. 'Are you still looking forward to the zoo?'

Ethan gave a nod, concentrating on his dad as he took a long drink of juice, the way he always did while he was eating dinner — stopping halfway through, downing the entire glass. As if working through his plate was as exhausting as crossing the desert.

'We're still coming here, aren't we? After the evening reception, I mean?' Grace said, back to the wedding. 'Mum said you're picking us up from the hotel?'

'Yeah, as far as I know...' Dan turned to me. 'It might be a bit full-on. The next few weeks...'

I agreed. It was like being part of some intense rehab programme, being in the middle of a stepfamily. Lots of day trips and visiting relatives. The weekends were starting to pile up with a stack of events and arrangements I only found out about after Dan remembered to tell me, and, he was adamant, everyone else made on his behalf. When you lived on the outskirts of somebody else's family, there were phone calls, texts, conversations, *situations*, going on above your head and under your nose the whole time. Arrangements being made. Events being planned. While all you could do was to stand on the sidelines, not sure whether to cheer everybody on, or roll up your sleeves. I was a cheerleader with two left feet. It was like that dance game I used to play with Grace. Never knowing where my next step was coming from until the very last minute. The moment you put a foot wrong, off went the alarms.

'So, if you do go out,' Grace said, not only keen on having an itinerary but always the first to devise a back-up plan, 'is Grandma coming over?'

'*If* we decide to go…' Dan took another mouthful of pasta.

'I'd really like to go if we could?' I tried not to sound too keen. 'I mean, if your mum's free to look after the kids and everything…'

'*Kids are what goats have*,' Grace muttered, taking a drink.

For a split second, I hoped she choked.

I knew asking Dan to give up a night with the kids was breaking an unspoken agreement. But the idea of spending the evening at the theatre, instead of in front of some God-awful game show only the kids liked, was growing on me.

'Yeah, I'll ask,' he said. 'Or, you know, you could go. If you want?'

I couldn't remember the last time we'd had a Saturday night out together.

Going out alone, turning up single, took the shine off it.

'Are you going to wear that dress?' Grace actually looked interested, far more interested than her dad. 'That long one you were looking at before?'

'I think so.'

I wondered if fashion was the way forward with her? Then remembered I knew nothing about it. Kim had always been my stylist. You could give Kim half a ball of string and an Argyle sock and she'd whip up something absolutely fantastic.

'Is it new or something?'

'No, I just haven't worn it in ages. In fact —' I glanced at Dan, the dress taking me back to that first night together — 'I think the last time I wore it was when we went to that retro cinema thing. Remember? *Movie Heist Night.* We watched *Ocean's Eleven*? Or it might have been *Twelve*? How many of those films did they make?'

I'd watched that film wrapped up in a gorgeous pashmina I'd borrowed from Kim. She'd let out a round of applause when I'd sloped back home to the flat, dodging innuendos. Trying to pretend I hadn't been missing in non-stop action with Dan for the last 24-hrs.

'I like those long dresses. That one of yours is really nice.'

'Do you think so?'

I was amazed how quickly Grace switched from deep freeze to oven-baked. She actually smiled and ate some of her food without acting like it was melting her teeth.

'But it looks kind of tight fitting.' She kept it deceptively light. 'It's like my bridesmaid dress. You might want to skip on these big meals, if you're still going to wear it...'

Chapter Four: Marigold Blues

I collected the dinner plates, relieved to have ten minutes alone. I wondered just how fat Grace thought I was, and why I'd suddenly thought it was my job to cook for the family? I couldn't do this stuff! I didn't know my arse from my oregano. I'd stumbled into the middle of a Bistro ad, horribly miscast as somebody's mother. I poured more wine and turned the radio back to our local station. I was tempted to finish the bottle, lock myself in there and turn up the old tunes. At least that way I'd be giving the children some time alone with their dad, because, let's face it, that's who they were there to spend the weekend with anyway.

I was grateful when my mobile began ringing on the counter. The perfect distraction, I smiled, as I noticed the Caller ID. *Kim.*

'Ella? This is Friday night calling!' I didn't half miss her sometimes. 'Get out here and show me a good time!'

I'd met Kim when the pair of us had been on a marketing course intended to help her launch her own jewellery line and give me some small hope of getting my foot in the door of an advertising agency. That was after my stint as a trainee journalist, commandeered by my mother and her army of connections, left me with carpal tunnel and an irrational fear of talking to strangers.

Kim always sat at the front of the class. Driving the tutor demented with her non-stop questions. And she was so *American.* She grew up in California. Moved there from Berkshire when she was ten. Heading straight back to Blighty after her 14-month marriage to an illustrator named Ben broke up. Her landlord put her place up for sale halfway through the course. She'd ended up moving in with me to the apartment on Lowe Street I'd left behind to move in with Dan.

'So, how did dinner go?'

I'd called her earlier from the supermarket. I'd been wandering around with a list of stuff I either couldn't spell or hadn't heard of, asking where the best place was to find béchamel sauce.

'Good. All good. Grace was the only one who hated it.'

'That *is* good. She should count herself lucky. I can still remember your bacon and egg pie,' she *yuck*-ed. 'Listen, I'm just on my way out. Are you sure you don't want to come? It's not too late to change your mind...'

Kim was going to a gallery opening featuring an exhibition of arty black-and-white photography called *Nude Headlines*. I heard her spritzing perfume and could almost picture her checking herself out in the hallway mirror, the way she always did before another one of her blind dates with destiny.

'Can't. Sorry. I'm on duty here.'

'Oh, nip out! They'll never notice. Did I tell you? Dominic knew Ben, my Ben, years ago?'

'Dominic? I thought you'd split up with him?'

I sipped my wine, wishing I could share the rest of the bottle with her.

'What? *No*! That was Oliver. Bloody hell, El,' she said. 'I split up with *Oliver* right after I got back from Sally's wedding. That was over the half-term.'

Kim was a primary school teacher. Although from the way she made it sound, you'd have thought she worked in the prison system. She'd flown back home during the school holidays to be her cousin Sally's chief bridesmaid. I'd seen the photographs. The whole thing looked like something out of

Dynasty, circa 1985. Kim thought it was hilarious, got into the whole puffy-sleeve and ruffle thing. Until she found out her ex-husband was not only invited, but actually planning on showing up. The only good thing was he didn't bring a date.

'Dominic's the guy who owns the gallery. The one I'm going to tonight? He went to university with Ben in Monterrey. Can you believe it? He used to DJ. They shared a place together. Junior year.'

'Isn't that a bit weird?' I thought it was. Especially as Kim was still calling him *My Ben* when they'd been divorced for nearly two years.

'No! I don't think so. Anyway, I'm not going because of that! Did I tell you how gorgeous the models are? *All male...*'

'Don't get your hopes up. They're probably *All Gay.*'

'Exactly! Out-of-bounds and bloody gorgeous! Exactly the type of man I need in my life right now. Enjoy your quiet night at home, Cinders!'

Mum's theme music was starting up as we said our goodbyes. I leaned against the counter, gripping my glass. I wished I could go back to the days when I only ate things that came out of packets and cooked in the microwave. Never needing to drain pasta, or have opinions on the price of dishwasher tablets. Not knowing that Marigolds came in different sizes, or why the hell you'd ever own a pair. I'd been expecting Dan's place to be more of a bachelor set-up the first time I came round. He'd been divorced for nearly four years before we met, but his house was a proper home. *A family home.* Bryony, the kid's mum, had been into entertaining. She'd kitted the kitchen out with state-of-the-art appliances and imported tiles. Even the kettle lit up. The only reason I was starting to feel more at home was because I'd stocked up on ready meals and already broken the lever on one side of the toaster.

'The weekend is finally upon us,' Mum was saying, sounding playful, sultry, and absolutely nothing like herself. *'And tonight, I've decided to do something a little different. Before I ask you to share your private lives with me, I'd like to tell you about the first time my sexual needs were met...'*

I switched her off. I didn't want to think about my mother's sexual needs being introduced, never mind *met*. Starky, technically, I supposed, my *step-poodle*, loped out into the kitchen and sat in front of me, tapping my foot with one soil-scented paw.

He was easy to love and even easier to feed. One bowl of dog mix and I was his hero.

'At least *you* love me, don't you, Starky?'

He panted a smile of agreement.

'And that's why Mummy loves you so much.'

I gave him a cuddle, even though I knew he was only checking in on the lookout for scraps from the family table. In a way, we both were. If a dog was for life, not just for Christmas, then a girlfriend was for fun, not just for family. Maybe if I sat on the floor and rested my head on her knee, Grace might show me a little affection. Or at least a little mercy. I'd joked about how I'd only moved in with Dan to be closer to Starky. So far, it had pretty much turned out that way. Starky had become my closest confidant. The one member of the family I could talk to about the other, less cuddly, family members. Starky knew how annoying I thought Dan was when he pretended everything was fine. He knew Grace sometimes stuck two fingers up in my direction when she thought no one was looking. He knew I worried Ethan was way too accepting. And how Dan's mum was never going to accept me. But most of all, he knew I had absolutely no clue what I was doing.

Except living, partially uninvited, and only partially house-trained, with someone else's family.

'You're so sweet, my Starky...' I pushed my hands over his ears, stroked his small, velvet face, as he blinked doggy-devotion into my eyes. Ethan had named Starky after Tony Stark, *Iron Man*, and with his kind, dark eyes, in the right light, he was just as adorable as Robert Downey Jr.

'Come on.' Dan was stood in the doorway, back from checking in with the kids about homework. His shirt cuffs were rolled up and his boots kicked off. Officially relaxed for the weekend. 'I said we'd play that charades game you got them.'

Dan had invented a new house rule this year. Every Friday we were going to spend time together *offline*. No computer games, tablets or anything with a screen involved. But ever since Grace had called me a bitch and burst into tears over a game of Monopoly a couple of weeks back, I tended to duck out of family games in favour of much happier times spent loading the dishwater or catching up on the laundry. Both a complete *hoot* compared to dealing with kids when they wanted to win at something.

'It's okay. You three go ahead. I'm going to clean up in here.'

'You okay?'

'Yeah.' I smiled. And I was. Now the wine had taken the edge off.

'Grace is funny about her food at the minute.' He lowered his voice, eyes shining in that way that made me want to believe every word. 'Don't take it too personally. I'm going to have to have a word with Bryony. She's got her *obsessed* over that bridesmaid's dress...'

'I'm not taking it personally.' I stood at the sink, rinsing a plate. 'I just don't want to leave the kitchen in a mess until the morning.'

'All right then,' he said. 'We'll wait for you.'

'Great,' I lied, reaching for my glass.

Chapter Five: S.K.S.

There was always one person who clung to the rules. In the absence of an official whistle-blower, that was Grace's job.

'Okay, first word.'

'You're not allowed to speak. It's Charades?'

I muttered a couple of *sorrys*, standing on the rug in front of the fireplace. Starky lay at my feet, as if he thought I was there solely to entertain him. Dan and the kids were perched on the couch, ready to aim guesses.

'Right, first word.'

'OMG! Is she thick?'

She must be, I thought. Standing there, feeling like a complete idiot while some stroppy kid called me names. Sometimes this stuff was fun. Other times, I remembered how weekends used to be about living a feline-existence. Prowling cocktail menus and captivating admirers alongside Kim. And who even said *OMG*? Wasn't that something you only put in texts? *SKS*, I thought: *Stepkids Suck*.

'Grace…' Dan gave her a warning sigh then turned back to me as I shifted from side-to-side like a goalkeeper in a penalty shoot-out, limbering up, tapping one finger against my arm.

'First word!' Dan shouted, Ethan giggling beside him.

I gave a nod.

'One word!' Ethan bellowed, wearing a broad grin on his ever-eager face.

I nodded then changed my mind and shook my head to start over again, rethinking my game plan, before I tapped out three fingers against my arm.

'Third word!' Dan smiled.

'No! I meant, it's only three words!'

'Is she for real?' Grace asked no one in particular, pulling her feet up beneath her. 'She just said, "*Three words*" out loud. Even Ethan knows how to play this…'

'Right, come on.' Dan smiled at me. 'We'll get there in the end…'

I waved my hands in front of me, making what I hoped looked like a 'go away' gesture.

'Queen!' Ethan bounced up and down on the sofa.

I shook my head again, moving my hands, *shooing* through the air.

'Stinky smell.' Ethe grinned. Starky trotted over towards him, jumping up on the couch for a quick snuggle and a ruffle of his ears.

'It's the name of a song, you doughnut!' Grace scowled.

'Yeah, well. It might be something about a song that stinks!' Her brother grinned. 'Like a stinky song!'

'But it's obviously not, dummy…'

'You're a dummy!'

'Hey! You two!' Dan interrupted. 'Are we playing this game, or not?'

I stood still for a second, all out of ideas. Glancing at the timer, I beckoned Starky off the couch, no words necessary. Wiggling my earlobe between my fingers, which I hoped still meant 'sounds like', I pointed down at him.

'Sounds like Starky?' Dan asked. 'Dog? Sounds like dog?'

Ethan giggled as I looked around, searching for inspiration.

I raised my hand. Wiggled my earlobe again. Took hold of Starky's paw, pretending to take his pulse.

'That's not even allowed, using Starks like that.' Grace threw herself back against the settee.

'It's only a game.' Dan told her. 'Sounds like … *doctor*?' He mulled it over, until, quite brilliantly, he shouted: 'Vet! Sounds like vet?'

'Yes!'

I noticed Dan's grin. Ethan's excitement. Even Starky, my loyal assistant, panting a smile of encouragement. Despite Grace's mood and a few pounds of uneaten pasta, I couldn't help but feel ridiculously happy. These were the moments I was in this for. The times that made all the petty annoyances completely worthwhile. No distractions, just each other for company. Having fun and hanging out. Acting like goofballs for the kids, the way we used to.

Before I moved in it wasn't difficult being part of the mix. The kids seemed to like having me around, and it was a great feeling. When somebody else's children take a shine to you, they make you feel like some kind of adorable aunty. And it was especially perfect that I happened to be crazy in love with their dad, and massively inclined to love both of them too. At least a couple of times a month, we'd set out on our adventures together. Seatbelts on. Chatting away. Visiting those weirdly themed places only parents knew about. All height-restrictions and crash mats, buying souvenir pens and wearing 3D glasses to the pictures. Saturday afternoons had slowly become ours, just the four of us. Me and Dan sat in the front of the car, singing along to the radio, while in the back, Grace updated us on Taylor Swift lyrics and Ethan made jokes which only ever made sense to him.

But as soon as I moved in, the fits of giggles and classroom confessions pretty much cooled straightaway. They were suspicious all of a sudden, guarded, now I was living there, in their old house, with their dad. Instead of being part of their weekend escape, I'd become part of the problem. *A big part of the problem, from what I could work out.* Any hope the children had of seeing their parents back together again vanished the minute I unpacked my knickers and accidentally claimed their mum's favourite armchair.

'Do you live here with my dad all the time now?' Ethan had asked. He only got to stay with Dan at weekends. That's something you want to fix. I'd mourned their broken home like a good, lapsed Catholic.

Every weekend became a long, drawn out, apology. I'd even noticed Dan keeping his distance. I could tell he was silently apologizing for being there with me, instead of with them, during the rest of the week. I was a stranger sleeping on the rubble of their broken home. The minute I stepped over the threshold I'd become *The Wicked Stepmother*. When, technically, I was a Step-girlfriend.

Ready or not, I'd joined the Stepfamily Robinson. And I really wanted to get it right for Grace and Ethan, because getting it right for them, meant getting it right for all of us. I knew I'd never be a proper relative. The kids would never come running through the school gates to meet me. Whether they used to see me as that lovely aunty-type or not, I was still their dad's girlfriend. I got that. I wasn't going to start acting like their mum — and if you ever met Bryony you'd have seen for yourself that I could never measure up. But I wanted them to like me. *Just a little bit. One day.*

'Time's running out,' Grace prompted.

Still confident from my 'sounds-like-vet' breakthrough, I tapped out *third word* onto my arm and mimed walking off towards the door, still waving, staring at Dan, trying to send the words to him.

'Three words,' Ethan swung one leg. The way he did when he was concentrating.

'*See You Later, Alligator*?' Dan rambled, growing more urgent.

I tightened my mouth, coaxing guesses from them with one hand.

'*Leaving*?'

I pulled a 'sort-of' face.

'*Bye, bye, blackbird*?'

I pointed at Starky. Tapped one finger against my arm.

'First word sounds like vet!' Ethan shouted, pushing his fringe from his face. His hair sticking up in one, thick, blond wave.

'Well remembered!' Dan squeezed Ethan against him for a second.

I carried on waving goodbye as Grace studied the timer.

'*Bye, Bye, Baby*?' Dan was paying full attention now.

'First word still sounds like vet, Dad…' Grace yawned, pulling the lace back and forth through her hoodie.

My eyes darted back to the plastic timer balanced on the arm of the couch.

'Third word — I'm waving.'

'Don't speak!' Grace barked.

'Time's nearly up!' Ethan rocked, resting on his hands, watching the grains disappearing through the seconds.

'*Get Out Of My Dreams*?' Dan shrugged again. '*Go Your Own Way*?'

'They're all more than three words, Dad.' Grace said, before firing her suggestion: '*Time To Say Goodbye*? Oh, no … that's four words, too…'

'*Bye, Bye Baby*?' Dan shouted, as if we hadn't heard him the first time. '*Baby, Come Back*?' he muttered, running out of ideas. '*Never Let You Go*?'

Grace twirled her earring between thumb and forefinger.

'*She's Leaving Home*!' Dan looked sure of his winning answer. 'Is it? Is it *She's Leaving Home? If You Leave Me Now?*' He trailed off, as I left him dangling.

Grace gave me a sullen look, which quickly broke into a smirk: '*Get Out, Girl?*'

Her eyes fixed on me with distaste. A bored cat. I was an easy target. I waited for her to take aim. I might as well have been stood there with an apple plonked on my head and a team of paramedics on standby. She smirked. Her expression growing from bad to worse, and right on cue piped up: '*It's Over Now? He's Over You? Love Runs Out? Love Don't Live Here Anymore? We,*' she sang, '*Are Never, Ever, Ever, Getting Back Together?*'

'*Let it Go*!' I shouted, stemming the flow, just as Ethan who, bored of the game by now, bellowed: 'STOP!'

I'd never had Charades down for an adrenaline sport until I met Grace.

'*Let It Go.*' I cleared my throat, noticing how loudly my heart was hammering inside my chest.

'Right.' Dan cut through the tension. 'Game over. Time for bed, folks...'

'Dad?'

'Grace, you're over-tired…'

Grace was always *over-tired* whenever she was in one of her moods, according to Dan.

'Urgh, it's not even half-ten.' She looked at her watch as her brother gave his dad a hug, before making his way over to me, leaning his head against my arm in a show of affection.

'It will be by the time you get into bed,' Dan told Grace. 'Go on. *Up*! You can have half-an-hour online. Seeing as it's the weekend...'

'Cool!' Grace sloped off the couch and grabbed her phone. I slipped my clue card back into the pack. 'As if we were ever going to guess *Let It Go* from something that sounds like vet,' she drawled. 'How were we even supposed to know it was from *Frozen*?'

Her brother yawned, oblivious, making his way upstairs after her. His tiredness almost on cue, as if he'd been waiting for permission to sleep.

'Yeah, I didn't realize it was a Disney number.' Dan raised his eyebrows in agreement as he stood to replace the lid. I wondered what happened to Games Night supposedly being fun.

'Well, I didn't know!' I plumped the cushions back onto the settee as he collected the kid's empty glasses. 'I've never even seen *Frozen*.'

'I know, I know,' he said, heading towards the kitchen. 'I'm just giving you a bit of friendly coaching,' he said. 'Raising your game for next time.'

'Next time?' I pulled a face. 'I didn't want to play in the first place...'

'Oh, come on, Ella,' he said. I dipped my fingers into a bowl of cheese puffs, slightly stale, the way I liked them. 'Don't be such a sore loser.'

Chapter Six: Room Service

Possibly because I'd ended up changing bedsheets and now knew where most of their things could be found (bunched up at the bottom of the duvet, or left outside in the garden, usually), supervising bedtime had become my thing.

Starky met me at the top of the stairs, eager to investigate as I headed into Ethan's bedroom, beginning the ritual. I actually liked it and had it down to a steady routine. The kids seemed fine with it too. Ethan was always first in the bathroom. His ability to wee on demand was possibly down to the fact he was always too busy playing to go to the loo without prompting. I rinsed his toothbrush and he put either too much or the tiniest smudge of toothpaste on it. Next, I knocked and went into Grace's room. She was unfastening her necklace, pretending not to notice, as I turned back the duvet. I caught a look at her while she brushed her hair. She looked so much older for a second. Some future version of the Grace she'd grow up to be. Leah from work was only five or six years older than her. I wondered if one day, when Grace was that age, we'd be having heart-to-hearts about her latest boyfriend. Or if our conversations would more closely resemble my attempts at office small talk with Heather Constantine.

I fluffed the pillows and switched on the bedside lamp. Grace's own personal maid at The Holiday Inn. Then I went back to her little brother, just in time to tuck him in. Grace had replaced him in the bathroom. His feet were an audible, flat-footed shuffle across the carpet until he stumbled across his bed.

'Goodnight, Ethe,' I whispered, his eyes half-closed as I planted a kiss.

Starky leaned up on the edge of the bed and gave a curious sniff as I drew the curtains. My eyes drifted across the blanket of clear, night sky. I was wondering what shameful tales Kim would be bringing back with her, as the wind rocked up against the window.

'Night, Ethan.' Grace stood in her brother's doorway.

Starky followed her out. By the time I wandered back around the bed, Ethan's breathing now relaxed into easy snores, I heard her say: 'Starky! Get out, you little mutt!'

Her bedroom door shut with an assertive click. I'd become some sort of well-meaning Nanny who Grace was planning on firing. *You and me both*, Starky seemed to agree. I carried him downstairs, ready to relax now it was Dan's turn to make an appearance.

'You okay?'

'*Phh…*' He slowly exhaled. 'Not too sure, to be honest. My stomach feels a bit off.' Just as worry gripped me, he broke into a smirk. 'Must be all of that delicious home-cooking of yours…'

'You're not funny.' I retrieved one of Ethan's plastic man-figures from in between the seats.

'I know.' He produced a bar of something delicious from behind his back before throwing down the remote and grappling me for a cuddle. 'But I've got chocolate…'

The next morning, we were both lying there in that silent denial that sometimes started weekends. The clatter of toys tumbling from inside Ethan's room sounding exactly the same way hangovers used to feel. Except, I'd never woken up so early with a hangover. Or without one, come to think about it, but my weekends weren't about recovery anymore. We were both awake, saying nothing, waiting for similar evidence of life from Grace. I was hoping for maybe twenty more minutes, just a little snoozette, as Grace's room blasted out with the soundtrack of Saturday morning.

'I'll make breakfast.' Dan turned on his back and held my hand beneath the covers. I searched out the time, already knowing it was going to be painful: *6:52 am*. I'd be glad to get back to work just for the lie-in.

I was officially all-out of Friday Feeling. No more coasting along towards my next night out, or looking forward to the next time I'd see Dan. I'd gone to bed with a man I couldn't stop thinking about and woken up with two kids in a three-bedroom house. My days as a girlfriend had been abruptly interrupted. I slumped against the pillow, mourning the fact we'd never had the chance to do that cosy weekend thing. There was no getting nicely tangled up in the sheets together. No lazy mornings, scrolling through a selection of the day's headlines with a mug of English breakfast tea. That's the way I imagined it would be when you lived with someone. Well, not exactly imagined, just seen in magazines or in those designer lifestyle look-books that still got posted, addressed to Bryony. Magazine mornings were full of eco-friendly, Scandinavian lap trays and matching, Fair Trade egg cups. Photos of children having pillow fights in organic hats and knitted slipper socks, their incredibly good-looking parents practicing pilates on Icelandic patterned throws, which you knew those same kids had been home-birthed and probably conceived on.

Downstairs, I was surprised Grace's breakfast hadn't gone cold with the amount of time she'd spent complimenting her dad on the eggs he'd spent less than a minute beating with salt and pepper before pouring into a pan. No browning or sautéing necessary. No complaints of imminent poisoning or sudden sickness. She caught my eye as she sipped her orange juice. We looked at each other for a second before she offered a shy smile. Timid now after a full night's sleep, as if to say: *Yeah, I know it gets old, but I'm only a kid, and you are who you are, so what can you do?*

The good thing was, once I'd brushed my teeth and dragged a brush through my hair, the morning felt like a fresh start. I left my bad mood behind me, opening the dining room doors to a day which held a warm, steady breeze that Starky was desperate to follow. Dan, the only one of us actually dressed as he sat at the breakfast table, took him off for a walk. I washed the dishes as Grace announced she was taking a bath. Meanwhile, her little brother pulled on shorts and a football top for a kick-about in the garden. I offered my face to the sun for a second, ignoring my mother's warnings about UV damage, which she said guaranteed a middle-age blighted by overpriced neckerchiefs and oversized sun hats. Neckerchiefs and over-sized sun hats didn't do Joan Collins any harm, I'd said. There's a big difference between you and Joan Collins, she said. Namely, the South of the France, and a Swiss bank account.

Despite Mum's voice lingering in my ear, it was a perfect morning. The sun was blazing, Dan was being a proper, hands-on dad and, as awkward as it was sometimes, I loved him for it. I'd never met a man so totally at ease with himself and his family. And not in a *Right-On* kind of way, or as if he was making some huge sacrifice he expected repaid in gushing graduation speeches. He wanted to spend time with his kids. He was good at it. I'd never dated anyone with kids before, but being a great dad brought out all of Dan's best qualities. Qualities I'd never found in other boyfriends, and never known from my own father. My single-parent family brought constant, daily reminders of the huge sacrifices my own mum had made.

The night before, we'd slouched in front of some over-sexed, under-written, French movie. Dan dozing off beside me, I'd realised how stupid it was to take the whole Step-thing so seriously. Fair enough, that might have been down to the half bottle of Châteauneuf-du-Pape and family-sized bar of Fruit & Nut I'd had all to myself, but I was convinced I could get good at this Stepfamily thing. Dan was great. The kids were great. At first, I suppose, I'd only been window-shopping. Enjoying the thought of instantly becoming part of the perfect family scene, in the perfect family house. I needed to stop trying to turn everything into my bright idea of how it should be. I needed to give everything time, like the Stepparent forums said. Well, some of them did. Most of them agreed you should run for the hills before somebody else's kids happily destroyed your life.

I was thinking these thoughts as Ethan sailed past into the garden, clutching a football and chatting about his favourite football players.

'I'm being a vet when I grow up!' he revealed, as I went back upstairs to fetch a batch of washing, glad Starky wasn't around to hear him using the V-word. Look at me, I thought, I'm wearing matching loungewear, while two perfectly content children spend the morning at home, alone, with me. *I'm a regular, contemporary Hausfrau!*

Chapter Seven: The Accidental Hausfrau

'Hello?' Grace shouted, fifteen minutes into her bath, just as I was hoping Dan hadn't noticed my shiny support knickers dangling outside the laundry basket like a memorial flag to my youth. At least Kim wasn't around to show me up with the tiny, netty things she wore that looked like dental floss and frequently ended up caught between some bloke's teeth.

'Ella, do I use the de-tangling conditioner or the stuff in the white bottle? It says,' she paused, with a splish-splash of bath water, 'for dry/damaged hair? I think that's *probably* your one…'

'The de-tangling one should be fine.' I smiled at what Dan called 'kids telling it like it is', but what was actually Grace being a little Cowbag. 'Have you got the wide-tooth comb?'

'Erm, no. Can you help me please, Ella?' She used the same tone whenever she was in need of assistance. That same tone I imagined the adult Grace using to terrorize unsuspecting shop assistants one day. 'I can't get the shampoo out of my eye.'

I'd noticed the bath-time chatter was starting to become our regular routine. She liked to sit in the bath, holding court. Telling me all about what she was up to with her friends at school, as if she had an appointment in a beauty salon. In fact, I think that's exactly where she was pretending to be. Any other time I showed interest, she warned me off with a blank look, or made sure I knew what a drag it was, tolerating my existence. *Save it for Dad*, she'd said one time, when I'd told her how great her school report was.

I gave a knock, recognizing the same polite *drum-drum* I used at the doctors, hovering outside the door, waiting to be summoned.

Grace sat washing her face with a Hello Kitty flannel. I averted my eyes from the mild breakout of kid-boobs partially submerged beneath too much bubble bath. Miley Cyrus and Hannah Montana rolled into one. That was Grace. Serving up a shit-storm at the dinner table one minute and struggling to rinse shampoo out of her eyes the next. She was like some kind of hormonally-fuelled time-traveller, adding and subtracting the years. She flitted between sharp-edged adolescent and innocent child, all in the same sentence. Her moods were a palpable fragrance to me, detectable throughout the house from Friday to Sunday: *A soft, feminine scent.* I played out the ad in my mind. *Capturing the floral lullabies of youth, with an unmistakable base note of ionized oestrogen. She's the girl, becoming the woman. She is … Baby Bitch by Calvin Klein…*

'It's really stinging me…'

'Here.' I dabbed two cotton pads under the cold tap, gently pressed them against her eyes. 'Any better?'

'Uh-huh,' she nodded. 'I'm probably allergic to your shampoo because it's cheap. Mum only buys the nice stuff.'

'Oh, that's good.' I wasn't really sure how to compliment someone else's choice of shampoo.

'It makes her hair really shiny.' She scrunched her face, holding the eye pads in place. 'It's long, too. Longer than yours.'

'I know. Your mum has lovely, long, blonde hair. Just like my friend, Kim.'

Grace squinted a look of confusion, searching out my reaction with one, periscopic eye.

'Some of Mum's hair is a weave though,' she added, matter-of-factly. 'You can get the fake stuff, but Mum only buys real hair. It costs about £600, but Mum says it's worth every penny.'

'Well, it looks really nice…'

£600? I nearly squawked. I'd spent less on my hair since the day I was born. Although, maybe that was why I could never do a thing with it.

'Do you want me to comb the conditioner through?'

'Promise not to get it in my eyes?'

'I promise I won't get it in your eyes.'

'Or on my face, please. I'm getting pimples.' She was rehearsing the part of concerned teenager again, wearing a nonchalant look that reminded me how this had to be the best age. Just about to turn thirteen. When you could pretend at being grown up and sophisticated one minute, then soft-land back into childhood the next. So much easier than when you got older and they pulled the bath mat from under your butt and it was sink or swim all the way.

'You are not!'

I grabbed the comb from the sink and eased a dollop of conditioner onto my hand.

'I am. Look…'

She pointed to a tiny cluster of flesh-coloured dots on her forehead, her fingernails chipped with a silvery, glitter polish.

'Mum says it's Puberty, but you still get pimples on your chin sometimes, don't you? Have you got special spot cream?'

She gave the game away, turning around to check she'd hit her target squarely in the feelings. I was desperate to tell her how I hardly ever got zits actually, but I kept schtum — hoping to deflect the playground power struggle until all she could hear was her own childishness. Sometimes you had to use silence rather than words to win the argument. At least, that's what my mum had said, after I'd called for advice when Grace started calling me Ella-phant.

Grace turned, silently offering the back of her head as I applied conditioner. 'Do you have anything I could borrow? Mum lets me put on her good stuff when I get pimples,' she explained. 'I don't want to be all spotty for the wedding. Mum's letting me get a spa treatment. I'm booked in with her for a deep-cleansing, Aloe aqua glaze.' She almost tripped over the words.

'Wow. How grown up is that?'

'It's not grown up.' She flinched at the notion. 'Everyone should start their skincare regime while they're young. I'm having a Mani-Pedi done too. Mum gets one of those fish ones done that eat the dead skin off, but that's way too freaky. Have you got any spot stuff or not?'

'No,' I said, but I recognised a good chance to bond when I saw one: 'I've got a face-mask you could use if your skin's a bit oily?'

'Yes, please,' she sighed. 'I need to look my best for the photos.'

Both of the kids seemed really excited about their mum's wedding. For some reason, Grace couldn't wait to see her mum getting married. She hadn't stopped talking about the whole thing over the last few months. And, although Ethan never brought it up, whenever Grace did he'd casually boast about his smart-looking suit, and how he was giving his mummy away. As sweet as they were being, I had a feeling they wouldn't have been quite so keen if it had been me and their dad getting married. I had a hunch Grace would rather feed her own feet to those fish than watch me walking down the aisle.

It was as if they didn't realise their mother was marrying Vic. That man would've been bad enough as some distant uncle who showed up uninvited to christenings or attempted to put the 'fun' back into family funerals with his endless, embarrassing jokes and taste for single malt. The thing was, and this was the thing everyone knew but nobody mentioned, Vic also happened to be very wealthy. *Seriously wealthy*, in fact. He owned his own business, importing footwear and he seemed very fond of spoiling Bryony. Her engagement ring held a diamond the size of a sugar cube, which Grace said her mother called 'ice'. Despite the fact they weren't particularly impressed with diamonds, Vic seemed to be the kid's favourite stand-in parent, which didn't say much about me, except that I was obviously useless with children. It's not as if Vic did anything special, either. His own kids, six-year-old twins from his first marriage, would've made ideal poster boys for opt-in hysterectomy.

'Here.' I grabbed my basket of bathroom kit from the cupboard, balancing it on the side of the bath. 'Visibly Clear. You only need a little bit on your forehead. Don't put it near your eyes —'

'*Ella*!'

Ethan's voice cracked from the bottom of the stairs, stopping me in my tracks.

'You okay, Ethe?'

'I can't believe he's shouting like that!' Grace sat up, riffling through an assortment of out-of-date exfoliators, unopened bath bombs and dried up teeth whitener. All fighting for dust in my age-old supplies. That's what hoarding three-for-two at Boots got you. 'Mum never lets him shout like that in our house...'

'Oh, right. I suppose not.' I turned towards the door. 'Erm, Ethan!' I called, rinsing conditioner off my hands. 'Ethan?'

'Yes!'

'Don't shout up like that, please!' I shouted, wondering why I was following their mum's house rules instead of making up my own, and if that was better or worse for the children?

'But my knee's all cut up!' I could almost hear him wincing. 'I've gotta shout...'

'He's such a baby sometimes.' Grace was applying the face-mask. Hardly aware of me now, as she caught brief, pleasing glimpses of herself in the bathroom mirror, playing at being the girl on TV.

'Back in two minutes.' I grabbed the towel and dried my hands. 'I'll just go and see to your brother. Then I'll rinse off your hair, okay?'

Ethan was sitting on the bottom step as I got to the top of the stairs. He was breathing so sharply I could see his little body, not much more than a ribcage, tense with effort. His face was pale and wet with tears.

'What have you done, Mister?'

'It hurts.' He grit his teeth as he spoke, blood trickling down towards his sock, wearing a face that took me straight back to the playground. 'I got caught up in that big sheet. On the washing line,' he managed, tight-lipped, until his sad, brown eyes found mine. They were the kind of eyes that helped puppies leave litters. The same dark eyes that meant Dan could crush or caress me with one glance.

As soon as I saw that look, I knew I had to make his knee better again.

'I fell over on the patio. That's why it's all scraped up.'

He almost held his breath as he examined the wound.

'Don't worry.' I stroked his mane of surfer-blonde hair. 'We'll get you all fixed up.'

'Okay…' He looked at me and right at that moment I saw something amazing: *Trust*. I almost gasped. Seriously, I don't think you could have looked at that little face and not felt exactly the same way. *I'm taking care of the children*, I thought, quickly finding the first aid kit under the kitchen sink. Grace was trusting me to do her hair. Ethan was trusting me to make him feel better. This is what it felt like to be a real-life, live-in Step-girlfriend! One little girl relaxing in the bathroom. One little boy waiting for his next *Hulk* plaster.

'ELLA!'

'Grace?' I shouted back upstairs. 'Remember what we just said? Don't shout like that, please.'

Bloody hell, I thought, unzipping the first aid bag, *I sounded quite good then. Calm, but in control. The kind of person your kids could have fun with, but look up to, like a nice teacher or a friendly lollipop lady.* Ethan wiped his nose on the bottom of his football shirt, offering me his wounded leg as I opened a Steri-wipe.

'ELLA! *My face is burning!*'

'Don't worry.' I balanced her little brother's football boot against my thigh, wiping a trail of blood and dirt on a cotton wool ball. 'It's just the face-mask thing doing stuff to your pimples. Wash it off, it'll be fine.' Ethan sucked the air through his teeth, half turning away, half watching, as I gently coaxed dirt from the bloodied wound. 'Be brave, little man. Nearly done.'

'It's not fine! It's your stupid cream!'

Grace's voice rolled towards us like thunder, followed by the sound of bath water randomly being splashed by angry girl fists.

'Can you hold on to this for two ticks, Ethe?' I pulled open a packet of gauze, placed a piece over the cut, which I hated to admit looked far worse than I thought. 'Let me see to your sister. I'll be right back.'

'Ckay,' he sniffed, lip trembling. 'I'll try.'

I gave his arm a quick rub for comfort and placed a quick peck on the top of his head as I took to the stairs, wondering how such a small girl could be so high maintenance when her little brother was being so brave. Grace was already out of the bath, clutching a towel around her, as I opened the bathroom door.

'My hair came out!' Her face was covered in angry-looking blotches and I knew she wasn't playing. 'Look,' she said shuddering, offering wisps of hair in one hand while stomping out a mini dance, suddenly a much younger child. 'Your cream did this to my *fucking* hair!'

Half of her eyebrow was quite clearly missing.

Time seemed to stop for a second.

'Where's the cream, Grace?'

'There!' she shrieked, nearly hysterical.

Oh.

Shit.

Not *Visibly Clear* but *Visibly Smooth* — an old tube of bikini hair removal cream I'd forgotten I even owned. I raked through the majority of Grace's fringe still thankfully attached to her head. 'Honey?' I heard myself stutter. 'I think that was the wrong stuff.'

'Yeah, I'd already *fucking* worked that one out!'

Grace cried fresh tears as I inspected her fringe, wondering how I was ever going to explain this to her parents, and more importantly, where to find a replacement eyebrow at such short notice, first thing on a Saturday morning.

Chapter Eight: Coffee with Columbo

After being very brave about his knee, Ethan found blood inside his lip, then told us his tooth felt all wonky. We piled into the car to A&E, making the journey in silence, radio turned up, until we reached the main entrance.

We sat on cold, plastic seats in an air-conditioned ward, waiting our turn for nearly three hours. Grace sat in stony silence, typing texts and harbouring grudges. Dan avoided looking at me at all, sitting Ethan on his knee. Ethan had told his dad all about his injury and I knew what Dan was thinking: *This wouldn't have happened if Daddy had been home.* And I knew he was probably right, but what else was I supposed to do? I sat there, feeling mortified, hoping Ethan didn't lose a tooth after his sister had already lost an eyebrow.

'You can't leave sheets hanging out on the line when there's a kid around playing football,' Dan said, making us coffee once we were finally home, over four hours later, both of the children given the all clear.

Ethan was tired of the whole thing by now, eager to catch the start of his favourite TV show, while his sister was up in the bathroom, applying the cold cream we got from the pharmacy.

'I know. I didn't think. I'm sorry,' I said, already wondering how Dan expected anyone to guess pegging out a sheet would end up with a trip to the hospital? It must be yet another wonderful piece of advice I'd missed in the *non-existent* handbook on how to look after someone else's children.

'I know, but this is the stuff you have to think about.' He opened and closed the cupboard with a thud as the kettle rumbled into action. 'It doesn't exactly look great does it? Taking them home, looking like that?'

'Dan? I said I'm sorry. I didn't know he was going to fall into the washing line or that Grace had the wrong cream.'

'I just hope that front tooth's okay.' His face was grim. 'That ankle still looks swollen to me. It was a nasty fall. He could have broken it…'

'I know,' I said, sick at the thought. 'But they x-rayed it, and it's fine.'

'But it could've been broken.' He opened the fridge and reached for the semi-skimmed milk. Everything I said he came back to with the worst-case scenario. It was like sitting next to a nervous flyer and something told me it was going to be one hell of a long journey. I'd started the day off at Trust and taken a detour into Totally Unsuitable.

'Okay, Dan. I get it. I don't like seeing Ethan hurt or Grace upset like that, either. I feel guilty enough as it is….'

'Yeah, well.' He stopped for a moment and I noticed him do that thing. Pushing his tongue against his teeth slightly, the way he did when he was annoyed. 'He said you were upstairs when he fell?'

'I told you I was. Bloody hell, Dan!' I said. 'One cut knee and it's coffee with Columbo. Why don't you go ahead and call the police?' I reached for the biscuit tin. 'Launch a full investigation…'

'Don't be childish…'

'You're making it sound like I turned Ethan into a…' I bit into my Jammy Dodger, trying to think of the word. 'A *piñata*, or something.'

'You weren't watching him!'

'No, I wasn't.' I stuffed the rest of the biscuit into my mouth. 'I was upstairs washing your daughter's hair. What was I supposed to do?' I dusted the crumbs off my top. 'Fit the garden out with CCTV?' *And they're your kids!* I wanted to say. *You're the parent! You're the one who knows how perfectly innocent household stuff is potentially dangerous to children.* The only experience I'd had with kids was back when I had been one, and funnily enough, I'd survived Mum doing the laundry without any lingering injuries. 'Maybe you should have conducted a full Risk Assessment before you left the house...'

'I'm just saying —' He handed over my cup — 'I don't know what the hell their mother's going to make of it.' He took a drink. He was using the Father's Day mug Grace had hand-painted for him last year. *Team Dad*, it said. Perfect product placement. Except it stopped me feeling guilty and irritated me instead. 'It'd be bad enough if it was just one of them going home like that. *Christ...*'

'I've already told Mum.' Grace was stood in the doorway. 'She wanted me to come home early, but I talked her out of it.'

I really wish you hadn't, I thought, noticing the look on her face.

'You *are* home.' Dan paused over the top of his cup. 'You live with your mum in the week. You live here, too.'

'Yeah, I know.' She softened. 'Do I have to go to school on Monday?'

'Yes, Grace. You know you do.'

'Mum says I don't have to.' She was rotating the door handle back and forth, toes craned over the step.

'And I say you do.'

'God, Dad! We break up on Tuesday anyway!' She walked into the dining room, one thumb hooked into her pocket, glaring at Dan. 'It's only, like, two days!'

'Then you'll miss the end of year assembly, won't you?' Dan dropped his teaspoon into the sink. 'You're supposed to be giving a reading, aren't you?'

'That's not the biggest deal, Dad. I'm supposed to be Mum's bridesmaid in *three weeks*,' she said. 'I don't even wanna go now! I don't want to go to Mum's wedding! Not after *she* did *this* to my face!'

'Grace, I'm sorry. I —'

'Oh, whatever!' she sneered, refusing to be cornered by any useless attempts at kind words. 'You burnt off my eyebrow! You should be sorry.'

Burnt off her eyebrow? She was turning this into some sort of folklore the older kids at school could pass on to younger generations. *The Eyebrow Burner.* Years from now, neighbourhood children would patrol the streets, shushing each other in fear, whispering the legend every Halloween. Their eyebrows would be covered with plasters as they dared each other to walk up the driveway and take their chances.

'I didn't *burn off* your eyebrow. I didn't check which cream you put on your face. I didn't even know that tube was in there. It was a mistake.'

'Well, you *should have* checked it!'

'Yes, I know —'

'What if it had got in my eye? What if it made me blind?'

She had my full attention now. Grace had really thought this through. I was distracted for a moment, thinking how proud Dan would be if she grew up to be an important spokesperson. Travelling the world, challenging the status quo, like Angelina Jolie, only permanently furious.

'And what about Ethan?' Her face flushed as the case against The Wicked Stepmother gathered momentum. 'He nearly broke his ankle. All because *you* haven't got a clue about looking after kids!'

'Ethan fell over. It wasn't Ella's fault.' Dan started out strong but ended with a voice so defeated it wouldn't even convince me of my own innocence. Not in the face of Grace's brilliant case for the prosecution. Until, I realised, this wasn't Grace at all. This was her mother's reaction. *This was Bryony.* I squirmed, feeling like a kid myself. Trying to think of excuses that didn't involve me not having enough common sense to be left alone with two kids for half an hour.

'You don't put washing out on the line where kids are playing.' Grace was hand-on-hip now, looking like a pocket-sized mum-machine. 'Even I know that, and I'm not even thirteen yet! You don't even know what stuff you keep in your own bathroom cupboard.' Her face soured, eyes accusing. 'Ethan could have used that cream, or whatever other *dangerous stuff* you leave lying around the place...'

'Grace!' Dan stepped in. 'That's enough.'

'It's only what Mum said. She said you're supposed to keep stuff like that locked away when there's kids around.'

Grace was playing parlour room clairvoyant. Channelling Bryony into the argument. It's a wonder the lights hadn't flickered on and off. She brought her mum into every conversation and criticism, letting me know how her mum's opinion still counted for everything.

'It *was* locked away!'

'No, it wasn't.'

'Yes, it was.' I tried to stay calm and act like an adult instead of running away and sticking on my headphones, misunderstood and bored of explaining, the way I wanted to. 'I only got it from the cupboard because *you said* you wanted to use it.'

'*You said* I should use it. You didn't even know you had that stupid hair removal stuff in there in the first place. You just said so yourself, Ella!'

'Grace?' I was determined not to add fuel to the argument in case it turned into a house fire. 'There's nothing I can say, except I'm really sorry.'

'I don't care if you're sorry! You're an idiot!'

She folded her arms, her chin jutting out at roughly the same angle as her elbows.

'I said — *enough*!' Dan glared at the floor, locked in temper.

'Well, it's true.'

'Grace, I didn't mean —'

'*I didn't mean*,' Grace mimicked.

'I didn't do anything to your eyebrow...'

'Actually, you did.'

'I didn't touch your eyebrow!'

'*I ... don't ... CARE!*'

'Grace!'

'I don't care, Dad. I don't have to like her! And now she's done this!' She dragged back her fringe. Revealing a pink, half-bare brow, slightly raised, curiously bald. 'She burned off —'

'*I didn't touch your fucking eyebrow!*'

Their mouths clamped shut.

I enjoyed the silence for a second, until I remembered how I'd caused it.

I watched Grace's mouth give way to a smirk, aging her young face by at least ten years. *Good*, I thought. Stay like that. Look as old and hard-faced as you act. 'She was the one who put it on!' I noticed Dan's expression, knew that wasn't the point, but got carried away with my own argument. 'I told her to put a *little bit* on her forehead. I told her not to put it near her eyes. And —' I knew I was losing the battle — 'she swore at me! Twice!'

'*Liar!*'

'I am not a liar! You said *fuck*. You said *fucking*, twice.'

'So!' Her eyes blazed. 'You just said it twice yourself.'

She gave her dad a nervous glance. I saw the look on Dan's face and knew I was getting the blame for swearing, when all I was doing was telling on his daughter. It was all so *fucking* unfair! 'Why don't you stop trying to make everything worse?'

'Ella!' Dan snapped me out of my meltdown like a stage show hypnotist, bringing me back to the room, where I was stood in the middle of a full-on slanging match with his daughter, like some bad penny in a TV drama. All I needed was a leopard-print coat and a pair of gold, hoop earrings.

'Little girls don't need to put cream on their faces.' Dan turned to Grace, his patience wearing thin, but his voice deceptively steady. 'No one's going to notice. Look,' he demonstrated. 'You can barely see it if I ruffle your fringe a bit.'

'My eyebrow's missing, Dad,' she reminded him, becoming twelve-year-old Grace again, rubbing her finger along what remained of her brow. 'Because *she* made me put the wrong stuff on it!' She turned to me. 'You stupid *cow*!'

'I said, enough!' Dan warned. 'Grace.' He grabbed his cup. 'It'll grow back.' He turned and went to say something to me, but thought better of it. 'There's nothing we can do…'

He left us standing there and went off to find his son. Escaping into the landscape of afternoon TV, leaving cries building behind his daughter's lips.

And me, not knowing what to do next.

'You're supposed to check the tube. It was *your* idea.' Grace dragged one arm across her eyes.

'Yes,' I said, tired of arguing. 'I know.'

'I can't believe this happened right before the wedding.'

She wiped her nose on the back of her hand.

'Your brother was calling me, you know that. What was I supposed to do?'

'You just don't get it, do you?' She lurched forward like a centre in a rugby scrum. *I'm a kid, too!*'

I held my breath as the teenage-version of Grace loomed behind her eyes.

She was wronged. Misunderstood. And she would never forgive my mistake. I could picture her in five years' time, towering over me in ten-inch heels: '*You made me bald, Bitch!*'

'And now,' she stuttered back tears, fixing her hair over her eye. 'Everyone at school's … going to … laugh at me.'

'No, they won't,' I promised, knowing full-well Ethan already found the whole thing hilarious.

'Yes, they will. *Stupid bitch …*'

'Don't call me that. It's not very nice.'

'Neither are you!'

I prepared myself for another onslaught of accusations, but with that her temper extinguished with silent tears, elbows resting on the kitchen counter, head hidden in her hands. I preferred it when she was angry.

'Grace, I'm sorry.' I smoothed one hand across her back. 'I feel terrible...'

'Big deal.' She wiped her face on her sleeve, sniffing away upset.

What I wanted to do was comfort her. Say the right thing. Throw my arms around her. I almost saw myself do it. Willed myself to, but then, I didn't. I *couldn't*. It was as if there was some biological electric fence between us, keeping me at bay.

'Do you want me to try and cover it up?'

'How?'

I sprinted over to my bag, relieved to think of something remotely practical, rifling through my makeup, before twirling the stick between my fingers. 'Eyebrow pencil.'

'No!' Grace scowled at me. 'You'll only mess it up worse.'

'It's the same one —' I was going to say it was the same one I used, but thought better of it — 'my friend, Kim, uses…'

She'd only met Kim twice, but each time Grace had followed her around, asking endless questions, obviously impressed.

'Why? Did you burn off her eyebrow, too?'

'No!'

'I was *jo–king*…'

'I know,' I said. I felt momentarily brave enough to rest my hand on her shoulder, but my own hesitation made it unconvincing, even to myself. I dropped my hand and popped off the lid of the pencil. 'If you don't like it, I can wipe it off.'

'You're sure it comes off?' she smirked, wiping her nose again.

'It definitely wipes off.' I dared to give a smile, quickly double-checking it wasn't my waterproof one.

Chapter Nine: Captain Ahab

I couldn't get to the office quick enough on Monday morning. I'd spent the night curled up on the far side of the bed. The space between me and Dan had harboured a ravine of cold, night air. No wandering hand traced the contour of my hip. No fatal kisses breathed against my neck. The silence added to the longest weekend of my life. *The 48-hour assault on my sanity.*

Dan had finally spoken five minutes after he'd snapped off his bedside light. I'd closed my eyes, waiting for the cure-all *I love you* to relax me into sleep.

'I didn't want to say anything in front of Grace,' he said. 'But I don't want you acting that way again. Swearing. Losing your temper. You can't do that. That was totally out of order.'

I apologised for the hundredth time and lay there like a scolded child, knowing he was right. The next morning after a sleepless night I heard Dan shut the front door behind him. There had been no goodbye kiss on the top of my head before his usual early start.

My plan had been to get into work early and finish those press releases Audrey needed about the new Gluten-free place we were representing ,until I heard the *ping*! of a text from Kim, just as I reached my desk: *Yr mum is quite the party animal!!!*

'Check your email, Ella.' Heather Constantine flounced in from the kitchen, dragging on her coat like a matador about to charge into La Plaza. 'I'm on my way to a very important meeting with Eric Bartholomew.' She picked up her handbag and headed to the door. 'I suggest you prioritize your workload!'

Prioritize my workload?

Leah shared a look of disbelief.

Ooh, Eric Bartholomew. *Yip-ti-doo*! I'd met him a while ago. An old, rich, tortoise-shaped man whose neck only appeared from under his collar to bark unreasonable demands or withering criticism. So what if he owned some fusty old department store nobody ever shopped in? Heather had somehow convinced him to spend *squidillions* on marketing and he was making her polish every penny.

'Drinks, anyone?' I ignored Heather's sneering, put my work commitments to one side, went into the kitchen and prioritized a call to Kim.

'I mean, she looked amazing. *Seriously.*' Kim was ablaze, telling me all about bumping into my mother at the gallery on Friday night. The pair of them ended up going to some new bar afterwards. 'Totally gorgeous dress. And have you seen her hair? I told her most women her age give up, but your mother is *banging* hot!'

Kim might think that was a compliment, but I didn't want my mum to be *banging* anything, funnily enough. 'What was she doing there? At a bar launch?'

'What do you mean what was she doing?' Kim laughed. 'She was drinking the bar dry with the rest of us!'

'Brilliant.' Even I could hear the disapproval in my voice, my tone bordering on Victorian. 'I mean, who was she with?'

'Work, I think she said. She didn't stay long. Said she was going to some sushi place I'd never heard of on Saturday…'

Sushi? Since when did Mum like sushi? The woman was allergic to shellfish.

I hung up. A couple of the digital team offered a synchronized chin-tilt of hello in my direction like some kind of Mexican wave as I served Harry's coffee. I was beginning to wonder if they were all controlled via some government force, or maybe a religious cult. An invading Alien Super Power even. I sat back down at my desk, Heather's name back at the top of my inbox, and was catapulted back into my own hellish reality:

Subject: INCORRECT FILES!!!
Re: Electronic copy of ALL *Steen* & *Heard* annual client account files as REQUESTED on FRIDAY!!!
NOW URGENTLY REQUIRED at the FIRST INSTANCE!!!

Electronic copy? She sounded like a self-service checkout.
Couldn't she ask me to stick the files on an email like everybody else?
At least Audrey wasn't copied in, for once.
Yes, Heather, I thought. I'll send the files back *electronically*. Unless perhaps, you'd prefer them transferred *telepathically*?
And, for her information, the files weren't *incorrect* at all. Why would I start sending her client files for the entire company? I sourced the attachments month-by-month. While in a parallel universe, I typed:

Subject: MY ARSE
Re: YOUR ATTITUDE
ADJUST IMMEDIATELY in the FIRST INSTANCE!!!

At twenty-past-twelve, confident I'd located everything Heather Constantine could possibly need, apart from a psychiatrist, I'd made the mistake of giving Mum a quick call. I was obviously overlooking the small fact that Mum was incapable of holding anything resembling a brief conversation. I pretended I was being helpful, reminding her about Ethan's birthday trip to the zoo on Saturday when what I actually wanted to know was what she thought she was doing going out partying with *my* best friend. Out 'partying' at all, actually.

'*Yes, Ella.* You invited me. I've got it right here. On the mobile app thing. There's no excuse for not being organized nowadays. Not with all this technology. Mind you, I still can't work out the timer on that new oven. Whoever writes those user handbooks needs to realize we're not all fluent in *Geek*. I thought I'd be able to muddle through using the illustrations, but not even the Egyptians could translate those bloody things…'

'So, we'll see you there then, Mum?' I balanced the handset between ear and shoulder, standing in the staff canteen, trying to navigate my way through a hedgerow of boxed salads.

'Yes, I suppose, but is it really going to make a difference? Me being there?'

'Yeah, of course it is!' Well, it was to me, anyway. I needed all the help I could get. Safety in numbers and all that. Although, the mood Dan was in I wasn't entirely sure either of us was still invited.

'So Ethan's eight? I'll pick up a card and get him some vouchers. And Grace'll be thirteen soon? *Wow*,' Mum sighed. 'You'll have your work cut out for you then...'

'What does that mean?'

I was used to Mum's unfaltering cynicism, but was curious nevertheless.

'What do I mean?' She laughed. 'Hormones, that's what I mean. Closely followed, in no particular order, by boyfriends, exams, peer pressure, drink, drugs, sex, STDs — and the possibility of unwanted pregnancy.'

As a result of her loyal listeners and dedicated research, Mum had turned into a walking encyclopaedia of romantic horror stories and cautionary tales of family life grown septic. I picked up a bottle of elderflower juice, wondering if it was too early to top it up with a double gin.

'I don't think we need to worry about all that just yet, Mum...'

'Well, you say that, but time goes by so quickly with children. Half of them decide they're transgender or pan-sodding-sexual by the time they start secondary school.'

'I'll remind Dan to ask Grace for his brogues back...'

'Very funny, Ella. I'm not trying to worry you,' she said, clearly affronted. 'Children are life's greatest adventure, but it's not all plain sailing.'

No shit, I felt like saying. *You're talking to Captain Ahab here.*

'Anyway, Mum, I'll have to go. I've got loads on today.' And I really wasn't interested in letting Mum run wild on this particular subject, not when I was already on the Stepfamily Robinson Wanted List.

'They say we can have it all, and I'd love to agree, but there're sacrifices involved,' she said. 'It's difficult enough making them for your own children...'

Mum planted seeds in our conversations as if my mind was her own personal allotment. Despite her popularity in trendy, liberal magazines, in reality, she couldn't quite get past the 'Step' part of my relationship with Dan's kids.

'Those children have been through so much. Parents divorced. Mum getting remarried. You living with Dan,' she told me. 'I doubt a day at the zoo's going to help them adjust to living with you...'

'Well, luckily,' I said, joining the queue, 'that's not why we're going...'

'Yes, I know, darling. I'm just saying. These situations, all this co-habiting, step-parenting business. It's a lot for anyone to take on board. Let alone the children. The last thing they need is you throwing me, another complete stranger, into the mix.'

'You're not a stranger…' The whole thing was difficult enough without being held responsible for ruining their childhood by my own mother. 'But if that's how you feel, maybe it'd be nice for them to get to know you.'

'Well, you're his girlfriend, I suppose. I'll be there, if you think I should.'

'Yes, I think you should! And I'm not just his girlfriend. We live together. I spend as much time with the children as Dan does.' I knew she'd have something to say about this next bit, but went right ahead anyway. 'And, I'm a Step-girlfriend, actually.'

'A what?' she almost-laughed. 'For goodness sake, Ella. Those kids must need a degree in Linguistics by now! What does that make me? Their *father's STEP-girlfriend's mother*? I can barely say it! Goodness only knows what they make of it.'

'You're my mum. I doubt they worry about what to call you. You're about the same age as their own grandma. They probably see you like that.'

'Thanks, Ella. Good to know I'm not wasting my time, paying out for dermal fillers twice a year. You're very passive-aggressive these days, I've noticed,' she was verging on hoity. 'You know exactly what I mean. I worry about how much you're giving up, that's all. How much you're going to *continue* to give up.'

'I'm not giving up anything.'

'Maybe,' she muttered, unconvinced, 'but it seems to me his family are doing a lot better out of this situation than my daughter.'

'Will you please stop calling it a "situation". I'm not a hostage! I love Dan.'

'Did you open my present?'

'Yes, I did.'

'And?'

'And — I put it away.'

'For a rainy day?'

'No, Mother. It's just that I didn't fancy putting a sex toy in the bin where the kids might find it.' The woman in front of the queue, I think she worked for the firm of accounts on the third floor, turned around with a sudden dash of interest in my conversation.

'Oh, of course,' my mother said. 'Even a grown-up discussion about vibrators leads us back to Dan's children. When was the last time you two went out, let alone at it, Ella?'

'Not as often as you, according to Kim. She said she saw you over the weekend...' I was curious why she hadn't mentioned her right out when I'd seen her for lunch. Usually she loved keeping me updated with her pulsating social diary.

'That's right. At the gallery. Rising Radio interviewed the photographer.'

'Kim said she asked you to go. You should've gone!' She sounded annoyingly blasé. 'You and Kim never used to let the dust gather.'

Kim and I never used to dust at all. We were undomesticated, unattached and uninhibited. Well, Kim was uninhibited, but she'd made my last days of being single worth remembering. It was hard to believe that was two years ago. Those days already felt like long-lost youth.

'That was when we were both single. I'm with Dan now.'

'Well, I know they call it settling down, Ella, but you two never seem to come up for air.'

'We have the kids at the weekend, you know that.'

'Exactly. So there needs to be more of a balance if you're both serious.'

'Of course we're serious!'

'Then it can't just be about his children. I mean, look at this zoo thing.' She was on a roll now.

'It's Ethan's birthday!'

'Yes, I know that, but I'd actually quite like to get to know Dan. That's why I texted you about the theatre, *two weeks ago*. I gave plenty of notice, and I've still not had a response. Presumably because Dan can't find a babysitter?'

'Maybe we don't want to go to the theatre. Did you ever *presume* that?'

'I was hoping to find out, that's why I invited you, Ella,' she retorted. 'Look, I don't want to argue. You're my daughter. I'm entitled to an opinion.'

'Yes.' I handed over a note to the woman behind the counter. 'But you don't have to share it. And that's all it is, Mum. Your opinion.'

'Okay, I get the message, Ella. I was minding my own business, when *you* called *me*, remember?'

'Don't start doing that uppity thing, Mum. It makes you sound ancient.'

'I don't sound ancient. I sound authoritative. That's what my producer says.'

'Your producer??'

'Anyway, see you at the weekend.'

'If I survive this one…'

'Ah, now we're getting somewhere.' Back to the talk show host again. Her professional interest ignited. 'So, tell me why you really called.'

'One cut knee and a missing eyebrow.'

'How did you manage that?'

'Not me. The children. Dan left them with me for half an hour and that's what happened.'

'Oh, for goodness sakes, Ella! Is that it?' No attempt to hide her disappointment. 'All children have weird and wonderful *minor accidents*, growing up. Remember that time you drank my nail polish?'

'You told me it was called Raspberry Ripple. That was different. You weren't my St—' I went to say it and realised what I was potentially parachuting into. 'You were my mum —
'

'Still am.'

'You know what I mean...'

'I do, but look on the brightside. It's hard work non-stop when they're your own children,' she said. 'You can't be held entirely accountable. Count your blessings you get to give them back after a few days.'

'Thanks for that wonderfully uplifting insight, Mother.'

By the time I finished lunch, I'd attached every single one of Heather's month-by-month breakdowns to yet another sodding email. Actually, I decided, she could have a hard copy too. Best to cover all bases before she complained about my lack of initiative. I'd even bind the thing and leave it on her desk with a fresh cup of almond milk tea. I pressed *Print*. A message appearing across my screen:

Remote Printer Out of Paper

Resentful Copywriter Out of Patience. I grabbed the keys to the stationery cupboard, the one concession towards career advancement I'd managed to keep hold of since Heather's return.

'What are you *DOING*?'

For a second, standing inside the small room of supplies, I thought Heather was photocopying her breasts in some early attempt at zhoosing up the Office Christmas Party.

'We're out of paper…' I said, as she turned, trying not to disturb the thick transparent wires leading from her nipples to a small unit on the shelf.

'This is an *Amanda Beau Cabuchi breast pump*! I've got a three-month-old at home. How dare you unlock that door!' she shouted, as I stuttered apologies. 'This is what a working mother looks like.' I went to step outside. 'No, no! Hold on, I need to talk to you. Wait right there —'

I stood in the doorway, dreading to think about what was going on back there.

'Keep your back turned, Ella. Not that you display any listening skills, or basic capability, but I need those reports urgently —'

'I was about to print them off.'

'I didn't ask for them to be *printed off*. I asked for you to email them. The correct information? If you think you can finally manage that this time?'

'The Steen & Heard database for the last 12-months. Attached to email.' I was attempting to speak in her native tongue. Devoid of human error. 'All yours.'

'It only took you all morning,' she huffed, as I clearly heard a slurping sound that I hadn't realised was physically possible until that moment.

'And,' she grew milder now, 'I'd rather prefer it if we kept this incident between ourselves.'

'Yes, of course, Heather.'

'Unless,' I heard her disassembling equipment behind me, 'you want Audrey to know I'm in here restocking the fridge with the 6oz of milk I expressed for my son at 7.30 this morning, which I presume you've been serving to the rest of the office during your impromptu tea rounds?'

Chapter Ten: Bad Words

From what Dan said, returning home on Monday night, a truce signalled by our usual smooch in the hallway, Bryony had gone ballistic about her daughter's missing eyebrow.

How the hell did Ella let this happen?

Does Ella actually spend any time supervising our children?

Grace was nervous enough about the wedding, without developing alopecia a few weeks before the ceremony…

'I wasn't in the best mood, last night.' He fixed my hair behind my ear. 'Sorry.'

'Me too,' I said, but there was a tiredness between us. Upstairs that night, after spending an entire day under the constant criticism of Hurricane Constantine, I was beginning to wonder if office life really was the right choice for me. Surely there were other jobs where defending yourself against eight hours of incoming attacks would be deemed heroic? The only small satisfaction I had was reminding myself that Heather was the reason I'd met Dan in the first place. She'd had a couple of meetings cancel one week and somehow managed to blame me, telling Audrey I should be bringing in business leads. That's when I'd gone for coffee with Kim, not looking for anywhere in particular, and spotted Dan's shop, Dr. Coffee. The first thing I'd noticed was how Dan's place wasn't like the usual coffee-chains, all bark-effect mugs and designer syrup. Dr. Coffee felt like a find. The kind of place Steen & Heard could work with, make into a 'Destination Location', as Audrey would say.

I'd been at the counter, Kim navigating her way towards a table, while I decided against the *Pain aux Raisin* because I still couldn't bring myself to use a faux-French accent without feeling like Inspector Clouseau. A sudden gasp brought everyone's attention to the middle of the room. A little girl sat clutching her throat. Her mother reached for her: *She's choking!* That was when Dan appeared, thumping the girl on the back until she sprayed beige-coloured mulch that turned out to be complimentary Biscotti across the table. The waitress brought water and napkins. The mother was still drying her eyes as Dan took his place back behind the counter.

'So's that why you're called Dr. Coffee?'

Great eyes. A dark smattering of stubble. He even had nice ears. Nice and neat. Kim said those were the kind of weird things only I'd notice.

'My dad was the doctor. This was his place.' His eyes briefly met mine. 'I don't think he'd have been quite so rattled by a bit of first aid. Happened to my daughter when she was about that age.'

I'd thought about the place for the rest of the week. I made notes about loyalty cards and asked Harry to mock up a template for Dr. Coffee receipts with *Your Prescription* printed in cursive along the top and *Just what the doctor ordered* scrolling along the bottom. I'd packed up Harry's handiwork and made the journey during my lunch hour, but Dan was out with suppliers and no one was sure when he'd be back.

I ordered a latte and sat alone with excuses and disappointment. The coffee was great, but deep down, I think I already knew I might just have gone back there to see the owner. *He'd said he had a daughter. Must have a wife to go with her.*

I was being ridiculous, but just as I was leaving, fiddling about with the derailed zip on my handbag, he appeared in the doorway and he smiled at me. Not just any smile. Once *the right guy* smiled at me, I knew the difference. My heart went off like a flashbulb, descending inside my chest, leaving me light-headed. *Ha!* I actually did feel a little light-headed, because it was a smile so familiar. I could've kissed him right then and there. I'd made some garbled explanation and handed over the paperwork, before heading off in the wrong direction, knocked sideways by the sight of him, following the drum of my own pulse.

When we finally did get together Dan didn't remember any of that. Not the same way I did. So I never shared the full, unedited version. But what he did remember was that when he'd finally called the office, I'd asked: *Saved anyone's life recently, Dr. Coffee?* like some flirty woman who went around saying things like that, when really, I was so nervous to hear from him. We'd chatted for a while. He'd told me how opening the place had been his father's dream. He'd taken early retirement as a G.P and come up with the Dr. Coffee brand. I loved that story. Before I knew it, one of Dan's new loyalty cards was tucked inside my purse, his name and number scrawled across the back, where my hand would sometimes find it and a smile would always follow.

While Dan sat in peace in front of the TV I stepped into the shower, finally relaxed, getting sentimental about how we got together. He looked like he'd had enough of step-girlfriends and ex-wives for one week. *So had I.* It had been so much easier when he was still Dr. Coffee and I was the Loyalty Card Girl he asked out.

I dried my hair, remembering how Kim and I used to turn Monday night into our Movie Night, both still recovering from the weekend. Kim would sit there in her rollers, while I painted my nails, eating sweet'n'salty popcorn. The worst it ever got with Kim was the occasional sullen silence over an overdue bill, a borrowed dress, a slightly pilfered fridge — usually, all down to me, but she cried when I moved out, so I can't have been that bad. I picked up my phone, about to cheer myself up with the photo Kim sent of herself, raising a toast, surrounded by a small crowd of half-naked model boys from the gallery, when I noticed a text from Mum: *We're going to the theatre. Plenty of time to get organized. See you next Friday! Mum X*

I knew she was right. It was exactly what I needed. Dan or no Dan, I needed a break from Stepfamily Robinson arrangements. And it was the perfect excuse to think about brilliant things, like what shoes to wear, hair up or down? I wrapped up the hairdryer and found my favourite dress in the wardrobe, which brought back all those memories of the first time I came back to the house. 'By the way,' he'd said that night, 'I've got every intention of calling you a cab. This isn't some weird kind of trap, getting you back here.' I'd looked into those blue eyes of his, hoping he was bluffing. Hoping it was definitely some kind of sexy man-trap. "I thought I'd let you see for yourself. I'm not living with my mother, or living it up in some bachelor pad. I'm boring. What you see is what you get,' he told me, as if that was a bad thing.

All of that came back to me the minute I put on the dress. Except, once it reached my ribcage I couldn't actually get the thing on. It wouldn't budge an inch. I pulled the fabric out from where it gathered across my chest and freed the lining, inching it down over my bust. I turned back to the mirror, gently easing the dress over my hips, slowly working the zip.

The Perfect Party Dress. And … *I was in!* A bit tight in places, but —

I heard the tear as soon as I took a breath out.

The dress was torn along the seam, literally gaping down one side.

I could barely stand to look. I slowly peeled myself out of it, before sticking it back on the hanger as fast as I could, hiding the evidence of its demise. I pulled my pyjama top back on and opened the wardrobe for another quick look. The torn remains of my dress were as depressing as a split condom.

Grace was right. How much weight had I put on? Without Kim nagging me to the gym, I hadn't exercised in months. I'd been relying on the stress of the kids to burn up a few thousand calories. I put my hand on my tummy and sat on the bed, analysing my thighs, before I heard Dan charting his way toward me across a pathway of switches and bolts.

'Given up on the TV?'

I tried to act as if I hadn't just found out I was twice the size I used to be.

Dan closed the bedroom door, still typing into his phone.

'Just had a text off Bryony.' He scanned the screen. 'She's doing some sort of buffet-picnic thing for the zoo. Told us not to worry about making anything for Grace and Ethan…'

'Bet she did…' I was busy applying hand cream, glad to see my fingers still looked about the same size. Hopefully there was no chance of them bursting through my gloves like the Hulk come winter-time. I was wondering exactly how bad a cook, girlfriend and general influence his ex-wife thought I was, as I got into bed. 'They've probably told her they hate my cooking.'

'She didn't mean it like that.' He sat on the side of the bed. 'She didn't want you to worry, that's all.'

Of course she didn't. Beautiful Bryony wouldn't want me to worry. The same way she'd never tear gut-first through a beautiful dress, or need a translator to read a recipe. I glanced at Dan, who was still mesmerized by his mobile, absentmindedly scratching his chest, deep in thought. I missed that look. When he wasn't worried or tired. Before I had moved in, we had talked, made plans. Now all we seemed to talk about was what to put in the fridge or on the TV until the kids arrived and the plans were made for us.

'Think I'm going to turn in.' He put down his mobile.

'Yep.' We switched off our lights. 'Me too.'

For a minute, I lay there, terrified we were turning into That Couple. Mr and Mrs Suburbia. All horrifically boring TV dramas and a cold mattress.

'So,' I propped myself up on one elbow, 'am I forgiven, then?'

'Forgiven?' He turned to face me and slid one thigh between my legs, before quickly dragging me on top of him. 'Yes. But I do think you need to vent that temper of yours.' He gripped my waist, pulling me towards him. His kiss sent a deep rush inside my mind as I felt him grow hard beneath me. 'And you do know what happens to bad girls who use bad words?'

Chapter Eleven: Browbeaten

'Bloody hell!' Leah called over as I made my way back from the printer. 'Someone's in a good mood this morning…'

'What?' I lovingly stapled together Heather's revised client list, as she took a conference call in Audrey's office. I'd already printed out her contacts sheet, updated all her email addresses and phone numbers, then caught up with my outstanding copy requirements for the week and still managed to check my horoscope, all before ten-thirty.

'You!' Leah said. 'Every time I look at you, you've got that bloody big grin on your face.'

'Caught up on my sleep,' I said. Using the International Girl Code for *up-all-night-in-various-states-of-undress-and-exhibitionism*. 'You're looking pretty chipper yourself this morning…'

Leah held my stare and shook her head.

'Nah,' she said, typing away. 'Just … normal.'

An Instant Message appeared at the corner of my screen:

Leah: *Stationery Cupboard. Now!*

I grabbed the keys, wondering what the news was, hoping she wasn't leaving, as I unlocked the door.

Harry Collins' face peered up at me.

For a second, I thought maybe he'd fallen over and got locked in there somehow, while replenishing his Biro collection. His voice growing hoarse from unanswered calls for help, as he uselessly reached for the door handle, pain telling him he was in desperate need of immediate surgery.

At that moment Leah appeared at my side and that's when we noticed he was lying on top of Karen. Our lovely receptionist. A jersey twin-set was pushed up around her chin, creating an obscene polo neck.

'It's not what it looks like!' He scrambled back into his trousers.

Leah let out a scream. I turned away, not risking the chance of seeing anymore of Harry, naked from knee to navel.

The clock finally crawled towards five as Heather emerged from Audrey's office. She'd been in and out of there all day, only pausing to tell Leah she hated her choice of font for the Steen & Heard blog post and could she change it immediately. That word again. *Immediately.* Everything in Heather's world was immediate. I should come to work in a toboggan, so I could hurtle through her requirements a little faster.

Leah and I watched as she switched off her computer, grabbed her coat, picked up a multitude of official-looking bags and left without a word.

'Ah! Another happy day on the calendar. Bye then, Heather.' I waved. 'Have a fantastic weekend! No, please, don't mention it. Just doing my job. You'll only embarrass me…'

'What *is* her problem?' Leah applied her lipstick now the coast was clear.

'No idea.' I reached into my handbag and took out my perfume. 'But I'm getting pretty sick of solving it for her.'

Friday night, finally at home, I made my way into the lounge, stopping as I heard Grace: 'It was, like, burning. I was screaming, but by the time she came it was too late. Bits of hair were already coming out in clumps. Ella was just going on about me not reading the label.'

'Oh, darling!' Pippa gasped. 'I know!'

I'd expected Grace to throw her heart into it. I didn't expect to be so shocked by her rendition, not when I'd actually been there. She was turning last Saturday into The Salem Witch Trials and doing just as good a job as Winona Ryder in *The Crucible*. Listening to Grace *I'd* have had me arrested.

'But Grandma —' She sniffed away tears — 'That was the whole point. I couldn't read the instructions. I told her, I had soap in my eyes.'

Wow. She was good.

She had more than just soap in her eyes. She had Soap Opera in them.

Lawyer, Activist, Actress, I thought. *This kid's going to do big things one day.*

'Well, of course not,' Pippa, who'd called around to drop off Ethan's present, so he could open it on his birthday morning, agreed. I found myself agreeing, too. *Who wouldn't?* I mean, we'd all believe the report of an innocent child over an incompetent adult.

'And the next thing, we thought Ethan had bust, I mean, *broken*, his ankle —'

'Ella was nice to me...'

A weak smile drifted across my face as Ethan spoke in his most solemn voice. He might've only been about to turn eight, but even he knew a stitch up when he heard one. His sister was manipulating the grown-ups quicker than he rearranged action figures.

'We didn't think he'd broken his ankle, Grace,' Dan corrected. 'I only said —'

'But you *did say* it looked badly swollen, Dad. That's why I panicked, after you said that. And it's Mum's wedding next week.' She broke into fresh tears, as my soul booked a one-way ticket to Purgatory. I wished Dan had never got her that John Grisham boxset for Christmas. Theodore Boone had a lot to answer for.

'Daniel, where were you when all this was going on?'

'What does that mean? *Where was I?*'

I took a seat in the lounge, not ready to brave the conversation just yet. The jury was out and I remembered an echo of my own grandmother. Something about people who listened in on conversations never hearing anything good about themselves.

'What are you doing?'

Ethan appeared in the doorway.

'I'm eating egg mayonnaise from the mixing bowl.' I was caught red-handed.

'That's dirty.' He scrunched his face in disgust.

'It was meant to be a private moment.'

'Mum says you can't expect privacy,' he explained, 'not with two kids in the house.'

'Yeah, I'm beginning to realize that.'

'Are you going to stop?'

'I'll stop eating this when you stop picking your nose.'

'I don't pick my nose!' He grinned.

'Yes you do…'

He shook his head.

'Everyone's picked their nose at least once.'

'Have you?'

'No.' I took another spoonful. 'I get to eat egg mayo from the bowl instead.'

'That's worse.'

'No, it's not. Picking your nose is much worse.'

'At least I don't eat it.' He shrugged, as Pippa's voice boomed from the hallway: 'Why was *Ella* looking after my grandchildren?'

Thanks, Pippa.

'Grandma's here.' Ethan ran back off into the hall.

'I do leave the house occasionally, Mum,' Dan was saying. 'I was walking Starky. Ella's perfectly capable —'

'Well, obviously not! Look at your daughter's face…'

'Mum, it was an accident. She's fine. They both are.'

'Fine? Hardly!'

Grace broke into louder sobs.

'Mum, you're upsetting her.'

'Oh, *I'm* upsetting her, am I? Name one time when either of the children has ever come to any harm in *my* care, Daniel?'

Harm? What was that about? I didn't like it. The definition was too intended. Too premeditated. It made me sound like some sort of Step-monster.

'It's only her eyebrow. It'll grow back,' Dan tried to reason with her. 'You can't even notice it behind her fringe.'

'What's left of her fringe, you mean!' Pippa pointed out. 'She's still got marks on her forehead. And what's this? Is this makeup?'

'Ella told me to draw on a fake eyebrow,' Grace said in her weakest voice, as if I'd tied her to a chair and attacked her with a kohl stick. 'I told her I didn't want to.'

But you asked to borrow it! I thought.

'This is ridiculous!' Pippa said and by this point I agreed with her. 'This is no way for Gracie to spend the summer,' she said, over sniffles from her granddaughter. 'And she's got the wedding!'

Perfect. So now I'd ruined Bryony's wedding. I sat back against the armchair, knowing I had to join the conversation but not how I was supposed to do it. It was like skipping rope. Every time I went to jump in I tripped over how to face Dan's mother, when, according to Grace, I'd left her screaming in pain, while I caught up on *E! News*, filing my nails, or something.

The door swung open. Ethan appeared again.

'Why are you sitting there?'

'I think I might be in trouble...'

'Uh-huh.' He nodded. 'My sister doesn't like you.'

'I know. Can't really say I blame her, I suppose…'

'She's always like this.' He shrugged. 'Even Mum says so.'

'Yeah? Well, I don't think that's going to help me. It's my fault.' I had to get out there and be a good influence, not hide behind doors, too scared to face grown-ups while in front of Ethan. 'But you do know I'd never do anything to hurt you, *either* of you, don't you?'

He thought about it for a second and gave a nod.

'Well then. That's all I need to explain to your grandma. Come on.'

I marched out before I could change my mind. I wasn't very good at being a role model. I'd never been one before. I'd never even been a Prefect, and even Janine Langley, who cut off her own ponytail in the school canteen using a butter knife, got to be one.

'Pippa?'

Ethan raced ahead, joining the congregation by the front door.

'I feel terrible. Ethan fell. Grace was shouting from upstairs. I was running between the two of them. I wish I could just rewind the whole weekend.'

Ethan turned himself into a robot, rotating his shoulders, walking backwards, as I said that. Meanwhile, his sister looked away with a pout that said: *Excuses are pointless when I've already told Grandma my version: Guilty as charged!*

'I know two children can be difficult to cope with Ella, but there's Bryony's opinion to think about here.' Pippa narrowed her eyes and tightened her lips. 'Do you think she's going to agree with the sentiment *accidents happen*. I don't think so...'

'Can you two both go upstairs and sort out your things, please?' Dan manoeuvred the children away as soon as Pippa started talking about their mother.

'I told Mum last week, I'm okay, Grandma.' Worry washed over Ethan's face. 'It doesn't even hurt anymore. Look.' He pulled up his joggers and showed her his plaster.

'You're very brave is what you are,' Pippa said, combing back his hair.

'At least he only fell over. Mine's worse.' Grace was never too keen on sharing the spotlight. 'He does that all the time anyway.'

'Exactly.' Dan agreed. 'And he's fine. You both are.' He fixed her with a look that soured her expression. 'So go and unpack your things, please —'

'Dad!'

'Grace, do as you're told. We've got to be organized and ready to get straight out to meet everyone at the zoo in the morning. Have you finished your essay for school on Monday?'

'No...'

'There you go then. Go and finish it before we have dinner.'

Grace looked to her grandma for support.

'Go on...' Pippa echoed. 'Ethan, up you go, too. You can't be distracted, not around his children,' Pippa continued, setting her sights back on me as the children traipsed upstairs. 'Your distraction could cost us our visitation rights.'

'Mum! You're completely overreacting...'

'Daniel, I just want Ella to understand that we're in the middle of a legal arrangement here.'

'It's not a legal arrangement,' Dan muttered. 'I'm their dad.'

'I know you're their dad, but whether we like it or not, that's exactly what it is. Both of those children went home in a state,' she reminded us. 'Any mother would have every right to be concerned. You have to be so careful in these situations…'

I took Ethan's makeshift seat on the stairs, realising I'd inadvertently sat on The Naughty Step. 'Maybe I could speak to Bryony?' I suggested, not wanting Dan to deal with 'the situation' alone. 'You know, just explain what happened?'

'It's fine,' he said. 'She already knows what happened. I spoke to her last weekend. It's done, Mum. She's fine.'

'Dad?' Ethan hollered down from his bedroom. 'I can't find my socks!'

'Yes, but the whole thing's my fault and I'm the only one who still hasn't spoken to their mum —'

'Ella, it's fine. Mum, they've had accidents before. They'll have them again.' Dan shuffled past to help his son.

'Well,' Pippa turned to me. 'What a mess.'

I remembered how Ethan had looked, crying on the stairs, while Grace was practically hysterical in the bathroom. Then Dan driving us in silence to the hospital.

'I've told Daniel a thousand times, I can be here in two ticks. Leaving them here, it's not fair on you. It's definitely not fair on them,' Pippa managed. 'Ah,' she said, with a sudden nostalgia, 'at least they're both looking forward to tomorrow. The zoo. That'll be nice for the children. We'll all get ice creams and watch the monkeys.' She looked at me now, expression softening. 'All I'm trying to say is, there's a great deal of trust involved for Bryony, having to hand over her children every weekend. We see so little of them both as it is. I'd hate for that trust to be broken.'

Burner of eyebrows. Breaker of trust. They may as well say it: *Danger to children.*

Mum mightn't think it was such a big deal, but I was learning pretty quickly: Step-girlfriends didn't get to turn childhood accidents into cute, childhood anecdotes.

Chapter Twelve: Zoo Day

Both of the kids were upstairs the next morning, hopefully getting dressed, although there was a good chance the birthday boy had snuck back onto his computer. Grace was messing around, straightening her hair and complaining about the results, still in her dressing gown. Meanwhile, I was busy loading up the cooler bag when Kim called. Kim had been in bed for the last two days with some stomach flu thing. I was hoping she might make an overnight recovery, or at least let me visit her while she was sick so I could catch it and have a legitimate excuse to get out of zoo day.

Dan wandered past, texting away, finishing his second coffee. I'd let mine go cold, trying to work out how you were supposed to construct a sandwich wrap without the help of some industrial-strength glue or a team of specially-trained experts.

'*I knew it…*'

'Seriously, Ella. I feel like I'm dying…'

So do I, I thought to myself. *On my arse.*

'I was throwing up all night…' She paused to sip a drink.

'Are you sure you don't want me to visit?'

Despite her seemingly-exciting single life, Kim had no one around when it mattered. No matter who you were, everyone needed someone to hold back their hair in the bathroom and run to the pharmacy every once in a while.

'Do you need anything? Painkillers? Shopping?' I listed every reason I could think of to bow out of the 'blended family' trip, which had the capacity to ignite like a Molotov cocktail.

'Honestly, no.' She sounded knackered. 'I just need to sleep.'

'Well, open a window. Let the germs out.' I heard myself issuing instructions from some sepia-tinted childhood illness. 'Are you sure you don't want to come out to the zoo with us? The fresh air might do you good?' I sliced through a tomato. A semi-domesticated girlfriend about to be released into the Wild. An endangered species without a keeper.

Bryony had said not to bother with food, but I'd followed a hunch that it was some sort of red herring. It was the same way people said *you shouldn't have!* when they were expecting that thoughtful bottle of wine on arrival or the 'Thank You' card through the post. It was exhausting trying to work the etiquette out between the lines.

'Right now,' Kim rasped, 'I'm not planning on leaving my bed. There's no way I could spend the day traipsing around, surrounded by kids, staring at elephants.'

'You're a teacher! You're surrounded by kids every day.'

'Exactly. So the last thing I want is to go looking for them. It's okay for you. You get to work with civilised human beings. People who tie their own shoe-laces, wipe their own butts —'

'Not all of them.'

'— I have to stand there in front of a lynch mob every morning.'

Kim's Tales from Kindergarten. It was exactly how I remembered school. I'd never have guessed most of my teachers probably felt the same way, not until I'd listened to Kim regretting the day she ever qualified.

'Well, I still think you should do something with those amazing jewellery designs of yours…'

'I'm getting there. I've been working on some pieces. But back in the real world nobody else seems all that interested in my *amazing* jewellery designs…'

'Oh, stop being such a miserable cow. The summer holidays are coming up.'

'I don't have summer holidays. I'm only ever in between OFSTED reports.'

'Okay, Kim. I'll quit trying to cheer you up.'

'Good.'

'I thought it was men who made the worst patients?'

'Good job I'm not a bloke then, isn't it?'

'Well, listen —' I checked my watch, knowing we needed to head off — 'If you need anything, give me a shout.'

'At the zoo? Like what? A koala bear keyring?' Kim sounded even worse when she tried to laugh. 'I'm more worried about you.' She paused to cough, holding one hand over the phone. 'Do you reckon their mum'll be funny about the eyebrow thing?'

'No idea,' I said, semi-casual, considering I'd been thinking that exact same thing all morning.

'Talk to her about weddings or something. It'll be fine,' Kim advised. 'Has it grown back yet?'

'No, but don't worry, if she brings it up, at least I'll have my mother there to make the whole thing even worse.' I kept an eye out in case Dan overheard. 'And if things get really bad I'll grab a bunch of bananas and dive head-first into the nearest gorilla compound.'

Our cars pulled up at roughly the same time. We were stepping out of our metal boxes to spend the day gawping at other creatures, looking just as bored in theirs.

'Ella! Hey there, dude!' Vic headed towards me, pastel pink jumper tied across his shoulders, golfer-style and a pair of Aviators perched on top of his head.

Bryony's soon-to-be-second-husband was the kind of 'dude' who dropped phrases like *Hit the ground running* and *Singing from the same hymn sheet* into everyday conversation. Whenever I saw him, which thankfully wasn't all too often, mainly dropping the children off on a Friday, he always made a beeline for me. It was as if he thought the fellow black sheep of the whole Stepfamily set-up was desperate for his company. I didn't think anyone had *ever* been that desperate.

Kids by their side, Pippa and Dan stood by Bryony's car: the gleaming BMW, or *Beamer* as Vic called it, that he'd bought her to celebrate their engagement. Ethan was jumping up and down, telling his mum what his dad had got him for his birthday by the looks of things. An adopted, new-born meerkat. The new-born meerkat I'd told Dan how much Ethan would love in the first place, but he hadn't even waited for me to get out of the shower before he gave Ethan the gift pack.

Grace was unfolding a map, Bryony and Pippa standing either side, presumably going over the itinerary for the day. I was unloading the boot as Vic lurched towards me. Practicing his usual sleight-of-mouth he aimed for my cheek then planted a cigarette-scented kiss squarely on my lips before standing back to give me his trademark, lingering once-over.

'Looking *fantastico* as ever.' He made a complimentary 'O' between index finger and thumb. His slightly jaundiced gaze was horribly fixated on my chest: 'Nice flats you've got there.'

I glanced down, in fear of a rogue nipple.

'A *trés* fashionable,' he said, by way of explanation, 'suede ballerina pump.'

'Oh. Right.'

'Size six?'

'Erm, yeah.' I wished he'd stop staring at my feet and hoped his eyes weren't travelling towards my bum as I grabbed hold of the cooler bag.

'Don't tell me. You can't've forgotten? I'm in the "shoe" business!' He placed his Aviators on the bridge of his nose, smuggling laughter through his nostrils like a round of asthmatic-hiccups, as he repeated the line from his latest radio jiggle. The same one he sang every time he saw me: *'There's no business like "shoe" business…'* He gave a jazz-hand wave without a trace of irony. 'Love that. Clever line.' He nodded. 'Clever line. You know, I can tell a lot about a woman by her shoes…'

'Really?'

Vic had followed in his grandfather's footsteps as CEO of *Heel the World*, importing overpriced designer footwear. I was wondering if Vic's groin had ever been punctured by a well-placed stiletto, as I spotted Bryony making her way over, blonde hair flowing, soft pink t-shirt revealing perfectly toned arms, as she handed over the car keys.

'I really don't understand your interest in everyone else's shoes, Vic,' she said. 'You've been wearing that same style loafer for the last two years…' She gave a quick nod in my direction. 'Nice to see you,' she said with a smile that avoided her eyes, presumably because Vic could do with a patch to disguise his wandering one.

'Ella?' Dan was helping Ethan into his backpack. 'Your mum's here.' He looked over towards the farthest side of the car park.

Mum raised a hand, pretty as ever in a floaty polka-dot dress.

'Nice arch…'

'*What?*' Bryony snapped, as Vic zoomed in, lowering his shades.

'Her shoes,' he explained. '*D'Orsey*. They've *got* to be Italian…'

Tickets at the ready, we'd just about made it through the entrance, washing up in a shore of similarly tired-looking family outings, before Vic realised his six-year-old twins, Philip and Theo, were still in the back of the car. They were staging some sit-in protest, Bryony said, refusing to leave the back seat.

While Ethan haggled with Dan over the price of some animal face-painting, Bryony and Grace were deciding which direction the group should head off in first.

'I bet you can't believe how big they're both getting,' my mum said, attempting light-hearted, mum-regulation conversation with Dan's mum.

'I certainly can't.' Pippa looked over at them. 'I can still remember Ethan fast asleep in his carry-cot, only a couple of days old. Gracie always stood up, sucking her thumb. My husband, Derek, used to say, *Turn around and they'll be jumping in the driver's seat next*, which is about right. Seems like only the blink of an eye, when Derek was here and Ethan was still in his baby-grow…'

Dan's dad had passed away nearly three years ago. His parents had been like salt and pepper, he said. Totally different, but you couldn't imagine one without the other. Dan was really close to his dad. Derek used to call him every day until he got really sick, still wanting to know how the shop was going. Chatting about sport, telling him the latest films to recommend to the regulars, or about his latest finds in the name of bird watching: *Only the kind your mother would approve of*, he liked to joke, too ill to venture out much, using his new binoculars as a window to the world.

'None of us knows how long we've got,' Pippa announced, before Mum piped up: 'I agree. Have to make the most of every moment. I said to Ella only the other day, you're only young once. She won't get these years back. Her twenties...'

'You've picked a lovely day to come to the zoo, Ethe.' I was trying to steer my mother away from anything too serious before she caused a family divide.

'He didn't choose today. It's his birthday,' Grace deadpanned, fixing her fringe over her slightly-shiny brow before turning back to her dad with the kind of expression that made me keep any other thoughtful observations to myself.

'That's our Grace!' Pippa laughed, holding her jacket over her shoulders, each hand on the opposite lapel rather than inside the sleeves like a normal person. 'Quick as a whip she is!'

And just as painful, I thought.

'*We're at the zoo! We're at the zoo!*' Ethan sped past with the twins, now freed from captivity, in close succession. Pippa linked Dan's arm. My mother gave me a nudge and linked mine as I felt the kind of dread usually reserved for wild, late-night African safaris.

Chapter Thirteen: Don't Feed the Animals

We made our way from the giraffes to the Monkey House, with Mum pointing out a particularly athletic chimpanzee. Pippa, Dan and Bryony strolled along, chatting, as Grace clasped her dad's hand and Ethan clashed two warring, plastic figures against each other, walking alongside his mother.

They looked relaxed. Happy. *They looked like a family.*

Dan, Bryony and the kids travelled a little further ahead, finally disappearing into the crowd. I looked at my mum, who was smiling inanely at the chimps. I was far too old to be spending a day out at the zoo with her, now that Dan had left me to it. The twins ran over to the other side of the enclosure, blowing their mouths against the glass, heckled by an ineffective Vic, who was fixing his hair, more concerned with his own reflection than keeping an eye on them.

'Hold on, hold on!' Pippa held a bulky old-fashioned camera at shoulder height. 'That's the picture!' She crouched, paparazzo-style, as Dan, Bryony and the children smiled for the camera, monkeys playing in the background. 'Look at Grandma! Happy Birthday Ethan … *and* … we've got it!'

Mum delved inside her pocket, offering me a lozenge for some reason, while Dan searched the crowd, raising his hand as he found me.

'Ella!' He waved me over to join them, but the moment was gone.

I followed Mum out, making my way towards the Aquarium, thinking that we must be the only species dumb enough to attempt this stepfamily stuff.

Sitting in the Picnic Area, only halfway through the day, our group took up two separate tables in front of the Outdoor Adventure Area.

Dan was sitting with the children.

Mum and I found ourselves lumbered with Vic.

'Daddy! We just laughed at the fat kid!'

Theo jumped up and down in front of his father as I nibbled at one of the chicken salad wraps I'd packed, opting for something healthy, even though we were sitting by a Snack Attack Shack serving the most delicious-smelling hot dogs with way too much ketchup and just the right amount of mustard. But no matter how gorgeously wrong they smelled, I wasn't letting the side down, not in front of Bryony. Definitely not in front of Grace. From that moment on, with the memory of the tattered remains of my favourite dress hanging in the wardrobe, it was rocket and pine nuts all the way.

'And then the boy cried!' Philip sniggered.

I was trying to pretend Philip and Theo were two innocent children, but there was something about them, something so undisputedly 'Vic', that was completely disturbing in their matching miniature form.

'I'm not down with that, guys,' Vic replied, more for our benefit than theirs, I thought, as he noticed us listening.

'It *was* funny.' Theo folded his arms.

'Yeah.' A huge grin spread across Philip's face. 'We was walking like this.' He waddled from side to side, air inflating his cheeks.

'You pair of rascals.' Vic shared that unconditional grin only parents fully owned, grabbing both boys for a group hug.

Ethan sat beside his dad at the next table, chatting about Lego. Grace sat across from them, huddled over the zoo map as she bit into an apple. Bryony rearranged plastic containers, oblivious to everyone, until she absentmindedly placed one hand on Dan's shoulder, giving his arm a quick pat as he accepted her offer of a sandwich. It was almost slow-motion, like watching some former moment from Dan's old life playing out right there in front of me. I decided to open my sugar-free yogurt, not wanting to catch any more tender moments between Dan and his ex-wife.

'Broke Derek's heart, really.' I reluctantly tuned into Pippa's conversation. She'd wandered over, making an effort with Mum, pouring tea from a flask and complaining about zoo prices. Vic and the twins, who refused to sit and eat their lunch, went back to monopolize the climbing frame.

I reached for my bottle of water, realising Dan wasn't going to eat a single thing I'd packed, not even after he'd seen me spend all morning preparing food.

There was no way I was going over there to offer him anything. I'd feel like I was competing over whose picnic he preferred, Bryony's or mine. And from the state of my sandwich wraps, I didn't need confirmation.

'We hoped they'd work out their differences, especially when there're children involved, but what can you do?' Pippa batted away a wasp, as my mother took a drink.

Rather than stuff my ears with my pimento peppers to avoid any more of Pippa's conversation I was actually glad to see Bryony, elegant and understated in a stylish maxi skirt, heading over towards us: 'Carrot cake?'

'Oh, no. Thanks.' I tried not to, but I was still picturing her hand back on Dan's shoulder. 'I'm trying to be good.' *Especially after your daughter's given me an eating disorder and what used to be my best dress looks like some sort of makeshift maternity smock.* I put my empty yogurt carton inside our designated rubbish bag as Bryony took a seat beside me.

'So am I,' she insisted, 'so *please* share the guilt. If you don't have some I'll end up demolishing the whole thing myself.'

Even her picnic was perfectly accessorized. Homemade cake sitting prettily on a doily. My wraps were barely edible, at least not in public. A tide of lettuce and tomato had washed up around my ankles, as if they'd been ripped from the clutches of the Malayan Sun Bears.

'Oh well.' I screwed the cap back on my bottle. 'At least it's got carrots in it.'

'Don't tell Ethan that.' Bryony glanced over at her son, who was sitting up on his knees, picking out his favourites from a bowl of sweets. 'It's just about the only thing containing vegetables I can get into his stomach these days...'

She handed me a plastic fork, her huge diamond engagement ring catching the light like a laser beam. She was so good at this. So prepared. The kind of woman who probably owned one of those weird clay pot things you cooked rice dishes in and actually knew how to use it. In fact, judging by the doily, she probably had her own kiln and made the thing herself, just in time for dinner.

'I feel as if we never get a chance to talk, you and I.' She cut into the cake, not the skinny-arsed slice I'd been expecting, but a proper mouthful. 'It's ridiculous, really.'

'Bryony, I feel so bad about last weekend —'

Mouth surprisingly full of calories, she shook her head.

'I went off on Dan. It was all the wedding stuff,' she said. 'I've been so stressed out. I'm refurbishing my Yoga studio. Still managing Vic's schedule. Coordinating 200 guests. It's in-sane.'

'I didn't know you had a Yoga studio.'

'Well, I don't. Not yet. It's just that, as Vic pointed out, I've been renting studios for the last couple of months, teaching classes and I may as well set up my own. I'm renovating a small unit.' She flicked her golden hair over one shoulder.

'At least you can relax after the wedding.'

'You're joking, aren't you? As soon as the wedding's over Vic's lined up a meeting for me with his friend who's interested in stocking a range of workout clothes I've designed. I've just had the samples delivered, actually.'

'Wow.' I was genuinely impressed, and permanently inadequate. 'That's amazing!'

'Nothing fancy.' She shrugged and took another bite. 'So, the whole A&E stuff with the kids?' She shook her head again. 'Dan caught me at a bad time. I'm going to pay for Ethan's physio myself. I've told Dan he doesn't need to worry about that, and Grace's skin looks fine since I got her those gel packs. The dermatologist gave her the all-clear. I've been massaging her brow myself. Re-growth's looking fine.'

'Well, thanks for being so understanding.' *Physio and a dermatologist??*

I took a big mouthful of cake to celebrate, grateful that at least one member of the family wasn't likely to press charges.

'Listen, it happens. Don't look so strung-out.' She smiled. 'I nipped the top of Ethan's ear once, trying to give him a home haircut. He cried for an hour.'

I would have smiled, but after Bryony saying we never got the chance to talk I was slightly worried I was taking part in some child-rearing suitability test.

'Come here.' She put down her plate and jumped up, suddenly digging her fingertips into my hair. 'You're a mass of blocked energy.'

'Oh, I'm fine.' I tried to back away, as she carried on backcombing my scalp.

I could feel people looking at us and hoped they didn't think she was checking me for tics. We looked like a pair of love-struck gorillas.

'Honestly, my energy's great.'

'It will be. Give me two seconds while I balance your Chakras.'

'I wanted to call you, you know. To apologise.' I tried straightening up, hoping that it might help improve my Chakras, but she was persistent. 'Dan was worried I might make things worse.'

'Was he now?' She started doing some weird tapping thing on the top of my skull. 'Well, that's Dan for you…' I was tempted to ask what else was 'Dan for you', but the thought of someone else being so close to him, close enough to know things I hadn't discovered, kept me quiet. 'I just mean,' she finally backed away from my barnet, 'he was never the best at talking. Not to me, anyway…'

I used to wish men came with references from their exes. *Too tight to buy a lottery ticket. Digs for ear wax while driving.* That sort of stuff. Those small complaints that gave you a strangely reassuring glimpse into why you were eventually going to break-up with them, but sitting next to Bryony (*perfect, Bryony*), I didn't want to know anything about her and Dan.

'So.' She threw a cautious glance behind her, finding her former mother-in-law had stolen her place at the bench, chatting to Dan. 'Pippa spends a lot of time with the children…'

'Every weekend.' I noticed Mum talking to Theo and hoped he wasn't threatening her.

'You get off lightly.' Bryony popped the last piece of cake into her mouth, eyes brightening with amusement. 'The thing about Pippa is.' She finished her cake. 'She likes to dish out the guilt; but things were always the same. Any excuse for her to wade in and take over. I was never good enough, that's for sure.'

'Really?' I hoped I didn't sound as relieved as I felt, but if Bryony wasn't good enough, maybe that meant I could stop trying as hard? 'She's always so nice about you...'

'I bet she is.' Bryony pursed her lips. 'Now that I'm out of the picture, you mean? God, I don't miss those days...'

'Mum!' Grace shouted over. 'Come and see this!'

'Right.' Bryony stood up. She pulled an unimpressed face that could have belonged to her daughter. 'I'd better go and see what Grace's up to. *Phew.*' She waved her hand in front of her. 'Really warm today, isn't it?'

'Grandma's found where the meerkats live!' Grace called.

'Good old Grandma.' Bryony waved over at her daughter as she got to her feet. 'Oh well, better go and see what they're up to. Might sit next to Pippa.' She wandered back off and turned with a smile. 'That ought to lower the temperature.'

'Enjoying yourself?'

I'd almost forgotten Mum was sitting there. I thought about being polite and lying, but I didn't have the energy or the inclination. Maybe my Chakras really did need balancing. Part of the reason I'd wanted Mum there was so she could see how it was with me, Dan and the kids, but with Bryony and Pippa present it looked like I was dating a bigamist.

'Did you enjoy hearing how disappointed Pippa is that Dan and Bryony ever broke up?'

'We all have to make compromises.' Mum swerved from her seat to my side of the bench. 'But —' I could see she was in two minds over whether to finish — 'Sometimes, I do wonder: what's Dan compromising for you?'

'My happiness?'

She leant her head to one side.

'That was a joke.'

'There are no jokes, Ella.'

'Of course not. Everything's *deadly serious*. Not everything needs a five year plan, Mum.'

'Maybe, but maybe I don't want to see my daughter co-parenting someone's children when these should be her fancy-free years. You're starting out in your career. I made sacrifices for your education, not so you could end up living like a glorified child-minder.'

'Mum!'

'Is he prepared to make some sort of commitment, if that's what you want?' she said, as if she was chairing one of her charity panels.

'He *has* made a commitment to me. We live together.'

'I mean, a romantic commitment, not a living arrangement.'

'Mum, we're not talking about marriage.'

Marriage was one of those things I thought might just happen one day, when I least expected it. All part of the same, steady evolution, that would leave me with grey roots and bifocals, carrying an endless supply of mints in my pocket.

'Exactly…'

'So now you're a traditionalist? You've never even been married!'

'Yes, I know. I *think* I'd remember, but I suppose if you're going to go ahead and jump in with both feet, I'd like to see Dan getting his toes a bit wet too, that's all.'

As a technicolour carousel of parents and children whirled past on repeat, I couldn't be bothered explaining. I didn't know where to start. Since I'd moved in everything had become so much bigger than those small things, like if we were planning on spending the rest of our lives together. I was still trying to get through the basic 'living together' part first.

'Mum, we've only been together a year and a half! And if I do ever get married, I can do without an arranged one, thanks!'

The words hung like bunting as Grace meandered over, getting a glass from the cooler bag.

'Maybe,' Mum trilled, 'but you don't buy the cow when there's milk in the fridge...'

'Well, if it makes you feel any better —' I noticed one of Grace's earphones hanging loose, freed from her ear — 'we run out of milk all the time, and we're both fine with it.' Grace headed off, wearing a puzzled look. 'There're worse things than meeting someone with children. What about that guy you dated who kept his dentures in his pocket?'

'I wasn't dating him! We went out for one meal to discuss a work project. Look, I'm not saying I don't like Dan. Quite the opposite in fact, but you've moved into his house, you've inherited the children —'

'I didn't *inherit* them, Mum. They're not a pair of earrings.'

'Oh, you know what I mean. You've bought into the whole family set-up.'

'It's not some dodgy timeshare, either.'

'You've made a commitment to his children.' She brushed an imaginary crease from her skirt and placed her hands either side of the bench. 'You're nearly ten years younger than him. No children. No baggage...'

'No interfering mother to worry about?'

She crossed her legs, elbow balanced on one knee, face propped on her hand. I had a premonition of her hosting some pseudo-psychological daytime TV show, looking exactly like this, giving tender-faced close-ups to the camera.

'I want whatever you want, Ella, but even the best of them are selfish.' She gazed over at the twins, both cheering as Vic got tangled up in the rope swing. 'He's an odd one, isn't he?'

'Vic?'

'I don't know what Bryony sees in him. She's very attractive.'

'Try: his own business, a holiday home in France, and unlimited designer shoes for starters…'

'Along with violent children, a perspiration problem and those God-awful, too-tight trousers.' She eyed his chinos with disdain. 'There must be specialist shops hidden away for men his age…'

'He's younger than you!'

'I'm a *very young* fifty-four!' She gave a wiggle of her hips. 'And I'd never date a man who wore trousers like that, no matter how old he was,' she said, clearly appalled. 'They're practically flesh-coloured. He looks naked from the waist down from where I'm sitting.'

'Not the best look for a children's play area…'

We were giggling over Vic's flesh-coloured pants when something so surreal happened I was almost convinced I must've dreamt it. Until I remembered there were witnesses — and forensic evidence.

Philip — twin one — galloped towards us without a word, pulling down his pants as if to wee on the grass verge, which was distracting enough, me and mum craning our necks in search of Vic, until he spun round, spraying urine straight onto my handbag. *Deliberately*. He actually took aim and fired.

Then Theo — twin two — appeared, carrying a packet of biscuits. A chocolate Hobnob dangling from his mouth, he danced around his brother in a protective circle, camouflaging any attempt at adult authority. Reciting Incy Wincey Spider at the top of his lungs, red-faced with delight at his twin brother's strange display of, what Mum later diagnosed in her professional capacity, the early manifestation of a sexual disorder. Only after Mum literally screamed: 'Stop that, immediately!' did they finally run away.

I couldn't help but think Kim would have crawled from her deathbed if she'd known what she was going to miss. There were shocked glances from surrounding tables. Vic arrived and the next thing I knew everyone was laughing politely, as if this was all some regular, unspoken occurrence at children's birthday parties.

Maybe it was.

Maybe it was yet another one of those fun facts only parents knew about.

At least Dan had the decency to stand up, grim-faced, as I tried not to reveal my true colours as someone who thought Vic's twins were a pair of psychopaths who needed locking up. Six-years-old or not, I'd've sent them straight to the nearest cell, where they could pee wherever they wanted.

I was relieved to see at least Grace and Ethan were freaking out and staying safely beside Bryony, who issued a long, disgusted glance at her fiancé's sons, before coming over to help, offering me a packet of baby-wipes.

'Even the Kray Twins wouldn't have pissed on someone's handbag,' she muttered, as I gently wiped at stain marks. 'Maybe they're going to take after their father and spend the rest of their lives obsessing over women's accessories. Count yourself lucky,' she said, 'God knows what I'm going to find in my shoes one of these days...'

Chapter Fourteen: Eatza Pizza

I'd made it through the day, relatively safely, and I was ready to limp exhausted across the finishing line when Bryony suggested we stop off for dinner on the way home. The Birthday Boy made the decision to dine at Eatza Pizza, which at six o'clock on a Saturday night was more frantic than the non-stop procession of prams, sugar-fuelled kids and dehydrated parents at the zoo.

Pippa was chatting with Grace and Bryony, nodding along politely, smile fixed, like a grandma in a sit-com, the way she always looked in front of her former daughter-in-law. The men folk wrestled their sons into line, discussing the afternoon's football results. All I wanted was to get home and dry out my handbag. Instead, I was surrounded by pop music blasting out from speakers, paper-crowned heads running past at waist-height and hands juggling plastic bowls or dripping with ice cream, precariously balanced on top of cones. Everywhere you looked it was the same scene. Parents lost control at tables, arms craned over wilting slices of jumbo-sized pizza. Smaller kids were crying out in high chairs, noses streaming as they tearfully chewed soggy mouthfuls of Eatza Pizza's famous fries. The place was permanently in motion, trays were stacked with discarded boxes and congealed remains and staff swayed past with platters.

Unbelievably, I'd started to think pizza places and pubs that still smelled of the 1966 World Cup Final were quite romantic after my first date with Dan. We'd met in one of the older bars in town: all hardwood floors and studded leather seating. We sat together in a corner booth. Dan was a few minutes late after dropping the children off with his mum. 'So,' he had broken the silence. 'Do you have kids?' I'd laughed, no idea what to talk about to people who did.

But, by the time we stopped off for pizza, nearly three hours, two life stories, and several gin and tonics later, I knew I wanted to see him again. 'Might throw you a bit with my choice of topping, though,' I'd told him, as we stood in the queue.

'Really?' He played mock-serious, scanning the menu, which was mounted full-length across the back wall.

'I've had some comments in the past,' I admitted. 'Kim, the girl I share with? She thinks it's disgusting.'

'Disgusting? *Really?*' He nodded in contemplation. 'That's a pretty serious observation.'

'Mmm-hmm,' I teased, still giddy from too much G'n'T. 'So I know it's not to everyone's taste...'

'Well, toppings.' He let out a long whistle. 'That's a potential deal breaker right there. You can tell a lot about a person by her choice of toppings.'

'Can you?'

'Oh!' He was so serious, so good at playing along. 'Believe me ... *a lot.*'

'Go on then,' I said. 'Guess!'

'You sure you want me guessing your choice of topping? You're sure you're happy putting that out there so soon?' He pushed his hands inside his pockets. 'Me? I'm your standard pepperoni type of guy, but every once in a while...' He paused and gave a wiggle of his eyebrows. 'I might throw a little blue cheese into the mix.'

'Blue cheese?' I grinned. 'That's quite a bold move on a first date.'

'You're right. You're absolutely right.' He nodded. 'But, just so you know, I don't go round throwing my blue cheese out there for just anyone. Not on the first date at least.' He smiled. 'It's strictly a third date choice of topping in my opinion. You, on the other hand …' He'd stood straighter, weighing me up. 'Let's see, you're playing it a bit mysterious,' he said, thinking it through. 'So, I'm going to pick from the chicken menu, but right when you least expect it, I'll throw it on it's head, add a little chilli chicken spiciness right there, just to keep you on your toes...'

'Interesting,' I said, but then tight-lipped, 'wrong.'

'*Wrong*?' His shoulders slumped, play-acting defeat. 'What then? Avocado? Calamari? Not anchovy?'

'Hawaiian.'

'*Hawaiian*?' he shouted, feigning outrage in the middle of the shop. I gripped his arm, laughing, trying to quiet him. 'No one orders the Hawaiian! That's just something they put up there,' he gestured to the menu, 'out of *tradition* or something.' He took another look at me. 'You think you know a person…'

By the time we left, rain splashing against the pavement, he'd hooked his jacket over my shoulders and grabbed my hand: 'C'mon,' he'd grinned that grin of his, 'let's make a run for it.'

That was the moment I knew I loved Dan.

The moment I knew I was leaving everything that came before behind.

And now, there we were, back to ordering pizza. Except this time around, we were sharing it with the extended family — without the side order of heart-dancing, grin-painting romance.

'I might have the Hawaiian…'

My eyes fixed on Dan as he worked his way back along the options.

'Hawaiian?' He studied the page, not getting the reference. 'Think I might go for the Mediterranean…'

'This is on me! This is on me!' Vic ordered the *Family Fun Feast* on everyone's behalf, as we sat in a red leatherette booth with unnervingly sticky seats.

'Hey! No.' Dan glanced over the top of his menu. 'That's okay, Vic. I'm getting this. Thanks.'

'First you won't let me pay for the zoo.' Vic was still harping on about picking up the tab. 'Now I can't buy the kids a bit of pizza?'

'Honestly, Vic,' Dan told him, 'we're good.'

'Come on!' Vic put one hand on the table, head swaying like a branch. 'I can't have you paying for this.' He reached for his wallet.

'Vic? It's Ethan's birthday.'

'I know that,' he whined. 'So at least let me get this?'

'Vic, I'm his dad.'

'Actually.' I closed the menu, handing it back to the demented-looking waitress. 'I'm going to go for the Slimline Trimline Salad.'

Grace hid a smile behind her menu. I realised ordering from the Healthy Options range was the same as declaring myself officially fat to the nation.

Bryony took off her glasses and folded her arms on the table.

'I need to run something past you both.'

I assumed she meant me and Dan. Turns out, she meant Dan and his mother.

'I only found out about this today myself —'

'My fault, my fault!' Vic held up both of his hands.

'Vic surprised me this morning. We're going on honeymoon after all.'

'How lovely.' Pippa offered a wavering smile, flicking open her napkin with shocking precision.

'Oz!' Vic was fishing ice from his glass as the twins blew paper covers off straws, spitting the ends onto the floor and taking aim at exhausted-looking waiters.

'Australia,' he clarified. 'Scuba diving in the coral reef included, so … you, er…' He popped an ice cube into his mouth and took a crunch. 'You could say —' Here came the laugh again — 'I'll be spending my honeymoon *down under*. Catch my drift?'

'For twelve days,' Bryony explained, ignoring her soon-to-be-husband's tasteless attempt at humour. 'We fly on Saturday night. The day after the wedding.'

'What about my birthday?' Grace was already deep in calculation. 'What about my birthday, Mum?'

'I'll be back in time.' Bryony took hold of her hand and gave her a peck on the forehead. 'We get back early Friday morning. The day before.'

'But I can't have it at our house now, can I? What about my gazebo?'

'Then you'll have it at your dad's place instead.' Dan's eyes flashed with purpose. 'It'll be fine. Mum said she'll be there.'

'Can we come?' Philip had given up trying to shove his straw down his brother's ear and was pouring sugar into Theo's outstretched hands instead.

'Don't see why not.' Dan looked to Grace for confirmation.

She gave Philip a clipped smile.

'Dan, that's great.' Bryony looked visibly relieved. 'I've started making arrangements, but this threw a complete curveball in them.'

'Curveball? A man wants to spend some alone time with his new wife?' Vic took a frothy slurp of his fizzy orange and raised his arms. 'So shoot me.'

If I'd had a gun, I would have taken it out of my piss-stained bag and capped him right there, in front of his horrendous children.

'We're going to have a great time.' Dan leaned towards Grace. 'It's not every day my baby girl becomes a teenager, now is it?' He turned to his son. 'It's going to be cool, isn't it?'

Ethan bobbed up and down in his seat — the small boy equivalent of Starky wagging his tail.

'Of course it will!' Pippa promised, snuggling against Grace.

'We'll have to work around my shifts.' Dan turned to his mother.

'Oh, we'll be fine!' she said. 'We'll work it all out between us, won't we?'

She put one arm around Grace's shoulders and gave her a brief squeeze.

'Can I stay with you, Grandma?'

'You can do whatever you like, Gracie. Actually,' Pippa mused, 'thinking about it, it would be far easier if I came to stay with you, Daniel. All their things are there. Saves wasting time, shuttling back and forth between two houses.'

I felt invisible. Not a flicker in my direction.

Maybe I'd died but nobody had told me.

'Makes sense to me.' Dan gave a nod.

The waitress appeared with our orders.

'Ughhh!' A sudden spray of lemonade splashed against my face.

The twins sat grinning opposite, long stripey straws dangling from their mouths, as we were surrounded by a horn-blowing Mariachi band, starting up with an ear-busting rendition of *Feliz Compleanos* for Ethan.

Chapter Fifteen: Bosom Buddies

Pippa arrived unannounced at twenty-past nine the next morning, surprised to find us still in the middle of breakfast. 'I said I'd call round after eight o'clock mass. I've been texting Grace!'

Dan was helping unload the car with preparations for her stay. I stood in the hallway, still in my pyjamas, without so much as a coat of mascara or an underwire bra to my name. 'Now, I've brought a few groceries.' Pippa handed over a couple of bags. Starky sniffed excitedly around them. 'I'm gluten and dairy-free, these days,' she told me, leading us into the kitchen. 'Saves traipsing the children around the supermarket. Daniel? You've put those lamb chops in the freezer?'

'Yes, Mum.' Dan was back at the kitchen counter, buttering toast for Ethan. He'd developed a craving for shredless marmalade ever since he'd watched Paddington. 'But you do know it's not this week you're staying? It's next week?'

'Oh, yes.' She paused for a second. 'Mummy's got to have her wedding first, hasn't she?' she said to Grace, plunging deep into a large, shopping bag. 'And I've brought my carafe. Yes, I know you think I'm being fussy, Daniel.' She noticed her son's amusement. 'But I need water in my bedroom, don't I Gracie?' Grace brushed up by her side. 'If you use a glass, it only gathers dust. And I can't abide those overpriced bottled things either. *Carcinogenic.*' She grimaced. 'Linked to *cancer.* I read that somewhere. Now, where am I sleeping?'

In your own house, 20 minutes away? the small voice in my head began to plead.

'In my room, Grandma!' Grace grabbed hold of Pippa's hand. 'We already worked that one out!'

'We did, we did!' Pippa chorused. *'We already worked that one out.'*

'Dad? Grandma's going to stay in my bed,' Grace updated him. 'So, can I have the blow-up one, if it's still in the loft?'

'Yeah,' he said. 'I'll get it down. Should be fine.'

Satisfied with the sleeping arrangements, Pippa marched over to the cupboard, rifling through bottles while I managed a quick bite of my once-warm teacake.

'No white wine vinegar?' She sounded slightly put out. 'Not to worry.'

'Don't tell me, you've brought your own?'

'There's no need for sarcasm, Daniel...'

Of course she'd brought her own. I wasn't the least bit surprised.

Pippa was an accomplished hostess who'd fully immersed herself in the 1980s *Tupperware* explosion. She'd gone on to successfully navigate New World wine during the 90s. And a few years ago, when Derek was ill, she went fully organic. She was a professional with a house like a hotel and no patience for amateur renditions.

'And it's a good job I did.' She delved back into her shopper. 'I've been meaning to do that porch...' She headed off towards the hallway, where 15 minutes later I found myself involved in a live demonstration of how to clean windows correctly. 'The trick is using newspaper, you see?' She crouched down, working at each pane, steadily turning the local gazette into papier maché. 'Look at that. Not a streak in sight!' She stood back. 'Here, have a go!' She handed over a wad of newspaper like a particularly pushy QVC presenter. 'Bryony showed me this. Works wonders. The newspaper trick.'

I rubbed at the window, inadvertently discovering it was physically possible to Twerk my own breasts and wondering if that was something QVC viewers would appreciate. Pippa cast a disapproving look at my runaway cleavage.

I quickly covered my chest with one arm.

'Not to worry.' She confiscated the newspaper. 'You're either that way inclined or you're not.' She threw a glance at the rest of the house. 'Daniel was going to get someone in after the divorce. A cleaner to keep on top of things.' She almost laughed. 'Never mind, we'll get the place back up to scratch. Especially if we're throwing Grace a birthday party. And Bryony's coming over too. She was always so house proud.'

By the time Pippa left, the porch might've been gleaming, but the loft was beginning to seem like the perfect place for me to spend the next few weeks.

Blow-up bed or not.

Away from any mention of white wine vinegar, dust-free carafes or frozen lamb chops, family life was doing wonders for my commitment to my job.

'Morning!' I was making my way to the lift when I noticed Karen sobbing behind her reception desk. 'Are you alright?'

'He gone!' she gasped from behind a handkerchief. 'Harry's gone!'

'Dead?'

I'd heard something about him having a dodgy back, but nothing more serious.

'No!' Karen sobered up, still clutching the tissue. 'They've fired him! Your boss has!'

I spent the lift journey wondering what Harry Collins could possibly have done to get the sack? Well, apart from being caught sprawled on top of Karen in the stationery cupboard.

Luckily for Audrey she wasn't the one with that image burned permanently onto the back of her retina. Apart from that, I was all out of ideas.

Leah sat talking with one of the digital team and waved me over just as Audrey appeared from her office.

'Ella?'

She was pale as death, despite the bronzer.

I hadn't even realised she was in there. The blinds were still drawn.

I couldn't think of anything I might have done. Not unless Heather had actually gone ahead and told her about me serving her breast milk in my tea round? Or maybe about the other week when she caught me letting Leah vote for *Celebrity Shoemaker USA* from the work phone?

It was nearly ten-to-nine. Heather's desk was still shockingly empty.

I wondered if she was lurking behind the blinds and had taken Audrey hostage, forcing her to pick off her own staff, one by one.

'Could you come in here, please?' Audrey perched on the edge of her desk. 'You accessed confidential files.'

'Confidential files?'

'If you're planning on leaving us, I'd appreciate your honesty at this point —'

'Leaving? I'm not leaving —'

'And your resignation.'

'My resignation?'

I'd imagined throwing in the towel plenty of times, but never like this.

In my version, I was majestic. At the top of my game. Audrey and Heather would be devastated by such a huge loss to the world of Corporate Communications.

'Those confidential files were compiled by yourself and emailed to Heather. You also sent them to print from your computer.'

'The annual account files? Heather asked me for those.'

'I don't doubt it.' She walked back behind the desk and took a seat. 'But that doesn't explain why this wasn't immediately brought to my attention.'

'I thought it was odd, but Heather *is* odd. I've still got a day's worth of emails, asking for everything except my birth certificate, blood type and fingerprints.'

'If you're planning on working for Heather,' she fixed me with the sort of look reserved by my mother, 'I've every right to ask for your immediate resignation.'

'Working for her?' I almost smiled. 'It's bad enough working *with* her.'

'I'm not singling you out. To put this into context, Ella, we found Harry Collins had been putting together artwork and templates for Heather's new website. But you say she hasn't approached you?'

'I'd be the last person Heather Constantine would head-hunt and the last person who'd be interested. Believe me, I'd rather smell severed feet for a living than work for her. I did think it was strange, her asking for the database...'

'Then why didn't you question it?'

'Because she acts as if she runs the place.' *And you let her!* I wanted to say. *You give her full run of the office. You can't go changing the rules and blaming the rest of us the second she finally turns on you.*

'I'm sorry to tell you,' she said, and for a second, I was convinced I was getting the chop, 'Heather Constantine will no longer be working for Steen & Heard.'

Somewhere, I thought, *a unicorn has just jumped over a rainbow.*

By the time we reached the end of the week, the whole office had been interrogated. Audrey was so uptight I was surprised the water-cooler hadn't been frisked.

'Close the door behind you, would you?' She'd summoned me and Leah into the office on Friday morning. 'Ella?' I was relieved to notice she had her usual faint reflection of warmth. 'Leah? Sit down, sit down,' she said. 'Bad news, I'm afraid.'

I braced myself, convinced I was going to be spending a lot more time at home with Pippa lecturing me on the burden of unemployment on the family.

'As you know, Heather Constantine resigned last week —'

Oh no. She was coming back. Snootier than ever. I knew it! It'd all been some ploy to bag herself a pay-rise. That whole week the only upside of Audrey's breakdown had been the sight of Heather's empty desk with nothing to remember her by except for the dent of her arse in her ergonomic chair.

'As you know, I became concerned regarding highly sensitive files, which,' she said, 'as you explained, Ella — and that's no longer an issue — Heather asked you to duplicate. To cut a long story short, one of our biggest clients had the decency to inform me that Heather approached him with this...' She handed us a print out. '*Bosom Buddies.*'

I scanned the logo Harry had designed.

Basically, two B's with a certain boob-like quality.

'It's an initiative Heather's been working on for quite some time. She's approached our three biggest annual spenders. Pitching the *Bosom Buddies* initiative alongside managing their PR accounts at a greatly reduced cost. Confidentially,' Audrey seemed pretty pissed off now, 'Heather expressly indicated to me she intended to dedicate her time to baby Apollo, with no imminent work commitments. I took her at her word, so there's no contractual obligation from her, unfortunately...'

I couldn't help but think 'Baby Apollo' sounded like some kind of space station. Was there even a baby? It might be some sort of code. Heather was fulfilling some lifelong ambition of running Earth from a station based on the moon.

'So.' I scanned across the print-out. 'What is it? *Bosom Buddies*?'

'Heather's encouraging suitable businesses; hotels, restaurants etc., to provide in-house breast-feeding facilities. These businesses pay Heather a monthly retainer, technically renting all facilities and merchandise.'

The image of Heather setting up shop in the stationery cupboard flashed across my mind, as Audrey handed over the local newspaper.

'Take a look. Page three.'

Page three? I was worried Heather had taken the launch too far and had posed semi-naked wearing only her breast pump and new company lanyard. Instead, she was sat with the baby space station, looking like an actual mother instead of a one-woman Franking machine.

'If you'll notice,' Audrey drew our attention to the *Promotional Feature* sub-head, 'it's paid-for advertising. I'm guessing the people behind this *Amanda Beaumont* range are heading up the bill.'

'So, she's working for them?'

'Heather being Heather,' Audrey explained, 'she's gift-wrapped their merchandise in this *Bosom Buddies* initiative. She's basically working as a rep for their company within one of her own initiatives.'

At the bottom of the piece, imaginatively headed: *Become a Bosom Buddy!* there was a list of local businesses signed up to support breast-feeding mothers.

'Any names you recognize as clients,' Audrey said, noticing us reading them, 'are now our former clients...'

'You're messing?' Leah took a closer look. 'So, if you don't join you look like you're anti-women or something? That's reverse sexism! She's basically *bullying* people into signing up!'

'Exactly,' Audrey agreed. 'The implication being that unless you're a *Bosom Buddy* you're somehow taking a stance against working mothers.' She blinked away irritation. 'It's a huge threat to our client base. Extremely damaging, potentially. Heather's offering to undercut us on overall representation. Almost a contra-deal, in fact. We simply can't compete.' She looked well and truly defeated. 'She doesn't have the same overheads. Doesn't have any premises or staff to worry about.' I flinched a little at that part. 'We have to reaffirm our position. Make a statement in the marketplace —'

'I know what you're going to say!' Leah's bum almost left her seat. 'I know what you're going to say. The whole breast-feeding theme?' she grinned. 'Topless Flashmob!'

'Er,' Audrey nearly smiled. 'Not exactly —'

'Naked Selfies?' Leah suggested. 'Not us!' she explained, as I looked at her, wondering why she was so eager to get naked for the sake of the company. I'd hesitate at the thought of getting my kit off for two weeks on a tropical island without at least six months' notice, let alone to help out the boss. '*As if!* Done professionally,' Leah assured us. 'With proper models.'

'No, Leah,' Audrey clarified. 'No naked selfies, I'm afraid.'

'Well, that's the stuff that goes viral,' Leah said. 'That's what makes a statement in the marketplace. We'd get loads of coverage...'

'Not enough coverage by the sounds of things,' I pointed out.

'I was thinking of something a little more,' Audrey searched for the phrase, 'in keeping with our clients' interests. That's why,' she turned her laptop around, 'I've been working on this.'

'*The Avington Food & Drink Festival?*'

'It's ambitious, I know.' We studied the on-screen proposal. 'But it's been in the pipeline for some time. These latest events have finally prompted me. It's our way of showing what a fully-established agency can offer, as opposed to Heather's one-woman band. We have to be ambitious!' She whipped off her glasses. 'Ella, you did a sterling job with Bartholomews' glassware launch. You'll be assisting initially,' she said. 'But I think it's high time we moved things along, before you decide to take your talent elsewhere…'

Talent? Audrey must really appreciate an orderly stationery cupboard. I'd given up trying to impress her since Heather had asked me to come up with a 12 month marketing forecast for Steen & Heard, and all I'd got was a 'good thinking!' and first choice from a tin of assorted biscuits.

'You want me on the festival?'

'Absolutely. I want you as project manager.'

Audrey relaxed in her seat as I looked to Leah, letting the idea sink in.

'Project manager?'

'You've more than proven yourself capable. Now it's time to head things up.'

She snapped forward and put her spectacles back in place.

I felt the weight of my career slump lift from my shoulders.

'So, with that in mind,' she toyed with her diamante encrusted pen, 'Leah, I think we should discuss how you feel about taking over Ella's current role.'

Leah smiled.

'Can't have you *temping* permanently, can we? Ella?' Audrey turned to me, as I tried to be brave and smile, 'You've a natural ability with clients. A highly organized approach. I've no doubt you'll do a fantastic job.'

Chapter Sixteen: Cleaning Inferno

'There's a world of difference between normal, everyday standards and what's good enough for your boyfriend's mother.'

I was explaining to Kim why I was in the middle of a cleaning frenzy on my first Friday night alone with Dan in months.

'She's only coming to stay, Ella. It's your house not a crime scene...'

Pippa came over to walk Starky, as she usually did while we were at work, but she had decided to spend the rest of the day scrutinizing the place with her *Pippa Vision*. She'd listed vital evidence against me on a telephone notepad, now installed in the hallway as part of her new regime. Audrey might think I had a natural ability with clients, but my 'highly organized approach' was lost on Dan's mum.

The first note, stuck on the hob, read: *Ella! Bicarb of Soda. Works a treat on the stove.*

'Actually addressed to me, not Dan,' I told Kim.

Then, I spotted another one: *Olive oil good for coffee table!*

And just as I thought the coast was clear, in the bathroom, stuck to the sink: *White vinegar = bathroom taps.*

Right then, I was making my own mental note for Pippa: *Boyfriend's mother = clearly insane.*

'What does Dan say?'

'Oh, he laughed the whole thing off. Told me not to worry, it's not like it's the first time his mum's seen the place.'

'Sounds good enough to me...'

'The thought of his mum noticing toothpaste splashes on the bathroom mirror or commenting on the hygiene standards of the toaster mightn't bother him, but it bothers me, okay?'

'I doubt his mum's going to notice if you've cleaned the toaster…'

Don't bet on it, I thought. Pippa would be inspecting the crumb tray with a torch, the first chance that she got. But, guess what? I'd already thought of that. *Clean as a whistle.* 'I'm not letting the side down. Not now.'

'What side, Ella? There isn't a *side.*'

'I'm just trying to show her …' I was trying to remember what it was I was trying to show her. 'I can do all this house stuff. That's all…'

'You don't have to show her anything, Ella. You're not dating *her.*'

Kim didn't realise it, but I kind of was. Her and the kids. Trying to sweep everyone off their feet so I could be with Dan.

'Well, don't forget, I'm living in his ex-wife's *perfect* house…'

I'd never said it out loud before and instantly regretted it.

Following in Bryony's footsteps was like mastering the tightrope in roller-blades — after Pippa had beeswaxed it.

'Ella, Dan doesn't need a perfect house. And if his wife was so great,' I felt myself cringe, hearing Kim use the wife word, 'he'd still be with her, wouldn't he?'

'Well, she was the one who taught Pippa how to get sparkling results on her windows, don't forget.' I was admiring my smudge-free reflection in the front door.

'And I bet Dan felt like the luckiest guy on earth,' Kim said, in that sarky-sounding voice she used. 'Unless she towel-dried them with her tits, I doubt he gave a shit. You said his mother's staying for two weeks?'

'Technically, its only ten days.' I informed her, more for my benefit than her own. 'And not at the weekends.'

'I told you,' Kim sighed. 'Never invite family over unless it's New Year's. That way the place is allowed to be untidy because it's just after Christmas. And if they really start pissing you off you disappear into the bedroom, invent a dead school friend they've never met and fake cry yourself to sleep. That gets them away just after midnight, depending on the wait for a taxi.'

'*I* didn't invite anyone, remember?' I pulled the long reed head-dress from the ornamental diffuser I'd spent way too much on, turning over the stems to perpetuate the myth of *California Beach* throughout the house. 'It's either I do it now or Pippa sees to everything. I'm just being practical. She'll be checking.'

'Checking?' I could hear Kim's smile. 'Checking for what?'

'God knows, but whatever it is, I won't let her find it...'

'Ella?' Kim laughed. 'Have you heard yourself? Get a grip.'

'Kim, she's packed the freezer with chops and brought her own carafe. And, I meant to tell you,' I needed Kim to understand what I was up against, 'when she called the other day, do you know what she said to me? She said: "Is Daniel *not there?*" No small talk. No, how are you, Ella? Just: "Is Daniel *not there?*" Bearing in mind, she'd already left all those housework notes addressed to *me*, like it's *my* job to keep on top of the house — not Dan's.'

'Maybe it was important?' Kim reasoned. 'She needed to ask him something?'

'No, listen,' I insisted. 'Before I could say he was out in the garage, she goes: "Thank you." As in, *you're dismissed!* She dismissed me!'

'Ella, you really need —'

'No, no, that's not it,' I said. 'Then, I realised, she never usually calls the house phone. Only ever Dan's mobile, but his phone was on charge.' I let the information settle. 'Don't you get it? She literally calls his mobile so she doesn't have to speak to me! She only ever wants to talk to *Daniel*. And I hate the way she calls him that! *Daniel.* It sounds so,' I gave the door handle a quick polish with my sleeve, '*judgmental.* Like her!'

'Ella? Can I get a word in? You're giving me brain ache.' I could hear Kim pouring herself a drink, and wondered if it was vodka, wishing she could pour me one. 'You seriously need to chill out. Dan needs to deal with this stuff, not you…'

'Oh, he did. He went and got the blow-up bed out of the loft. *Whoopie-doo!*'

'Ella?'

'Yeah…' I was scribbling myself a quick reminder on Pippa's new notepad about ironing her pillowcases. 'What the *fuck* is wrong with you?'

'You know what's wrong with me.' I arranged the pen neatly back on the table. 'I'm stressed out of my mind.'

'Look, your place has nothing to do with his mother. Does she know you don't give the faintest fuck about any of this stuff?'

I wrapped up the call. I had no time to explain to Kim why she was wrong. Maybe I never used to care, not when we shared the flat, but I was single then. That was before Dan, with his grown-up house and his grown-up life, kids, and co-parenting mother. Dan lived in the real world, with real responsibilities, real commitments.

Dan had nipped out to get us a takeaway. I grabbed a couple of plates, wondering if Vic had managed to work his jingle into his wedding vows. Talking of which, I noticed the time and switched on the radio.

Mum was involved in a spirited explanation of how the women's sexual revolution of the 70's resulted in a preoccupation with the female orgasm. This, Mum was saying, as I grabbed myself a beer from the fridge, noticing the shelves could probably use a quick wipe down, was at the exclusion of real intimacy. Ultimately, this led to the commercialisation of female sexuality, she explained. Resulting in a prevailing culture which exiled the emotional panorama of women's sexual needs.

'Big deal,' I said to the radio, exhausted just listening to her. 'What about who does the dishes?'

Two minutes later, Dan wandered in with a bouquet of peonies and two takeout pizza boxes. One Hawaiian, one Peperoni, for old time's sake.

Maybe I was growing up, I thought, wrapping my arms around his neck. Maybe I was abysmally dull, but mostly, I was in love. Starky gave me a look from his basket: *Who cares about the cleaning? It's all good from where I'm lying.*

We chatted over pizza and cuddled up in front of a movie without uncertain glances from Ethan. No Grace plonking herself between us, nudging me to one side with a casually pointed elbow or carefully jutting foot, wearing that look that silently said: *Keep away from my dad!*

'I can't believe how much you've done.' Dan put his arm around me as we slumped against the settee. 'The place looks great. Have you hoovered?'

Hoovered? Try steam-cleaned. Try hand-scrubbed.

Hoovering was for L-plates.

I wished I could visit the parallel universe where you saw only finished results and surface appearances. *The magical world of being The Bloke.*

He didn't care that the fridge needed cleaning. Or know what limescale was. Or realise the bathroom mirror wasn't self-cleaning. And neither had I, I remembered, not until I met Pippa and joined a proper family set-up, in a proper family house.

It was a cruel law of nature. I'd literally woken up and realised all this stuff mattered. *Really* mattered. And I was determined to become the invisible force behind it. The Goddess of Household Chores, whoever that poor, bare-knuckled bitch was, had apparently visited sometime in the night, telling me I should care about what Dan's mother thought. My brain had been hot-washed to a domesticated setting. The same way I'd probably wake up one day, retired, with a collection of felt hats, support tights and an ornamental teapot I didn't remember buying.

'I love you, you know, but I don't love all the stressing, and I don't love all the cleaning,' he said, as I gave him a warning look. 'Well, I don't...'

'I don't love it, either, Dan.' I paused the movie before we missed Alan Arkin's final scene, closing the lid on my half-eaten Hawaiian. 'But someone's got to do it.'

'I said I'd help. *I did!*' Dan argued, as I almost dared him to continue. 'I said just let me know whatever needs doing...'

'But by the time I have to explain *how* to do it,' I collected our beer bottles, 'I may as well do it myself. I just don't think it's okay, your mum doing the cleaning. Pointing out how much of a mess she thinks the place is...'

'She wants to do it!'

I gave him that look he'd recognize as potentially dangerous. He tried to backtrack as I carried the pizza boxes out into the kitchen. Too angry to look at him, I emptied the fridge, piling the sink with plastic containers, loading worktops with milk, chicken, salad, and what I hoped was an old lump of cheese, as he followed me out.

'What are you doing?'

'The fridge needs cleaning.'

'At,' he glanced at his watch, 'quarter-to-nine in the middle of watching a movie? It's Friday…'

What do you know about having fun on a Friday night? I wanted to say. Playing some board game. Then falling asleep. That's how our Fridays usually went.

'When am I going to get another chance? Your mum's moving in tomorrow.'

'Ella,' he put his arms around my waist, 'she's not moving in. She's looking after the kids. Will you stop over-worrying?'

He gave the side of my head a quick peck as he let me go.

Over-worrying? Well, maybe it was his *under*-worrying that had caused the problem in the first place. Had he ever thought of that?

'You make all these arrangements.' I whacked the tap onto full velocity, spraying myself with cold water, which did nothing to douse my mood. 'And now,' I said, as he offered a dry dishtowel to thin air, 'I'm the only one worrying if the fridge's clean enough, or if we've got enough guest towels —'

'Guest towels?' He chucked the dishcloth onto the worktop. 'What's a guest towel?'

'See?' I shook off a tray and opened the fridge. 'You just don't get it, do you? Your mum goes out of her way to remind me, all the cooking, all the cleaning's down to me, because *Poor Daniel's* so exhausted all the time, running the business…'

'Where's all this come from?' He nodded towards the radio. 'Your mum been lecturing you on women's rights again?'

'Don't bring my mother into this…'

I shoved the egg tray back into the fridge, fighting to place the lid back on top.

'But you can say whatever you like about mine?'

'No.' I took the egg tray, or whatever it was called, back out, trying to lock the container together. 'Haven't you noticed?' I dragged one arm over my forehead, my hands sweating inside the rubber gloves. 'I'm making a huge effort for yours…'

'*O-kay…*'

I ignored him and grabbed an armful of condiment jars, wishing I could use them for target practice but reloading the refrigerator instead. We didn't even use half of this stuff. Chili seeds? Garlic mayonnaise? Mint sauce? That's what I was, I thought, bloody mint sauce, waiting for Pippa to point out my expiry date.

'I'm sorry.' He leaned against the counter. 'That was out of order.'

'You didn't even *ask* me, Dan! You made all these arrangements with your mum and just expected me to hop to it.'

'All I was expecting was for you to eat some pizza, put your flowers in a vase and watch a movie, like the complete *shithead* I am —'

'And, for your information, I didn't invite my mum to the zoo just so we could straggle behind your family all day, hearing about your *heart-breaking* divorce.'

'Who said that?'

'Who do you think? Bryony, practically hand-feeding you.' I scrubbed at a stubborn milk stain, erasing the memory. 'And where was I? Stuck with Vic. Sat there like a moron while your ex-wife criticized my Chakras.'

'Do you think I enjoy spending the day with Vic and those psycho twins? All I want to do is spend the day with my own kids.'

'What did Vic's kids ever do to you?' I gave him a half-look over my shoulder. 'It's *my* handbag Philip pissed all over.'

'Yeah, I know...' He paused. 'What kind of kid *does* something like that?'

'Somebody else's?'

'Look, I'm just saying,' he grabbed a tea towel, picked up a shelf from the draining board, 'I wish all this was easier. For you, as well as me.'

The inane buzz of the radio broke the silence just in time for my mum to invite listeners to call or text with their thoughts on genital piercing.

'It would just be nice if people treated us like a couple,' I said, the fog of crazy cleaning lady finally clearing. 'Instead of me spending the whole day with my mum, trailing behind you and Bryony.'

'I'm divorced. I can't change that,' he said. 'I've got two children. I wouldn't want to change that. I spent my son's birthday with him. I want to spend as much time with both of them as possible. That's the way it is, but what I feel really bad about is how you don't feel like we're a couple. That's news to me.'

'Because that's what I mean, Dan! You don't get that it's not just you who has to live with everyone else's grand plans.' He reached over to me and everything was better the moment my face rested against his shirt, my worries soothed away by the clean warmth of him. 'I don't feel like part of your family. I either feel in everybody's way, or on the way out...'

'Ella,' he kissed the top of my head. 'You're not on the way out.' He tilted his face down to mine. 'You're not on the way out, okay?'

For some reason, possibly because being in love makes you incredibly shallow, I looked at his face, my favourite face, and had the urge to kiss him. I'd almost forgotten what we'd been fighting about as his stubble lightly grazed my skin, decisive lips finding mine. Before I knew it, he had me sat on the counter, ignoring the sound of his mobile as he quickly worked at my clothes.

'I'm sorry. I've been going mental about the stupid house, haven't I?' I sighed in between kisses. 'What about the film?' I smiled as he dragged down my jeans.

'I think this is going to have a much better ending,' he said. 'Don't you?'

We were hip-locked in seconds. All thoughts of kitchen hygiene were erased as my naked arse repeatedly bounced off the formerly pristine worktop.

I'd highly recommend giving Dan a little undivided attention…

I was vaguely aware of my mother's advice echoing against my mind. She'd been absolutely right. I had every intention of shoving aside that ornamental bamboo centre-piece I'd bought to impress Dan's mother and making him do me at high-speed across the dining room table. He was manoeuvring me onto the floor, my thighs clamped around him, just as the voice sounded from the hall: *'Daniel?'*

With the sudden slam of the front door, he left me in a heap, pulling his clothes on in one, swift move. I wrestled with my jeans, finally doing up the top button as Pippa walked into the kitchen.

'I've been calling you.' She was carrying yet another shopping bag. 'You're having pizza at this time? I've told you, Daniel, there's chops there, in the freezer. They're very *trendy-looking* trousers, Ella...'

I realised I'd pulled them on inside out. All the white cotton pockets were hanging out with weird seams on display. Anyway, I didn't care how 'trendy-looking' Pippa thought my jeans were, I was more concerned that I'd just noticed her son had managed to hoopla my knickers around the hot tap.

Pippa just had to see Grace in her bridesmaid dress, she said. *She'd love to surprise the children. Turn up to collect them with their dad. And it would be so late after they got back. She may as well stay over. Save Dan the drive.*

Chapter Seventeen: Merry Men

Gravel crunched beneath tyres, headlights illuminating our way, as we drove closer to the venue, trees merging overhead.

'Oh, it's magnificent.' Pippa gripped onto each headrest, perched between driver-side and passenger seats, ogling the view like an eagle searching for its young. 'Absolutely magnificent…'

Paper lanterns decorated the garden and fairy-lights hung like brilliant jewels against the night. Up ahead a few people were stood on the terrace, jackets discarded, ties loosened now, as they chatted, trading cigarettes and laughter.

I spotted Vic among them, nodding along, the way he did, one hand in his pocket, counting his change, as my mother would say. Then, two seconds later, after Dan texted to say we were parked, Grace appeared, looking out across the driveway and spotting her dad's car as Pippa clambered out from the back.

Grace's hair was pinned up in loose curls with a garland of flowers perched on top. Her champagne-coloured dress caught the light. She offered her dad a shy smile, anxious to see him. She looked so beautiful standing up there. The sight of her that night, standing there at her mother's wedding, almost made me wish her parents had stayed together. Until I remembered I was sleeping with her father.

I made my way out of the passenger side, following the Robinsons up large, stone steps, flowers tumbling down either side, as Grace shouted in surprise at the sight of Grandma.

'Ethan's still inside.' She kissed her dad, giving her grandma a big hug and offering me a wave. 'Even some of the grown-ups are going to bed, but he's still wide awake!'

We huddled together, until Bryony emerged from behind curtained doors, music escaping. She left a huge room filled with guests and I could see white polka dots of dining tables skirting the crowded dance-floor. A sleepy Ethan, shirt damp, half-hanging outside his smart, grey trousers, stood with a yawn at his mother's side. The bride, wearing a long, beaded dress, the same shade as her daughter's, rested one hand on his small shoulder.

Bryony made a beautiful bride. *But Dan already knew that.*

'Congratulations!' he said, followed by a pause so long, I wondered if he was temporarily stunned by the sight of her. He leaned in for a hug and then suddenly stalled, unsure. They broke into laughter, which became a barely-there kiss on the cheek.

'Well done!' Pippa offered Bryony a light pat on the arm. The same cautious technique she'd used to pat the two-humped camel at the zoo, I noticed.

'Thanks, Pippa.' Bryony turned to greet me.

'Congratulations!' I stepped forward to kiss the bride, out-of-place and under-dressed in housework jeans (no longer inside out) and makeshift ponytail. 'It looks amazing. *You* look amazing. You all do.' I looked at the children.

'Oh, I'm probably a bit too old for all this jazz, but hey,' Bryony said, 'if you're going to the trouble of organizing a wedding. *Again...*'

'Oh, it was no trouble when you two got married.' Pippa grinned, adjusting her handbag onto her shoulder.

'Grace?' Bryony interrupted her daughter, who was chatting loudly with her dad about her little brother's stint on the dance-floor. 'Can you help me get your stuff, please?'

They wandered inside. Ethan rested his head against Pippa, too tired to say too much as he nodded along with Pippa's enthusiastic coaxing of wedding details.

'*Guys!*' I folded my arms against the breeze as Vic appeared from Smoker's Corner. His hair was damp and curled slightly. There were moist patches beneath the arms of his shirt and his eyes were more jaundiced than usual. He was also wearing *bright green* brogues with pale blue laces, I noticed, staring down at his feet. He took my hand and for some reason, possibly because he was Vic and tended to do unnecessarily creepy things, bent to kiss the back of it with a *schmack* of relish.

'I see you've noticed the shoes.' He took a slightly unsteady step back. 'Something old.' He pointed to himself. 'Something new.' He stuck his hands inside his trouser pockets, buffering the fabric. 'Something borrowed.' He offered his wrist, angling a cufflink which read, *If found...* then a second one, which read: *Return to wife.* 'And, that all-important finishing touch. Something,' he pointed at his feet, grabbing one shoelace... '*Blue!*' He laughed at the joke, which I guessed he'd been telling all day, as he turned to Dan and offered his hand. 'Thanks for coming! Come on in.' He slapped Dan on the shoulder. 'Come and have a drink.'

'Driving. Sorry.'

'Just one drink!' Vic whined. 'Not gonna hurt...'

'Honestly, Vic.'

'Come on, Dan.' The groom took a step forward. 'Don't be like that, dude.'

'Sorry, Vic. I'm just here to pick up my kids…'

I wasn't sure what was going on, but something was definitely happening. From the way Dan was acting he may as well have turned up dressed as a Father For Justice. I instinctively peered along the road, wanting to leave as soon as possible, away from Dan's cameo appearance as a divorced and slightly bitter Caped Crusader.

'Hey, I was only saying thanks for coming.' Vic turned to his friend, who was chain-smoking at the far side of the terrace. Must be his best man, I decided, as I noticed their matching green shoes. 'It's my wedding day, dude…'

'I know it's your wedding day,' Dan told him. 'You're marrying my ex-wife. *Dude.*'

'Ethan?' Pippa chimed. 'Let's get you into the car, shall we?'

'I want to say goodbye to Mum first.' He yawned.

'Do me a favour, mate?' Vic took a step closer. 'Don't talk about my wife like that…'

'I'm not talking about your wife.' Dan tucked his hands inside his jeans, suddenly casual. 'I'm talking about my kids…'

'My wife, your wife.' I smiled, predictably desperate to lighten the mood. So, as usual, I settled for the first thing that came into my head and I did what any other idiot would do, bursting into song as if we were all having a right good time:

'*You say Tom-AY-to!*' I pointed at Vic. Then to Dan: '*He says Tom-AR-to…*'

'*Tom-AY-to!*' Vic sang, wagging his finger, stooping slightly.

'*Tom-AR-to!*' I tried to sound enthusiastic.

'*Po-TAY-to!*' Vic rang out, arms outstretched.

'*Pot-AR-to!*' I sang on tip-toes.

'*Let's call the whole thing off!*' Vic crooned as the door swung open behind us to reveal the bride, suitably unimpressed by her new husband's choice of song.

'Good one,' Vic chuckled, walking off to rejoin the smokers as Grace appeared.

'Check out my case, Dad,' she said. 'Mum got it for me, for when I stay over at yours.'

Pippa gazed up from the bottom of the stairs, Ethan waiting beside her. 'Oh, that is smart!'

'Grown up, isn't it?' Bryony shared a smile with Pippa. 'And here's little man's stuff. Some games. I know he's got plenty at yours already...'

'Take it easy, you two!' Vic called over to the children, following his guests back into the party. 'We'll have to have that drink some other time, Dan.'

I didn't bother checking Dan's reaction, but held onto a friendly smile, folding my arms as the night air whispered around me.

'Mum?' Grace said, as Dan grabbed hold of Ethan's bag, walking off downstairs to a *bleep-blink* of the car alarm. 'I'll miss you...'

Grace propped up her suitcase and lay her head against Bryony's collarbone, eyes tightly shut, flower garland dropping to the floor. I picked it up as Bryony placed her hand on the back of her daughter's head, brushing away silent tears.

'I'll miss you too, my good Grace.' She tried to compose herself. 'And my Ethan.' She smiled through tears as he trotted back up the steps to say goodbye, leaning his head against her chest, that small, down-turned mouth, making him look even more vulnerable, as she ran her fingers through his corn-yellow hair.

'Now, you two, be good for your dad, do you hear?' She put her arm around her son, gripping him closer. 'It's just a little holiday. I'll be back before you know it. And I'll have a tan and you won't — *ha*!' She took Grace by the shoulders. Ethan managed a smile, looking out towards his dad, who waited by the car with Pippa.

Chapter Eighteen: Shit Sticks

'A fairytale wedding. That's what they call it.' I'd had a running commentary of Bryony's wedding ever since I'd wandered into the kitchen the next morning. I'd been following Starky's orders after he'd fetched me from sleep, bypassing Dan's side of the bed to let me know he was desperate for the garden. Even the dog thought I was a dogsbody.

'I know,' Grace sighed. 'It was just like a fairytale. I'm glad you saw me in my dress. Properly, I mean…'

'I told your dad, I *just have* to see her!'

I'd found Pippa and Grace huddled over Grace's phone at the dining table. I'd hovered over photos with them while the kettle boiled, barely wincing as Pippa recited stories from Dan and Bryony's wedding day.

'You couldn't be there, of course,' she giggled, as Grace played the video of Ethan's break-dancing again, only half-listening.

They'd kept me awake, chatting for ages. Grace was happy on the camping bed, while Pippa took the single. Unable to sleep, my mind wandered to the promising start Dan and I had almost got off to in the kitchen, knowing there was no chance of finishing what we'd started. Not tonight. Possibly not for the next fortnight. I lay next to him like a grumpy parent, wondering when the girls' were going to keep the noise down and get to sleep.

'Ethan's had three retweets already!'

'What's a retweet?'

'On Twitter, Grandma. You know, social media.' Grace got busy on her mobile again. 'You need an account!'

'Oh no, Grace,' Pippa giggled. 'I'm long past all that stuff!'

'Don't say that,' Grace said. 'Have you got one, Ella?'

'A Twitter account? No…'

'But isn't that kind of your job? All that stuff?'

'Erm, no. Not really.'

I wondered if Grace had been listening in on my last performance review. I'd told Audrey I was about to become a digital whiz kid. Then Leah started at the agency and I had been off the hook. I didn't like the idea of it. Chatting away to nobody. It was like those silent discos, everyone alone, grouped together.

'Right, I've set you up!'

'What?' I wandered over to Grace, who sat grinning at the dining table. 'How have you done that?'

'Just needed your phone number. Your password's *starkydoespoos*. And now I'm following you. You can see all Mum's Australia pictures.'

'Thanks,' I said with no real intention of getting involved.

'We've been thinking about Grace's birthday party.' Pippa sat in a quilted house robe, about to sip some tea, before she jerked away the cup. 'You couldn't top that up with some more hot water could you, please, Ella?' She handed me back the cup. 'It's far too strong.'

'Could you do mine, too?' Grace offered the slightest of glances, following Pippa's protocol, working away on her mobile, her concentration fixed.

'We've got the guest list down to twenty, or thereabouts,' Pippa informed me, as I re-boiled the kettle, my feet growing colder on the tiled floor. 'It'll be as busy as your mum's wedding, the way we're carrying on,' she said to Grace.

'Some of my friends won't be able to come, *obviously*,' Grace adopted a drawl I hoped was ironic. 'I know for a fact three of them are on holiday.'

'And we thought Ethan might like to invite some friends along, didn't we?' Pippa reminded her. 'Save him getting bored?'

'He may as well.' Grace was plaiting a small strand of hair. 'Especially if Philip and Theo are already going. We don't even like them.'

'Now, now,' Pippa said, and I wondered how long I'd last if I tried talking to Grace in toddler-speak. 'You're all family now.'

'No, we're not.' Grace's eyes were suddenly wide, unblinking. 'I'm having nothing to do with them. Neither is Ethan.'

Pippa looked at me pointedly now, sucking in her top lip for emphasis.

'I know I've got to have them at the party, but that's only because it's going to be more like a family party, not just my thirteenth,' Grace explained. 'I want it to be like the ones you told me about, Grandma. The parties you used to have in the olden days.' Pippa laughed at that. 'Like when you were growing up in a big family,' Grace said. 'And kind of a welcome home for my mum, too.'

'That's so sweet of you, darling.' Pippa covered her granddaughter's hand with her own. 'It'll be a day we'll never forget, won't it?'

I refilled the cups and let Starky back into the house. After drying off his paws, I made my way back up to bed, finding Ethan snuggled up next to Dan. There was no space for one more and my own cup of tea had grown as cold as my feet.

'I'll see you all tomorrow!' Pippa called as Dan saw her to the door. 'May as well sleep here on Sunday night. Saves me driving over first thing Monday morning.'

Grace was back at the kitchen table, installed at the computer. Pippa had suggested it might be fun for her to design her own invitations to her birthday, which apparently, wasn't a birthday *party* at all. Not the way I'd said it.

'Kids Ethan's age have *birthday parties*.' Grace fixed her attention back on the screen. 'And Daddy said I can still *defo* have a gazebo...'

Too old for birthday parties. Young enough for Daddy?

Grace typed away as the rain started up, either a disgruntled CEO or a trophy wife in-training, I hadn't quite decided, and her unmade bed caught my eye. *Room Service*, I muttered, opening the curtains. Housewife extraordinaire, Pippa, had left her own pillow neatly propped against the headboard, her duvet crease-free. The only thing out of place was the small stack of photographs lying on top. A collage of smiling faces grinned up from the bed. Bryony on the beach. Sunglasses askew as she pulled a face, gripping a multi-coloured straw that dangled from a coconut-shell cocktail. The next, Dan and Bryony at the house, him working the barbecue and wearing a straw hat as he held up a steak, while Bryony pretended to take a bite. Then Grace and Ethan sitting beneath a Christmas tree, in the space where the TV was now, their mum hanging a bauble with an expression that said: *Hurry up and take the picture, for God's sake!*

I put the photos to one side, feeling strangely adrift for a moment, like some tiny fragment of Dan's life. They'd been a family. A mum. A dad. A couple of kids.

They still were, I thought, as I made up Grace's makeshift bed. My mind filled with those images until they formed a thousand tiny punctures, quickly dotting together in my one, deflated attempt. I was taking another glimpse of the Dan I never knew, until the sound of Ethan charging uphill disturbed me.

'I hate her!' He ran past, throwing himself on his bed with one leg dangling, as he lay, face-first on top of the covers.

'Who do you hate?' I already had a pretty good idea.

'Her! *Grace*! She's always pushing me around!' His face reddened as he propped himself up on his elbows.

We should start a support group, you and I, I thought, tempted to burst into tears, lie down and thump the pillow beside him. Instead I rubbed his back. His skinny little body made me smile.

'Oh, come on, sulky! She's your sister. Don't fall out.'

'I only said she's done too many invites. 'Cause she has done too many! Then she kicked me like this.' He kicked one trainer against the divan, shoelace dangling. 'And she called me dumb. Mum's already told her about that. She's a big, stinky … *shit stick*!' He half-turned to gauge my reaction.

'What's a —' I decided not to repeat it. 'What's that?'

'It's a stick with all poo on it, *like her*!'

'Ethan?' I managed to keep a straight face. 'That's not nice, is it?'

He collapsed back against his pillow, face half-hidden.

'You don't hate her.' I lifted his deceptively heavy foot, retying his shoelace. 'You just don't like it when she's mad at you.'

'Yeah, but she kicked me!'

'I know.' I rubbed the back of his leg. 'She shouldn't kick you, but that doesn't mean you get to say bad words.'

Although, *shit stick* was a pretty brilliant epithet. Simple, but effective. I liked it.

'Yeah, well,' he sulked. 'I only say stuff like that when she's being horrible.' He rested his chin on top of his hand. 'She's always saying bad words.'

'Well, then, two wrongs don't make a right, do they?' I nudged him hip-ways, prompting a response. 'So that makes you both bad, doesn't it? She's mean to me, too,' I reminded him. 'But I can't just go around, calling her a shit stick now, can I?'

He rolled onto his back, looking at me, wide-eyed, holding his breath for a second, until his tummy boiled over with laughter. 'You said *shit stick!*' he grinned, feet swimming in mid-air. 'You called her a *shit stick!*'

'No, Ethan. I said, I *can't* go around calling her a shit stick.' I gave him a wink.

'I'll say it for you,' he gabbled. 'Next time she's horrible to you, I mean.' He fastened his lips, stared at me and burst into giggles that fizzed like lemonade.

'No, you won't!' I told him. 'I only said that to cheer you up, okay?'

He smiled.

'Feel better?'

He gave a procession of nods.

'Can I have Monsieur Monkey?'

'Huh?'

'Grace said I can't have Monsieur Monkey at her party,' he said, staring up at the ceiling. 'But Grandma said it's a shared party, so I can, can't I?'

'What's Monsieur Monkey?'

'You know. Off the telly. *The funniest monkey in zee 'ole of Fran-cey!*' he said, in his best French accent. With his face flushed from anger and laughter, his hair damp and overheated, he looked like a miniature drunkard, the way he was rambling on.

'Howie had him at his party. And now Lucas wants him at his. He's got a unicycle. And he's really, really funny. And he's got this like,' he tried to remember, 'garlic grenade-thing made for *zee stinkage!*'

'Don't see why not,' I said. 'I'll speak to your dad and see what I can do.'

'*Woohoo!*' he said, making his hands into fists like a mini Superman.

'I only said I'd speak to your dad. Don't get carried away.' I gave his knee a shake. 'Right, you don't want to lie up here all day, do you?' He shook his head from side to side against the pillow. 'And neither do I. Shall we go downstairs? You can show me what you've been making.'

He slid himself off his bed, tummy-first. And then, when I least expected it, he did something he'd never done before. Ethan took hold of my hand.

It wasn't the first time we'd held hands, but right then none of those other times counted. All those other times, I'd reached out to him. Steering him clear of main roads. Helping him out of the car. This time, his slightly clammy fingers wrapped tightly around my own. I didn't say a word, afraid to scare him away and spoil the moment. *Ethan*, I wanted to say, remembering the family in the photographs, *I know this isn't how you want things to be, but please don't blame me. Please don't turn me into a shit stick.*

We reached the bottom step, his hand still gripping mine. The gesture was as delicate as a tiny bird perched on my fingertips, until he sped off into the garden.

Dan was pacing across the patio as Ethan ran up to him, mobile against his ear, like some sort of battery-pack to his thoughts. Still at the table, Grace was using a ruler to carefully fold each invitation in half, making them into cards.

'Did you finish them, then?'

'U-huh,' she muttered, still concentrating. 'See?'

She held up one of her homemade invites.

Thanks to the advance warning, I smiled. The front of her card was one of those old pictures, scanned and printed with a loud, neon, birthday font. Grace, her parents and Ethan on a beach. Dan's arm was around Bryony, her head leaning against his neck. His other arm was around Grace, who looked a much happier version of herself, while a toddler-sized Ethan stood at the front, distracted by ice cream. Behind them the horizon melted into a volcanic shade of orange.

'That's a nice picture of everyone...'

'That was my favourite-ever holiday. To Barcelona.' She handed me the card. 'I was nearly eight. Ethe's only about three. Mum said it's her favourite picture of us together. Dad looks so handsome on it.' She inspected her handiwork.

'He always does.' I felt strangely relieved as Grace threw a look of disapproval.

Chapter Nineteen: Lunch for the Lonely

Taking a break from my new part-time job of price-checking gazebos and wondering how to transform the house into a thirteenth birthday wonderland straight out of Grace's imagination, I'd spent the morning finalizing arrangements for The Avington Food & Drink Festival.

I'd managed to find a number for Ethan's Monsieur Monkey impersonator. It turned out *Monsieur Monkey* went by the name of Steve and was also available as a Country & Western-style wedding singer, complete with authentic Tennessee cowboy boots and a castrated Shetland pony. I'd been finishing my email to Monsieur Steve, hoping he wasn't the kind of 'children's entertainer' who'd be sitting naked while he read it, when Audrey gave me a shout.

'I really need you to man the fort for a couple of hours. I've got that luncheon thing,' she said. '*Lunch for the Lonely*. Eric Bartholomew's wife, Dominika's going.' She pushed one of the local Society magazines towards me. 'Can't get out of it…'

The annual Lunch for the Lonely was a highlight in the local business calendar, a chance for companies to give back to charitable causes supporting the homeless. Although, from the way Audrey described it, business cards flowed down a river of wine until the whole thing turned into a Dance for the Destitute at around 7 o'clock, the generous attendees ignoring the plight of the homeless as they spilled past them into taxis and bars across town.

I studied the Society pages. Dominika was not the type of woman I'd ever have imagined being married to Eric

Bartholomew. More importantly, I couldn't believe the rather gorgeous guy in the photograph could possibly be Eric's son.

Saul Bartholomew, according to the caption.

He sounded like something out of *Game of Thrones*.

He actually looked like something off *Game of Thrones*.

Maybe he was adopted?

'We're expecting Council confirmation on the festival before two. No later than three. I need someone here to take their call.' Audrey put on her jacket, opened a drawer and took out some perfume. 'Don't want you missing it. Feel free to set up shop in my office while I'm gone.'

How had I gone from watering plants to managing projects? I wondered. The rest of the office were now out on lunch as I wandered back to my desk. I suddenly remembered I needed to 'borrow' some envelopes for Grace's invitations from the stationery cupboard — until I noticed my keys were missing.

Walking over, the door was shut. No keys dangling from the lock.

Great. Audrey would have us all on Red Alert the minute I told her, paranoid Heather was setting up another rival franchise in there, which wouldn't have surprised me at all, to be honest. I noticed the time and grabbed my laptop and half-finished carton of orange juice, determined not to miss the incoming call from the Council.

I waltzed back into the sleek sophistication of Audrey's room.

Alone under the spotlights of Steen & Heard Communications.

Maybe this *was* what I was good at? Destined to use my brain for business. No children's parties, teenage girls or critical grandmothers to worry about.

In fact, barely two minutes after stepping into the sophisticated-looking office of someone far more successful, I was already reclining in Audrey's seat, imagining I was highly successful myself. The office looked so much better, far more impressive, when you were presiding over it.

The Steen & Heard sign lit up in light bulbs on the back wall.

Our cosy, orange seats and busy desks were suddenly very cool and photogenic.

In fact, I decided, this was exactly the kind of thing I should be documenting on my new Twitter account. I stood at the window and pointed my phone — as Leah and one of the Digital triplets came giggling and shushing around the corner. She made her way over to my desk — returning the keys to the stationery cupboard — as Love's Young Lumberjack pulled on his coat, grabbed hold of her hand and they made their way out the door. *What a little minx!*

I took a quick snap, wondering if I was the only one who'd managed to keep my clothes on in that cupboard. I opened the Twitter app and was quickly presented with wedding pictures and updates of Bryony's flight. I uploaded my photo and wrote:

Office Life: Monday morning in Marketing. #Steen&Heard

Bryony might be the world's most glamorous mum, but I was a bona fide career girl — just look at my new Twitter account, people!

I watched my photo appear with the speed of a paper aeroplane.

I could be anybody on Twitter. *Successful. Accomplished.*

I was practically Audrey already.

So maybe that's why I made myself at home, sneaking a look inside her top drawer. Breakfast bars, a sunglasses-case, insoles claiming to prevent blisters and some sort of self-help book: *Leading the Bitch Behind: A Guide to Women in Business.* I picked it up, not too keen on the sentiment, until I opened the cover and all became clear:

To Audrey,
Wishing you well.
Heather.

Audrey's glasses sat on the desktop and for some reason I stuck them on as I picked up her perfume bottle. No quick-buy, emergency desk fragrance. It was that lovely expensive one from the commercial where the shaven-headed couple rolled around on a bed of hot coals. A big 100ml-sized bottle left for dead in a desk drawer. *Such a waste!* I couldn't resist a quick spritz for luck. Then I noticed Audrey's signature baby-pink trench, hanging on the coat stand, with that charcoal grey trilby I loved perched on top. I took a quick glance out the window, before I walked over casually, as if approaching a stranger. I slipped into the coat, impressed by the label before I belted up. I popped the trilby on top, admiring my reflection in the glass of Audrey's awards and certificates — just as the phone rang. I froze for a second and quickly attempted to change out of my fancy dress costume, yanking at the belt and undoing the top button.

I couldn't miss the call. I stopped fumbling and cleared my throat. Relying on Audrey's glamorous attire to bolster my new-found authority, I answered:

'Audrey Heard's —'

'I'm on my way to the hospital.' The voice was low, distracted. 'Peter called. Joanna's in labour.' I recognized James Steen and tried to correct him, but before I could I was caught on the telephone line like a fancy-dress fish — just as Audrey walked back into her office.

'I'll see you at the hospital,' he was saying, but I was barely listening as I took off Audrey's hat and pulled her glasses from my face.

'Hello? Sorry, this is Ella Shawe.' But perhaps the phone-line wasn't that great, because James continued: 'Let's not get into this, Audrey,' he said, 'but Peter wants you there, I know he does.'

'No, sorry. Mr. Steen?'

I couldn't look up, couldn't face the sight of Audrey, facing the sight of me. 'Sorry, Mr Steen? This is Ella. Audrey's....' *About to fire me?* I thought, before I decided to say, rather optimistically given the circumstances: 'new Project Manager.'

Audrey closed the door and took a seat opposite me. The same seat I took when she was the boss and I wasn't pretending to be her.

'Wait one second, I'll just put Audrey on.'

'No, no, can't stop,' he said. 'I'll get her on her mobile.'

He signed off as I stood still for a second, not wanting the call to end, wondering what the hell Audrey was going to say. How was I ever going to explain that I'd blown my six-day promotion getting carried away, impersonating the boss?

Could I be charged with that?

I hung up as Audrey studied me, looking quite relaxed, considering.

'Well, the hat looked a little too big and my coat's far too long ...'

'Audrey, I'm —'

'As you know,' Audrey said, one hand outstretched. 'I left my glasses.'

I handed them over.

'Anything important?' She raised her eyebrows towards the phone.

'Oh, yes.' I'd almost forgotten about the call. 'It was Mr. Steen. He said —' I knew I really needed not to mess this up — 'Peter called. Joanna's gone into labour —'

Audrey closed her eyes and sat back in her seat.

'Mr. Steen said he's on his way to the hospital and Peter definitely wants you there. James said,' I carefully repeated, 'they both definitely want you there.'

'That's what he said?'

Worry clouded Audrey's brow. She looked even more shocked than when she'd walked in on me wearing her clothes.

'That's what he said.' I nodded, hoping I hadn't botched that bit up too and wondering why Audrey was taking the news so badly.

'I think you can take off my coat now, Ella…'

'Oh, yes … your coat…'

I was thinking of what to say next as I hung it back up on the stand.

'I don't know why I tried your things on…' I tried to sound light-hearted, as if Audrey was Kim, or some friendly changing-room assistant. 'I mean, I've always liked that coat, but —'

'So James is on his way over there now?'

Audrey took a bottle of water from her bag, sipped it and burst into tears.

The pause seemed to last for minutes as I sat back down on her chair.

I didn't know what to do, except offer her one of her own tissues from the chrome-plated box sitting on top of her desk.

'Thank you…'

'Are you okay? Can I get you anything?'

'No, no.' She shook her head. 'Silly, really. *Family.*' She blotted the corners of her eyes. 'Peter's my stepson. At least, he would be,' she explained, 'if we were married.' Her eyes brimmed over again. 'Joanna's not due for another three weeks. Well,' she took a breath, blew her nose, 'this is embarrassing…'

'At least you're not wearing my clothes…'

'Is it worth me asking what you were doing in them?'

'No idea,' I admitted. 'Bad weekend? My boyfriend's mum's been staying with us. I've sort of got step-kids too…' I ran out of excuses, but Audrey gave a nod of understanding. 'I suppose I wanted to know what it felt like to be someone else for a while…'

Someone successful and competent, who wasn't afraid of family gatherings or considered a danger to children.

'I can't say I appreciate finding you dressed in my clothes, Ella. In fact, it's *extremely* odd and unbelievably unsettling, so I'd really rather you didn't do it again.'

I looked up from where I'd been zoning out onto the polished desk and nodded in agreement.

'But, you've always seemed fairly sane in the past, so, since I'm hardly the model of composure myself,' she said, 'let's say we're even, shall we?'

I attempted a smile, but thought better of it.

'How old are his children?'

'Ethan's just turned eight.' I couldn't help but think how funny he'd find this story, once he was old enough to understand it. 'Grace is about to turn thirteen.'

'My stepson, Peter, is expecting his first baby,' Audrey told me. 'Our first grandchild. Well,' she clarified. '*James* is expecting his first grandchild. Peter just about tolerates me.' There was a dash of a smile. 'I've been in his life since he was 10, but he's made it quite clear that this baby has absolutely nothing to do with me.' She inhaled, her lip trembling slightly.

'Well, James, Mr. Steen, said Peter definitely wants you there,' I said, full of sorry optimism.

'I've learned the hard way,' she sighed away tears, 'whatever it is James *thinks* Peter wants and what his son actually wants are two *very* different things.'

The phone rang. We both looked at it then back at each other.

I wasn't sure whether to take the call, involved in some kind of silent, telephone duel with my boss, before she nodded permission.

'That's wonderful news.' I watched her expression brighten. 'Yes, that's right,' I said. 'I'll be looking after the event.'

Chapter Twenty: Grandma in Residence

I stood in the porch, key slotted in the door as a dense wall of TV-sound came from the lounge. Two small figures ran across the end of the hallway, just about visible through ripples of frosted glass. It was like going to my own surprise party.

Except I knew what the surprise was and I didn't really fancy it.

I wished I'd hung around at Dr. Coffee and got a lift back with Dan, so we could arrive home together. Starky trotted towards me as I stepped inside. His curly face panted hello as he nuzzled his head against my leg.

'Oh, hi.' Pippa nodded politely, a quick glance at the empty glasses she held in each hand, as if I was a next-door neighbour she'd inadvertently clashed timetables with.

I wandered into the lounge, Starky bouncing proudly ahead, eager to show Mummy the adventures waiting inside. My once perfectly clean and tidy lounge was a tip, filled with so much communal clutter you'd have sworn it was Christmas Day. The coffee table was stacked with side plates and discarded napkins. A collection of old DVD cases were lying vacant on the floor. Someone's jumper and shoes had been discarded. A micro scooter I'd never seen before was propped against an armchair. Pippa's reading glasses and a collection of boiled sweet wrappers were lying on top of a newspaper, folded on the seat.

'Don't stroke him. That's *her* dog…' Grace mumbled instructions just a little too loudly to the girl sat by her side. They cast smiles into the air, holding a Selfie stick.

Ethan sat cross-legged on the floor with another boy, surrounded by Lego. He gave me a brief look, hands busy with plastic intricacies. The other boy was searching among miniature pieces of debris. Starky, intrigued, settled himself down between them.

'Daniel's home in half an hour.' Pippa flinched at some cartoon-coloured Sit-Com, finally locating the TV remote inside a discarded trainer. She lowered the volume and collected plates. I picked up half-empty glasses and left the kids to it.

'Starky's had his walk. I said to Daniel, it saves dropping him off every morning, me being here. I've got sausage casserole on the go,' Pippa said. 'Cheese crust. Daniel's favourite.' She slid the casserole dish out from the oven. 'He always loved my sausage casserole. The way to a man's heart.' She lifted the lid, inviting me to enjoy the aroma of home-cooking, but as I looked into the earthenware pot, I couldn't take my eyes off the sausages, bobbing away in there like missing fingers.

So that's why *browning* was so important, I thought, gaining another notch on my kitchen-skills apron.

'Looks lovely,' I said, but it really didn't. I'd never heard of anyone putting a cheese crust on a casserole before. It was bad enough knowing there was a load of boiled sausages floating around in it. If that was the way to Dan's heart, I'd happily settle for his crotch. 'Thanks, Pippa. You didn't have to make dinner for us.'

'Of course I did.' She took plates from the cupboard, examining each one like some expert on the Antiques Roadshow. 'The others are getting picked up any minute.'

'Oh, okay.' I realised she meant the children. 'Don't think I've met them before…'

'Well, you wouldn't have, would you?'

I glanced at her and felt a slight prickle in my direction.

'Janelle and Lucas. Friends from school. The girls started together. Lucas is a little younger than Ethan, but they've been no bother, no trouble at all...'

I could see that. The house looked like one of those Indoor Play Centres. All that was missing was a ball pit, a rogue nappy and an outbreak of nits.

No wonder she said she'd mind them at Dan's place. Pippa would never have left her own house in such a mess. It was way more untidy than usual, way more untidy than before I'd given myself a hernia, setting to work with brushes, cloths and good intentions. The floor was covered in muddy footprints. Every surface was littered with the evidence of Pippa's cooking. Various plugs, extensions and wires from the kid's stuff had been left for dead across countertops. Even the garden was covered in cast-off toys and clothing. We may as well have installed a bowling lane and opened a roller disco out there.

'Would you like a cup of tea?'

'No.' Pippa almost sounded offended, as if I'd suggested a quick slug of Absinthe. 'No, thank you. Never touch the stuff after six. Won't sleep a wink if I do.'

'I can do you a decaf, if you like?'

'Oh, I can't be doing with all that nonsense. It's like those vegetarian sausage things,' she told me. 'No idea what's in them, but if you're still wanting a sausage, you're hardly a vegetarian, are you? Made my sausage casserole for Bryony once and she didn't know the difference. And she never could resist my Sunday lunch either.' She looked pleased. 'We always had Sunday roast together. Roast chicken, and all! So much for meat-free! Oh, that's what I meant to ask you.' She waved her hand and ticked off an invisible list, mid-air. 'Could I borrow your sewing kit?'

'My sewing kit?'

'Ethan's collar's come away at the seam.' She gestured to her neckline, rattling one-handed around the cutlery drawer. 'It'll only take two minutes.'

'I don't think I've got a sewing kit...'

'You haven't *got one*?' Pippa sounded so surprised you'd have thought I was talking about my vagina.

Right at that minute, I was delighted to hear Dan come in. Pippa gravitated towards him like the moon orbiting the sun.

'Your friends' mum and dad are here, I think? They're parked up outside,' he told the kids, and I was glad to see him looking as confused as I was.

Grace hopped on tip-toe, engrossed in her iPad, kissing his cheek.

'Dad, look!' Ethan offered his latest creation.

'Oh, that's great! Hi,' he said, as the other two kids appeared, one wheeling past on the scooter, the other pulling on her coat.

'Thanks for having them.' A woman appeared in the porch, gesturing towards Pippa as her children muttered *thank yous*.

'Oh, they were no bother at all. We'll be seeing you at the party, won't we?'

'Yes! Wouldn't miss it.'

I felt the woman's scrutiny. The high street dismissiveness.

'Bryony mentioned you were having Grace's party here...'

'We'll all catch up properly then,' Pippa said, as the children followed their mother out, shouting goodbyes as she waved behind them.

'There's stuff everywhere.' Pippa gave a half-laugh, picking Ethan's jumper from up off the floor.

'*Ow!* Watch where you put your Lego.' Dan stood on a tiny yellow brick.

'Just like old times, isn't it?' Pippa gripped Grace's shoulders, while Ethan followed his dad's instructions, tiding up the sea of toys in the lounge.

Grace sat at the dining table, scrolling through her iPad.

'You've got new followers,' she told me. 'On Twitter.'

'Oh good.' I poured tea as Pippa checked the oven.

'Mum's posted a picture of Australia already,' Grace said. 'Look!'

Perfect sunset here in Melbourne, Bryony had written. And it was, except for the sight of Vic. Roughly the same colour as cod, frolicking about on the horizon.

'Can't believe you've made your casserole, Mum…'

'Thought my favourite son might like his favourite meal when he got home…'

She made it sound like she was flirting with him.

'No, Mum. I was all about your chili, remember? Casserole was Dad's favourite.'

'Chili?'

'Yep,' he reminded her. 'Not that I'm complaining. You used to make your casserole for Dad. Chili was my favourite.'

'Umm…' she muttered, unconvinced.

'But aren't you supposed to brown the sausages?' He peered into the pot. 'Looks like someone's lost their hand in there…'

'Oh, for goodness' sake!' Pippa placed her hand on her hip. 'How's that happened? I'll just have to stick them under the grill.'

'How's the food festival going?'

His mother continued to chide herself, as Dan turned to me.

'Might be worth me taking a look. Any other coffee places signed up?'

'Oh Daniel,' Pippa said. 'Your father tried all that nonsense.' She fished for sausages, lining them up on the rack. 'They're extortionists. Making you pay for the privilege of handing over a day's profit…'

'People respond really well to the businesses taking part.' I took up the challenge, reciting what I could remember from Audrey's press release. Pippa pulled on a silicone oven-glove in stony silence. 'I mean, you're not in the centre of town like the bigger places, but knowing you're a family business, only a few minutes away? It might increase footfall, convince people you're worth making the trip…'

'Hey.' Dan gave my hand a squeeze. 'You've convinced me.'

'Well, it's not you who needs convincing, now is it?' Pippa slid the sausages under the grill as Ethan came tumbling in, reaching an abrupt halt next to his grandma.

I grabbed placemats, setting them out on the table. I was eating that casserole, mutant sausages or not. I'd only realised I hadn't had lunch by the time it got to half-past three and by then the canteen was out of anything decent. I'd grabbed a bottle of Ribena from the vending machine and nabbed the last, semi-stale doughnut from the counter. But just as I sank into the jammy bit, Bryony, looking sensational in a sequined bikini, started following me back on Twitter. I'd brushed the sugar from the top of the doughnut, took one last, decent bite and then retweeted something about quinoa, before I got back to making phone-calls.

'Ethan, out of the way, please. Oh,' Pippa carried on muttering to herself. 'I know where there's a needle and thread. I'm sure Bryony's got a basket somewhere in that little cupboard…'

'Hey, don't take it to heart.' Dan joined me around the table, setting out cutlery. 'Took me long enough to convince her on those Loyalty cards…'

'*Urgh.*' Ethan scrunched his face. 'Are we having *that*?'

'Ethan?' Pippa reached for the ladle she'd brought with her especially. 'You're going to eat your dinner.'

'But I don't like vegetables!'

'Now, don't be silly,' Pippa told him. 'You know full-well that's a jacket potato.'

'They're cool. They new?' Dan asked, as we'd settled in the lounge after dinner. He glanced at Grace's feet, glad of the chance to fill in the blanks between Monday-to-Friday, all those small, weekly details he missed. The casual observations, fleeting over-night likes and dislikes the children lost interest in by the weekend. Watching him, sometimes over-eager, other times, unsure, I wondered if the kids ever seemed as foreign to him as they did to me. Half the time I needed a translator: the *Rough Guide To Step-kids*. 'Your trainers?' he said.

'We got those today, didn't we, Gracie?'

Pippa sat in the armchair, quietly occupied. I was relegated to the couch next to Ethan, as Pippa sewed yet another button on to yet another polo shirt. She'd installed herself as the in-house seamstress. Dan had nipped to the counter shop to help her stock up on needles and cotton, after she had discovered Bryony had packed up her sewing supplies along with her Decree Nisi.

'Mum, you can't keep buying them stuff…'

'I'm allowed to spoil my grandchildren every now and again.' Pippa tied a knot, snipping at cotton with her nail scissors.

'They're not trainers, Dad.' Grace looked semi-embarrassed on her father's behalf. 'They're netball shoes.'

'Oh right.' Dan glanced over, quietly amused. 'So, feeling good about the match on Saturday?' He balanced his elbows on his knees like a sports coach prepping the dressing room. 'Going to finish the season on a high?'

'Uh-huh,' Grace replied from deep at the back of her throat, his encouragement barely registering across her bee-stung expression. She was a winner, a successful competitor. Confident in her approach, unfaltering in her self-belief. She didn't need the pep-talk. You could see that from the way she laced up her trainers. Tightening them like reigns, saddling up, preparing for combat.

I was trying so hard, but the longer I spent with her, the more I remembered that I'd always been a huge fan of the underdog. The only thing I'd ever competed for at school was first dibs on the last piece of cheese and onion flan.

'Oh, we're totally winning that cup,' she announced.

The way she said it, for a moment, I secretly hoped her team lost.

Yes, I know that was wrong of me. She was Dan's daughter. This was important to her. It's not as if I even knew anything about netball, or was a big supporter of the opposing side, but because if she wasn't winning, controlling or deciding, it would be so nice, just for one minute, for me to get to know Grace without the gum shield.

Chapter Twenty-One: Jekyll & High School

Instead of the sophisticated 'ten-to-two' I'd been aiming for, without Kim to draw them on for me, my wonky-armed attempt at liquid eyeliner ticks read at twenty-past ten. Around the same time the kids were supposed to be in bed on a Saturday night, in fact. I secured my earrings into place and heard Grace shouting from her bedroom: 'My tummy still hurts! *I said*, I'm going to *PUKE!*'

'Coming, honey!' I switched off the bathroom light. 'Do you need another hot water bottle?'

'I don't want *you*! *I want my dad…*'

'I'm here, Gracie.' Dan was getting changed, his footsteps sounding across the landing.

'I want my *mum!*'

So do I, I thought, or at least someone who knows how to deal with kids *and* have a social life. It was the first tummy ache I'd ever known Grace to have. I couldn't help but wonder if it had something to do with our one-and-only date night.

I went into our bedroom, put on my perfume and caught a glimpse of myself in the mirror. I'd gone for the stretchy jeans and smart jacket combo, thinking that was the kind of semi-stylish look Audrey would go for if she was at least 10 pounds overweight. When Dan and I had first met I'd pick out cute outfits and spend ages in front of the mirror, smoothing scents all over my body, choosing sexy little pieces of underwear I knew I'd soon be standing in back at his place, until there was nothing left to remove except my inhibitions and a nice pair of heels. I slipped into my flat, ballerina shoes, feeling bad for not tolerating the pain and making an effort and at least going for a nice, tight skirt for a rare night-out with Dan. But, on the one weekend we had somewhere to be, after a week when I'd been caught dressed like a drag version of my boss, taken full responsibility for an entire food festival, and put up with nearly two hours of Grace's insults and threats of projectile vomiting, I could barely be bothered to put on a pair of my good knickers.

'Mum's home soon,' I heard Dan say. 'And Grandma'll be here any minute.'

'Why can't I come with you?'

'Because Ella and I are going out.'

I could hear the reluctance in Dan's voice.

The only break Grace would allow us to go on without a fight was a perpetual guilt trip.

'You know how much Grandma loves spending time with you and your brother...'

I let their voices dissolve and for some reason I had a Cinderella-moment. I wished my torn dress could go to the Ball as I took it from the wardrobe, wondering if the rip really was that bad. *It was worse.* The dress would have to go. I folded it, knowing it wasn't even fit for the charity shop, not in that state, but as I did, I felt something sharp against my palm.

One side of my favourite dress had been stapled together.

A perfect line of metal teeth exposed as they bit through the fabric.

Grace?

She was my first thought.

I stood perfectly still, examining the handiwork.

Grace asking about the dress a few weeks ago.

Grace bitching about my weight.

Grace with the makeshift office supplies — including a perfectly innocent-looking stapler.

I stood still for a moment, a murmur of conversation coming through from the bedroom next door: 'Why'd you have to go out with *her*, Daddy?' I shoved the dress back into the wardrobe and switched off the bedroom light, my mind racing with possibilities. Maybe Grace thought I should do a Liz Hurley and go for the sexy, safety pin look? Or it was a fun, Punk tribute — perhaps with the right encouragement, Grace was all set to become the next Vivienne Westwood. Or maybe she just hated my guts and decided to make me hate them too. *Stop.* I tried not to get upset about it, as I noticed the light on next door. I popped my head into Ethan's room. Ethan who was never demanding, always so sweet. Although, the thought occurred, he was happily distracted by a universe of Marvel make-believe, probably putting the emotional scars of sharing his dad with me on hold until his teen years.

'What are you up to?'

He was lying in bed, balancing a cardboard book on his forehead.

'Nothin' much,' he huffed. 'Just doin' this thing with my dinosaur book.'

'Wowzers,' I smiled. 'You're making a cool shadow on the ceiling. Look!'

I collected super heroes from the floor, placing them on a heap of similar figures inside his toy chest. 'It looks like a scary, dinosaur creature, just like the one on the cover. See?'

'I know.' Ethan gave his usual downcast smile, before shoving the book across the bed, turning on his side and wriggling beneath the duvet in one swift move.

'Goodnight, favourite boy.' I switched off his lamp and placed a kiss on his head.

He pushed one hand under his jaw, the way he did when he was tired, giving the same thoughtful sigh his father sometimes mustered. Until his eyes flashed open: 'My sister hasn't really got a sore tummy.'

'I know, Ethe.'

'Hmm.' He gave into a series of absentminded sighs as he closed his eyes again. 'I liked dinner. There weren't any vegetables.'

'Thank you.' I wiped lip-gloss from his forehead, pleased he'd enjoyed my first attempt at Enchiladas. 'I liked making dinner for us.'

The doorbell rang.

'El?' Dan called, still busy negotiating with his daughter. 'Can you get that, please?'

'That'll be Grandma. She's come back to mind you both,' I told Ethan. 'We'll see you in the morning.'

'Night,' he breathed, mouth already slack as he formed the word.

I heard the thud of the door before I made it to the bottom of the stairs.

Pippa and her set of spare keys.

'Oh, hello Ella.' She was always so surprised to see me standing in the house I'd been living in for over six months. 'Thought I may as well let myself in. Where are the children?'

'Ethan's settled in bed, just about asleep. Grace's in her room. She's got a bit of a tummy ache.' *And a mean streak*, I thought.

'Oh, poor thing. I'll nip up and see how she's doing.' Pippa handed me her jacket. 'It's all the stress of that netball match this morning, I'm sure. Ah.' She stopped briefly at the foot of the stairs. 'Such a shame. They should've won…'

I felt a pang of responsibility. I'd thought losing might have done Grace good. Given her a healthy dose of *you can't win 'em all, honey*, just to soften her edges, but disappointment only enraged her.

'Ella didn't cook the chicken right and now my insides feel like they're rotting,' Grace was explaining, with a voice far younger than her years.

'She's gone off Ella's cooking.' Dan's tone shifted from child-friendly to fully-fledged grown-up. As if that way, Grace couldn't understand him.

'Well, it smelled disgusting.' Grace found me hovering inside the doorway. 'Like that stuff she dishes out to Starky.'

'He ate all of your leftovers,' I said. 'So, maybe you're right…' I forced a casual smile, which I hoped said, *Kids, hey?*

'Well, maybe I could get you something that you *do* like,' Pippa soothed, as Grace wiped her nose with the flat of her palm. 'Do you think chocolate milk might help?'

'The hot chocolate that you make?' Grace wiped her eyes.

It was amazing. One minute, Grace was twelve-going-on-terrifying, the next, she adored chocolate milk from Grandma. One of those entirely different personalities I could probably handle. It was the combination of both I found unsettling. She had a bad case of Jekyll & High School.

'Yes, Gracie. I remembered how much you liked it last time.' Pippa turned to Dan, exchanging a smile, before she looked over, suddenly concerned: 'Better get a move on, you know,' she said to me. 'You haven't got much time to change.'

'I'm as ready as I'll ever be,' I said, quite cheerfully, considering I was mortified. 'I was going to wear my dress…' I looked over at Grace. Dan and his mum were discussing what medicine they had left in the cabinet. 'But someone's ruined it…'

She held my gaze, pout slightly trembling and snatched her hoodie from the bed, pulling it roughly over her head. 'Hope you feel better soon,' I said, leaving the room. *Deal with it, Grace*. I thought. *One-all. It's a draw.*

'She'll be fine,' Pippa assured us, as Grace eased her feet into her fluffy slipper boots, burrowing her head against Grandma's shoulder.

But Grace wasn't fine. We made it halfway through the door before she'd beckoned Dan back for a hug. Five minutes of crying and clinging to him later, there was no chance I could ask him to go anywhere. Instead, Grace was now installed on the settee, snuggled under a chenille throw while Pippa placed a cold flannel on her forehead, loving the chance to love her more.

'I said all along you don't need me to go. Make it a girls' night out. Go and see your mum.' Dan was fixing Pippa a Saturday night Mojito and pouring himself a Guinness. 'Why don't you ask Kim?' He bailed ice cubes into his mum's glass.

'*Kim*? Are you joking? I need to be there in half an hour.'

'You're going to the theatre. She's round the corner from Basnett Street. You're always saying you never get the chance to see her...'

I didn't think there was much point, but I took out my mobile anyway.

'You look great by the way.' He took a sip of his drink, relaxed, dark stubble already shadowing his face since this morning. I loved how Dan used a cut-throat but could still be bearded within twelve hours. There was something reassuring about it. That and it felt great against my thighs.

'No I don't,' I said, feeling guilty, wondering if Dan might've been more interested in Saturday night with his girlfriend if I'd worn a slinky dress and hadn't cancelled my blow-dry. 'Your mum's right. I look too casual.'

'My mum wears hats to the supermarket,' he mock-whispered.

'Well.' I checked my volume. 'You're standing me up to have a date night with her, so maybe that's where I'm going wrong…'

'Grace is sick!'

He sliced through the lime Pippa had bought with her especially.

'Yeah, and let's see how long it takes before she's feeling better…'

'Are you saying she's making it up?'

He stopped slicing now, focused on me.

'As soon as the taxi comes,' I said, getting to the point of not really caring how I sounded, not now I knew what Grace was capable of, 'my guess is, she'll make a full recovery…'

'You don't think she's ill?'

'Do you?'

'Just leave it, Ella.' He went back to playing bartender. 'Or maybe wait until the middle of the night to start with the complaints, the way you usually do…'

That silenced me. Until my phone pinged with a response.

'Kim's coming!'

He walked past, carrying their glasses without a word.

'Ella?' Pippa called from the lounge. 'I think your taxi's here…'

I shouted goodbye and gave Dan the chance to offer me a kiss, but he stayed with his mother, shouting for me to have a good night instead. As the cab pulled away from the kerb, I glanced back at the house to find Grace in the window, looking so triumphant, I actually laughed. *GA or GD?* It was getting difficult to work out who was playing Goal Attack and who was playing Goal Defence, anymore.

Chapter Twenty-Two: Lover's Layne

I made my way along the aisle, side-stepping knees and feet. Up on stage, the cast of *The Rock'n'Roar of Thunder* thrust themselves into a particularly energetic instrumental number. 'Sorry we're late,' I half-shouted, half-whispered, over the whine of electric guitars, pounding drums, and from the sounds of it, some sort of kazoo, as Kim took her seat beside me.

'Hello. Sorry. My fault!' Kim leaned towards Mum with a quick raise of the hand. Mum leant forward, mouthing an overdrawn *hello* and handed me a gift bag: 'To share. VIP's only. Chocolates are divine.'

I opened the chocolates straightaway, relieved I could actually have one now that my phantom weight gain had turned out to be a big, fat lie. As I offered the bag to Kim, a booming voice cut through the music, drawing our attention to the stage, miles away from crazy kids and doting grandmas.

'So, as I was saying!'

'Jesus, Ella.' Kim grabbed my arm, delving one-handed into the truffles. 'He's alright, isn't he?'

Jeremiah Layne, lead actor and It-boy of the moment, looked out across the auditorium. His muscular torso glistened under the lingering eye of the stage-light. He was wearing some sort of spandex costume, unclipping his microphone, all backcombed hair and sprayed-on trousers. His face was contoured with the same thick poster paint that reminded me of taking Ethan to *Make & Create*.

'I believe in love at first sight — at least once a night!'

He caused an outbreak of applause with one serpentine flick of his hips. He was trying to be provocative and androgynous, but so far looked more like a style-conscious wrestler than Ziggy Stardust. According to Google, Jeremiah first sprang to fame and out of his trousers playing a mute but dangerously attractive farm-hand in one of those period dramas full of heaving chests and quivering buttocks. Nowadays, he was as famous for seducing his leading ladies as he was for seducing the camera.

'There's nothing like the allure of a beautiful lady to tempt this lonely vagabond off-course...'

The crowd gave way to an anonymous alert of wolf whistles. I popped another truffle in my mouth, slowly realizing that Jeremiah was sashaying his way towards us, the long microphone cord let loose between his legs.

'He is *hot*!' Kim butt-shuffled in her seat, giddy-knickered. 'I'm loving this *interactive* bit.'

By the time Jeremiah had fixed his flirtatious gaze on her, we were both snorting with laughter.

'There are some women who catapult innocent prey like myself, onto the mantle formed by the bucking horse...' Here came a gasp: *'of Love...'*

Kim gave me a nudge, unable to unlock her eyes from his, until he finally raised one arm with a flourish: *'Everyone! It's your turn to humour me, if you will? This is Renée,'* he shouted, taking my mother's hand, as the audience gave a round of applause.

My mother's hand?

Kim and I stopped laughing.

How did he know Mum's name?

And why was he drooling over her?

She was old enough to be his mother!

She was *my mother*!

'The beautiful Renée has inflamed my vision with her presence...'

From the look on his face, I guessed that wasn't the only thing my mum had been inflaming. Meanwhile, she was doing her *sexy lady* face. Calm and confident. The same one she used in restaurants, or, weirdly enough, when she was driving.

'*I do declare!*' He placed a kiss, which turned into a lick, on the back of Mum's hand. My mouth gaped open, neck swivelling back to gauge Kim's reaction.

'*Renée…*' he growled, as an electric guitar started up on-stage, and, with the briefest of looks, 'You don't mind, do you, lovely?' He plonked himself down on my knee, overlooking the bag of assorted truffles in my lap, as he sang: '*Renée, I wanna stay … in your sights … share further delights. Won't you be mine? For you're so di-vine … naked … under your beauty —*'

By this point, I was terrified he was actually going to mount her in front of us.

'*— I long to … recline…*'

Mum pulled her hand from his grasp with a ladylike smile, as the band started leaping around in an incidental jam session. Jeremiah pounced back onto his feet: '*Oh, you love it!*' He blew Mum a kiss and scampered off back onstage, where a troupe of dancers lay at his feet, miming that old, Improv chestnut: the hands-climbing-rope move.

Mum leant towards us, looking coy: 'Isn't he the sexiest thing ever?'

'He's bloody scorchio!' Kim grinned, before she noticed my expression, remembering it was my mother she was talking to.

'You're *seeing* him?' I asked, one eye still on him as he cavorted around.

'Jeremiah's my friend.' Mum smiled, defiant and demure all at once. 'And he happened to co-write the show. He's very talented…'

I tuned back into Jeremiah's performance. The rest of the mock-rock cast harmonized along while he sang something about a nipple piercing unleashing his molten desire. How very *talented* of him.

'He's got the most amazing voice…' Mum half-shouted, bypassing me in favour of Kim's more appreciative attention, as he writhed against the lead guitarist.

I picked up my flattened truffles, half-melted by Jeremiah's arse, and quickly stuck the remains of one shattered chocolate into my mouth.

'I can't remember the last time I went to the theatre,' Kim was saying, as we stood in the backstage bar, apparently reserved for VIPs, most of them more drunk and disorderly than the perfectly nice people drinking at the perfectly nice bar downstairs.

'Kim? My mum's *shagging* that guy. I'm not really all that interested in the theatre right now.' I neck-craned, trying to find my mother, who claimed to need the *Ladies* but who, I had an awful suspicion, was actually backstage in a slightly damp dressing room, getting slightly overheated with some *shit* actor who had to be at least twenty years younger and who dressed like Axl *fucking* Rose. 'I thought it was going to be a nice night. Instead, I've just sat through 90 minutes of *My Mother's a Groupie — The Musical.*'

'I really don't think it's like that,' Kim said. 'He was only having fun. She's probably interviewed him or something.'

'Kim, he practically humped her, right there, in front of us. It's disgusting!'

'Well, I doubt it's serious.' Her face broke into a smile. 'Can't quite imagine him as your stepdad…'

'Don't…' I gazed back into the crowd and I couldn't believe it, as I caught sight of Heather Constantine among the theatregoers. She was trying to be charming, I could tell. Giving that weird, squinty-smile that made her look like she was in pain. She stood next to Eric Bartholomew, which wasn't good news for Audrey, or anyone in the office who fancied keeping their job.

'What are you gawking at?' Kim followed my gaze. 'Have you spotted your foxy mother yet?'

'Clients, that's all…'

A face in the crowd seized my attention, and I tried to piece together every last detail of him before I looked away. Saul Bartholomew was standing next to his father.

Tall, slim, in a white, fitted shirt. Ridiculously good-looking.

'And, by the way,' Kim said, breaking his man-spell. 'Your new Twitter account's bullshit.'

That got my attention. 'You've seen my Twitter account?'

'Apparently it's yours.' I felt my face flush. 'What's with all the healthy living crap?' She folded her arms, unconvinced. 'No way have you ever been that excited about salad. Have you ever even *eaten* a salad?'

'I didn't know you were on Twitter.'

I felt exposed. Invaded. Like that time, back in the early days, when she'd let slip to Dan about my sinus problems, while I was still trying to be feminine and mysterious. Still too uptight to blow my nose in front of him.

'I'm not. I got an email alert telling me you'd joined. Although.' She tilted her head. 'Looking at it, I thought you'd been hacked by Jennifer Aniston.'

'I *am* eating healthier!'

'Good for you. But what's with the Mindfulness Meditation, Ella?'

'I can have new interests, you know?'

'Honey, there's an Indian Cymbal company following you…'

I didn't even know what Indian Cymbals were.

'Is this for the ex-wife's benefit?

'No!' I'd blown it.

'So, it's just a coincidence that the only two people you're following are her and Dan's daughter? I saw the wedding photos…'

'I'm just trying to get to know them better, that's all.'

'By faking your entire personality?'

'I'm not faking! I'm finding common ground!'

'By being someone else?' She grinned. 'So, how is life on Walton Mountain?'

'Grace hates me.'

'Because of the eyebrow?'

'I've been bending over backwards.' I felt the tension spreading at the mere mention of the bloody eyebrow. 'Trying to make it up to her…'

'Well, you're not going to do that until you stop bending over backwards for her father, honey…'

'I'm not in the mood for your vile innuendos…'

'*Oh, come on.*' She toyed with one long, emerald earring. 'If you think that's bad, how'd you expect Grace to feel? That's what her problem is. You're fucking her father, for God's sake…'

'Shut up, Kim!'

I remembered the look on Grace's face a few weeks ago. She'd walked into the bedroom, chatting away to her dad and had caught me fresh out of bed, grabbing a robe to cover my nakedness. Maybe that's what had pushed her over the edge.

That was the moment she'd reached for the staple gun.

'She *knows* you sleep with her dad, El.'

'So what am I supposed to do? Sleep on the couch?'

I wasn't entirely ruling out that option, not if it gave me a quieter life and saved the rest of my wardrobe.

'What I mean is,' she explained, 'it's only natural she's going to be a little … y'know, *prickly*.'

'She stapled my dress together.'

'What?'

'She stapled my favourite dress together. All down one-side. It's practically torn in two-pieces.'

I decided not to explain how it was all part of some game plan to give me Body Dysmorphia. Kim would only piss herself laughing, which completely missed the point.

'She'd be better off dealing with the real issue. Stapling your knees together.'

'Very funny.' I faked a smile. 'I don't know what to do. She won't even eat anything I cook. I make an effort. Find recipes. Stand there, *dicing* stuff.'

'You *diced* something?' Kim put on her Marilyn Monroe voice: 'Jeez, honey, why didn't you say?' She called out to the crowd: 'Can Nigella Lawson please return my friend to the foyer? So,' she smirked, 'you're pretending that your idea of a good time is cooking, and you want everyone to love you for it?' She raised an eyebrow. 'Listen, you need to stop pretending and serve up who you really are for dinner, Toots. You'll piss her off even more with the whole "Stepmum" routine. Teenage girls are moody little bitches. Remember?'

'She's not even a teenager yet. We've got the grand unveiling next weekend,' I reminded her. 'You're still coming?'

'Put my name down.'

'Good. I don't think I could take another day like the zoo. At least you'll be there if the twins decide to give me another golden shower.'

'It'll be fine.' She glanced at her watch. 'You just need to stand your ground. Where *has* that insane mother of yours gotten to?'

'I don't want to stand my ground.' I was contemplating calling a cab and leaving my mother to it, until I remembered the atmosphere back at the house and decided I might be better off staying for a drink. 'And it's bad enough coping with Grace, without the twins. They're like the devil in duplicate. And,' I said, thoughts tumbling out of my mouth, now that I had my best-friend to confide in, 'Grace's never going to get over it, because I'm not her mum...'

'No, you're not, and you're never going to be like a mum to her.' Kim got straight to the point, as ever. 'So, how about you stop trying to dress like one?'

I glanced down at my outfit for the hundredth time. And noticed the melted chocolate smudged all the way down one leg. *Melted truffle.* I was dressed like a binge eater.

'It's the flat shoes, isn't it? And the bloody chocolate...'

You may as well have rolled me in caramel and sprinkled some hazelnuts on top.

'I was joking!' Kim rummaged inside her handbag. 'You look great. Except for all that dead truffle down your trouser leg. Here.' She handed me a tissue. 'Look, seriously, if Dan wasn't with you, he'd be having the exact same problems with someone else. Trust me, the daughter will come around.'

'I hope so. Oh, and, don't forget,' I rubbed at my leg with the tissue, picking up the pace as I finally noticed my mother making her way through the crowd, 'is Grace's bangle nearly ready?' Kim had gone back to doing what she loved. Making pieces of her quirky jewellery, in between hating her day job. It was quite an achievement, finding the time to do anything else other than teach, she reminded me. But since she'd been living alone, she had to find some way to tide over the boring nights on her own, she'd said, in a mock-sulk. 'Yep.' She looked pleased with herself. 'Gonna be gorge.'

'Oh, there you are.' Mum offered us each a glass of wine.

'Thank you!' Kim said, as I carried on scrubbing at my trousers, which was doing nothing except sticking grubby little bits of tissue all over my leg.

'I meant to tell you — I got my first overseas commission!' Kim grinned. 'A customer back home.'

'Woo-hoo!' Mum gave a celebratory jiggle, which I knew was all about her and Jeremiah and nothing to do with Kim.

'That's so great.' I took my glass, trying not to look at my mother, knowing that if I did, words would engulf us.

'Only a friend of my cousin,' she explained. 'But you've gotta start somewhere, haven't you?'

'You certainly have! More power to you.' Mum gave Kim a clumsy rendition of a fist-bump. *Jeremiah again*, I thought.

We stood, listening to Mum tell us about buying a new wok after the handle snapped off her perfectly good one, followed by her thoughts on China as a super power. (She enjoyed the cuisine, not so keen on the Communism). Her preference for strawberry conserve over a simple 'jam', (Much fruiter, therefore healthier and far better value). News of her latest passion for growing Orchids. ('A lady only dips her toes in water,' being the rule of thumb when it came to watering), until, I knew Kim couldn't resist asking: 'How do you know Jeremiah Layne, then?'

Mum actually blushed. I couldn't stand it. Why couldn't she get back to her Orchids and stop skipping about like she was in season?

'We're friends.' She used the exact same tone Pippa told Ethan to eat his greens with. 'He's very smart. And funny. I enjoy his company.' A slight look in my direction. 'It's not all about the sex —'

'But we can soon change that.' Jeremiah held his champagne flute aloft, grinning into my mother's face like a sexually aroused vampire, his face still streaked by stage makeup. 'Can't we, gorgeous?'

Mum fixed her hair back in place, becoming practically *girlish* in his presence.

'This is my daughter, Ella, and her friend, *our friend*,' she corrected herself, 'Kim.'

'Oh, shit. Forgot you were coming,' Jeremiah offered his hand. 'Delighted to meet you, and your friend.'

Kim almost fell into his eyes. I could barely look at him.

'We already met.' I was glad Mum looked uncomfortable. 'You sat on my knee, remember?' He swayed as if on board a ship and took another swig from his glass. 'When you sang your little song ... *to my mother?*'

'Oh, yeah! Yeah, great to meet you!' He swallowed a deep belch. 'Anyway,' he turned to Mum. 'Table's booked. Car's waiting, doll.'

Doll?

'We're going to hit up this new place Jeremiah's been telling me all about…'

Hit up? Since when had my mother started talking like that? What next? A gold tooth?

'*A-huh.*' Jeremiah slid his hand around her waist with a sickening familiarity. 'Dim Sum.' He broke into a hiccup.

'You're both more than welcome to join us?' Mum added, as I took a mouthful of wine and placed my glass on the nearest window ledge.

'I've got to get back…'

'*Ella?*'

'Kim? You ready to make a move?'

'I am, actually.' Kim found a stable surface for her own untouched glass, as I noticed gorgeous Saul Bartholomew breaking into laughter at the bar. The longer you noticed him, the more handsome he got. And he laughed a lot. It put a smile straight on your face. 'I've got to be up and out tomorrow.'

'Okay, cool!' Jeremiah was tapping out a text.

'I'll catch up with you in the week, Ella.' Mum pecked us both goodnight, European-style. The way she did when she was trying to be chic. And then, according to surveillance reporting by Kim, Jeremiah's hand, complete with chipped, black nails, made its way down to my mother's arse and proceeded to stroke it.

I hadn't noticed.

All I'd noticed was Saul Bartholomew, noticing me.

Pippa was rinsing teacups as I arrived home just before midnight.

'Dan only went up half an hour ago. Everybody enjoy themselves?'

'Yes, thanks.' I smiled, fresh from ranting about my mother's love life in the back of the taxi all the way to Kim's. Then continuing the conversation, texting Kim about it all the way back home. 'How's Grace?'

'Fast asleep. Waited for her hot chocolate to cool, drank half of it, then asked to go to bed,' she said. 'We were more worried about Ethan, to be honest.'

'Ethan?'

'He woke up very upset. Had a bad dream. He said,' she turned towards me, 'you'd been playing a game? Something about dinosaurs hiding in his bedroom?'

'Oh, it wasn't a game. There was a dinosaur-shadow, that's all...'

'He's fine now,' she said. 'But that probably wasn't the most sensible thing to put in his head before bedtime.'

She gave me that *look*. I wouldn't mind, but Pippa was the one who'd bought the bloody dinosaur book in the first place. I'd practically been framed.

'Anyway,' she said. 'All's well that ends well. It was lovely. All of us spending Saturday night together. Been a long time since we did that...'

'Well, thanks for looking after everyone.'

'*You* don't have to thank me.' She was offended. 'They're my *family*.'

For some reason, when I should have been vowing never to go to the theatre again, or possibly thinking about the best way to let Mum know jumping into bed with an infamous, alcoholic womanizer — we'd thoroughly Googled him in the back of the cab — wasn't the smartest move for an expert in the field of Love and Romance, from the minute I walked upstairs, the only conversation I replayed over and over again, was my conversation with Pippa: *All's well that ends well...*

What was that supposed to mean?

Dan was asleep as I reached the bedroom. Not a murmur as I negotiated my way to bed, finding him sprawled, just about enough room to lie side-on, legs bent around his shape as if I'd fallen from a great height. *All's well that ends well...*

Pippa's message was loud and clear: Dan was a good dad who wouldn't be abandoning his children on a Saturday night *for me* anytime soon.

Dan would be spending his time with his family.

Not some *useless-around-children* girlfriend.

He turned over, tussling with the duvet, interrupting my thoughts.

'Come here.' His hands were against my skin, breathing me in, until his parched lips softened my thoughts. 'I missed you.'

He kissed my neck, sending a rash of sensation through my body: *'Dan…'*

The weight of sleep in his kisses. The silence between us, pulling closer.

Until the sound of Pippa's cough barked its way across the landing, hurtling against my subconscious like stones against a window. His kisses slowed.

Lying there, my eyes flashed open as I counted back the days.

I caught my breath. Our kisses become staccato.

My period was late.

Nearly two weeks late.

Chapter Twenty-Three: Family Planning

As rain whipped against the windows on Sunday afternoon, I hoped next weekend wasn't going to be tornado weather. Not with a gazebo and a dozen kids involved. Pippa had insisted on making a proper Sunday lunch. She was peeling potatoes while Dan and I played commis chefs, rinsing and chopping our way through rations of parsnips, carrots and turnips, piled high around the sink like a Victorian Christmas.

'Can you hear us?' Grace and Ethan congregated around the dining table, propping themselves up around the computer.

'Are you Skyping Mum?' Dan asked, rinsing the colander, before a tinny rendition of Bryony's voice wavered across the kitchen.

'I miss you guys...'

'We miss you too!' Ethan sat up on his knees, smiling broadly at the screen.

'Have you got a tan, Mum?' Grace looked sceptical.

After a moment's delay, we heard Bryony: 'It's too cold to sunbathe here.'

'I thought you said —'

'It's sort of spring here, I suppose. Probably better at home.'

Bryony sounded more like Major Tom than a new bride.

'No,' Grace told her. 'It's raining...'

'It's been raining all day,' Ethan said, as Starky swept past his legs, trying to taunt him into playing with the stuffed penguin he'd been slobbering over all day.

'I'd rather be back home with you two...'

'Mum?' Grace asked, as Dan dried his hands. 'Are you crying?'

Dan went over to the computer, standing behind the kids. Starky had run off now, squeaking out an oblivious tune on his slightly mauled penguin.

'Everything's fine here.' Dan looked over. He seemed worried. 'We're getting ready for Grace's party on Saturday, aren't we, you two?' He was in full-on Parental Guidance mode. The kids stayed mute. Ethan's interest made its way to the window, where the rain picked up at speed. 'Where's Vic?'

'In the bar. Boring everyone shitless about his sandals…'

Dan glanced at the kids.

'You'll be home soon,' he reminded her. 'We'll see you at the party.'

I swept the vegetables into the steamer. Pippa was gently humming along to an obscure, 70s-sounding song on the radio.

'Mum?' Grace asked, as Ethan sat back on default-setting, flicking the switch on one side of his model car over and over again.

'What time is it there?' Dan was trying to change gear, shift the mood, get the kids back onto an even keel before Bryony signed off.

Pippa sang the words to the song. Something about the captain of a ship.

I thought of Dan, steering the conversation. Charting a steady course back to child-friendly.

'Half-eleven.'

'Well, try and get some sleep then, hey?'

'Yeah, you're right. *You usually are…*'

Bryony sounded drunk. *Really drunk.*

'I miss you, guys. All of you,' she slurred slightly. 'Remember our Sunday afternoons? Remember how we used to bake? Daddy always made the best butterfly cakes. Didn't you, Danny?'

'You don't know who people are, who they'll turn out to be,' Pippa was telling me, polishing dishes that had already been dried to perfection in the dishwasher, handing them over for me to put away, 'not until the kids arrive...'

Except, I kind of knew Dan was a great dad, I reassured myself, anticipating the result of the pregnancy test I was going to have to take as soon as I got to the nearest chemist. Or maybe in a couple of days, once the idea of being an actual *mother* sank in. All of this was intermittently swimming around my head as I'd left Dan in the lounge, Grace wedged up next to him, ordering helium-filled balloons from a place I'd found online. Ethan sat at their feet, console hooked up, nagging his dad to join him on a racing game he was slack-mouthed engrossed in.

Dan looked so relaxed without the usual siren of weekend activity. No need to jump-start a week's worth of family time, running against the clock until Sunday evening. Dan was always quiet on Sunday nights. Frustration at saying goodbye to the kids masked by a sudden, brooding impatience. It felt so strange the minute the place became abruptly childfree on Sunday evening. The children's bedrooms fell silent. Tell-tale signs of their visit — the crush of Ethan laying on top of his duvet, the trail of hair slides, bobbles and brush across Grace's dressing table — preserved until next weekend. This evening, a purposeful kind of happiness had settled across Dan's face.

'Daniel had taken over the coffee shop. Lost his father.' I rejoined the conversation with Pippa. 'Two children at home. Then all that business started. The *divorce*,' she mouthed, as if the word was a curse. 'Ethan was only a baby. Three years old, bless him. Bryony put nothing but pressure on him. Daniel, I mean,' she said. 'The house wasn't good enough for her. Too much work, not enough holidays. She didn't want to work in the shop. Then decides she's going to run it. That's what all this was for.' She swept a glance across the kitchen. '*Catering.*' She gave a huff of disbelief. 'Mine and Derek's business. Daniel's inheritance. Then, next thing, she wants out. Wants to go off to Australia, of all places.' Her eyes darted with annoyance. 'Doesn't do anything by halves, that one, never did. Wanted to uproot the whole family. That's where her father was from, did you know?'

I didn't, but the significance of the honeymoon wasn't lost on me.

'Expected me to sit back while she took my grandchildren to the other side of the world.' A china bowl was bearing the brunt of her frustration. 'I don't think so! Derek's dream was opening that shop, and it didn't come easy,' she informed me. 'Not half as easily as we'd imagined. Barely knew what had hit us, let me tell you. Then madam comes along, expecting to cash in her chips. I don't think so...'

While Pippa polished the gold-plating off her gravy boat, I realised I'd learned more about Bryony and Dan's relationship in that half hour with her than I had in the last year and a half with Dan. Dan had been young, twenty-one, when he met Bryony. A dad by the time he was twenty-three. Bryony was a couple of years older, 'and light-years ahead of him,' Pippa added. 'She was never going to settle down,' she said. 'It was Daniel who had the right to be flighty, but even with the best of intentions, it wasn't going to work. Not with those two. Let's hope she's made the right decision with this new bloke. At least for the children's sake. Vic seems nice enough, but those boys of his!' She shook her head as I carried on loading up cupboards. 'I said to Daniel, I'm sorry, but I don't want Ethan influenced by them. Such a shame,' she sighed. 'The parents break up and it's the children who suffer. For poaching eggs,' she explained, as I inspected a weird rubber cup thing.

'Men are made by women,' she continued, reaching down into the cutlery basket. 'We create the babies. The lives we want to lead. The men we want to love. We do.' She examined an already gleaming fork. 'We mould things into shape. *Nurture* them. But it's the men who shoulder responsibilities. At least, if they're decent. Those children need their father. I know you love my son.' I paused, dish in hand, as I realised she was talking to me. 'But it's important that you learn to love my grandchildren.'

'I do love them!' I closed the cupboard door, as I heard my own words and really felt them. I'd felt it before. Felt some hidden doorway slam whenever I disappointed Grace. Felt distances between me and Ethan knit together with a rush of affection.

She nodded and closed the drawer.

'Next Saturday'll be nice. Grace's birthday.' She brightened. 'Did Daniel tell you, he's ordered that gazebo? And wait 'til you see her dress! I'm so glad we got to do this.' She said these last words almost to herself. 'We wouldn't have got a look-in otherwise, not at their mother's place. Well, you know how it was at the zoo,' she pouted. 'All about Bryony. And those twins running around! We're practically treated like strangers. Daniel's *only* their father. Anyway.' Her features restored themselves back to grandma-mode. 'Did you say you wanted that hot chocolate?'

I headed into the lounge to see if Dan fancied a cup. Pippa shared out her luxury cocoa powder before leafing through a double glazing catalogue, the same way I devoured the Showbiz sidebar.

'Dan? Do you want a cup of hot chocolate?'

He was deep in thought, typing into his mobile.

'Hey, are you even listening?' I sat next to him, ready to snuggle up and catch up with that boxset we'd downloaded. 'Shall I text you instead?'

'No, thanks. I'm fine…'

'You okay?'

I wriggled headspace against his shoulder, hoisting his arm around me.

'Yeah,' he said, semi-convincingly. 'Just texting Bryony.'

Chapter Twenty-Four: To The Rescue

Audrey called the office first thing Monday morning, announcing she was taking Paternity Leave. 'Well, James is, so I am too,' she'd laughed. 'Only a couple of days, to help everyone settle in with the baby.'

'Good for you!' I'd said, until I realised that meant I'd be managing the food festival single-handedly — as well as trying to handle my mother. I'd run off and ruined our night at the theatre, she'd text me. Although, from the look on her face as soon as Jeremiah was near, I seriously doubted it. I'd ignored her messages, all five of them, but about 11 o'clock, once I'd settled the first onslaught of work, I caved in and called her. As soon as I heard Mum's voice down the line I realised that if I could handle her mid-life crisis, I could handle it all.

'You were rude!'

'Oh, as if he noticed.' I was wading through Audrey's emails. 'He was drunk, *belching* all over everyone...'

'He wasn't belching. He gets hiccups after he performs. It's some kind of delayed stage-fright we think.'

'Well, it's some-kind-a vile.'

'I thought you'd at least have a little empathy for other people's anxiety issues, but if you're going to insist on being so childish...'

'Childish? He's only three years older than I am. You seem fine with how *childish* he is! Anyway, what's that supposed to mean? I don't have *anxiety* issues...'

'*You* don't have anxiety issues?' She gave a humourless laugh. 'You're not coping at work. You're cleaning around the clock —'

'I am coping *at work.*' I scoped the office. 'I wanted the house to be nice for Pippa, that's all. It's called Spring Cleaning. Although, I needn't have bothered. The bloody lounge looks like Lost Property. You'd think there was a school trip going on, the amount of shoes and bags left all over the place...'

'I've never met a happy woman with a tidy house, Ella.'

'You must be permanently ecstatic then,' I said. 'Where do you get all this stuff from, Mum?'

'It's not selfish to put your own feelings first, is all I'm saying. You're showing classic signs of Anxiety. Dusting away doubt. Polishing every surface. Marking your territory. Trying to clean away the ex-wife —'

'I am not —'

'Oh Ella! You've hit the duster the way some people hit the bottle. It's all in the mind. The emotions. You know that. That's what you need to spring clean...'

'So, everyone who cleans is unhappy?' I was stumped for a second, worried Mum might be making perfect sense. 'I'll tell John the cleaner you're so concerned when he clocks on at five.'

'That's entirely different. That's work. There's a skill-set involved.'

Talking of which, I still had a backlog of Public Liability Insurance certificates to cast my eye over. Meanwhile, Leah had spent all morning planning some kind of trip — printing out tourist details while I pretended not to notice.

'Mum, I've got to go. I can't talk. I'm at work.'

'You don't seem able to talk at home either, nowadays...'

'It's your interrogations I don't like...'

'Don't be so ridiculous,' she said, then lowered her gear from warp speed. 'Everything on track for the party?'

'Pretty much,' I told her, though really I hadn't a clue what was going on. Every time I asked the To-Do list grew longer. 'Only the food to sort out.'

Dan was supposed to be sorting out catering, until it turned out Grace didn't want her dad's coffee shop cramping her style. The other girls would think that was excruciating. *Excruciating* was the new word for anything lame. And it was *excruciating* how much Grace used it when we suggested anything that wasn't already on her wish-list.

'Didn't you say you were organizing a food festival?'

Actually, yes. *I was*!

How the hell hadn't I thought of that?

'Well, let me know if I can do anything,' Mum said, 'but, Grace is Dan's daughter. I'm sure Dan's mum will want to help out. She's living there with you now, isn't she? Pippa?'

I was barely listening. My computer screen filled with exhibitor profiles, all research for the report I was putting together, as I called up the page for Rice'n'Roll. They'd signed up the week before, supposedly with the most fantastic lunch menu. Audrey was a big fan of the vegetarian options. *Perfect for Bryony.*

'Yes, I told you Pippa was staying with us...'

I located the order page, pulling down options and ticking boxes, wishing everything in life could be this simple.

'And who's idea was that?'

'It wasn't really an idea, Mum. It was either Pippa looks after the kids, or we leave them home alone for a fortnight.' I clicked inside the dots, ordering one Vegetarian, one Meat, one Fish Platter. 'And look how Macaulay Culkin turned out.'

'Pippa's not planning on moving in, then?'

'Not that I've noticed…'

'*Really?*'

'Mum? Why are we talking about this?'

I noticed Leah flagging me down, waving over for my attention.

'Eric Bartholomew on line two,' she said. 'Not happy.' She pulled a face. 'Shall I put him through?'

'You're avoiding the issue…' Mum said.

'I'm avoiding this phone call.'

I gave Leah a nod, pressed *Send* on the order form.

'Love you Mum. Gotta go. Bye!'

Eric Bartholomew. Our biggest and arguably most difficult client.

And not an Audrey in sight.

'I can't have this kind of situation developing among the staff,' he insisted.

Leah was right. Eric really wasn't happy. Not happy at all.

'It's affecting Business Practice. When practice is affected, there's an immediate impact on productivity. Our lack of engagement with a campaign heralded in the local press as being supportive of working mothers puts us in direct opposition with at least 70% of my workforce. You're putting me in a very precarious position in terms of Union action.' His speech reeked of Heather Constantine. 'What do Steen & Heard propose to do? Because, unless you provide the support we're paying you to provide, and despite my personal friendship with James,' he wavered. 'I'll have no choice but to take my business elsewhere. It's simply untenable.'

'We understand your concerns, Mr. Bartholomew. The team here at Steen & Heard are not only aware of your position, but we're actively working on a solution.'

Leah gave a thumbs up, watching from her desk, looking as tense as I felt.

'Which is?' He was growing more agitated by the second. 'Miss Shawe? I'm on my way to the airport. It would be nice to have a response from you before I reach Italy.' The last thing I needed was to let Audrey know we'd lost another account while I was the one in the hot seat. 'Which is…' he repeated. I was leafing through Audrey's notes, trying to work out an answer, as Leah held up her notepad:

TOPLESS FLASHMOB?

I gave her a look: for God's sake, not *that* again.

She went back to scribbling: *FREE STUFF?*

I shrugged, shook my head.

She tore out a page, held up: *BLOW JOB?*

'We're developing our own initiative,' I told him, which wasn't strictly true, but I'd been thinking the exact same thing, listening to Heather on Rising Radio Breakfast that morning. Her plans to hoist her *Bosom Buddies* initiative all over Avington were already all over the airwaves.

'Go on…'

'*Breast Friends*!'

Leah's eyes widened as I blustered out the only semi-decent idea I'd semi-recently thought of. The downside was I hadn't thought of it with Audrey. In fact, she had no idea I'd been having ideas. Especially ideas about this particular client, who'd been playing golf with her husband and been a client for the last decade or so.

'Brea—' Eric couldn't bring himself to use the B-word, which wasn't particularly encouraging. 'What exactly do you have in mind?'

'We're keen to offer our clients other options,' I rambled, reading out Audrey's notes. 'Along with our expertise —'

'Yes, yes,' he ushered me along.

'The *Breast Friends* initiative will work at a Human Resources level to ensure your business meets approved standards.' I didn't know where any of this was coming from except the dark recesses of my imagination.

'Which is exactly what *Bosom Buddies* is offering,' he pointed out, 'but at *half the cost* of your representation…'

'30% of the *Bosom Buddies* fee is spent renting products to secure outrageous commission for their representative, Heather Constantine.' I was quoting Audrey again.

'I see.' He sounded vaguely interested. 'But you're still asking for double the investment of your former colleague, who did a superb job managing our account, while still working at your agency.'

'Mr Bartholomew,' I said, aware of Leah's eyes on me. 'If you feel confident about a one-person operation representing your business, a business your family has built over 45-years, we respect your decision. But, if you're making that decision based solely on a marketing fad in the local gazette … Steen & Heard have worked alongside Bartholomews' for the last decade. Heather's work represents only a small fraction of what we can offer. Heather was part of our team. A successfully tried and tested team, who gave Heather a huge amount of support and direction.'

Leah made a silent clapping gesture.

'*Breast Friends*?' Eric sighed. 'Send over some literature, would you?' he said. 'I'll be in touch.'

I hung up and slumped forward, as if I'd completed that 15-minute workout app Bryony had been tweeting about. I felt like I'd done 20 minutes of cardio working out how to download the damn thing.

'Woah!' Leah high-fived mid-air. 'That was so good!'

Before I could respond with a thousand reasons why it really wasn't good at all, my mobile started up. For a second I thought it was Mum calling me back. I was planning to pretend she was a PPI caller and hang up to speak to her later, but when I glanced at the screen it was Grace. Grace who never called me.

'Everything okay?'

'Not really,' she said. 'Me and Ethe are at the pictures and Grandma's not answering her phone.'

'Where is she?'

'I dunno.' Worry clogged her throat. 'She's not answering. She dropped us off to watch *Kung Fu Kid's Kamp*. She should've been back here now to pick us up. I told her what time it finished. Ethan!' She suddenly broke off. 'Come here! Stop chopping him! The Security Guard said he'd wait with us…'

'Good,' I said, as Audrey's phone rang. I hoped it wasn't another disgruntled client, as I wondered what the hell to say to Grace. 'That's good…'

'I would've called Dad, but Grandma said not to tell him…'

'You've spoken to her?'

'No, she —' There was a pause. 'Don't say anything, okay?' She made me promise. 'When we took Ethan to the Lego Store last week Grandma forgot where she put the car keys. We were walking around the car park for ages in case she'd dropped them. Then it started to rain. We had to call a taxi back to her house to get the spare set. She said Dad would only worry about her minding us if we said anything to him…'

'Wait right there. I'll be with you in half an hour.'

'Where are you going?' Leah asked, as I went into Audrey's office, finding the keys to Heather's old company car. 'Don't you need to get that paperwork across to Eric?'

'What paperwork? It doesn't even exist. Not yet.'

Chapter Twenty-Five: Reach For Your Feet

I'd tried calling Pippa myself and put Grace on speakerphone, finally in the driver's seat.

'Ella!'

'Are you okay? Still waiting with the security guard?'

The line went dead. I tried Grace again. Her phone went to voicemail.

Bloody mobiles, I thought, urging the traffic lights to change.

Up for a quick gossip? Get through first time. Genuine crisis? No reception.

Precisely twenty minutes later, I arrived at the cinema. I was nearly out of my mind by the time I made it to the foyer. I didn't think the kids had ever looked so pleased to see me before, until I realised Pippa was jogging behind me.

'Grandma!'

'Ella?' Pippa caught up. 'I thought that was you. What're you doing here?'

'Grace called —'

'Instead of calling Dad…' Grace explained.

'Sorry about that.' Pippa patted down her collar. 'I went with my friend to the doctor's. She hasn't been feeling so good lately. Completely lost track of the time…'

'Everything's okay?'

'Of course it is! I wouldn't've left them here!'

But you did, I thought. *You did.*

Once I'd made it back to the office, got in touch with Audrey, who gave a rather curt seal of approval, sent the proposal to Eric, and replied to the latest email from Health & Safety, it was nearly 9 o'clock before I finally made it home.

'You look tired.' Dan was leafing through paperwork.

'Yeah, I am.' I went over, kissing the side of his head as he wrapped his arm around my waist, still eyeing printouts. 'Your mum alright?'

'Mum?' He looked up. 'Yeah, she's watching some dance show thing she recorded. Why?' I knew Dan would want me to tell him about Pippa, but Grace would never forgive me. And, let's face it, I was risking a lot worse than my dress being stapled if I opened my mouth and dragged Grandma into it. Anyway, it would be unfair. I was hardly a dream babysitter myself.

'Oh, you know.' I yawned. 'Just being busy with the kids and stuff.'

I made my way up to shower and found Grace's bedroom door open with strange music coming from her room.

'What are you up to in there?'

'Mum's Reach For Your Feet class!' She was sat on the floor, legs stretched out and fingers and toes pointed. 'We do this one.' She got on her tummy, stretching her arms behind her back and reaching for her ankles. 'This is Phase Two. And the last one.' She bent herself into a triangle. 'Downward dog.'

'Downward dog? I've never seen Starky do that…'

She rolled her eyes. 'D'you like my t-shirt?'

I did, actually. Oversized grey marl with *Toned by Bryony Malone* splashed across the front in neon yellow.

'It's Mum's new merchandise. Look.' She dug inside her new wheelie case. 'There's Yoga pants and body suits too. Built-in sports bra, see? Cool, isn't it?'

'Yes, really cool.'

'Try it on if you like.'

'Oh —' I handed it back to her, but she wouldn't take it.

'Go on. It's your size. It fits Mum.' Grace seemed to be making a point of telling me I was slim all of a sudden. 'It's too big for me.'

'I don't even know how to do Yoga.'

'I'll show you.' She pushed an elastic headband up over her fringe. 'It's really easy. If Grandma can do it, you can. *Please?*'

'Yeah,' I said, half-heartedly. 'We'll do it at the weekend, when it isn't so late —'

'Mum says it's never too late!'

'I think she means too late in life.'

'Oh, come on, Ella. Don't be so boring!'

Boring? 'Oh, go on then…'

I did as I was told, while Grace made me close my eyes and concentrate on my breathing as she bullied me into the Lotus Position.

'I've got a skirt on. This is fine,' I insisted, legs stretched out in front of me as I curled my toes into something called Staff Pose.

'And remember, you're only one Yoga class away from changing your life…' She used a strange, breathless voice, rattling off New Age-isms like Oprah Winfrey serving up fortune cookies. 'Right.' She sounded more like Grace again. 'That's how you're supposed to breathe! Now, get changed and we'll start!'

'I don't need to get changed.' I got to my feet. 'Can't we call this a practice class?'

'Go on! Go and put the stuff on,' she coaxed. 'You have to move freely, Mum says. That's why she's doing her clothing range. I'm trying it out for her. It's called market research…'

Grace was so enthusiastic that before I knew it I was getting changed into what was basically a leotard with baggy, festival pants featuring the *Toned by Bryony Malone* slogan embroidered across the back. They were a little on the tight side. My bum didn't exactly look like the best endorsement for Bryony's exercise regime, but I was soon doing Upward Facing Dog. Followed by a Low Lunge and finally the Lion Pose. *Who knew I could be so flexible?*

'Look at you two!' Pippa gave a light tap on the door. 'Wondered what all the chatter was. You teaching Ella your Yoga, Grace?'

We were sat on the bed. Grace was insisting we take selfies, eyes-crossed, tongues sticking out, to send to her mum. I hadn't been in that state since Kim's last birthday.

'Show her your Half-Forward Bend, Grandma!'

'Well, let's see.' Pippa bent forward without a second's hesitation. Her back was almost a perfectly straight line. Her hands were wrapped around her calves with not so much as a frown of discomfort, as if it was the moment her life had been leading up to. 'I'm getting quite good at this, aren't I love?' My hamstrings ached at the sight of her. 'What's my best one called?' She stretched her fingertips down until they almost reached her ankles.

'Wide-Legged Forward Bend, I think.' Grace leafed through her booklet of Yoga poses. 'Do you know that one?'

I shook my head, concerned that Pippa was about to fracture something, as she spread her legs, her head now hanging between her knees.

'Come on,' Grace said, joining in, a slightly less flexible version of her grandma.

'Well, you know, it's only my first class —'

'Come on!' Pippa lifted her head, stretching out her neck. 'You can do it! Marvellous for the spine…'

I stood beside her, taking note, shuffling my feet apart, not sure how low I could go. I got about halfway, but unlike Pippa, my spine wasn't rendered from plasticine.

'I think this is me!'

'Just relax!' Pippa instructed. 'Ease yourself into it. Inch down, inch down.' She stood to flatten my spine. 'Isn't this music wonderful!'

'Smile!' Grace pointed her phone at us, taking more shots.

'Grace.' I could barely speak, blood was filling my head and my lungs were crushed against the bend of my body. 'I don't think —'

'I'm just taking a photo,' Grace said, as Pippa gave me another helping hand. 'Cool! Now I can get your face in, Ella!'

Grace uploaded the photo before I had chance to beg her not to.

It was hard to tell whether I was being eaten by my own arse, or giving birth to my own my bright red face, before my knees had given way.

Pippa squealed with laughter. Whichever way you looked at it, my Arse-Face picture was now all over Twitter. Even in Melbourne. Bryony gave me a retweet. Kim said she was sending it straight to Moonpig.com.

Chapter Twenty-Six: Party of One

'Bryony just called.' I wound up the vacuum cleaner, following Dan's voice into the hallway as he jogged downstairs. 'Said I'd pick up the gang.' He opened the porch, finding his running shoes.

'What happened to *The Beamer*?'

'Vic's playing Golf. Picking them up later.'

'You're leaving now?'

'I'll have to, won't I? If I'm going to get back in time…'

'But we've still got stuff to do. Can't they get a cab?'

'A cab?' He gave me a brief look, leaning against the door-frame as he pulled on his trainers. 'Bryony's only twenty minutes away. Then I'm going to swing by, get the twins…'

Swing by? Dan was playing Tarzan to his ex-wife, while I was left to grapple with Monsieur Monkey. 'The twins are definitely coming now?' *Great*, I thought, sticking the vacuum cleaner back in the cupboard with a heavier hand than strictly necessary. *I'll go grab my wellies.*

'What was I supposed to say, Ella?'

There were a million things he could have said. Maybe something about having a house-load of people arriving shortly and a girlfriend with no experience of children or parties left to fend for herself. 'What time will you be back?'

'Shouldn't be too long…'

I was only half-listening, trying to recalculate the numbers. Pippa had already called Dan three times since 10 o'clock with last-minute additions to the guest list. Meanwhile, I had been distracted by unpacked party bags, mini cake boxes and stacks of party decorations, still unwrapped.

Twenty-past one. Exactly two hours and ten minutes until my attempt at Grace's birthday party became official. And with those additional guests added to the list, nearly thirty people were due to arrive at the house. Two of which, the twins, were seriously demented and capable of destroying the entire day. Make that three, if I included myself.

I heard Dan looking for his keys in the marble bowl, where I knew he wouldn't find them, because I knew exactly where he'd left them. They were on the arm of the chair, but for some reason, perhaps because he'd coaxed me onto this rollercoaster of party food and parents, then abandoned me at the first plummet, I didn't have the slightest inclination to tell him. I went back to planning, trying to concentrate on what was left to be done. I was highly organized, I reminded myself. Audrey had told me so herself.

'So,' I shouted, keeping it chirpy. 'That takes it to thirty of us.' I was convinced he still hadn't fully comprehended the size of the crowd about to descend on us.

I tried to ignore my misgivings and think of the best possible outcome instead. *Visualising the Positive*, it was called. I'd read about a man who survived a deadly fall down a mountain by imagining his own rescue. He waited for days on end for help to arrive with only two broken legs and 30 inches of snow for company. I was starting to wish I could spend the whole day just like him. Lying there, making snow wings, instead of feeling like an unwelcome guest at a party I had no business giving, in a house with a colder climate than an alpine tundra.

'Well, at least Vic's backed out of it. Playing golf, supposedly. And there's plenty of food,' Dan said, as if that was all there was to worry about. He wrapped his arms around me and, feeling so close, I reminded myself I was catering for a teenager's party, not Elton John's Ruby wedding.

'Please get back soon. There's still so much to do.' I rested my chin on his chest, wishing I could stay there. 'I still need to set up the cake stands —'

I glanced out into the garden as I said this. It didn't look any different, except for the few extra bits of patio furniture Pippa had donated.

'Before you have a meltdown,' Dan said, because even Starky, tail slunk down low as he sloped from the room, had worked out that's what I was on the verge of. 'I was about to put the gazebo up when Bryony rang —'

'The gazebo's not up? The balloons are in the shed, and the gazebo's not up?'

'I'll put it up when I get back. It's fine.'

'In two hours? Everyone's going to be here by half-past…'

Except I mightn't be, I thought. I might dig a tunnel through the kitchen floor and escape to France using a set of salad servers before the first set of parents arrive.

'I'll get the cakes, too.'

'Very funny,' I said, until I noticed him looking flustered for the first time all day and realised he hadn't mentioned them.

He was actually serious.

'I forgot to pick them up with the rest of the stuff. I got the tonic water, cucumber and lemons.' He sounded quite pleased with himself. 'I drove straight back from the supermarket. Look, I'll get them…'

'This is a joke…'

'Look, as soon as I —' By this point I was floating out of my own head, not sure I cared anymore. 'I've got Mum calling me.' I tuned back into whatever it was he was saying. 'Then the kids are on. Now Bryony…'

I looked at my lovely lanterns, grouped together on the kitchen floor, ready for tables with the pretty, polka-dot tablecloths, tea lights, neon-coloured plates and plastic-sculpted glasses. All dressed up with no gazebo to go in.

'I'll call at the bakery. We probably should've booked somewhere, I know. It's…' He checked through his wallet, finding Pippa's cupcake receipt. 'I didn't expect this many people.'

'You can't get the cakes now.' I sounded slightly eerie, a ghost haunting my own nightmare. 'You'll be late…'

'I'll have to.'

'No.' I took the receipt from him. 'I'll get them. You haven't got time, not if you're picking everyone up. Anyway, it's best if I get them. If they're sat in the car for too long there's a good chance the twins might take a crap on them.'

'How are you going to get there? I'm taking the car.'

'I'll call Kim, and if she can't make it…' I plotted the journey towards Grace's cakes like Steve McQueen leading a bakery breakout fraction at Slimmer's World. 'I'll give your mum a ring or something…'

'Okay, well, let me know. I'll try and set the gazebo up as soon as I'm back…'

'You'll try?' I actually smiled then, wondering if Dan realised the whole day was as much about Grace eating designer cupcakes under a gazebo as it was about her turning thirteen.

'Look, I'll be back in an hour or so…'

Or so. Meaning at least two hours. Dan's sense of time was about as sharp as my sense of proportion. How the hell was I going to set everything up in that time?

'It's fine,' I said. 'It's not as if we've got thirty people turning up, expecting a party. Go get Bryony…'

'Ella, what was I supposed to say?'

'You don't think I could use a little help, too?'

He stopped and looked at me.

'Ella, she can't rely on Vic to sort anything out, apart from lying on his arse on a beach for two weeks. I'll be back as soon as I can. *I promise.*' He placed his hands on my shoulders and tried to sound reassuring. 'Look, I've got to make a move. Go and get changed.' He gave me a quick kiss. 'All this … *chaos*, it's half the fun!' He grabbed his jacket. 'It's a party, remember? And that curry's really good,' he called, heading off out through the door.

That was a weight off my mind. The gazebo was lying on the lawn, still unpacked. The specially ordered, designer cupcakes Grace had set her heart on were going stale on a shelf somewhere, but the curry was a real winner.

Brilliant. I thought. We'll all sit under *the curry*.

Grace can blow out the candles on *the curry*.

The party was a disaster, they'd say, but *that curry* really was something.

The car roared into life as I surveyed party props, interrupted by Starky, who sat at my feet. I swore he could read my mind as he grinned a slobbery grin of tongue and teeth that said: *Face facts, honey. You're stuffed…*

I knew I had to do something, maybe start crying, but there was no time.

I grabbed my phone, rang Kim, who reminded me why she was my best friend in the entire world by making her way straight over with no awkward questions while I went onto *HowYouDo.com* and typed:

How the hell do you put up a gazebo all on your bloody own?

And quite brilliantly, the search box ignored my frustration and produced a video which someone — the absolute boy-genius! — had uploaded of doing exactly that, at some sort of paint-splattered, European festival.

'Come on,' I said to Starky, stepping outside. 'Looks like it's all down to you and me…'

We were finally making our way to the bakery, and after all the heroic activities which had taken place during the last fifty-five minutes and counting, we could quite easily have been flying there wearing Ethan's Superman cape.

After I managed to single-handedly assemble the gazebo, Kim had arrived. The pair of us had hardly said a word as we turned the garden into a 60-minute makeover, arranging patio furniture, attaching ribbons to balloons and nearly garrotting ourselves on a mile of innocuous-looking bunting.

'Remember Tuesday, when there were only sixteen of us coming?'

Kim slowed at the lights, on our way to Operation Cupcake.

'There's about thirty people coming over.'

'Ella!'

'Ethan's friends are too young to stay on their own, apparently, so their parents are staying with them. I didn't actually think of that until Pippa mentioned it this morning. How stupid of me,' I said. 'So that takes it to at least a plus-two with each child. And, Vic's twins …'

Kim gave me a look.

'Exactly, but at least Vic's off playing golf. No chance of him hovering around, hoping for a toe job. Oh, and all of this happened right before Dan left to me to it. Off to play *Disney Dad*. Rescuing Bryony, when I'm the one who needs saving…'

'How the hell've you ended up with that many guests coming over to the house for a kid's birthday party?' Kim said. 'Dan should've hired somewhere.'

'I've been trying to tell him that for the last two weeks, but Grace really wanted it at the house. And it's not just a birthday party, remember? We're supposedly throwing a welcome home party for Dan's ex-wife too. Oh, and, let's not forget,' I said, 'it's got to be just perfect and breath-taking enough for Pippa.'

'No one expects it to be perfect.' Kim took a left off Crank Road. 'It's not a contest.'

'Yes it is,' I said without thinking, because that was exactly how it felt. 'And I don't care what anyone's *expecting*. It's going to be perfect. At least it was, until it all went to shit…'

'Ella? Will you just relax? Do your own thing, your own way.'

'Kim, I haven't got a *thing* or a *way*. They've had at least *twelve years'* experience of all this.' I leaned back against the headrest, wishing she'd offer to drive me straight to the nearest hospital and have me sedated and left under quiet observation for the rest of the day. 'This time last year I didn't even live with Dan, remember? How the hell does he expect me to know about all this stuff?'

'There's only so much you can do. It'll be fabulous. You do this for a living.'

'No, I don't, Kim! The food festival's the biggest thing I've ever worked on, and from the way today's going, it'll be the last. Up 'til five minutes ago, I'd spent my entire career writing very nice things about very nice things people paid me to be very nice about. Jotting down notes, approving adverts. I liaise with clients, not kids! Pippa was quick enough telling Grace she could have every last single thing she wanted. Didn't stop to think about the finer details, like how any of that's supposed to happen, exactly. I mean, why didn't she stop me? Why didn't Pippa step in and supervise all this, the same way she insists on supervising everything else?'

'Why'd you think?' Kim took the next right, suddenly slamming on the brakes behind a removal van. 'She's not soft.'

I jolted forward, palm-slapping the dashboard. 'She's having a blow-dry while you're having a breakdown. *That's why.*'

Traffic zoomed past as two burly blokes held a settee inside the van, pausing as they noticed us stuck there behind them.

'And can you believe not one of them's cancelled?'

Kim hit the horn, lowered her window and stuck out her head.

'Don't people turn down invitations anymore?' I said. 'Pippa keeps calling us, *thrilled*, adding to the numbers, as if we're totting up *fundraising*, or something —'

One of the men rapped against the passenger window.

'Gerra a move on, love.' He took a step back. 'Gorra a van to unload there.' He spat onto the pavement.

'Urgh.' I turned away from him as Kim lowered my window, leaning across me.

'And you're illegally parked, mate. So unless you noticed a set of propellers on my roof, move it…'

'What I am moving,' he sneered, 'is the contents of that *va-ahn*.' He pointed a fat, stubby finger towards the abandoned sofa. 'Into that *har-se*. It's called overtakin'. Give it a try…'

His friend gave a laugh, sitting on the steps outside the va-ahn.

'And that's called on-coming traffic, sweetheart,' Kim said. 'So you'll need to shift your arse and move your *va-ahn* so we can get past…'

'We've got to get some cakes.' I tried to reason with him.

'Yeah? And my bacon sarnie's going cold, love.'

'My friend here,' Kim shouted as he turned away, 'has taken an overdose!' He stopped and turned back, looking mildly concerned. 'So, unless you move roughly four metres or so down the road, we're going to be stuck here, waiting for her organs to fail, which should give me roughly enough time to note down your number plate and have you done for manslaughter.'

'Jesus Christ.' He looked at me, backing towards his mate. 'Thought she looked a bit outer it…'

Kim pressed her hand flat on the horn.

'Alright, keep your 'air on.'

He shouted his friend to attention and jumped up into the cabin.

'I thought Pippa was making the cake?' Kim took her sunglasses out of the glove box.

'Kim? You just told that bloke I'm suicidal!'

'Yeah,' she said, restarting the engine. 'Because your *we've got to get some cakes* line wasn't going to get us to the church on time, was it?'

The removal man parked up ahead, his arm appearing from the driver's side a moment later, waving us on. 'Off you go, girls!' he shouted. 'Good luck!'

'*GO TAKE YOUR FACE FOR A SHIT!*' Kim called from my window, blasting her horn and speeding past as I froze. 'Right.' She turned to me, perfectly composed, pushing her sunglasses back onto her face. 'Where the hell are we going, and why did you have to order these cakes from the other side of the globe?'

'Kim! That's the most disgusting thing I've ever heard anyone say in my life! Have you gone mental or something?'

'No, but you, my friend, are about to, so I ain't holding back.'

'Take the next right,' I said, realizing my stress-levels were proving highly contagious. 'It's up here somewhere. Pippa ordered them from this special bakery. It's where all the cool gang get their cakes from apparently… That's it, that's it!' I noticed the sign as we cruised down the road, spotting a car reversing out from a space almost outside it. 'It's Grace's birthday.' I was already unfastening my seatbelt. 'I'm not giving her any excuse to criticize. She's *getting* her cupcakes.'

'Try not to make it sound so much like a threat, honey.'

'Right, I'll be back as quick as I can.' I took a deep breath as Kim came to a stop. 'Thank you! Thank you so much for today!'

'Nothing to thank me for.' Kim rested her hands on the steering wheel. 'Happy to be of service.' She fixed her sunglasses on top of her head. 'How's Dan coping?'

'Dan?' I grabbed my handbag from the back seat. 'Dan's looking forward to it. The chaos is half the fun, he said. Can you believe that? Meanwhile, I've still got seven more chairs to find. That's the stuff he doesn't think about. Then looks at me like I'm mad for stressing…'

'Ella, in a couple of weeks, we're going to laugh about all this.'

'Kim, in a couple of weeks, I'll be repressing this, along with most of my childhood.'

Chapter Twenty-Seven: The Arrivals

My Thai curry stood on the hob in three pans of descending sizes — because who owned a pan big enough to hold lunch for at least a dozen adults, nine teenage girls and six small boys? And more to the point, who wanted that many people, half of them complete strangers, traipsing around the house in the first place?

After planning the thing, shopping for it, following the recipe and cleaning the blender — inventing a new, thoroughly obscene swear-word, after nearly losing a fingertip dislodging stubborn sweet potato from in between the blades — I'd now learned why anything stored in a box at the back of a kitchen cupboard should be left there, indefinitely. The one thing I didn't expect, though, was the highly palatable result, and all I had to do was gently heat it once the guests arrived. Tasting the curry, Kim blinked in delight, disbelief even: 'It doesn't taste like shit!'

That was good enough, more than good enough, for me. Although I did have a subtle, '*Well, I won't be buying that again,*' lined up for Pippa, in case it went untouched.

It was quarter-to-three as I applied lipstick, ready for the doorbell to ring. I felt relaxed for the first time in days, like a fairytale-version of a step-girlfriend, making family wishes come true. I wandered through the house, staying afloat on a rush of pre-party endorphins, double-checking everything was in place. Kim set out glasses, distributed flame-free candles and stacked plates outside. The gazebo was up! I was so proud of myself! And my idea about attaching helium balloons to Dan's old golf tees, pining them on long ribbons to the lawn, creating a floating-fence had worked brilliantly. Hopefully everyone would love it, especially Grace. And the best part of it was that in a couple of hours the guests would be leaving. Bryony would be officially back from honeymoon. We could put the blow-up bed back in the loft and get back to being normal — which is why what happened next felt like such a drop-kick to the gut.

The first thing I noticed were the splatter marks rising against the wall as I walked downstairs. A fine, orange spray across the front door, before I spotted the puddle in the middle of the carpet, forming what looked like a big patch of rust.

My gaze fixed on the mysterious filth.

I didn't notice the smell until I got closer.

Then came the noise.

It sounded a bit like an egg being cracked, over-and-over again, against the side of a bowl. I was fairly certain Kim wasn't making pancakes, and if Pippa had hired a mobile Creperie, it must've been a surprise, because she definitely hadn't mentioned it. I followed the noise, correctly guessing what I was going to find, as Starky vomited, not onto the parquet floor, because that would've been way too easy, but straight onto the Persian rug I'd had since college.

He looked at me briefly, his eyes harbouring sadness and what had better be regret. Then he threw up another miniature swamp of shredded chicken. 'Starky! No!' I grabbed him by the collar, leading him into the kitchen, almost knock-kneed. 'What have you done? And why did it have to be on the carpet?'

I scrambled to open the backdoor, spotting Kim in the garden on her phone before I confirmed the source of Starky's sudden illness. The hob was drenched with the remains of one entire pan of homemade Thai curry, which I remembered tasting, but not replacing the lid on.

But Starky had never done anything like that before, I thought, in his defence.

He might like the occasional nibble of scraps, but he wouldn't —

The thought hit me as he scampered out across the lawn towards Kim: *I hadn't fed him that morning.*

And if I'd forgotten, there's no way Dan would have remembered.

We set to work, tucking our maxi dresses into our knickers, scrubbing down paintwork and scooping hot, dog vomit up into carrier bags. Starky watched, reticent now, as if he might've shrugged: *A dog's gotta eat…*

Rock salt and lemon, another top tip Pippa had recently shared, sprang to mind. Ideal for neutralizing smells and stains, I remembered, just as the doorbell Dan had recently repaired — and right then, I really wished he hadn't bothered — gave a jovial chime, signalling the start of The Arrivals.

'Ella! The door,' Kim called from the lounge, up to her elbows in wet sponges and tea-towels.

Oh please let it be Mum. She'll be expecting this kind of crap. I pulled off my rubber gloves and stuffed them into a carrier bag along with the gloop, taking a quick, terrified look out of the window, like a hermit at a house party.

Bryony stood at the door with Vic's twins. Dan slammed the car boot, following down the path, arms loaded with bags and gifts. The last time I'd kind of spoken to Bryony was after Grace uploaded my butt picture on Twitter and I pretended I thought it was funny. She stood behind the frosted glass and some saying about when the past comes calling popped into my head like I was narrating a Hammer Horror.

I didn't know where my suddenly sunny disposition had risen from, but I opened the door as a much calmer version of myself. I stepped to one side, just as everyone's eyes were simultaneously drawn to the hall carpet, which by now smelled exactly how you'd imagine the inside of a dog's stomach to smell. Only with an exotic, homemade Thai twist.

'*EURGH*! What's that?' a twin I decided was Philip shouted, pointing a finger towards the stain and nudging his brother to attention.

'It looks like poo!' the other one, possibly Theo, said, before the two of them ran off into the house to further investigate.

Bryony stood, reciting excuses: 'Vic's playing golf. Coming over later.'

'What *is* that?' Dan's eyes fixed on the mess, placing the bags on the stairs.

'Oh, just the dog.' I rolled my eyes at Bryony in a *what-can-you-do* kind of way. 'He ate some of my curry. How was the honeymoon?'

'Great, thanks!' Bryony gave a look which started out as polite, until she stared back at the carpet. 'I can't wait to see the kids.'

'Jeez, Ella.' Dan shook his head. 'You couldn't make this stuff up…'

Don't get me started, Dan, I thought. Not after you've left me for hours so you could flirt with your ex-wife over your Soft Rock playlist, because there's a good chance I'll rugby tackle you, right here, in front of Bryony, who your mother's already told me kept the house pristine, and I'm guessing, made far nicer Thai curry than I ever will!

The twins ran back through the door, Kim following behind them, as they scouted their next move, home invasion clearly on their minds.

'Right.' Dan nodded hello to Kim and took off his coat. 'Mum's just set off with the kids. I'll sort out the gazebo.'

'She's done it.' Kim placed a few layers of kitchen roll over the carpet. 'She was out there, wrestling with poles, when I arrived. I'll check how Starky's doing.' She pulled a face that said she wasn't confident his stomach had subsided.

Bryony side-stepped the puddle and grabbed her bags from the stairs.

'Shall I take these into the kitchen?'

'Oh, yes, please,' I said, keen to avoid Dan's eye. 'Here, I'll grab the rest.'

'You put the gazebo up?'

I nodded, busy with bags as Dan stood, gripping the stair post.

'How?'

'Boys!' Bryony shouted, one eye on the pair as they disappeared from view, possibly booby-trapping the place, as we followed them into the kitchen.

Dan cleared a space on the worktop as the gruesome twosome crouched in front of the dining room doors. They turned with matching grins on their matching faces: 'The doggy did it again!'

Starky stood on the deck, brewing up a long slobber of bile. Kim was rubbing his back, feeding him ice cubes as he crunched away appreciatively. Theo turned, bored now, as Starky recovered. The little boy's eyes narrowed. He scrunched up his face, resembling a shrunken gargoyle. 'We don't like you, lady!' He pulled at his brother's coat sleeve. 'She made that dog do sicks!'

'Don't be silly, Thee!' Bryony smiled at him as he glared at me, despite my best *I'm-a-lovely-grown-up* face. 'You do like

Aunty Ella,' Bryony told him. 'She invited you both to the party today.'

Nothing to do with me. The evil little bastards invited themselves, I thought, as Dan offered Bryony a drink, tagging on a quick: 'You don't want one, do you?' in my direction, grabbing a couple of glasses.

'Here, I've brought my Pinot.' Bryony opened a canvas bag with a sketch of Sydney Harbour Bridge woven on the side. 'Just need a corkscrew.'

'You're still drinking that stuff?'

'Yes, it's my favourite! Remember?'

'I know, I just...' He pirouetted the bottle, examining the label.

'Well, we still don't like her!' Theo shouted, stamping one foot for emphasis.

Dan and Bryony's attention darted back to the indignant twin, both of them bursting into laughter. I was suddenly desperate to step outside and clean up after Starky. I urged Kim inside and told her to grab a drink before the fun really started, locking the twins safely behind me as sun broke out between the clouds.

Starky loped to the far side of the lawn, settling in his favourite spot under the Rhododendron as I hosed down the deck, washing away thoughts of Dan and Bryony's unmistakable lifetime ahead, despite the divorce. A beginning, a middle, and not exactly an ending. They laughed together in *their* old house, in *her* old kitchen. I stood with wet patches of dog sick stuck to my knees, gawping through the window like The Ghost of Christmas Past. Starky was sunbathing, almost asleep, as I turned off the water. I heard the slam of car doors and chatter emerging from the front of the house, announcing the arrival of Pippa and the kids.

I stepped inside as Ethan appeared, almost at a run. He was suddenly shy at the sight of his mum as he allowed kisses and scrutiny. His sister followed, slower, grinning, led by her dress.

'Oh honey, it looks even better than the pictures!' Bryony grabbed her daughter, silently holding onto both children, her sense of relief palpable.

'Oh dear…' Pippa stood at the counter, checking the order form still taped to the top of the cake box. 'I think I got my numbers mixed up…'

'Happy 31st Gracie!' Dan grinned, tilting the top of a cupcake to show her, while Bryony stifled a smile.

Chapter Twenty-Eight: Parental Guidance

I stood in front of the window, washing my hands, as I watched the lawn become a garden of continents with people gravitating towards each other. Starky and the children were travelling between them like curious interlopers.

'I'm Samson's dad...'

'We're Avery's parents...'

'This is Janelle and Lucas...'

'Howie's our boy...'

The doorbell chorused with a non-stop delivery of guests, name-dropping their kids for entry. I gave up on the introductions and left Dan and Bryony to greet the guests. What was I supposed to say, standing there beside Grace's actual parents? *'Hi, I'm Ella. I'm sleeping with the birthday girl's dad. Party sausage, anyone?'* When you grouped parents together, they spoke a different language. They even looked the same. I was glad Dan at least still dressed like himself. The other fathers looked like older, disappointed renditions of their sons. Hoodies, t-shirts, trainers. Same clothes in different sizes. A matching set from Adult to Junior. Their own names remaining a mystery, as they accompanied mums in pregnancy-defying jeans.

'Grace?' I finally tunnelled upstairs, desperate to change out of my dog-sick-scented dress. 'Your friends are here.' I pulled on my jeans. *And I'm not going through all this for nothing*, I thought. 'Grace?'

I decontaminated myself with Tom Ford and reapplied lip-gloss for good measure. Grace's door remained closed, a new drama lurking behind it. I hoped it wasn't something to do with the eyebrow. I dreaded having to go through all that again; it had almost grown back and was barely noticeable now.

'Grace?' I knocked again. I heard nothing but the rustle of bedcovers and didn't believe for one minute she was in there making her bed. 'Come on, Birthday Girl, you're missing your day!'

'*Go away…*'

'Go away? What? And leave you here, ignoring 30-odd guests?' I couldn't believe she was doing this now, not after all the fuss she'd made about wanting a party. 'Your friends are waiting downstairs and you're up here, sulking in your room?'

'I'm not sulking!'

'Oh, okay then. Fine…' I'd learned that the longer I stood there, giving Grace an audience, the longer the show would go on. 'Have a nice birthday.' I crossed the landing. 'I'll save you a cupcake…'

'Ella?'

'Yes?'

'Can you come in here a minute, please?'

A low soundtrack, the insistent murmur of voices, floated through the window, reminding me of all the people I didn't know, grouped outside, as her door unlocked.

'I got my period.' Grace turned to reveal a wine-coloured stain on the back of her dress. 'Will it come out?'

'Not right now, honey,' I said. 'Not today.'

'Oh God.' Grace placed her palm on her forehead. 'Is it ruined?'

'I don't think so.' Her chin gave way to a wobble. 'Oh, don't get upset, Grace. It could be worse.' I put my arm around her shoulders. 'It's not like someone stapled your dress up so you would burst out of it like a fat pig in a blanket. They didn't even dream that one up in Mean Girls.' She checked my reaction. 'That's the last time we watch Edward Scissorhands.' I smiled. 'Come on, time's a'tickin'. You need to get changed,' I said. 'It's the Party of the Year, don't forget? You're Guest of Honour!'

'I can't get changed.' She pulled at her ruined skirt. 'Grandma'll ask.'

'I think Grandma knows all about periods, Grace. Probably more than you —'

'No way…' Her eyes inflated, voice final. 'I am *not* telling my grandma.'

'Why?'

'*Because…*'

'Shall I get your mum, then?'

She shook her head, shifting the dress around.

'She'll only act all weird. Then we'll have to talk about it loads. I'm not in the mood. Have you got anything? You know? A thing?'

'Yeah, of course. Are you feeling okay? Do you need Paracetamol?'

'No, I'm okay.' She shrugged. 'It doesn't hurt or anything, but do you see why I couldn't come down now?'

A ripple of laughter from the garden grew louder as I went into our room, wishing I was sat in a beer garden somewhere with a group of childless friends. I opened the drawer, knowing I only had tampons, not convinced they were the right thing to give her. I remembered the first time I'd tried to use one at her age: my crotch ended up like some botched attempt at a school recycling project.

I'd opened a new box that morning, unprepared for the disappointment I felt at that unmistakable cramping sensation. I obviously wasn't pregnant, but I'd almost figured out how I was going to tell Dan. I was almost looking forward to it. Now, I was scared what that meant.

I routed through ruptured hair bands, half-used cuticle cream, those free shampoo and conditioner sachets I occasionally unstuck from magazines and found a trial-sized sanitary towel, just as the doorbell rang. I was happy to leave that to someone else, as I noticed my special birthday present for Grace standing on the dressing table. I'd planned on handing it over when everyone was having cake, but right then, with just the two of us, it seemed like the right moment. Out of the whole family, from the pick of the entire guest list, Grace had finally chosen me to be the one to help her.

'Here you go.' I stepped back into her bedroom, where she stood, typing away on her phone.

'I think someone should invent an Emoji for starting your periods.' She smiled. 'Do you think I could wear my bridesmaid dress instead?'

'Great idea!'

'Really?'

'Perfect,' I said. 'But with those shoes,' I pointed at the pumps in the corner, 'not with your sandals. And how about that little cardigan you've got somewhere?'

'Weird… I was just thinking I'd put that cardie on over it…' Grace wandered over to her door. 'I didn't even really like this dress that much, you know?' She looked down at the skirt of yellow cotton. 'Grandma chose it for me.' She scrunched up her nose. 'I hate that. When someone buys you something you don't really like, but then you have to let them, because you know they're really buying it for themselves.'

'Is that what you think?'

'I s'pose,' she said. 'I only really thought about it now.'

'Hold on a minute.' I was smiling at her take on it all. 'Don't you want to open your present?'

'From you? But...' She took the small box, wrapped in pink chiffon, tied with a satin bow. 'You already did my party...'

'Oh, stop being so polite and open it!'

She actually gasped at the silver bracelet, adorned with delicate charms.

'Kim made it. Look!' I showed her. 'A cupcake so you remember the ones you got for your birthday.' Grace studied its silver shape, taking in every tiny detail. 'Your initial,' I explained, turning the bracelet between my fingers. 'And that's Peridot. Your birthstone, which weirdly,' I pulled a face, 'sounds a bit like Period so we covered that too.' She gave an awkward smile. 'Anyway, Kim reckons it's supposed to be magical, because she's a bit loopy like that.' I held up the stone and it shimmered against the sunlight. 'And, see? I chose three things so you'd always remember the bracelet was for your thirteenth.'

'It's amazing...' she said, as I fastened the catch around her wrist, her eyes still fixed on each individual charm.

'Happy Birthday!' I quickly pecked her head as if blowing out a candle.

'I love it!' Grace stretched out her arm, admiring her new jewellery.

'Good!' I combed my hand across her shoulders. 'We better get down there. You okay?'

'Ella?' Grace bit her thumb slightly, then wrapped her arms around me, leaning her head against my collarbone. I wrapped my arms around her too and closed my eyes, holding her tight, knowing I needed that hug, probably more than she did.

'I'm sorry about what I did to your dress.'

'I know, Gracie...'

I gave her a tighter squeeze, knowing it wasn't about the dress.

It was about the hurt. The change. The disappointment. Wanting to staple the pieces of her family back together. Wanting to let me know that I was part of the pain.

'No use crying over split seams, hey?'

'Do you think I had P.M.T?'

'Yes.' She looked at me. 'If you mean, Pretty Messed-up Teenager?'

Chapter Twenty-Nine: Ella for Leather

Pippa stood next to my mum and, as if the day couldn't get any more surreal, Mr Jeremiah Layne, himself. The three of them were contemplating the soggy tissue in the middle of the carpet as if it was some sort of Modern Art installation. And while I could just about cope with him wearing leather trousers in the middle of the afternoon to a kid's party, I found it a little more difficult to accept my mum wearing bright blue, *wet-look* Jeggings.

'The dog?'

I nodded.

'I did try to tell her.' Mum shared a giggle with Pippa, more appropriately dressed in a navy trouser suit and her favourite pearl earrings. 'She gets her culinary *prowess* from me, I'm afraid!'

'I don't think it was my cooking that made Starky sick, Mum.'

'Yes, Ella. I know,' Mum said. 'I was making a joke…'

'How about we stick the rug over it?' Pippa suggested. 'The one in the lounge?'

'He got that, too…'

Pippa's attention darted to the stairs.

'Gracie! Is that your bridesmaid dress?'

'I got changed…'

'Oh, she's lovely!' Mum grinned. 'A beautiful dress for a beautiful girl! Can't have one without the other.' Mum gave Grace an affectionate wink which I found strangely irritating.

'Oh, now, sweetheart, you're not going to wear that today, are you?' Pippa was obviously disappointed. 'No one's seen your lovely buttercup dress. We got that especially, didn't we? Took us all week running round shops to find something nice,' Pippa told Mum. 'And there's me, with arthritis in one knee.'

'Grace was saying she might wear this, weren't you?' I tried to provide an alibi. 'Everyone else is wearing summer dresses. She was worried she'd never get to wear this again, weren't you?'

'What's going on?' Dan strolled out, relaxed as you like, beer in hand. 'You're missing your party.'

'Hi Renée.' He kissed Mum on the cheek. 'I didn't realize you were here.'

His eyes hovered on Jeremiah for a second.

'Sorry, mate,' Jeremiah said. 'I'm —'

'Jeremiah's my friend,' Mum explained.

I hadn't told Dan about Jeremiah. I watched him playing along like the rest of us, pretending he didn't want to blurt out: *Bloody hell, Renée. Are you actually* shagging *him?* Grace gave a sympathetic raise of her eyebrows. We both know what *that* meant. I raised an eyebrow in agreement, just as the doorbell rang, along with my mobile: 'Dan? Can you get that? I don't know who anyone is…'

'Neither do I.' He sounded slightly put-out. 'Bryony's the one who knows all the parents.'

'We'll go get the door, shall we?' Pippa suggested, placing her hand on the small of Grace's back. 'You can introduce everyone…'

I didn't recognize the voice or the number: *'Hello? Ella, is it? This is Rita. Steve's wife. Monsieur Monkey? Steve can't make it, I'm afraid. Slipped a disc at a Holy Communion. We'll refund your deposit. He does send his apologies.'*

'But —'

'Nothing more we can do. Must go. I've got a bar mitzvah to cancel.'

'Great…'

'What is it?'

Pippa and Grace led more unidentified guests past us, out into the garden.

'The Monsieur Monkey guy can't make it…' I told Dan, just as Ethan came tearing around the corner.

'Monsieur Monkey?' Ethan's face found mine, a spark of excitement suddenly doused.

'I'm sorry, Ethe. We thought it would be a nice surprise…'

'Oh, but this is boring, this is.' His shoulders sagged. 'Everyone's saying it's just for girls, this party…'

'Boring?' Jeremiah piped up, obviously a man who liked a challenge, which must have been the case if he was dating my mother. 'We can't have that, now can we?'

Ethan stared up at the leather-clad stranger.

'You know what you need when there's too many girls?'

Ethan harboured a half-smile, shaking his head, while I dreaded to think what the answer to that one was. Jeremiah squatted down in one swift motion: 'Zombie Apocalypse!' he shouted, taking off after a screaming Ethan, Mum gazing after them both, wearing a smile.

There was a murmur of people nursing drinks, making conversation; it was like somebody else's house, except, worse than that, it was somebody else's life.

'Oh, I love this one!' Mum shimmied away on Grace's makeshift dance floor, the girls turning up the music to encourage her. Jeremiah pulled up at my side as I delivered bowls of Doritos and stuffed peppers.

'Isn't she magic?' he grinned.

'Who's singing this?' Mum called, swinging her hips to the bassline.

'Pharrell!' one of the girls shouted.

'Colin Farrell?' Mum looked bemused, snapping her fingers to the beat. 'The one with the eyebrows? I didn't know he could sing, but he's very good-looking…'

'Just say if you need a hand.' Dan put his empty beer can in the bin, following me back into the house. He actually looked as if he was in party mode. 'Everyone's starving.' He eyed the quiches cooling on the worktop.

'You mean, *you're* starving…'

I took a tray of cheese tarts from the oven, the heat scorching my face.

'Don't blame me! People are starting to ask about food.' He smiled light-heartedly, which pissed me right off. 'Don't fancy taking my chances, talking them into your curry.' He smirked over at the tower of empty pans.

'That reminds me,' I said, ignoring him. 'Those platters should've been here half an hour ago.'

'Give me the number. I'll call them.'

'It's fine. I'll call them myself.'

'You okay?'

'Yep…'

'You sure?'

'I'm worried about your mum.'

'About my mum?'

'Getting mixed up with the cakes?'

'She's fine.'

'She seems a bit confused to me, recently.'

'She's been confused for as long as I can remember. What about you?' He bowed his head slightly, avoiding my gaze. 'I saw the thing.'

'What thing?'

'In the bathroom?'

For a minute, I thought it was something to do with Grace.

'The *pregnancy test*, thing. Is it, you know?' He was almost holding his breath. 'Is everything okay?'

'It was negative.'

'Oh, okay.' A flight of relief. 'Look,' he said, as I tried to remember where I'd put the oven glove. 'I know you're stressed out with all this stuff. We'll talk about it properly, okay? These look delicious.' He took a tart from the cooling rack and demolished it in a couple of mouthfuls. 'I'm just glad Mum didn't see it,' he said, 'or, you know, one of the kids…'

'Will you just…' I didn't know what to say, I only knew I wanted him to stop talking. For the last few days, I'd actually thought we might be having a baby, but Dan was obviously much happier without one. 'Will you just, please, stop going on about the curry?' I found the glove under a sheet of tinfoil. I retrieved another batch of canapés as a couple of girls wandered past, off upstairs with Grace, caught up in birthday chatter. 'There was nothing wrong with it…' I trailed off, feeling ridiculous as Mum walked in, mid-meltdown. 'You said it was nice before Starky got at it.'

'You can't serve that curry. Not now!' Mum was adamant, catching us midway in conversation. 'Not after a dog's vomited it all over the house.'

'I know that!'

Mum gave Dan a look: *What's her problem?*

'I'm not serving the curry. I threw it away —'

Mum turned her attention to me. 'Anything I can take out with me?'

'Mini quiches, if you don't mind?' I pointed at the tray, resisting the temptation to suggest she take Dan as far away as possible, for his own safety. 'And these tartlets need to go out, too.' I stretched up to reach a pair of ornate china dishes from Pippa, which I never thought I'd use as long as I lived.

'We're Zombies now!' One of the twins, Philip I think, ran out, breathless, his fringe stuck to his forehead. 'We're going to Zombie you, Uncle Dan!'

His brother appeared, a wet-patch of slobber down the front of his sweatshirt.

'Yeah, Uncle Dan!' the slobbery one, who must have been Theo, said. 'We don't like you anymore!'

I don't like Uncle Dan anymore either, I thought, as Dan negotiated his way from the twins and out of the kitchen in one piece, promising to join in the game once he'd helped Aunty Ella. I wished he *was* helping Aunty Ella. Aunty Ella wished she could be more like Starky, running for sticks and digging up borders. And, more than she would ever have imagined, Aunty Ella wished Dan had been a little more helpful with his daughter's sodding party, and a little more disappointed about the negative pregnancy test.

Chapter Thirty: Bending Forks

The girls were scanning topics from party décor to deranged boys from what I could hear, as they sat cross-legged on the patchwork floor cushions loaned from Mum. Assorted couples, some I'd briefly met at the door, exchanged small-talk. Various children were drawn to their sides like tiny magnets. Dan nursed a beer, chatting steadily with one of the other dads, as I kept things flowing in the garden.

Pippa and my mum sat next to each other, smiling fondly at the jumbling map of children. 'There's goat's cheese and tomato as well.' I divided my attention between tables, making room for filo-wrapped cheese parcels and rearranging table-tops.

'Oh right.' Mum eyed the filling. 'I wondered what that was...'

'There should be some sandwiches arriving soon...' I reminded myself to call Rice'n'Roll and check on the delivery again, wondering if it wouldn't have been easier to just buy some buns and start spreading the Lurpak.

Pippa was chatting away, turning the stem of her glass between her fingers as Mum suddenly bolted from her seat, attention diverted. I followed her gaze. Jeremiah was crouched in the middle of the lawn, being steadily kicked by Vic's twins, who rang out in a chorus of *Stranger danger! Stranger danger!* while the other boys, including Ethan, drifted into retreat by the borders.

Mum leapt to the rescue, breaking up the fight as parents herded children away from the scene. 'We thought he was the bad man!' one of the demonic duo panted in explanation, exhausted by what I hoped was his first attempt at prolonged assault.

'They're very aggressive little boys.' Pippa leaned towards Bryony, occupying the neighbouring table with her equally glamorous friends.

'They're only kids, Pippa…'

'Umm.' Pippa sat, unconvinced, examining her napkin. 'Ethan was so placid at their age…'

'Well, like you were always telling me,' Bryony took a sip from her wine glass, 'divorce affects every child differently, doesn't it?'

'Well,' Pippa laughed. 'Those two are *definitely* different…'

Ethan appeared at the sight of fresh food, refuelling, before a taller boy ran over: 'Which one's your real mum, again?'

'I told you,' Ethan managed in between chews. 'Her,' he said, nodding his head toward Bryony, now thankfully chatting with one of the other mums. 'Not her,' he nodded over towards me.

'Isn't it strange?' one of the women was saying to Bryony as I moved a vase of tulips to one side, placing a dish of spring rolls I'd tried to arrange as neatly as you could possibly arrange parcels of pastry. 'I remember you moving into this house when Ethan started Glenn Park.'

'David and I are thinking of putting our house up…' a head of Blonde Highlights turned to say.

'No! Really?' said the same mum who had collected her kids from the house the other week.

'We've seen this house,' the blonde extended her fingers, decorated with a cluster of rings, blinking her eyes shut in disbelief, 'just come on the market,' she said. 'Absolute dream in *Channing Place*.'

'That's around the corner from us!' Bryony said.

'Oh, yes! You're on Swanton, aren't you?'

'Sterling,' Bryony corrected.

'Sterling, yes,' the Blonde nodded. 'I'll have to come round.'

'I know, I know. I've been so caught up with the wedding,' Bryony said, tilting her chin towards me in hello, as I made way for a dish of slightly battered-looking blinis. 'I won't know what to do with myself once I've sorted all this studio and clothing stuff out.'

'Start decorating the nursery?'

'Tamara! We've got *four kids* between us already!'

'I'm Celiac,' the woman with blonde highlights said, inspecting the platter.

'Ella,' I said, pleased at least one of them had acknowledged my existence.

'Not the same as having your own though.' Blonde Highlights gave me a slightly sceptical look for some reason. 'Does Vic want kids?'

'He'd love a little girl…' A chorus of coos rose from around the table. 'What if I end up with twins?'

'Do they run in his family?' A brunette picked up a chocolate-dipped strawberry, examining it as if she'd never seen one before in her life, before popping it into her mouth.

'His dad and his great-granddad...'

'Bryony!' The women chorused in laughter.

'Don't they look amazing?' The Blonde gazed over at the helium fence, slowly swaying in rows of pink and silver.

'I know,' Bryony muttered. 'Grace's favourite colours...'

The football was now out in the garden. Small boys were looking on with heckles, or standing around professionally, hands on knees, as I wandered back across the lawn. Ethan was attempting a goal attack, gurgling with laughter as Dan threw himself into one last dramatic attempt at a save. Starky ran circuits around them as Dan fell, grinning with his son, sharing ruffled hair and grass stains.

'Excuse me?' A man in a chunky knit jumper and toe-capped boots, despite the heat, walked out checking a piece of disgruntled notepaper, loosely scribbled in his hand. 'Which one of you's Ella Shawe?'

One of the dads drifted out behind him, checking my face for signs of recognition.

'Yes, that's me,' I said. 'I'm Ella Shawe...'

'Could you sign this for me, please?' He loosened the paper from his grip, holding a large, oval tray. 'Soon as we've got that, we'll bring out the rest of the table.'

I took the note. It was an order form.

'Is that real?'

Every boy at the party seemed to descend at once, a few of the girls looking on, repulsed, in a communal: '*URGH!*'

A large, eyeless pig stared back at me, as much as an eyeless pig could stare, from the middle of a silver platter.

'Hog roast? From Medieval Meats. Did you not order the centre-piece?'

'It's a pig with no head!' one of the twins shouted. 'I mean,' he bumped his palm against his forehead, 'a head with no pig.'

Jeremiah strolled over, taking a long stride forward, crouching low, scrutinizing the pig's face, before turning to the small gang of boys.

'Lads?' He took out his mobile. 'Who's up for taking a Porkie?'

Kim didn't understand how I could've possibly pressed *Send* on the wrong order form, not until I'd explained how I'd been juggling The Avington Food Festival with planning the party — and had my mother on the phone at the same time.

'Hi!' Bryony said, with wine-infused zest, as Kim and I worked at the sink. 'I'm Grace and Ethan's mum. I love that necklace!'

'Thanks.' Kim fondled the stone-encrusted creation. 'Made it myself.'

'You're joking…'

Kim unclipped the piece and handed it over.

'Kim made the bangle I got Grace for her birthday,' I told Bryony, as she stared straight through the stones as if focusing on her own reflection.

'For Grace?' She looked at us blankly.

'For her birthday…' I said, before Kim and I exchanged a look.

'Oh, I'll have to get her to show me.' She handed the necklace back. 'She's been off with her friends,' she explained. 'You know what they're like at that age. *This age*, I mean.'

'Cup of tea?' Kim wandered over to the kettle.

'Don't you want Prosecco?' *Please have a Prosecco and give me an excuse to get smashed and give up*, I thought.

'I'm driving, remember?'

'Aren't you having a drink-drink?' Bryony asked. 'I'll just grab my Pinot.' She looked surprised to find herself without a wine glass. 'I'm still recovering from that pig...'

Bryony had been horrified and tried to blame the whole debacle on Pippa: 'She never respected my being vegetarian. Always obsessed with conning me into eating poultry…'

'I'm actually glad I'm driving. Don't want to end up in that state,' Kim said, amusement lightening her expression. 'She's going to have to cancel any plans for tomorrow...'

'I didn't realize she was that drunk.' I watched Bryony walk over to Pippa and Grace, her emerald-coloured blouse billowing as they stood beneath the Sycamore tree. Grace offered up her wrist for inspection. 'Actually, can you make me a cup, too?' I said. 'You know you make the best tea…' I used the same old excuse, back from the days when we were flatmates and spent our weekends doing nice things like shopping and drinking cocktails.

'What's Dan up to?'

'Still playing with the boys, last time I looked.'

'Well, I don't suppose he gets to hang out that much with his son. Where're the teabags?'

'Top left. Yes, that one. Polka dot caddy.'

'*Caddy*?' Kim pulled a face as she popped the lid. 'That Pippa's having quite the influence on you…'

'Hey, don't laugh. I've learned how to backstitch and my hospital corners are second-to-none. Wife skills,' I said, making a 'W' shape with my hands thumb-to-thumb. 'Do you know,' I told her, 'you're the first person to make me a drink all day…'

'Do you mind if I take my shoes off?' Bryony made a surprise return, leaving her friends from the school gates outside. She slumped onto a seat, pulling the stripy heels from her feet with that almost suction-cup sound only women understood to mean pain, and Vic probably found arousing.

'My feet are killing me. Think they're still swollen from the flight.'

'Oh yeah, you've been on honeymoon.' Kim placed one foot down on the pedal bin, disposing of teabags.

'Still haven't caught up on my sleep. It's about,' Bryony peered at her slim, gold watch, 'three o'clock in the morning in Melbourne.'

'No wonder you're tired.'

'I'll be fine. Thanks, you know, Ella.' She peered at me a little too intently over the top of her glass. 'Doing all this. For my Gracie…'

'Don't worry about it. It's her birthday.'

'I know, but…' She held my stare. 'I'm her mum…'

'Is that a tattoo?' Kim placed a mug down in front of me, pulling out a seat.

I'd never noticed the trace of black ink on Bryony's shoulder, not until Kim mentioned it. I'd've never had Bryony down as the tattoo type.

'I keep thinking about getting them removed, but this …' Bryony pulled down her top, turning to reveal bold calligraphy engraved on her shoulder, 'was for Grace. It's the Tibetan symbol for Strength. And, God knows, I need all the strength I can get with her at the moment. You want to hear what I have to put up with.' She fixed on Kim: *'Ella gives me my own set of towels. Ella makes her pasta sauce from scratch…* Big deal, I said to her. I made two kids!' She gave a breathy giggle. 'No offence,' she said, as I sat down, wondering if she was making the whole thing up to make me feel better. 'Oh, believe me.' She noticed my expression. 'Don't be fooled by the hormones. She was always her daddy's girl, but she thinks you're cool as fuck.'

Kim glanced at me, a faint smile crossing her face.

'It's me she thinks is the complete shithead. And, then, this,' Bryony continued, scraping back her chair to stand flat-footed on the tiles, toes painted in a vibrant, holiday coral. I avoided Kim's eye as Bryony fussed with her waistband, pulling skin-tight jeans down over one hip, 'is the symbol for Wisdom. I got that done after Ethan was born — that was my reminder — *Wise up! Don't ever go through childbirth again.* And then,' she said, fixing her clothes back into place, 'Vic's two rolled up,' she sat back in her seat, 'and I wondered if childbirth was all that bad, compared to putting up with other people's kids.' She watched the twins running around Dan in the garden, probably about to launch another vicious attack. Either that, or take a quick whizz on his trainers. 'They threw a lit match over the fence, you know?'

'What?' I grabbed the arms of my chair. 'Just then?'

'No! Not here,' Bryony said, as we tried to keep up with her runaway thought-train of conversation. 'They threw lit matches onto my neighbour's trampoline. Burnt a hole straight through it. They'd been banking on a bonfire.'

'You're kidding?' Kim relaxed back into her seat as if she was watching The Real Housewives of Avington.

'Philip said it was burning his fingers and he panicked. Yeah, right.' She laughed. 'I suppose that's why he'd left a dozen dead matchsticks lying in next door's borders. *Failed attempts*,' she said. '*Little shits. £300* it's going to cost us to replace it…' Kim and I took simultaneous sips from our mugs. 'Do you know, I have to lock my own kid's bedrooms every weekend, just to make sure those two don't stick a landmine under someone's bed,' she said. 'Then I've got his ex on the phone, having a go at *me* for raising my voice at her *perfect sons*.' She took another drink of wine, toying with one earring.

'What did Vic say?'

'Oh, that's the best part.' She raised her glass. 'Apparently, leaving a box of matches on a kitchen shelf was really stupid of me.' She gave a snort. 'I said to Vic, if I'd known we had a pair of fucking arsonists staying every weekend, I'd've never left them there, would I? Then he looks at me like I'm the one who hasn't got a clue about kids! Honest to God.' She took another drink. 'Thinks he's the dog's dick, that one.'

'Bollocks,' Kim corrected.

'He does! You don't know what he's like…'

Kim hid a smirk behind her cup. I couldn't help but think how different Bryony was now from the elegant bride at the wedding, the capable mum at the picnic.

For some reason, I felt disappointed. 'So, Vic's okay with it?'

'Oh, are you ready for this one girls?' She cleared her throat. 'Vic said, at least the neighbour's kids weren't on it at the time.' She almost laughed. 'Like that's supposed to be a comfort? No one's up for manslaughter, he said.' She drained her glass, set it down on the table and peered back into the garden, maybe focusing on the twins, but it was hard to tell. Her pupils were barely bobbing to the surface. 'I tell you what, it'll be me facing two life sentences at this rate. Did I tell you, their mother tells them they don't have to listen to a word I say?' Her voice gathered pace. 'Not that they ever listen to Vic. Not that I blame them.'

'They are a bit … intense.'

'Intense? I can barely sleep when they're in the house. Wondering what they're up to. What they're planning next...'

Kim sucked in her cheeks, fighting a smile.

'Look!' Bryony drew our attention to one twin, possibly Philip, standing over in the corner of the garden, holding a fork, fixed in concentration. 'Look at that.' She half left her seat, leaning on the table. 'What the fuck's going on there?' She pointed at him. 'What's with the fork?'

'Don't worry.' I got to my feet. 'It's only plastic.'

Kim let out a cackle over the top of her cup.

'I swear to God, if he stares at that thing long enough,' Bryony said, oblivious to the funny side, 'he'll probably bend it.'

Chapter Thirty-One: All Fall Down

I wanted Grace to have the best day, but once that first set of parents announced they had to get going, I was thanking them for leaving, not for coming over.

After that first couple rounded up their kids, a magical domino effect wove its way across the lawn: dads herding children while mums collected discarded sweat tops and rogue pairs of trainers, all thanking Grace for a lovely day, while I pretended to be sad the party was over. I still wasn't fully convinced half of them even knew who I was, not until Bryony's friend, the brunette one, who I now knew was called Jules, piped up: 'I'm so sorry, Ella. Didn't realize you were Dan's girlfriend. That gazebo was *a-mazing*.'

'Ella!' Pippa lurched at me like David Attenborough in his prime, ploughing her way through the balloon fence. 'Everyone! This is all a bit late in the day, I know, but I just have to thank Ella, my son's partner, who made all of this happen. To Ella.' She realised she was empty-handed and raised an imaginary glass instead. 'And a day we'll never forget!'

Her son's partner? That sounded like a promotion, I thought.

Bryony had waited until the last of the guests left before falling sideways off her chair, trying to help Ethan into his coat. She vomited loudly in the downstairs bathroom and Dan stopped to grab a glass of water for her, making excuses, blaming it all on the jetlag. Pippa pretended not to notice the casualty, happily engaging the children in premature sentiment about the afternoon.

I was about to make my way into the lounge when I heard the murmur of my own name.

'What about Ella?'

So, I did what any other slightly paranoid step-girlfriend would do. Whatever eaves were, I dropped mine at the door.

Bryony gave a gentle laugh. 'For Christ's sake, Dan…'

'I know, I know…'

'Hopefully she'll agree,' Dan mumbled. 'If you could keep the kids out of the way for the weekend? I just don't think it's fair…'

'No, I totally get it.'

'I don't want them feeling uncomfortable. And I don't want Ella feeling like we're all in on it…'

All in on what? I was trying to stay positive. Maybe it was a surprise party? Except my birthday was in February and ever since Mum 'surprised me' with an *Emotional Intelligence* seminar, hugging strangers and eating what looked and tasted like algae for two days, he knew exactly how much I hated surprises.

'What are you going to tell Vic?'

My heart paused for a second.

'Vic?' Bryony sniggered. 'I'll think of something. He's the one who stormed off, left us stranded...'

Silence. I held my breath. I heard nothing I could pinpoint as I imagined them in some tender embrace. I wondered if I should burst in and catch them at it. Except I didn't think I could move my legs.

'The kids'll be fine,' Bryony said. 'I think they'll be relieved, to be honest.'

'Yeah, maybe,' Dan agreed. 'The last few weeks haven't exactly been easy. Do you want me to get your things?'

'Yes, please. I can't face your mother, not right now. I don't need a lecture on the perils of daytime drinking. My jacket's still out there. My sunglasses are still on the table, I think. Could you pass me a tissue?' Bryony said. 'I can't believe I got that drunk in front of our kids…'

'It's a party. They'll be getting drunk in front of us before we know it.'

Us?

'Yeah, I know…' I could hear her smile. 'Thanks, Dan. Well, it looks like my husband's finally on his way over. *My husband!* It always seems funny, saying that, with you standing there. Here I go again, swimming with the tide…' she trailed off. 'I had this flashback at the wedding. Déjà vu, or whatever they call it. I stood there, thinking, if you and me couldn't make it…' A gentle laugh from Dan. 'Do you think Ella's half expecting it?'

'It would make it a damn sight easier if she was.' He gave a half-laugh.

'We're off.' Mum linked Jeremiah.

'Just wanted to say, we're both really proud of you. Of today,' he told me, placing his hand on my shoulder. 'What you did out there? Those kids loved it. Amazing it was. Anyway, gotta go *walk the dog*.' He winked, sidling past, before paying a quick visit to the bathroom.

I waited until he'd left the room and noticed Mum looking sheepish.

'You could have told me you were bringing *Jim Morrison* with you…'

'You know full well we're seeing each other.' She threw her tie-dye scarf over one shoulder. 'You should've been expecting him.'

'Expecting him? Sorry, who's my mother again? Kate Moss, is it?' I tried to keep my voice down. 'You're fifty—'

'Don't you dare bring my age into this. You're being ridiculous.'

'Oh, I'm the one being ridiculous, am I? What next? A motorbike license? A tattoo? You going to start living in a Kabutz, headlining next year's Glastonbury? And what's with him? *We're proud of you?*'

'He was trying to be supportive. Trying to be nice to my daughter.'

'Well, he needn't bother,' I told her. 'Are you actually having a breakdown? He's wearing leather pants to a kid's party!'

'I enjoy spending time with Jeremiah, if you must know.' She rearranged the contents of her handbag, searching for car keys. 'We happen to enjoy each other's company. Regardless of my age,' she said. 'Or his trousers.'

'So you thought you'd bring him to Grace's party? Was that really the best idea, Mum? And are those *wet-look* Jeggings you're wearing?'

'Jeremiah ran around entertaining those children all afternoon.' She pointed a finger, back in mum-mode. 'And I happen to look great in these Jeggings!'

'You look like you're on a scuba diving trip!'

'Do you know what, Ella?' She adjusted her bag firmly onto her shoulder. 'You're nothing but a hypocrite!'

'A hypocrite? You're the one who said wet-look anything was common!'

'You expect Dan's children to accept you, but you won't give Jeremiah the time of day!'

'Oh, for God's sake, Mum! It's not the same!'

'Actually, Ella.' She gave one of her curt head-wobbles. 'It *is* the same. I've been seeing Jeremiah for quite a while now. The fact is, he makes me very happy,' she informed me. 'I'm not asking for your permission. The only reason we're having this conversation is because *you're* not happy with your own boyfriend…'

Jeremiah stepped back into the kitchen as if following a particularly gripping *Wimbledon* final, looking to each of us, unsure of his next move, while we stood at Love-all. 'Look,' he said, assessing the tension, hands outstretched, as if negotiating an armed robbery. 'Don't want to step on anyone's toes here, but I'd really like it if we could be friends?' He peered at me a little too intently. 'Yeah?'

'Let's go.' Mum correctly guessed that wasn't going to be the best approach.

She took Jeremiah's hand, leaving in silence.

'Why do they do that?' I noticed Grace outside the kitchen door, carrying dishes back into the house. 'Why do they say, "This is my friend," when it's so *not* just their friend. It's ex-*cru*-ciating…'

Kim stood on the outskirts of the bedroom as I loaded up my bag, collecting essentials, retracing my steps. 'Are you sure you really want to do this? I don't know if this is the best idea.' Kim watched as I grabbed my hairbrush, shoved in my makeup bag and tightened the lid on my face cream.

'Ella?' Dan opened the door. 'Mum said she couldn't find you. She wanted to say goodbye…' He slowly took in the scene, looking to Kim for answers. 'Are you *packing*?'

'I'll wait downstairs…'

Dan stood aside, letting Kim past.

'What's going on?'

'I heard your conversation…'

'What conversation?' I folded my jeans and tucked them down into my bag. 'With Bryony?'

'So you do know what conversation I mean. And funnily enough, it involves her…'

'What did I say?'

I moved quickly, opening drawers, anything except looking at Dan. I had no idea how I'd gone from picking up cupcakes to packing an overnight bag.

'Ella? What are you —'

'I'm going.'

'Bryony's drunk. We didn't say any—'

'Dan?' I motioned for him to stop. 'I'm going to stay with Kim for a few days…'

'No, you're not,' he said, as I stopped, challenging him with a look. 'I mean, you don't have to do that…'

I double-checked my bag.

'Ella? You're over-reacting.'

'Overreacting?' I spun around. 'Overreacting to you making plans with your ex-wife? Telling her we're over. After I did all your dirty work, arranging this party?'

'Nothing's over, you know that's not true…'

I turned away and picked up a recently divorced sock, a hair slide, an old copy of Red magazine, anything I could get my hands on.

'All I know is I didn't move in with you just so I could keep house or look after your kids. But I tried. I did my best, and I've finally figured out what was wrong with that picture.' I rearranged my packing, sliding a paperback down one side. 'It was expected. All of it. And I'm too young for this! I don't want to act like your mum.' My voice grew louder now. 'I'm sick of trying to behave like somebody else. Someone I'm not. I'm not some child-friendly neat-freak. My mother's dating Russell Brand, wearing wet-look trousers, and I'm standing around, fussing over miniature quiches. It's not right!'

'Ella? I don't want you to act like anybody —'

'I kept thinking about what you said to Vic. About him marrying your ex-wife. What does that make me, Dan? The it'll-do-for-now? Playing house so you can still have your perfect family of four every weekend?'

'That man puts me down every chance he gets!' Dan said, angry now. 'With his wallet, his constant remarks, *flirting with you*. Doesn't exactly bode well for Bryony or the kids, does it?'

'Maybe you shouldn't spend so much time worrying about Bryony. Maybe you should be more interested in your own life, instead of dropping everything, including me, the minute she calls.'

'I didn't drop everything for her!'

'Dan, you practically ran out the door to *save her* today.'

'I was helping her out! What was I supposed to do?'

'It doesn't matter. I'm not staying here. I'm not waiting around for you to decide when I should leave. Not one thing in your life changed.' The tears had started now. I raised my voice over his, not wanting him to interrupt me. '*Not one single thing*. I'm here, like an idiot, while you're *plotting* —'

'Plotting? I wasn't —'

'I don't want to be anyone's second choice. I'm not last year's Christmas present.' I zipped up my bag. 'I'm sick of living with your ex-wife's rules and your mother's arrangements. So whatever you and her were talking about? *Go for it…*'

'Dad?' Ethan stared at my bag. 'Vic turned the car around. I forgot my trainers.'

'You've got everything now, though?' Dan said, back to being Dad.

Ethan nodded, looking solemn, and I hated all of it. I hated doing that to him. I hated *us* for doing that to him.

'You're sure?'

'Uh-huh.' Ethan looked over. 'I liked it today. The party was good in the end.'

'Good.' I could barely look at him. 'I'm glad you had a nice time.'

'See you next Friday.' He backed out of the room and galloped downstairs.

I stood still, gripping my holdall, until the front door closed.

'Here.' Dan reached up and took a washbag down from his wardrobe, took out a brochure and placed a ring box on top.

I tried to convince myself that ring box was everything except what it was. A set of ear-plugs Dan had finally picked up, taking the hint about his snoring. A designer dog whistle only Starky could hear for next time he ran off chasing birds. Pippa's front door key. Returned. In case we ever wanted to have spontaneous sex again.

'There's the big secret. That's what I've been *plotting...*' I looked at him now. 'I picked it up this morning, which was why I forgot to pick up the cakes. That was what I was talking to Bryony about,' he told me. 'I almost proposed today. The kids thought I should,' he nearly smiled, 'seeing as I had the ring, but I wanted to wait until it was just about us.'

I was still trying to process the word, *Propose.*

'Bryony talked to the kids a while ago. I wanted to test the water. Didn't want it to come as a huge surprise to them. She was going to have them while I took you away for the weekend. Pretend it was a thank you for today.' He tried to gauge my reaction. I was still trying to convince myself about that dog whistle.

'So, go on,' he said. 'Aren't you going to open it?'

I stared at the box.

'*Dan...*'

My eyes found his face.

I left.

Chapter Thirty-Two: Rotten Bananas

I went over to the window, the familiar smell of takeaway places rising up from the street. I never knew egg fried rice could smell so much like home.

'Thanks, Kim.' I folded my coat over the back of the chair.

'For what?'

'Being there on the worst day of my life.' I rooted in my pocket for a hair tie.

'Want me to make you feel better?' She pulled on her slippers, settling down on the couch, putting her legs up beneath her.

'An all-expenses trip to Lourdes with Dr House couldn't do that right now.'

'Guess what?' She waited until she had my full attention and opened her antique cigar box. She produced a photograph and started waving it around: 'I'm pregnant!'

I thought it only happened in Agatha Christie novels, but my jaw literally hinged open. I walked to the settee and lowered myself onto it as she handed over the ultrasound scan.

'That's its face?'

I couldn't take my eyes off the figure eight in the photograph.

'Yes!' She laughed. 'It's a baby!'

I glanced at her tummy, suddenly suspicious.

'Who's —'

'Ben.'

'*Ben?*'

She nodded.

'Your Ben?'

I was so shocked. She may as well have told me the baby was mine.

'Just when you thought I couldn't get any crazier…'

'You're having your ex-husband's baby?'

'Told you I'd make you feel better, didn't I? Yep,' she sighed, 'it's the most stressful news I've ever had, and I can't even chain-smoke my way through it…'

'But …' I was scrutinizing her now. 'You don't even look pregnant!'

'I've just gone 13 weeks.' She suddenly looked very pregnant as her hand instinctively cradled her abdomen. 'And, from the very first moment I found out,' she said. 'I'm just…' She smiled. *Completely in love…*

I stared at her, until I remembered what you were supposed to say to people who were expecting. It's just, I still couldn't believe Kim was one of them.

She'd once flashed her tits at a troupe of elderly Morris Dancers.

She'd danced on the tables at parties, barely a thong to her name.

She could open beer bottles with her teeth. And, one time, using only her cleavage. And now she was somebody's mother?

'Congratulations!'

'I've only told you and Ben so far. Still figuring out how to break the news to my folks…'

'Maybe wait until the baby can tell them itself?' I suggested, used to hearing about her family's high expectations. They had been disappointed enough when she had gone into teaching instead of taking over her father's IT consultancy. "Give it a few years," Kim's dad had said, "and computers will be taking over from teachers." "Well, for both our sakes," she told him, "let's hope they take over from daughters, too."

'What does he think?'

'Ben?' The front door jutted open. 'Perfect timing. You can ask him yourself.'

I wasn't quite as relieved as I should've been when Audrey arrived back Monday morning. The whole Batholomews' panic was still hanging over me. There had been no real word of response to the proposal I'd sent over, but I knew Eric would've contacted Audrey by now. Leah and I had put our heads and notes together and I hoped the proposal made sense, or at least explained why I'd decided to put forward the campaign. Leah said it probably would have been smarter to go with her suggestion and give Eric that blow job.

I knew what Audrey was going to say: I should've referred Eric to her, not taken it upon myself to start wheeling out business strategies the moment she left and they happened to pop into my head.

'I leave the business for a few days and come back to an absolutely tremendous response to our competitors. One of our oldest clients is positively raving about you.' She tapped her notebook. 'Eric was most impressed.'

'And that's without the extras,' Leah muttered, giving me a nudge.

'What was that, Leah?' Audrey looked up from our paperwork.

'We took a look at the Bartholomews' spend.' Leah quickly changed the subject. 'For the last few years Heather's increased their digital investment and they've still kept hold of a decent print budget.'

'We thought it was time to review that approach.' I tried to sound convincing. 'Reduce their existing spend in digital and press, and gradually increase our profits in the process.'

'Reduce their spend?' Audrey said. 'I don't quite see how that adds up for us?'

'There's a lot of wastage in online advertising for a store like Bartholomews'. It's probably something they thought they should do,' Leah said, and I guessed her Digital Lumberjack had been helping with our homework, 'just because everyone else was doing it. Their customers are like, proper old. Some of the magazines they're advertising in are totally the wrong for them too. And those websites they're advertising on?' she explained. 'There's no talkability.'

'Talkability?' Audrey nodded.

'So, that's when we started looking into radio advertising. Bartholomews' needs a new approach to branding.' I stepped in. 'A more heritage-led approach, which breaks down the demographic. We need to portray them as a great, special occasion department store, for a more discerning, as opposed to an older, clientele. I've seen the listener demographic. Local radio fits perfectly…'

'This sounds absolutely fantastic.' Audrey leaned back in her seat. 'But I've looked into radio advertising in the past. It's hardly a low-cost option.'

'We've worked it out. It is, if we reinvest Bartholomews' budget. And the station's willing to cut us a deal.' I was almost excited by now. 'We've spoken to some people over there at *Rising*. They're really interested in working with us. I think we can negotiate them right down in price. Especially after we explain that we've got a whole food festival to promote. A full rota of local clients to potentially advertise with them. Obviously, we'll need to persuade Eric that his existing spend would be better used predominantly on-air. We'll need to maintain his original budget, but that move should start to generate some active profit.'

'Ella, you'll be presenting this at 8 o'clock tonight.' Audrey straightened her back and folded her arms along the desk, as I nearly swallowed my pen. 'Apologies for the late shift, but I spoke with Eric this morning. Got us a slot.'

'You want me to present?'

'Absolutely,' she said. 'You came up with the proposal. Led the research. I'm happy to hand over to you while I concentrate on finalizing the food and drink festival. Eric's away on a buying trip. He's handed the marketing over to his son, Saul.'

'Saul?'

'Ella?' Audrey fixed on me. 'We cannot lose this account.'

Chapter Thirty-Three: Good Girl Voice

My brain ticked over with last-minute platitudes, reeling off stock phrases as I stood outside the glass façade of the empty department store, strip-lit in silence.

Steen & Heard are actively working on your account…
Your account's our number one priority…
We can assure you, we'll do whatever necessary to retain your business…

The brass bell reverberated beneath my fingers as Saul Bartholomew came to the door. He was carrying a delightful-looking bunch of keys, like something from the Dark Ages.

He looked right at me.

BLOODY HELL…

'Ella Shawe?'

'Yes?' I tried not to make it obvious I was momentarily distracted. Eyes averted, trying not to melt the buttons off his shirt. 'I mean, yes. I'm Ella Shawe.'

'Saul Bartholomew.'

He looked like the actor from that film my mum cried over every Christmas. Except contemporary. *And utterly shaggable.*

He waltzed off across Ground Floor Accessories like he owned the place, which, I reminded myself, he did. The lift doors opened and he stepped in, not so much as a glance in my direction and pressed the top button. How had Eric Bartholomew's reptilian DNA not extinguished such an exotic, leather-booted, vision of a man? God bless Saul's beautiful mother.

'I was just finishing off.' He glanced at me with the darkest of eyes. 'In my office…'

A burning heat washed over me, exploding inside my ears. I took a deep breath, but the lift was filled with the scent of black pepper and leather.

Dear Lord, please send help…

'Oh right… Well, I appreciate you seeing me.' I followed him through the doors, which opened with a chime and a stolen glimpse of Saul's lovely arse. 'I mean, with it being so late…'

Man, I was boring. I couldn't think of one single interesting thing to say to him. My personality had been overruled by every cell in my body simultaneously gasping: *TAKE ME, YOU SAVAGE!*

You should've seen the look he gave me, like a threat tied up with a ribbon.

'I work better at night…'

I had a sudden need to swallow. A slight tremble of the lip. *I know you do*, I thought, with a visual of him airlifting me onto the nearest hard surface.

'I like to set things in motion before morning…'

Another velvet glance in my direction.

I am here for a business presentation, I tried to reason with myself.

Except everything Saul said washed up in a sea of innuendo.

He had me drifting off into weird, antiquated sex fantasies.

I was losing track of my mind, following him around corners.

Adrenalin high-tailed its way around my body.

I could barely focus from behind a cloud of pheromones.

It felt fabulous!

Grow up! The better version of me, the Good Girl Voice who still cared about all that silly work stuff, snapped at my heels. *Clear your head immediately! Listen to the man.*

She was absolutely right, of course. But as we came to a stop, his arm brushed against mine. The sensation tightened my stomach. My heartbeat reached Olympian levels. I needed a chair before I fell at his feet.

'I usually end up here until late. I'd only be checking emails at home otherwise.' I found myself standing in his office, which looked far more like a hotel suite. Everything on the table had been planned and placed with precision. The laptop was at a sleek angle with a tall glass of water to the right. A fountain pen rested on top of a leather-bound notebook, a photograph of his parents stood behind it.

'All I seem to think about 24/7 is the store.' He took a seat at the mahogany desk. A piece of abstract art hung behind him, framing him as its subject.

'I used to have a lot more fun staying up all night...' he half-smirked.

'Me too,' I said, as his eyes met mine. I really wished I hadn't spoken, but then it got even worse. 'I mean, I've been working on you day and night.'

Shit. Did that sound slutty?

'On your account, I mean. On the store's account.'

'I know what you meant.' One side of his mouth twitched with amusement.

And I wanted to lick it...

No! Not lick it! Good Girl Voice was back. *Listen to him! He's a client!*

Yes, I agreed, as he noticed me looking at his parents' photograph.

'You've met my father?'

'Yes, I have. And, that's your mother?'

Saul's eyes. Saul's cheekbones. Saul's thick, black hair.

Oh, Saul! Good Girl Voice grew weak. *We think we love you!*

Shut up, I told Good Girl Voice. Shut up and be *good* like you're supposed to be!

'Mum's from Brazil. They met on a train. Dad gave her a business card, trying to impress her. She tore it up in front of him.' He looked suitably impressed. 'Quite a woman...'

And he was quite the Man-Cat! And he knew it. He knew he was sexy. I almost hated him for it. He was vain. Arrogant. Privileged. Cold. Everything I usually found a complete turn-off, wrapped up in one man who was hopefully unaware of the x-rated images he was provoking, as I tried to look business-like and composed.

God damn it! Good Girl Voice panted, trying to calm herself. *Oh Saul...*

We were doomed. I knew that night might just be the night I cracked open the Duracell, admitted defeat and took The Pulveriser out for a quick sex drive.

'I'm not going to play games,' I said, like the Good Girl Voice told me to say. Even though she was slipping into something a little more comfortable and basking on a chaise lounge at the time.

Wicked Whisper lit a cigar: *Unless they're strange, sexual ones...*

'Your account's our number one priority.'

Saul gave a long sigh and sat back, pushing himself away from his desk with one biker boot. Then, arching his perfectly-formed brow, he leant forward, asking me: 'Am I supposed to be flattered?'

Wow. I'd gone up in flames under my dress.

Oh, Saul! Good Girl Voice ran her fingers through her tousled hair. *You sexy, department store-owning, bastard!*

He had to be doing this deliberately. Was he *flirting* with me?

Because who sat back like that with their head all tilted and those hold-your-breath, do-me-to-sleep eyes? I was on the run, being hunted down by my own libido.

'Ella, I need a strategic plan.' He tapped each word out onto the desk with his index finger and I swear I was being hypnotized. 'Not some hand-holding exercise.'

I nodded, barely able to swallow.

'Do you have anything for me to take a look at?'

How about you take a good, long look at her while she lies naked across your desk? Wicked Whisper suggested, a great, big, dirty grin on his face.

But, by this point, Wicked Whisper fell on deaf ears — because I'd decided I actually hated rude, mean, demanding Saul Bartholomew.

'It's right here, on my iPad —'

I began the daily rummage inside my handbag.

'Email it across.' His focus shifted back to his laptop, distracted, impatient, as I fidgeted. 'I'll expect it first thing…'

Chapter Thirty-Four: Dress Rehearsal

Kim's Ben had gone to dinner with some long-lost uncle on Friday night, so Kim decided to start getting ready for their new arrival, beginning with a complete rethink of her wardrobe.

'Gotta make room for those elasticated waistbands and hilarious *Baby on Board* t-shirts.' She was already mourning her days as a wild child as we loaded everything she owned out of her wardrobe and on to the bed. 'Take it. Take it!' She held out her infamous zebra-print mini as if donating her pulmonary vein for an emergency transfusion.

'Are you sure?'

'Zebra-print's not a look you can pull off when you're pregnant,' she said. 'Or with a pram.' I folded the skirt and put it in a cardboard box headed for eBay. 'I feel like I died,' she said. 'This actually feels like I'm preparing my own funeral.'

'The Girl in the Zebra-print Skirt…' I remembered how that tiny skirt had been our pass into every aftershow party, VIP lounge and underground club in town.

Kim's zebra-print mini had known a wilder existence than the Maasai Mara.

I held it up in admiration. 'Keeper?'

'Keeper…' she agreed, voice calm, eyes pleading.

As well as being useless at helping Kim transform her wardrobe from wild child to fun mum, I caught up on her situation with Ben. Apparently, after spending the last month or so on the phone, Ben had only let Kim know he was booked onto the next flight as he boarded from California. He said he was going to check into a hotel for the next few weeks as he didn't want to overwhelm her.

'I'm three months pregnant and he thought *that* was going to overwhelm me?' She'd told him to cancel the hotel and get over to her place instead.

'But, now that you're staying.' She was examining a jersey top with a worryingly plunging neckline. 'The spare room isn't so spare anymore…'

'Hey, if that's a problem, don't worry, I can —'

'Hey, I'm not complaining. I love having you back here.' She chucked the top in my direction. 'But do you know how hard it is to pull once you're pregnant?' She grinned. 'He knocked me up,' she said. 'The least he can do is sleep with me.'

I noticed the time. I instantly wondered what Saul was up to and if he'd be staying up late doing it. He'd replied pretty much straightaway to my follow-up email that morning:

Ella, thank you for visiting me last night. I'm pleased to see our plans seem highly compatible. Once we put our heads together, I'd like to imagine taking this further. Hopefully an ongoing arrangement will satisfy my business needs, and your own. SB.

'So.' I shook my head from Saul's seductive debut in my inbox for the thousandth time that day, as Kim held up a horrendous, ruffled dress that looked like it had once belonged to a magician's assistant. 'Are you two going to get married again then?'

'I think we need to hit up the Delivery Suite before thinking about another walk down the aisle, Ella. We both said we'd almost gotten over the divorce.' She scrunched up her nose at an old Maroon 5 t-shirt. 'But it *was* kind of funny. Calling him my "ex-husband" in front of the sonographer.'

'Only you would end up married to the same man twice…'

'Well, I've always loved Elizabeth Taylor.' She nodded towards the Warhol print hanging over by her window.

Kim told me she'd been absolutely certain she was pregnant in July. 'How could I not know?' she said, after I asked how all that Earth Mother instinct stuff she was talking about could possibly be true. 'I'd missed my period. Vomiting yellow bile every morning. Then I start crying, *sobbing*, at the Year Six Leaver's Mass.'

'Did you know you were pregnant that day? When we went to the Zoo?'

'Hanging out of bed, wanting to throw up, didn't feel like the *nicest* way to break the news,' she said. 'Thought I'd wait until I was looking all peachy and you'd see for yourself that I was with child!' She placed one hand on her chest, imagining her glorious pregnant alter-ego. 'So far, all I've got is a major breakout of back-ne and I'm convinced my nipples have already changed colour…'

'Your *nipples*?'

'I read it someplace,' she said, sorting through enough pairs of tights to make a bungee for the Burj Khalifa. 'Did you know they can turn almost black once the baby's born?'

'Your *actual* nipples?'

Kim motioned approval to binbag an old pair of joggers.

'Will you stop saying *nipples*! Yeah, like rotten bananas,' she told me. 'And pretty much the same shape from some of the pictures I've seen. Some of those baby books.' She blew the air from between her pout. 'They read like psychological thrillers. I'm just grateful I can still shave my legs, see my feet, and laugh without peeing myself. That reminds me,' she said, chucking her winter beanie collection onto the bed. 'Let me show you this…'

She pushed aside some space from the assortment of coats, tops and jumpers multiplying on top of her bed and rested her laptop on a pillow.

'Can you believe I'm doing this?' She was busy scrolling through baby-related gadgets. 'I thought this would be you with the shock baby news. Oh. Sorry,' she said. 'It's just, you know, Dan's already got kids...'

'So one more wouldn't hurt?' I realised I didn't want my baby to be a one-more-wouldn't-hurt baby. I wanted a big fuss. And for Dan to think I was an absolute Goddess. To take wonderful black and white photographs of me holding our baby. Looking all fresh-faced and well-rested. Crazily enough, I thought, remembering his reaction to the pregnancy test, I'd've quite liked him to want the baby, too. Not look as though he was playing a poker tournament. I still hadn't properly spoken to him. He'd sent a text saying he'd give me some space. I wasn't sure how much space I needed. At that point, outer space wouldn't have felt like enough.

'I suppose so.' Kim mused it over. 'Oh, that's it! Look at this!'

The screen filled with a woodland-themed nursery, silver birch wallpaper and a little bird night-light.

'I thought I might be pregnant, a few days ago...'

She snapped the laptop shut.

'Only until last weekend.' I realised how stupid I must sound to an actual pregnant person. 'Nothing like this...'

'Why didn't you tell me?'

'I thought I might be.' I shifted over on the bed and dislodged a stiletto from my bum cheek. 'Then I wasn't.'

'What did Dan say? Did you tell him?'

'Sort of. He found the test.'

'So, what did he say?'

I shrugged, trying to untangle one of Kim's old corsets from my cardigan.

'Well, if that's how it is, maybe you do need to find someone who hasn't done it all before…'

'Like who? Dan, fifteen years ago?'

'I'm not sure Dan would've jumped at the chance of two kids before he had them, Ella,' she said. 'Look, I told you, it took Ben a month to get his head round all this. I wasn't even fully convinced myself, not at first. If it were up to the blokes, the world would be extinct. That's why God invented crazy pregnant women.' She grinned. 'Like me!'

'I still can't believe it.' I glanced down at her tummy.

'Well, believe it. And I'm the happiest I've ever been,' she said. 'Until, you know, the stretch marks. Haemorrhoids. Terrifying labour.' She reeled off the list. 'See? I'd've never've had me down for any of this, but it's like,' she settled back against the headboard, 'the best thing I never knew I wanted. And now it's happening.' She contorted her mouth. 'I sound super smug, don't I?'

'You're allowed to be,' I said, as I started to rummage through an assortment of discarded heels. 'And I'm going to be an aunty!'

'You'll be the best aunty!' She grabbed my arm. 'Please don't go deleting me from your phone when I'm boring you to death about grape juice and cradle crap…'

'I won't! Of course, I won't!'

'And promise me you won't let me get too boring.' She looked genuinely concerned. 'I don't want to be one of those parents who only talks about their kid.' She closed her eyes, slowly contemplated her fate. 'But it's inevitable.' She slumped. 'I know it is. *NO!*' she screeched. 'Not the *Fuck Me* boots!'

I dangled the offensive items over the donation box and released them from my grasp.

She smoothed one hand over her tummy. 'I'm never going to wear another sequin again!'

'And this can go, too.' I held up her black, ¾ length jumpsuit.

'I need that!'

'You're not keeping it!'

'It's got long-sleeves!'

'Kim, it's crotchless!'

She watched another piece of her glory days head for the dustbin. 'You know one of the best bits about having this baby?' She inspected a pair of tiny denim hot pants and threw them in my direction. 'It's already happened. Not the kind of thing you long for after your divorce.' We both smirked. 'But, like I said, life decided for me. So, have you decided anything about life? Before it catches up, shatters any plans?'

'Well, I'm not sure what life's decided for me. All I know is, before all those cogs lined up, at the right time, at the right place, and me and Dan finally met, some other woman had already come along, married him, and had his babies.'

'Fuck,' Kim said, opening a packet of chocolate digestives she'd stuffed in her bedside table on stand-by for sugar-cravings. 'That's dark.'

It was dawning on me. My ideal version, the version of Dan I wanted, was probably the one without the weekends.

'It's the truth, that's why,' I said. 'I don't even like saying it…'

'Stay here as long as it takes.' She shoved the biscuits towards me.

'Well, you say that, but I'd better work it out before this baby of yours arrives.' I stuffed half a biscuit in my mouth. 'Unless you want me cluttering up your designer nursery. Be honest, is Ben really pissed off with me being here?'

'No!' she said. 'I already told him, it's practically your place anyway. Still is, if you need it?'

'What? With you and the baby?' It suddenly occurred to me: 'You *are* staying in England?'

'I'm going home.' She smiled, tight-lipped. 'It's where Ben is. Where my family are.'

'You're leaving?'

''Fraid so. Aunty Ella's going to have to fly transatlantic…'

We sat in silence until I found the strength to chew the rest of my digestive.

'Oh well.' I decided to change the subject, not ready to be enthusiastic about my best friend flying back home. 'Think of all the cute baby stuff we'll be able to buy once we clear out this lot…'

'Yeah, but,' she smirked, 'what if I don't want my baby to be cuter than me?'

Chapter Thirty-Five: Electric Dreams

Kim and Ben had already gone to bed when I meandered around the kitchen that evening. I was opening cupboards, knowing there was nothing to snack on and knowing exactly what I intended to do next. I locked the bedroom door, casually drawing the curtains.

Nothing to see here. Absolutely nothing to hide.

I crouched down and opened the drawer, just like any other night.

Except, after a few seconds, I was digging down beneath t-shirts and jumpers like a puppy dog unearthing a bone. The Pulveriser sprang from its box, landing firmly in my hand. I was armed. And this thing looked potentially dangerous.

GO ON! Good Girl Voice, now a slightly huskier rendition, entwined in the tattooed arms of Wicked Whisper, said: *Switch it on! Hook. It. Up! Lie down … or perhaps*, she laughed like a lunatic, *standing up?*

Wicked Whisper grinned: *We DARE you!*

I studied the rubber-rocket and almost changed my mind.

It was so basic. So functional. Almost humiliating.

It was *exactly* how I imagined sex with Saul!

'Come on, you little love machine!' I actually gnashed my teeth, maintaining eye contact with the thing as undid my jeans. 'Let's see what you can do to me!'

Batteries. I keyed the word into my phone. Perpetuating the myth that these were only regular, household items when really they were gorgeous, zinc-fuelled bullets of guaranteed sensation beyond all previous comprehension waiting to fire me up. That Pulveriser had shown me such a good time, I had almost poured him a whiskey and lit a cigarette. That's right. I said, 'him', not 'it'. He deserved a little respect.

That Pulveriser had my heels pushed against my own windowsill. I'd left teeth-marks in my Cath Kidston headboard. And finally, when I knew I couldn't take much more, I'd strapped my legs around my chair, because it wasn't my dressing table chair anymore, it was Saul's big leather-number, and I was rocking my biggest, sexiest client into a Digital Revolution — until The Pulveriser stopped. My relentless ride machine left me all alone. Devastated. With only a pair of dead batteries for company and not so much as one last, sodding buzz goodbye.

'Oh, I only needed one! More! Minute!' I begged, exhausted, emotional, and wonderfully dehydrated, as I slumped arse-first onto the carpet. 'Come back to me!'

I gave him a shake. I needed to get him reloaded as soon as possible.

Wire him to the mains if we must! Good Girl Voice pleaded.

Thank God for Wicked Whisper, who ushered two words before taking Good Girl Voice down for another tumble: *TV Remote…*

I'd pressed snooze on Monday morning, grabbed my phone and was scrolling through emails, only to find myself almost in bed with the real Saul. He'd messaged at three that morning. Around the same time I'd fallen to sleep, cradling his battery-operated substitute, he was inviting me for an 10am meeting.

'Did you take the batteries out of the remote?' Kim was sat on the couch, starting to look a little more pregnant, wearing one of Ben's oversized sweat tops.

'No!' I ducked into the fridge.

'Ella? Why're you hiding?'

'I'm getting the milk.'

'By the way, your room sounded like a war zone all weekend.' Kim went over and switched on the TV. 'You used your mum's vibrator, didn't you?'

'It's not my mum's!'

'Ella's in *luh-uv*! Ella's in *luh-uv*!'

'Yes,' I snapped, closing the fridge. 'I tried it.'

'Sounded like you did a lot more than try it…'

'Oh, God. Could you hear it?'

'Put it this way.' She tucked back into her cereal. 'I've managed to convince Ben he's got tinnitus.'

'Oh God,' I cringed. 'I'm sorry! I'm so sorry…'

'No, honestly. We're really happy for you both…'

'There's this guy…'

'And you're packing plastic?'

'There's this guy.' I took a seat next to her. 'And he's just … so … sexy.' I bit my lip. 'It's ridiculous! As soon as I met him, I wanted to roll around with him. My body turns into a magnet. I've never known anything like it! I can't switch it off.'

'I heard…' Kim smirked, chewing on her muesli.

'He's everything that turns me on, just walking around, like he's normal!'

'Jesus, are you okay?'

'I don't think so.' I broke into a grin. 'I don't think I am! I've tried snapping out of it, honestly I have, but all I can think about is finishing off what he's started…'

'Wow.' She nodded. 'What's he look like?'

'He's a Man-Cat, but a bit like a long-legged sexy horse too…'

Kim sniggered: 'You wish…'

'A dark, Brazilian racehorse,' I pictured him in his office, 'with black, Brazilian eyes. Shiny, Brazilian hair. Long, Brazilian fingers...'

Kim gave me a look.

'His mother's Brazilian. I look at him and he says sexy things. He makes me want to take off my clothes in very important meetings.' Kim looked unconvinced. 'And I know if I did he'd carry on as normal, completely disinterested. He's a right bastard. I know he is, but I don't care. In fact, I like it. I like sexy, Brazilian bastards.'

'*Get a grip*! He sounds like your run-of-the-mill *shagger* to me. He'll end up a dirty old man, putting his hands up nurses' skirts, peering inappropriately at teenagers from his wheelchair. And no one's going to care whether he's Brazilian or not.'

'But —'

'He's a dog.' She finished her tea. 'First the teeth. Then the fleas. You've been warned. And, anyway,' she relaxed back against the cushion. 'What's the latest with you and Dan? You know, your sort-of ex-boyfriend? You guy's getting engaged or what?'

'After such a romantic proposal,' I sipped my coffee, 'how could I refuse?'

'That wasn't his fault. You should've stuck the ring on your finger!'

'Kim?' I gave her a look. 'It wasn't that simple.'

'Everything's that simple,' she said. 'Don't do what I did with Ben. You love him. He loves you. All this stuff with The Boy From Brazil? It's not going to change what you need to sort out with Dan. Deal with it. His kids were always going to take time getting used to the whole thing.'

'And what about me getting used to them? That's the bit nobody talks about.'

'You put too much pressure on yourself, that's why. He sees them, what? Two, three days a week?' She shrugged. 'You can't just jump in without causing a bit of a splash, babe. You all got on fine until you moved in. You get him to yourself the rest of the time.'

'I don't want to take him away from them…'

'Honey, that was the picture long before you painted it. They already have to live with their mum's bloke —'

'Who's a big tit.'

'Who's a big tit.' She nodded. 'And those creepoid boys of his. I mean, come on, Ella. No wonder Grace occasionally loses it…'

'I know.' I leant back against the settee. 'But, we're this normal couple, then the weekend comes along and I turn into Mrs Doubtfire.'

'Ella, you can't throw mum-skills out there and instantly expect everyone to think you're great. You have to give it time, so they know you're not going to do this,' she said. 'Pack a bag. Bugger off the minute you have your first argument…'

'Is that what you think?'

'He gave you an engagement ring and you left.'

'I was shocked!'

'So was he! That's why he blew the lid off the whole engagement.'

'Kim, if you want me to go —'

'No.' She reached over and grabbed my hand. 'Don't turn this into a thing. I just mean, the occasional sulky step-kid? He wants to marry you, Ella. I mean, you two,' she grimaced. 'I was kind of *jealous*, for a long time…'

'Jealous of what?'

'You were having this big, love thing,' she said. 'I was alone. My best mate was gone. I was still missing Ben.'

'I'm sorry.' I remembered the formality of settling bills, our friendship reduced to flatmates by the time I moved out. 'I was so caught up with my own thing with Dan. I should've been a better friend.'

'Hey,' she said. 'You're a great friend. You gave me a place to live. You put up with my shit when I was a total mess.'

'Yeah, but you were always such a fun mess.' We smiled. 'Do you think I'm meant to be with Dan?'

'Give me a break. It's not about what's meant to be.' Kim never had any time for soppiness. 'It's about what you want.'

'How can you say that? Look at you and Ben.'

'I'm on the brink of popping out his kid. It wasn't fate that got me pregnant. It was fourteen hours of drinking and a slow-dance to Burt Bacharach that got me here.'

Chapter Thirty-Six: Saul Over Now

I'd been warned.

I. Had. Been. Warned.

But once I was in his office I wanted Saul to seduce me, so I could climb him like a spider monkey. I'd promised Kim I'd concentrate on business, but as he gazed out of the window his voice became white noise. I fixated on the paper knife on top of his journal, imagining what he'd do if I picked it up, popped off every button on that tight, white shirt of his, *and ate them.*

'… and it's this manufacturing aspect which I feel puts us in a position —'

My imagination crawled towards him on all fours. Making her way across his desk. Inciting him to splinters, doing exotic Brazilian things to my Brazilian.

Oh hell! He was still talking and I'd completely lost track. I *wanted* to listen. He was very compelling if you weren't resisting the urge to undress him.

What the hell was I thinking? *I was turning into my mother!*

'So, you're available for the rest of the day?'

'Umm?'

'The manufacturer? I know it's short notice, but I'm due there today, so…'

Apart from a lingering awareness of how empty the car park was, our footsteps echoing against concrete, I managed to get through a 15 minute car journey without hitting Adolescence. The lack of eye contact definitely helped. I was usually far too busy exploring that great face of his to give a shit about his profit margins. And then there was the guilt that, unbeknownst to him, I had a *kind-of* boyfriend who I still kind-of needed to talk to.

This is not how you want Mr Bartholomew to think of you now is it? Good Girl Voice returned with an unflinching work ethic. *You want his professional respect. And his beautiful babies…* She sighed.

'You know.' His eyes hit the rearview mirror. 'Technically, we can turn up any time. Do you fancy something to eat? Or maybe a coffee or something?'

Coffee. I stared out from the window, thinking of Dan as I sat on Saul's heated cream interior, wondering if he'd ever had unprotected sex on the backseat.

'We don't have to.' He glanced my way. 'But there's a great place along here. My favourite place, actually. Brunch on the patio?'

I realised, as Saul parked up, he didn't really ask questions. He was only letting me know what was happening next.

I followed him up the steps as it dawned on me: most people wouldn't have the keys to their favourite brunch spot.

'Welcome to my humble abode…'

We stood in the circular entrance hall. A sweeping staircase entwined, high above our heads and a tall, slender woman with raven hair was standing at the bottom, arranging long, purple flowers in a glass vase which held court on a marble table.

'Darling!' She smiled, arms outstretched. 'Oh.' She noticed me. 'A friend?'

'Mum, this is Ella.' Saul shut the door. 'Ella? My mother, Dominika.'

'Hello, Ella.' She took my hand, taking in every detail. 'It's not very often I meet my son's friends.' She looked over at him. 'Or that he brings them home … during the daylight hours.'

'That's because I didn't expect to find you here, Mother.' He gave a tight smile. 'Ella's been working on some amazing ideas for our relaunch.'

'Oh,' Dominika groaned, leading our way up the staircase. 'Thank goodness! I've been begging Eric to let Saul have his way. My husband.' She shot a look towards us as we climbed to the first floor. 'He's such a silly, stubborn man.' I couldn't help but smile. 'With silly, stubborn ideas.' We reached the top and stood in front of a large oak door, left slightly ajar. 'Lovely to meet you, Ella.' She clasped my hand in both of hers. 'A very beautiful name. Very Ella-gant.' She gave her son a look. 'Wouldn't you agree, Saul?'

'Do I ever disagree with you, Mother?'

We left beautiful Dominika to her morning and took the next set of stairs, Saul explaining how he still lived in the family building, occupying the top floor. 'While my mother attempts to marry me off.'

He led me into a huge, open space with tall, boxed windows. Marble floors. A coffered ceiling.

'It's beautiful…'

'It's not much.' He threw his keys onto one of a matching pair of settees which framed an imposing fireplace. 'But it's home.' He offered his hands. 'Your coat?'

'Oh, yes.' I was still slightly startled, not sure how I'd ended up back at Saul's place, when we were supposedly having a meeting. He took us into the kitchen. All granite worktops and copper pans. He opened the French doors overlooking a balcony, where a table was already set. *For two.*

'My mother would be pleased to know I'm making you her favourite recipe. Persian eggs.' He rolled up his shirt sleeves and heated a pan. 'Cumin, chili, dates?'

'You're making it?'

'My mother says British men can't cook. She had me take lessons before university.' He was already beating eggs, as I admired an extravagant fruit bowl, piled high with multi-coloured tiers of citrus. 'She hates to cook. She told me: *If you wish to make love to a woman*,' he adopted Dominika's faux-English accent, pouring the eggs into the pan, *'first she must eat from your plate…'*

'Oh!' One tremble in the wrong direction and I sent fruit tumbling across the floor.

'Happens all the time.' He smiled, busy stirring and sprinkling exotic-looking things into the exotic-smelling dish. 'So, Ella? Who are you?'

'Who am I?' I put the last lemon back on top of the fruit bowl, which was a lot less ornamental-looking since my visit. *Who was I?* 'I don't know…'

'Nobody does.' He reached for a pair of champagne flutes. 'But we're all here to help each other find out.' He stepped towards me, and for a second I thought I'd made it onto the Breakfast Menu. 'Pass me an orange, please?'

Our fingers touched as he took the fruit from my hand, his dark eyes never leaving mine, as a smile shadowed his smooth, wide mouth. 'Thank you, Ella.'

No, thank you, I thought as he sliced through the orange with military precision, tightly squeezing each half in his palm, through a sieve and into our glasses.

'Why don't you take a seat?' He gestured towards the balcony as he topped up orange juice with chilled champagne. 'Food's on its way…'

I gazed across rows of equally grand-looking buildings, the traffic moving steadily as I sat sipping my drink, thoughts drifting across the city. Until my attention hit a red light: *Castle Street*. Dan's place. Where I'd found Dr. Coffee that day.

And Dan in there, right now.

'Here we are.' Saul appeared, carrying plates. 'Breakfast in Persia.'

'This looks incredible.' I unwrapped my cutlery. 'Thank you.'

'It's basically scrambled eggs with a little twist.' He took a drink. 'I can do much better.'

Self-praise is no recommendation, I could almost hear my mother saying. Although, if Dominika insisted Saul learnt to cook, there was a pretty good chance he'd taken instruction on how to make love after he'd flown the object of his affections to Persia via the frying pan.

I remembered Dan making scrambled eggs for the kids.

How much Grace loved her dad's breakfasts.

Ethan with his shredless marmalade fixation.

'Have you ever been skiing, Ella?' Saul attacked his plate. 'I'm taking a week, next month. Switzerland. Always far nicer with company…'

Did he mean me? 'Ow-fuh!'

'You okay?'

I took a stone from my mouth.

'One of the dates?'

I nodded, checking my molars were still intact.

'Must've slipped through the net.' He looked more concerned than strictly necessary. 'I pitted them all myself this morning.'

When he was planning on getting you here, intuition told me, in the absence of Good Girl Voice, who was reclining on the rug in front of Saul's fireplace. Deep in bliss with Wicked Whisper, neither of them any use to me at all.

'So, we're going to the manufacturers?' I concentrated on my plate, determined to get back to business. Although, not necessarily the kind of business Saul seemed interested in, as he finished his champagne and casually replied: 'If you'd like?'

He was acting as if it was some kind of after-thought.

'I don't want to make you uncomfortable, Ella.'

'You don't.' I almost sounded convincing.

'Don't I?'

'No.' I felt suddenly defensive as he sat eating his weird, spicy egg thing, so calmly. 'Why would you make me uncomfortable?'

'Because from the moment I saw you, Ella.' He held my stare until I completely lost my appetite. 'I found it very difficult to care about marketing plans. Quite frankly, I'd rather be spending time alone with you, doing this.' He looked out across the rooftops. 'Well.' A slight tick of amusement. 'Not this, exactly, I admit…'

'This was lovely.' I studied my plate. 'Shall we go to the manufacturers, then?'

'Of course,' he grinned. 'We can do whatever you want, Ella.'

I hadn't been so tense inside a car since Dan took me on a Rally Driving Gift Experience the kids had got him for his birthday last year.

I felt Saul's eyes on me as we stopped at the lights. Neither of us spoke. I'd tried making conversation about the road works on Portland Street, but he'd given me a look that screamed, *Not Interested*, and put his foot down. It was like being locked inside a shuttle. Speeding straight towards bed. He turned into an industrial estate, parked up, leaned back as if exhausted and moved to face me: '*Ella…*'

His hand traced my cheekbone, his eyes engulfing any rational thought under cover of their consuming darkness. I realised we were kissing. How had that happened? I made myself wake up to it, acknowledge the moment, but as I did, his kisses seemed brutal, ransacking my mouth, until I pulled away.

It's in his kiss, another one of Mum's sayings blurred in the back of my mind.

It was not the way I'd imagined kissing him would be. There was no slow descent into weakness. No surrendering my pleasure to his imagination.

Instead, Saul bashed his face against mine, his tongue prising open my mouth. His need to take whatever he wanted horribly obvious, leaving him oblivious to the fact he had to be the worst kisser in the entire world. Stuff the Persian eggs. Dominika had underestimated the importance of an introductory course in Cultivating Desire. He unfastened my seatbelt and unclicked his own.

Weird. I kind of liked it. Maybe he was genuine and caring, after all? *Or possibly into Bondage?*

'It really is a work of art.' He was back in professional-mode as he opened the warehouse door. The large, square space was filled with people working reciprocating machines, walking past with fixed looks of concentration, taking calls, making notes, checking orders. And when I say it was filled with people, I realised I meant women. There were so many sexually charged or just gorgeous-looking women in Saul's warehouse, I wondered if he wasn't storing them in it.

A wall full of intricate-looking sketches, Saul began to explain with an entirely straight-face, were for future boning. As well as the wall-to-wall Nymphets, swatches of intricate corsetry, mesh knickers and seamed stockings began catching my eye. I felt like we were touring the Moulin Rouge.

'And, I think if you experience the garments for yourself —'
'For myself?'

'Yes, like I explained? Back at the office? You'll get a more personal insight into why we get so excited by our lingerie range.'

'Oh, no. I'm fine. Honestly.'

'Colette? Could you measure Miss Shawe, please?'

Before I could tell pouty-lipped, spaghetti-strapped Colette, that I really didn't want to be a bother, her tape measure was whipping its way across my nipples.

Saul left us to it, walking over to peruse the displays.

'Let's try her in a corset,' he told an older woman in a tight suit and dangerously high heels. 'Not the Harringate. The Akana range.'

'Thong or half-brief?' she asked, specs perched on the end of her nose.

'Thong.'

'Poppers or sewn?'

He glanced over as Colette crouched, measuring my hips.

'Poppers.'

Suddenly, the last few weeks of lust left me, right when I needed them.

He was making me to order. I couldn't do this. He was a client!

A client who'd taken me on some unofficial date to an upper-class Ann Summers where I was about to be undone by a poppable crotch and a bra that I'm assuming would barely contain his excitement.

I couldn't manage his account.

We'd been playing a weird, business sex game all along.

I faked a prior appointment and managed to get back to the office without spending the rest of a rainy afternoon soaked in Saul's darkest desires. I shook out my umbrella, my suede boots limp with the weather. My favourite leather ones were still back at Dan's house.

'You're popular today.' Leah stood by a large cardboard box at the side of my desk. 'Your coffee's gone cold now, though.' She held up a Dr. Coffee takeout as I noticed the scrawl across the cup: *Free top up anytime. D xxx*

'Scissors!' She handed them to me, waiting for the grand unveiling. 'Your bloke said they'd been delivered to the house. He thought you'd enjoy them more at the office. How nice is that?'

The box yawned open with Cabbage Roses and dusky-pink Peonies.

'Now!' Audrey was standing over by Digital. '*That's* what we call a bouquet.'

I placed the flowers on my desk and propped the little envelope next to them, not ready to read whatever Dan had to say. The whole time we'd been together, he'd never sent flowers to the office. Now that it was over, everyone was suddenly interested in my boyfriend, way too late. It felt like wearing a clown-nose to a funeral. The envelope sat there accusingly as I started my computer. I finally logged-on and gave in:

Dear Ella
Thank you for the most amazing party ever
Thank you for everything you do for me and Ethan ☺
Love from Grace — The P.M.T!!! X

'Ella?' Audrey appeared at my desk, snapping me out of it. 'Have you got a mo, please? I need to update you on the food festival, and I wanted to catch up with this morning's meeting with Saul?'

I slipped the card into my drawer like an unpaid bill and grabbed my notebook, following Audrey into her office.

'The Rising Radio quotes look manageable.' She sat a little straighter. 'Would you mind going over the proposal once I've put it together? Between you and I, James is delighted I'm loosening my grip on some of the accounts, which is all very well for him, but,' she craned across the desk, 'it really didn't help our cause once he took his foot from off the pedal. Sorry.' She broke off, looking over my shoulder. 'I've got to ask. I'm sure it was earlier in the year,' she said. 'We haven't missed your birthday, have we?'

'The flowers?' I glanced at the multi-coloured globe on my desk. 'No, they're a Thank You from Dan's daughter, Grace. We had her birthday party last Saturday.'

'How lovely!' Audrey sat back and folded her arms. 'Can't say I ever had that level of appreciation from Peter, growing up, but,' she said, as I held my smile in place, 'I don't think I've ever seen anyone look quite so unhappy to receive such beautiful flowers.'

I didn't reply. I couldn't.

I sat there, waiting for the deep pull of sadness to pass.

Audrey pushed the tissue box towards me. 'Do you need to take a day?'

'Sorry.' The wave of emotion quickly became a tsunami.

'Don't be sorry.' She got to her feet. 'We're all human. Some of us even during office hours.'

'I don't know how to do it,' I told her, the words on the card catching up with me. 'The step-kid thing? I think we've split up…'

'There was a moment, after Shoshanna was born.' Audrey handed me a tissue. 'When everything became very clear to me. We went into the room, at the hospital. Anna, James's ex-wife, sat cradling the baby. I kept my distance. Trying to fathom my place in the pecking order, as you do. James and Anna had earned that moment as grandparents. James was taking a look at the baby, falling in love with her.' She sipped some water. 'Anna looked over at me, and do you know what she said? She said, "Audrey? What are you doing over there? Shosie wants to meet Grandma Heard." I think that was the moment when I realised, all that time, there was no magical way to fix it. We all had to accept the past and move on. Nothing like a baby to remind us, the future starts now. And, from what I can see, if his daughter sent those flowers, you must be doing something right...'

I shook my head. 'I made this huge effort. The party and everything. I didn't even feel part of it.' I dried my tears. 'Dan's ex was there. Their friends. Their family. Half of them didn't even know who I was...'

'Ella, this thing? It's so much bigger than you. Remember that,' Audrey told me. 'You have to bring the children closer to their dad, closer to each other. They'll be in his life forever.' Her tone grew more serious now. 'They need to trust you. That's something you earn. Once they feel you're a positive part of their lives, they'll relax. But until then,' she said, 'you have to be a small part of it. Not the cause. Not the cure. The smallest, most insignificant part. My relationship with Peter has been more tempestuous than my relationship with his father. It's taken me this long to realize, he was riddled with guilt. Trying to protect his mother. Thinking he needed to hold onto his father. Do you love him? Dan, is it?'

'Yes,' I heard myself answer. No hesitation.

'Then there's your answer.'

Chapter Thirty-Seven: Paws For Thought

'Hi, Ella. Hope you don't mind. Something's come up. Mum's not too good. Well, she wasn't too good. Nothing to worry about. She's fine now, but I could use a hand with Starky? Is there any chance Kim could help out with Starky while I'm at work? Friday and Monday?'

I replayed Dan's voicemail. The last two weeks felt like months as the familiar voice emphasised the distance between us. I was home-sick with the sound of it.

'What happened?' I sounded self-conscious as Dan picked up. 'Is your mum okay?'

'She fell down the stairs but she managed to stand up with just a few scrapes. They were surprised there wasn't any real damage. She told the doctor it was down to having a Wilton with a decent underlay. She couldn't stress that enough.' I heard him smile. 'She had a blackout, they think.'

'A blackout? What made her have a blackout?'

'She's been having tests for dementia —'

'Oh God!'

'She's fine. She's absolutely fine. She said she'd been noticing things. Her memory being off. Feeling disorientated. She'd been worrying herself sick since her neighbour got diagnosed a few months back. You know what she's like. She doesn't talk about anything.' I remembered our chat in the kitchen. How Pippa talked about everyone except herself. I felt guilty. I hadn't even thought to ask. 'Then she had the kids to look after. Her head was spinning. Turns out it was a vitamin deficiency.'

'A vitamin deficiency?'

'Mum cannot live on lamb chops alone. Vitamin D, apparently. Doctor said she needs to get back to eating dairy and get out in the sun. I'm sending her to The Lakes for a long weekend. It was supposed to be our weekend, actually...'

I realised he meant it was where we were supposed to get engaged. I had a vision of us in some parallel universe, actually together, all morning walks and afternoons spent undressed in our room. Not waiting it out, like this, until we became strangers.

'She's going Friday to Monday. Meeting her sister for a bit of a break. Sorry, I know it's short notice. I'm not sure if it's even the right thing to do, calling you —'

'It's fine. Kim said she's here all day.'

'You're working out custody of the dog?' Kim had said. 'It's always the pets who suffer...'

'That's brilliant. Thank her for me, will you? I'll see you Friday morning.'

I was stepping out of the shower as I heard Dan at the door, congratulating Kim. I hadn't told him I'd taken a half day. I showed my face in the office for the morning before leaving to spend the afternoon in the park with Starky.

Starky rushed up, tail wagging, balancing his paws against my knee as I made my way into the hall, as if to say: *We've found you! Let's get out of here!*

Dan gestured to come in.

'Oh, course. Sorry.' I put Starky back on four paws and kissed Dan on the cheek, as our little pooch galloped off to make friends with Kim and Ben.

'He seems happier already.' Dan gave his formal version of a smile. The polite, dealing with customers, kind of smile. How had we got to that smile so quickly?

He massaged the back of his neck. 'I brought you some stuff…'

At first, I thought he meant for Starky, but Kim had already shuffled off, carrying the bed and bowls. 'I'm not sure if this is everything you need.' He gazed down at the large canvas shopper we used for groceries. 'I just grabbed a few things. Your boots are in there.' He riffled through. 'Took some tops from the wardrobe. Hey.' A sudden smile. 'I took Ethan to Kung-Fu last night. Grace came as well.'

I'd sent Grace a text after I got the flowers. Got a smiley face back. I hadn't asked Dan what he'd said to the kids. Grace wasn't stupid. Ethan would've mentioned something about me packing that day.

'That's good. How come?'

'I'm trying to mix things up a bit. Mum was a bit down. Going back to the whole see-you-at-the-weekend thing. She asked if she could have them on Fridays. I'll get them Saturday morning. I'm trying to break the week up. Not leave it so long between seeing them. We thought Kung-Fu might be fun. We'll see how it works out. My eternal quest for compromise...'

He wasn't using his hair stuff. His hair was fluffy. School-boy fluffy.

My-girlfriend-just-left-me kind of fluffy.

'I didn't bring the ring,' he said, as I remembered the day I moved in with him. I'd expected our things to blend together the same way we had, but I'd found myself fighting for space against someone else's life. Suddenly everything I owned seemed like vital pieces of everything I was, everything I'd ever be. 'Sorry, bad joke.' He rested his hand against the door.

He looked so lovely right then, the way he was looking at me. A sadness weighed across his shoulders. A flicker of trust was still visible in his inquisitive blue eyes.

'I'm sorry…'

'What would you have to be sorry about?' he said, but his expression said something completely different.

'I'm sorry.' I avoided his look. 'That I can't be that girl.'

'What girl?'

'The right person.'

'Probably wasn't the best time to do it. Proposing.' He met my eye and almost smiled. 'Not when your girlfriend's packing. Ella?' He took a breath and cast a look to the floor. 'My life's … it's a bowl of spaghetti.' He tapped his hand along the architrave. 'I wish I didn't have all this baggage.' We heard Sparky in the lounge. Kim calling to him as he squeaked a toy. 'I'd like to have you, just for me. I love you. You know that.'

'I know.' I nodded, certainty gripping my chest. 'But I couldn't make everyone else happy, Dan. It just doesn't work.' We fell silent as I looked to the lounge, willing Starky to come bounding out to chase away the gloom from between us with some stupid stuffed toy dangling from his mouth.

'Well, if that's how it is, I wish I'd spent longer making *you* happy.' He focused on me until I felt the bruise. It was so composed, so final. 'I wanted you to feel like part of a couple, like you said. And part of the family. I know how much you care about everyone, not just because it suits me or anything like that.'

'Those two things. Us, *this*, and the family.' I shook my head. 'I can't fix everything, Dan…'

'Ella, it's scary. I know. I've got a teenage daughter a hundred steps ahead of me. I'm struggling to help my eight-year-old with his homework. I don't know what's going to happen 10 days' from now, let alone 10 years' from now.' He folded his arms and stared up at the ceiling. 'I'm not exactly an eligible bachelor, I know that. I didn't plan on meeting you,

Ella. Believe me,' he said. 'I had no plans bringing anyone else into all of this. All I know is, I wanted you. Maybe I was selfish, but I wanted to be with you. Even when you were freaking out over cakes, or gazebos, or something else. Some other thing I'd forgotten to do.'

Remembering all that made me realize how quickly you could walk through the next door and realize that everything you had, everything that used to be second-nature, had slammed shut behind you. I'd spent so long trying to control the future and now I didn't know what to do except kill time, racing ahead to a better conclusion.

'I wanted the kids to have a good relationship with you, and with their occasionally crazy mother.' He raised his eyebrows. 'I'm trying to look after my own occasionally crazy mum, too. It's not perfect, Ella. My kids aren't perfect. I'm definitely not, but don't...' He searched for the words. 'Don't finish it, just because it didn't start with us.'

I was determined to enjoy my stolen afternoon. The leaves were beginning to rust as I walked Starky across Avington Square, the soon-to-be home of the Steen & Heard food festival. Dan's words walked alongside me, but it wasn't that easy. If I went back I had to stay back. I couldn't change my mind. I couldn't do that to the kids. Couldn't do that to us. It wasn't just about love. Life wasn't that simple, was it?

'Hey!' I turned, stomach sinking, as Bryony jogged over, pulling out her headphones, head-to-toe in designer running gear. 'Only thing worse than running into your ex?' She was slightly out of breath. 'Has to be running into your ex's ex?'

'Yeah,' I admitted. 'Especially when your dog's taking a dump at the time.' Our eyes darted to Starky, stooping over a bed of pansies.

'What are you doing round this way?'

'My new Yoga place's down Cobden Road.' She fiddled with her iPod. 'Well, I say my new Yoga place. It's nowhere near opening. *Bloody builders.*' She stretched each leg back by the ankle. 'Thought Starky was still with Dan?'

She said it casually, as if it was old news.

'He asked me to look after him while Pippa's away.'

'Oh yeah.' She pulled a face and let out a long breath. 'That was horrible, wasn't it? The kids were so upset.' She took out a bottle and had a drink of water. 'Well, that's cool of you, minding the dog. I'm not sticking my nose in, by the way. Dan only told me you moved out because the kids were asking questions.'

'No, I know.' I stooped to clean up after Starky, wondering why I couldn't have seen Bryony while I was smartly dressed, on the way to some sexy business meeting with Saul, or at least not scooping up dog shit.

'Listen, nothing's perfect.' She shrugged, as I knotted up the little black bag. 'I'm going through my own stuff with Vic. That's why I'm here, avoiding well-meaning neighbours, who're just *dying* to hear how fabulously unhappy I am. Not even married five weeks and it's all gone to shit. Great, isn't it?'

'It'll work itself out...'

'Yeah.' She looked out across the park. 'Let's keep telling each other that. Right?' She noticed Starky pulling on his lead, eager to finish his walk. 'I'll leave you to it. But, hey,' she gave my shoulder a rub, 'I hope everything works out. Whatever that means, and, just so you know,' she untangled headphone wires, 'you've been great with my kids, and, Jesus, I know step-kids aren't easy.'

'Think I might've got a better deal than you there.'

'My kids can be annoying, but try playing happy families with Ronnie and Reggie every weekend. I'll end up paying them protection money at this rate.'

She wandered next to me in the direction of the nearest bin.

'Will you do me a favour?' I asked. 'Don't mention seeing me to Dan, will you? We haven't properly talked yet. I just wanted a day to myself to catch up with Starky.'

'That's why I started running. I probably need a shrink.' She fixed her long ponytail. 'Or maybe I should call your mum's show?'

'My mum? Bloody hell, Bryony. Things can't be that bad,' I told her, as Starky barked impatiently, tail wagging, bouncing on his hind legs as a sudden flight of birds emerged overhead.

Chapter Thirty-Eight: A Step Too Far

After that very apt number from Sister Sledge, now seems as good a time as any to reveal the hot topic for next Friday's show. Blended families. Step-families. Whatever the terminology, the issues remain the same. Or do they?

Mum gave her light-hearted, late-night phone-in laugh. I turned up the radio.

Join me, Renée Shawe. Same time, same station, for next Friday's show One Step Too Far?

'I knew you wouldn't be able to resist, Mother…' I said to no one in particular. Kim and Ben were out at the cinema, catching Nancy Meyer's latest, while I set up shop, not wanting to play gooseberry, centre-stage at the ironing board.

Step-families? She better not even think about name-dropping her daughter on next week's show. I still hadn't told her I'd moved out. I wasn't ready to be grilled. I couldn't stand the thought of the in-depth cataloguing of everything that was wrong with my last relationship. It was bad enough Bryony mentioning that Dan had custody of the dog without my mother throwing statistics at me.

Until then, we'll take our final call for this evening, as we ask the question: Are your partner's hobbies harmless fun, or hurting your relationship?

I ironed my linen dress, each crease becoming personal, wishing I could smooth out everything between me and Dan, until Mum's next caller stopped me in my tracks:

Katie, is it?

That's right. Katie…

And you're newly married?

Less than a month.

I listened over the hiss of the steam iron.

It was! I was pretty sure…

And you previously lived together, with no signs of your husband's very unhealthy habit?

I knew he was a social smoker —

It was Bryony.

I switched off the iron and sat next to the radio, zapping up the volume.

Ah, Mum said, with that knowing tone that made her sound like she was wearing her glasses. *Was that his choice of expression?*

Erm, yes. I suppose so…

Interesting turn of phrase for such an anti-social habit, Mum said, turning Freudian. *And, can you tell our listeners, please Katie. How has this become a problem in your marriage?*

Well, he… Bryony paused. *He likes to smoke before he goes to bed* — Mum interrupted with a tut. *I mean, he brushes his teeth and everything, but I can still smell it.*

And he does this secretly?

He makes excuses about putting out rubbish bins, that kind of thing. I got fed up with all the sneaking around. Decided to go downstairs and let him know. I mean, I'd rather he smoked in the garden if he really has to…

And, you told him this?

No. We got into an argument…

Classic avoidance technique, Mum clarified. *I'm sure that will resonate with many of our listeners who've had to confront their partners. You can find yourself veering off course into an unnecessary argument, or in fact, debating a completely unrelated topic. And, was this the case with your husband, Katie?*

Yes, Bryony sounded quite emotional, but I didn't understand it. I'd seen Vic smoking loads of times. I don't suppose I'd ever seen him having a fag while she was around, now I thought about it, but it was hardly a secret. Not the kind of thing you'd get my mother involved in. *Yes, it was.*

So, you caught your hubby smoking, and you're calling tonight for some advice with helping him quit?

No. Bryony took an audible breath. *I'm calling because he was wearing sling-backs at the time...*

I ... see. Mum sounded uncharacteristically thrown. *And, the sling-back wearing? Is this something you feel you could move forward with?*

Not really...

You feel you need to step away from the marriage?

I can't walk away, Bryony said. *Not this soon. It's my second marriage, but I'm not sure it's worth digging my heels in if I'm going to have to live with his behaviour. I just want him to stop...*

In that case, Mum suggested, *you're going to have to put your foot down.*

I've tried, but he won't talk about it. The last few weeks, we've both walking on eggshells. I know I have to leave him if we can't work this thing out.

Does he know you're prepared to give him the boot unless he starts talking?

I think so, Bryony said. *We've been tip-toeing around it, but like I said, every time I try and talk to him, he runs away...*

Well, he won't get very far. Not in heels, anyway, Mum said. *And on that note, I'm afraid we're running out of time, Katie. Please stay on the line and we'll give you some information which will hopefully be helpful.*

Music slowly ebbed, signalling the end of the show.

Enlightening stuff, I'm sure you'll agree. A big thanks to everyone for listening, and to play us out, it's Sam & Dave with Soul Man...

'Oh, it's you!' Jeremiah cracked a smile as I stood on Mum's doorstep early the next day, wondering what the huge white van was doing on the driveway. 'Thought it was the guy with the desk. Your mum's out.' He took a step behind the door and spun on his heel. 'Do you want to come in?'

'She hasn't replied to my texts. I got her voicemail. I was worried,' I said, exaggerating slightly. I was only there to confess about Dan and put the brakes on any mention of us on the radio. 'I tried the house phone this morning...'

'The phone? Oh yeah.' I followed him down the hallway. The heavy tread of footsteps and sounds of work, overhead. 'That might've been the other guys. We've speeded up the broadband thing for her. You're probably wondering what all this is.' He made his way into the lounge and practically launched himself onto a large white corner sofa. 'Did you want a herbal tea? We're decaffeinating at the moment.'

'I'm okay, thanks.' I scanned the room. 'Is that new?'

'This? The settee?' He reclined, popping his arms along the back. 'Do you like it? We love it. We're trying to create that whole sunken lounge thing. Once the fire's lit, it's total chill-out. Renée says it's like having our own honeymoon suite at home...'

'Yeah, it's nice,' I said, not wanting to hear about their makeshift sex retreat. I noticed a stone Buddha beside the bookshelves and a red, lacquer cabinet in the corner of the room. 'It's just not what I would've expected Mum to go for. What's going on upstairs? Does Mum know about all this?'

If she didn't, he was in for a shock. Mum had lived on her own so long, she couldn't handle the thought of someone changing a lightbulb without her express permission.

'Um.' He tightened his mouth and moved his head slightly from side to side. 'Yes. And no. You know how Renée...' He blinked away the faux pas and started again. 'You know how your mum procrastinates over everything? She's been getting round to redoing her office for months now. Thought I'd surprise her.' He arched a brow and gave me his famous, front-cover grin. 'You do know she's away for the day?' He hitched one thumb over his shoulder. 'Driving to Oxford? She was up and away first thing. Giving a lecture on The Male Gaze. Having dinner over there.'

'No, I didn't realize.' I was still gawping around the room, amazed at the transformation from standard, mum-regulation sitting room. I gave in and had to ask: 'Are you living together?'

'Ah.' He loosened his hands, balancing his fingers against each other, as if he was the one in the lecture theatre. 'You two haven't spoken in a while, have you?'

'Not really,' I admitted, standing over by the fireplace, still not entirely comfortable sitting with Jeremiah there, making himself at home. 'Haven't spoken to her much since the party, really. So, that's a yes, then?'

'Not technically. Technically, I still have my own place.' He rested one arm along an oversized cushion fashioned in peacock feathers. 'Do you want to sit down? You're making me nervous.' He grinned. 'Or is that the intention?'

I cast my eye along the old photographs on the mantlepiece, noticing a new addition, clearly there for Jeremiah's benefit. It was one of Mum, about twenty. Young and gorgeous. Pre getting pregnant with me. Wearing sunglasses, head thrown-back in laughter.

'Secondly.' He was thinking it through, working his mouth as if he gargling. 'I don't want this to sound patronizing, or insincere, or anything like that,' he said, 'but, the thing is, I really care for your mum. For Renée.'

'I know.' I turned to face him. 'That's what I came here to tell her. That and, well, I don't know if you heard the show last night?'

'Yeah, course.' He looked calmly bewildered, as expecting me to launch into a full-blown character assassination any minute.

'The step-stuff? I just don't want her bringing me,' I said, 'you know, my *private stuff*, into it. Apart from that, I get it. I'm happy for her. For both of you.'

'Really?' He sat forward, hands on his knees, alert now. 'Don't think that's the impression Renée's got. Or er,' he paused, still navigating my reaction. 'Me. To be truthful…'

I was distracted as Jeremiah picked up one of Mum's silk scarves, discarded on the floor, probably during wild, bare-knuckle sex, and wove it around his neck.

'You are a lot younger.' I rested my hands on top of Mum's reading chair. 'And, you're, well, you're *you*, aren't you? Actor, pin-up, whatever…'

'Cheers!' He flashed the grin again. 'Yeah,' he nodded. 'I get that, and Renée said, with your dad being a lot older, and like, *married*, and stuff, she thinks there's a massive head-fuck going on there. For you, with the age gap, I mean…'

'Maybe.' I didn't expect to hear Jeremiah talking about my dad like that. It had always been the great unspoken thing in our family. Mum had an affair with a married man and after she told him she was pregnant with me, he'd gone right back to being very married again. Right until the day my grandmother died, she was only just about on speaking terms with Mum. Everyone seemed to have something like that, lurking in the branches of their family tree. Kim's older brother was gay. Her parents told everyone he was this ambitious bachelor, too career-driven to settle down. 'He settled down ages ago with a guy called Sam from Boston,' Kim told me. 'I guess they think if they wait it out long enough, maybe Troy'll trade Sam in for a nice, respectable Samantha, one day...'

'And,' Jeremiah looked more comfortable now, 'you and the kid's dad? Your boyfriend? She reckons you're kind of, like, working through your own father-issues.' He monitored my expression. 'I'm not saying that's how it is or anything,' he backtracked. 'That's just something Renée mentioned a couple of times. No offence. But,' he grinned. 'I think she's brilliant, your mum. Her mind's like,' he gazed off into the distance, folding his legs beneath him. 'She's like an ocean of,' he searched. 'Frozen truth.'

'Weird. That's what I've always said…'

'Really? Oh, right. Renée said you sometimes repress anger through sarcasm.'

I'd forgotten how annoying it was having Mum captioning my every moment. Especially to him. I'd felt like some sort of case study growing up. One that, from the looks of things, Jeremiah had labelled: *Handle with Care.*

'The thing is.' He unfolded his legs, resting his elbows on top of his knees. 'I've sort of said it before, but to be absolutely straight with you, I'm in love with your mum. Look at this.' He jumped from the couch, halfway upstairs, shouting me to follow, before I had a chance to leave the lounge.

He was like some sort of springbok, bouncing around one minute, horizon-gazing the next, I decided.

'It's basically an installation. She's been looking at it for months.' He turned in a full-circle flourish. 'Tracked it down to this artist in California. And,' he pulled his phone from the pocket of, for once, relatively normal, grey trousers, 'this is the writing desk.' He showed me a picture of a wooden desk with a rounded, leather seat. 'I thought that was them, delivering it, when you arrived.'

'She'll love it.'

'Do you think?'

'Of course she will.' I looked over at the marble-effect wall in shades of blue and silver. 'Who wouldn't?' It was Mum's dreamscape. I knew it.

'Yeah.' He bit down on a grin, fastening away excitement. 'Let's do this more often, hey?' He stood, hands outstretched. 'You love her. I love her,' he said. 'Is that too much? I dunno.' He gripped his bearded jawline. 'It is kind of awkward, isn't it?'

'Only if you make it that way. At least, that's what everyone keeps telling me,' I said, as Jeremiah noticed me noticing the tattoo on his arm.

'My tatt? Yeah, I know.' He shook his head. 'Your mum told me not to do it, but,' he pulled the arm of his t-shirt up over his bicep: *Renée*, 'it feels right though, you know?' he explained. 'Like, this way, she's always there. Right under my skin, the whole time.

'Try being her daughter. You get that for free…'

'Ah, the sarcasm again,' he pointed out. 'Tattoo a bit much?'

I smiled and nodded.

'You will visit her, won't you?'

He was springboking again.

'Are you kidding? She'll be inviting me over straightaway. Dying to show off her new headquarters.'

'No,' he said. 'I mean, L.A. You'll love it. I do!' He was off again. 'Have you been? I couldn't believe it when Renée said she'd never been.' He morphed into surfer-pose, jumping side-on, negotiating an invisible wave. 'City of Angels, baby!'

'*L.A?*'

'Ah,' he stopped. 'That makes sense,' he deduced, chewing on his thumb. 'She hasn't told you yet…'

'*Tell me.*'

'*The Badge.* I'm filming a pilot over there. My character, Archer, he's really complicated, right? Like, he's this really artistic guy. Grows hydroponic plants, rescues a dog, total loner, that kind of thing. Anyway, he's bit tortured but cool. Really cool,' he explained. 'Going to have to lose my locks. But, you know, them's the breaks.'

'So,' I was trying not to freak out. 'Back to Mum?'

'Oh, yeah.' He snapped back to the point. 'The thing is, I've got a rental.'

'A rental?'

'Sunken Jacuzzi. Japanese garden. California-King-size bed with built-in Facetime and surround…'

'She's going to L.A? What about her show? What about this place?'

'Only for three months. They're going to hook her up. ISDN, or something. And it's brilliant, right, 'cos they're going to syndicate it. See if it gets picked up. She's not too bothered, I don't think. She's going to write, she said. She's already got contacts out there. Think she's planning on staying busy. The woman amazes me.' He let out a long whistle, his legs spread like a Musketeer.

'So, the whole thing's happening? She's actually doing this without saying a word to anyone?' And by anyone, I obviously meant her one-and-only daughter.

'It's not like, forever…' he clarified, trailing off. 'That's why she's storing some of my furniture. I'm renting my place out, but it depends on what happens with the show. Your mum thinks it'll be massive. She's the one who read the script. Told me I had to do it. She's got great instincts…'

Except maternal ones, I thought, as Jeremiah leapt back into action with the ring of the doorbell.

Chapter Thirty-Nine: Old Friends

'Parcel for you here, Ella!' Karen-From-Reception handed over a glossy gift bag tied up with a long, black ribbon. She gave me a curious look. 'Posh one an' all.'

Once I noticed the picture of the corseted gazelle, spilling out of her lacey cups on the cover, the lipstick-blot logo on the tag, I had a pretty good idea where it had come from, and I had every intention of sending it straight back to the warehouse.

'Just so you know,' Karen said, her desk uncharacteristically free from chocolate biscuits, cup-a-soup and multipacks of choux buns. 'Today's my last day...'

'I didn't know you were leaving.'

'I thought it was the right time,' she gave a pointed look, 'with everything that's gone on...'

'Oh, look. Forget about that, it won't go any further...'

'*Karen!*' Harry Collins spun through the doors, gripping his man-bag.

'*Harry!*' She got to her feet, wrapping her cardigan across her ample chest.

'Don't do this for me!' He gripped the desk. 'Don't leave because I left!'

'Oh Harry, for goodness' sake!' she snapped. 'Stop causing a scene!'

'I can't live without you, Karen! I told her.' He threw a furtive look in my direction. 'My wife. I told her everything! I told her I'm in love with you. She said I'm all yours!'

No wonder, I thought, noticing his ruddy little cheeks, the desperation in his eyes, and from the look on her face, Karen-

From-Reception had started to feel the same way. 'Harry,' she pointed a dangerously sharp, diamante-encrusted talon at him. 'I'll not let you do this to me, not anymore! Three years of loving you. Three years of waiting and hoping!' She looked close to tears. 'I'll not let you make it four. I've met someone.' Harry shut his eyes in defeat. 'Someone who takes me out in public. Calls to say goodnight. Says he loves me, and not only as he ejaculates —'

'Urgh…' I clasped my hand over my mouth.

'And he most certainly doesn't have a wife, Harry Collins!' she bellowed. 'From now on, you can order your own bloody stationery. And post your false promises right up your backside. *First class!*'

'Oh, come on!' Bryony broke into a smile, taking my hand, keeping it semi-business-like. 'This is absolutely cray-cray!'

'Do you two know each other?'

'Bryony's Grace and Ethan's mum.'

'Oh, yes. I see.' Audrey extended her hand. 'Lovely to meet you.' She took her seat. 'Saul.' She gave a curt nod from behind her desk.

I'd been dreading seeing him again, not only because I'd run out on his personal lingerie fantasy, but because, since then, Audrey had explained that Eric was still undecided on whether to go with us or Heather Constantine's company. The final decision was all down to Saul.

'Audrey.' Saul was back to being his professional, department-store heir alter-ego. 'Nice to see you. As ever…'

'So.' Audrey returned his handshake. 'Bartholomews' plans on stocking the *Toned by Bryony Maloney* range?'

'I've been collaborating with Bryony over the last few months,' Saul explained. I remembered her mentioning some important potential Buyer while we were at the zoo. 'Her collection's a big part of our revised strategy.'

'Saul's father is a friend of my husband.' Bryony rolled her eyes. 'Golfing buddies.'

I tried not to think about the damage Vic's stilettos must be doing to The Green, or vice versa.

'At Stringwood?' Audrey brightened. 'That's where my James plays.'

'Oh!' Bryony put up her hand and leaned across the desk, offering a bemused-looking Audrey a high-five. 'Golf widows of the world unite.'

'As the range is very much at the forefront of this new drive on Bartholomews' behalf,' Saul continued. 'I wanted Bryony to accompany me today. It's important she feels her collection has found the right home —'

'Ella,' Bryony interrupted. 'The deal's yours.' She turned to Saul. 'You should've seen the birthday party she threw for my daughter. Believe me,' she turned to Audrey. 'This girl can handle anything.' She winked.

The meeting wrapped up just before lunch. I led Bryony and Saul to the door, until he suddenly stopped: 'Ella, have you got a moment?' He was giving me that look again. Erasing my brain cells one second at a time. 'I wondered if you had those templates ready?'

'The new web-stuff?' Leah piped up from behind her computer before I could lie and get him to leave. 'Yeah, they're ready. I think Matt put them in the stationery cupboard.'

'Well,' Audrey said, once our guests had left. She looked at her hand like she'd recently discovered it. 'Don't think that could've gone much better, do you?'

'Audrey?' I knew I had to speak up now or forever hold Saul's peace. 'You know I've been totally onboard with retaining Bartholomews' account and everything? Well.' I had no idea how to put it. I had absolutely no intention of telling my boss I'd been involved in some kind of corporate mating-ritual with the son of our biggest client. 'I can't continue on the account…'

Saul had followed me into the stationery cupboard. I'd kept my back to him, exploring shelves, chatting gibberish to keep him at bay, until his hands found my waist, his voice in my ear, suggesting we do things in there that I doubt Harry and Karen had ever dreamt up in their entire three years together, including a very creative idea involving my new lingerie and the laminating machine.

Audrey clasped her hands. 'Go on?'

'I really don't see eye-to-eye with Saul Bartholomew.'

More like thigh-to-thigh! Wicked Whisper chuckled, back to his usual sex-obsessed self.

'Really?' She looked thoughtful. 'Well, that must be a first for Saul…'

It was.

He'd looked at me as if I was insane when I'd told him I wasn't interested.

'Ella?' He had whipped out the whole stroking-the-cheekbone move again. 'You can feel it. I know you can. It's inevitable, Ella. Don't let this moment pass. I can't think straight. There's something between us.'

'Yes, there is,' I'd told him. 'He's called Dan and he's my boyfriend. That's what's between us, Saul. So please stop acting all sexy all the time. And please don't send me any more knickers!'

Audrey went quiet for a second and finally asked: 'Brunch on the balcony?'

I nodded, too stunned to speak.

'A quick visit to the, erm,' she closed her diary. '*Manufacturers?*'

'How do you —?'

Her clipped smile told me everything.

'Had a lucky escape myself,' she told me, voice lowered. 'Can't say I wasn't bloody tempted, must admit. Wait until he sends you the underwear. Perfect fit…'

'Guess what?' Leah ushered me into the kitchen. 'Me and Matt are going to Alaska!'

'Oh, you and Matt?' I was grabbing a breakfast bar for lunch. 'You and Matt who haven't officially told me you're dating, yet?'

'Oh, like you told me about you and that Saul fella?' I gave her a blank look. 'We're going for a month!'

'A month?'

'Touring around the National Parks. We're going to see the Brown Bears!'

'Does Audrey know?'

'Not yet.' Leah placed her hands on her hips. 'Do you think she'll go mad?'

'No, but that means I'll get lumbered with covering all your stuff, so *I* might.'

'Has anyone seen my daughter?' I was disorientated for a second as my mother wandered in, acting as though she could usually be found hanging around the staffroom of a lunch-time. 'She visits my boyfriend,' she told Leah. 'Doesn't so much as return a phone call to her own mother. Don't worry.'

She must've noticed my expression. 'I'm not stopping. Jeremiah's in the car. We're on our way to buy a Futon.'

Leah made excuses, taking that as her cue to leave.

'So, Jeremiah's told you about L.A?'

'Oh, yeah.' I'd almost forgotten. Somewhere between not being with Dan; almost being seduced by a Brazilian department store owner; Kim being pregnant, and working non-stop to keep an office roof over my head, Mum's latest, glamorous news had temporarily escaped me.

'I'm not being made to feel guilty —'

'Good. I don't want you to feel guilty. I want you to go.'

'You do?'

I think it was the first time in my life, apart from that one time I admitted to watching porn, I'd managed to shock her.

'Well,' she said, slightly suspicious. 'I know you don't approve of —'

'Jeremiah? He's great.'

'He is?'

'Isn't that what you've been trying to tell me?' I unwrapped my cereal bar. 'Let's face it, Mum. What's the alternative? Dating someone your own age? Calling it *Companionship*? Can't quite imagine you settling for something that practical. What would you do? Visit obscure tourist attractions? Buy postcards of derelict mines with some middle-aged man, with a middle-aged name, drinking soup from a flask?'

'Exactly!' Mum said. 'And believe me, you don't know how accurate that description is, darling. Jeremiah said you'd bonded. I wanted to check the feeling was mutual, before I got my hopes up. So,' here came her turn to surprise me. 'Dan? The almost-engagement? And then this mysterious client you find so alluring?'

'How do you —' I managed through a mouthful of frosted flakes.

'Bryony told me about Dan,' she said. 'Between you and me, she's going to be coming to me for some counselling. Confidentially,' she paused for emphasis. 'She's been having a few problems with that husband of hers. Then I called Kim.'

I groaned at the mention of own best friend, betraying me.

'She was worried about you. And,' she grinned. 'How exciting about her move back to California! We're all going to meet up over there. Me and Jeremiah. Her and Ben.'

'Hello, there!' Audrey walked in, cup in hand. 'You must be Ella's mother. So pleased to meet you.' I swear, Audrey almost curtsied. 'Huge fan of the show,' she went on. 'Listen every week.' Did she? She hadn't mentioned it. 'In fact, I, er,' she flinched at little as she looked at me. 'I actually called and spoke to you once, a couple of months back.'

'Oh?' Mum was in her element. She loved meeting her fans, especially when I was there to witness it. 'Really? Well, thank you. The show? What was…?'

'Oh, it's silly really,' Audrey seemed a little flustered, self-consciously vague. '*Keeping the Love Alive*, was it?'

One of the Digital triplets, not Leah's one, came in to retrieve his lunchbox.

'*Keeping the*..?' Mum pondered. 'Oh yes! The sex toys!'

Digital boy developed mental myopia, leaving what he pretended to be an empty kitchen as quickly as possible. Meanwhile, I insisted on taking Audrey's cup and loading up the dishwasher. Confirming my mother's observation, I realised, that in times of high stress, I reached for the detergent.

'One in particular, actually,' Audrey muttered, words barely audible. Yet they rang inside my ears like church bells. 'That … Pulveriser thing?'

'Ah,' Mum laughed. 'Yes. That's Ella's favourite too, according to her flat mate. They've barely got a battery left for the doorbell.'

Chapter Forty: Newly Bilingual

The morning of the Avington Food & Drink Festival arrived a little earlier than planned. Audrey called at five-thirty. The Decadent Delicatessen couldn't make it. Their baby was arriving well ahead of schedule. The owner's brother was turning up any minute to unload stock and a business partner was getting in from Birmingham at about 10 o'clock to take over, which in layman's terms meant it was all down to me to retain their fee and set up shop. I sat up, still in bed, trying to negotiate, mouth glued by sleep. Maybe his brother could handle things? But five-a-side football was at the start of the season, Audrey explained. The stall-owner had been quite insistent, because didn't they pay Steen & Heard to manage exactly this kind of thing?

By ten-thirty I was out in Avington Square. Everything from Artisan chutney to bite-size oatmeal crackers had been unloaded and there was still no sign of the business partner.

'I've left him a voicemail. Told him you're manning the fort. I'd love to help out myself,' Audrey said, 'but I really should be using today as a networking tool...'

Unless she was networking with the guy who'd just pulled up in the Candy Floss van, I didn't know exactly who Audrey was planning on meeting with.

'He's definitely on his way, isn't he? I can't do this all day.'

'Oh no, no! Of course not.' Audrey tilted a jar of lemon curd to a more intriguing angle. 'I've put a call in to the husband. Explained the situation. No joy as of yet, I'm afraid. Not that we can expect too much, not with him at the hospital.' She glanced at her watch. 'Tell you what. I'll grab us a coffee while you display those cheeses. Lady Mayoress is due any minute…'

Not only was it freezing that morning, but as soon as I'd put the cheeses out, placing them under a glass dome I thought Audrey would approve of, it began to rain. A portly man, who I prayed was the business partner from Birmingham, approached me, fishing his glasses from the end of a neck cord, clipboard in hand.

'Excuse me, young lady.' He peered over his reactor-lights. 'That's a breach.'

'That?' I rearranged the label at the end of a strategically placed cocktail stick. 'Oh, I think you mean *brie*?'

'Breach!' He pointed a pen in the direction of the cheese. 'Food hygiene breach.' He tapped his clipboard with the butt of his biro. 'No apron.' He used the pen as he recited his checklist. 'No hair net.' He assessed me like some life-threatening specimen. 'And, no.' He scribbled. 'Disposable gloves.'

I took my hand off a small wheel of ginger-infused cheddar.

'The thing is, I'm just helping out. The —'

'Well, if you're helping out.' He rolled forward onto his toes and produced a plastic-wrapped pack from the depths of a nylon bag. 'Let's make sure you don't become a hindrance to food hygiene,' he said. 'Follow the instructions and you'll comply with UK regulations.'

He ticked off his checklist as I applied hand sanitiser. I searched for Audrey in the crowd as I pulled on thin blue plastic gloves with a matching plastic apron. Finally, the dreaded hair net, which looked like something your great-grandmother might've used for contraception.

'Oh, smashing!' Audrey appeared a few minutes after Captain Clipboard had gone on his way. 'Don't you look the part?'

Part of what? I thought. A fertility clinic?

All I needed was a white coat, some goggles and a pair of Crocs.

'There you go,' she handed me a takeout coffee. 'That ought to warm you up.'

I never thought coffee could be so depressing.

I couldn't even look at a disposable cup without thinking of Dan.

The love of my life made biodegradable.

'Any news?'

'The brother's on his way. Only thing is, he's reached a bit of a stop-start on the M40,' Audrey mock-whispered, diverting my attention from the wonders of the Continental meat platter. 'Can't see him making it 'til at least eleven-ish, realistically. Anyway,' she said. 'Told him we'd muddle on...'

'Excuse me?' Captain Clipboard was back, pen in hand. 'You are going to change those gloves once you've finished with that coffee, I take it? Transferable bacteria, you see.' He noticed Audrey, his expression softening as her famous trilby-and-coat combo worked their magic.

'How awful,' Audrey agreed. 'Can't have that.'

'Well, no. Exactly.' He teetered on the edge of an actual smile. 'There was one case.' He sidled up to her. 'One minute, everything was right as rain at an unregulated buffet. The next.' He clicked his fingers. '*Listeria.*'

By the time midday arrived, I'd resigned myself to spending the afternoon in the rain, chopping pork pies into quarters, pouring organic cordial into polystyrene cups, and hoping I'd be struck dead by lightning as soon as possible. What I hadn't banked on was not being able to use the bathroom all morning. On the bright side, at least Captain Clipboard had made sure everything I had on was waterproof.

'Audrey?' I waved her over, spotting her perusing the Real Ale stand.

She waved back, a couple pushing a pram making their way alongside her. She handed a shopping bag over to James Steen, who peered inside and gave an appreciative nod.

'Ella, how're you getting on? No more news, I'm afraid.' She pulled a face, brandishing her mobile as the pram came to a halt, steered by a man I assumed was Peter, Audrey's sort-of step-son. A pretty blonde woman linked his arm, both of them offering polite hellos. 'This is who I've been telling you all about. This is baby Shoshanna.' Audrey gazed, clearly besotted, down into the pram. 'And these are her parents. James' son, Peter, and his wife, Joanna.'

I smiled at the baby, her tiny, rose-blush face frowning in sleep, one mittened hand striking out in a fist as James Steen approached.

'Ella, isn't it? Audrey said you were going above and beyond for us today.' He held out his hand, which I briefly took, hoping the weirdo with the clipboard hadn't noticed I was still wearing my hygiene glove at the time. 'Congratulations on the new role. Sure you'll do a cracking job. Although,' he said, with a faint trace of amusement. 'Audrey tells me how much you remind her of herself at your age, which I'm not entirely sure is any great cause for recommendation...'

'And this kind of chit-chat is exactly why James is now banned from the office.' Audrey playfully pursed her lips and examined her phone, distracted as ever.

'We're going to head over to that organic stall, Dad,' Peter said.

'Been hearing fab things about coconut oil,' Joanna explained. 'I'm dying to give it a go.'

'My friend, Kim, swears by it,' I told her. 'Cooks with it. Puts it on her skin, everything.'

'Told you,' Joanna said to Peter.

'Come on then,' James said. 'Let's wheel ourselves over to the coconut shy.'

'Catch you up in five,' Audrey told them.

'Say goodbye to Grandma.' Peter gazed at his sleeping daughter, before the group headed off with a quick, 'Nice to meet you!'

'*Grandma*,' Audrey said. 'Gets me every time. Finally had a text response,' she said. 'Good news: the brother's less than half an hour away.'

'Brilliant!' I said, 'but, I was going to ask a favour? I really need the bathroom.' I squished my knees together. 'Would you be okay to stand in for five minutes?'

I pulled off the gloves and untied the apron.

'What the…?' Audrey gazed past me. 'Is that?'

'Have you seen her?' Leah, Chief Photographer for the day, ran over. 'She's put it all over Twitter.'

'What's all over Twitter?' I asked, stepping out from behind the counter.

'*DEAR GOD!*' Audrey gasped.

Heather Constantine suddenly appeared, parting the crowds, a herd of followers trailing behind her. She led the pack, megaphone to her lips: '*Bosom Buddies are best for business! Bosom Buddies are best for business!*' Which was distracting enough, but even more distracting were the fake plastic boobs they'd strapped to their chests.

'Excuse me! Excuse me!' Audrey marched past gaping festival-goers, turning their children away. She flagged Heather down. 'Kindly remove yourself from this family-friendly festival!'

'I've every right to be here, campaigning against businesses that don't support women,' Heather boomed out through the megaphone as the surrounding stalls slowed to a halt. 'Where are the breast-feeding facilities?'

'Over there, actually,' Audrey pointed towards our dedicated Mother & Baby area. 'Despite the lack of over-priced merchandise or representation from you, everyone here is a *Breast Friend…*'

Captain Clipboard reappeared, this time with a council-branded baseball cap and his very own megaphone: 'Cover your breasts and please leave this festival immediately!'

'My breasts are covered, you idiot!' Heather sneered. 'This is a peaceful protest on behalf of breast-feeding mothers.'

'What this is,' Captain Clipboard did his little toe-roll again, 'is a food festival. Not a topless Mardi Gras. In my official capacity, I'm instructing you and your friends to cover yourselves,' he reached for Heather's coat, 'and be on your way!'

'Get your hands off my breasts!' Heather ordered.

'Get your breasts out of my borough!'

'Heather?' Leah shouted, snapping a picture as she stood, red-faced and bare-chested. 'Put them away, love! You're making a right tit of yourself!'

Once I got out from behind the stall the festival didn't seem all that bad. In fact, I couldn't quite believe our little agency had made all of it happen. The rain finally stopped and sunshine rolled out as I noticed an oversized monkey's head wobbling on top of a unicycle and realised Monsieur Monkey had made a full recovery.

Back on slightly muddy ground, small children sat on top of their parents' shoulders. Pram handles swung with shopping bags, weighed down by locally sourced, gluten-free, organically grown produce. Assorted walking boots and raincoats made their way across Avington Square and onto the surrounding lawns. Squelching footprints and threads of conversation flowed through the air.

The line for the Portaloos ground to a halt as families waited, pacified by rucksacked mums offering uplifting observations, wet wipes and hastily unwrapped lollipops.

'Dad said you're not old enough to go by yourself. When I was your age I still had to go in with Mum.'

'But I don't want to use the *Ladies* one.'

'Well, Dad's not here.'

I heard their voices before I spotted them.

'Get off me, Grace!'

'Pack it in, Ethan!'

Ethan swung loose, yanking away from the grip and glare of his sister. A few shoulders ahead in the queue, their attention quickly fell on me as he came to an embarrassed stop.

'He's being really *babyish* today,' Grace explained, as Ethan stared at his shoes.

'Hey, Ethan,' I grinned. 'Did you see Monsieur Monkey over there?'

'Yeah. He's a bit rubbish now…'

'Have you got a stall here?' Grace took hold of her brother's hand.

'Yes, but it's not mine,' I said. 'I'm just helping out.'

'What have you got on your stall?'

'Erm, cheese, things like that.'

They both looked unimpressed. Ethan covered a yawn.

'Yeah, not the most exciting of things. Not for you two, anyway…'

'Do you have to keep that thing on your head the whole time?'

I reached up and pulled the hairnet I'd completely forgotten about from over my ponytail. 'Not the whole time. Only when I want to look a complete dork in front of people I know.' I stuffed the white net into my jeans. 'Who're you here with?'

'Janelle and Lucas. They just got picked up. Dad's waiting for us in the car. Ethe needed to go the loo first...'

The children were happy to let me jump the queue once I'd explained how I'd spent the last hour almost cross-eyed.

'Go on, Ethan,' Grace instructed, as I stepped down from the cubicle. 'Your turn. And hurry up,' she said. 'Dad's waiting for us, remember?'

'Urgh,' Ethan scrunched his face. 'But I don't wanna smell Ella's poo-poo smell.' He broke into a grin.

'Don't you dare be so disgusting!' Grace called, as he clambered up the steps. 'And make sure you wash your hands, you little germ-bag! Sorry about that,' she said. 'He's been showing off all day. So, you liked the flowers then?'

'Loved them,' I said. 'I've been looking after Kim. She's preg—'

'Look, Ella, I don't hate you or anything. I mean.' She glanced up at the bathroom door. 'It's just stupid, because everyone gets on everyone's nerves sometimes. You just,' she stared off into the distance. 'You always used to act like, if I was pissed off, it had to be about you. But *it wasn't*. Not the whole time. That used to bug me, because I have got my own life, outside of Dad's place, you know?' She flashed me a look. 'So, I did like you, okay?' she said. 'And so did Ethan. And Dad obviously does. I already said, I was sorry for being a big bitch. Mum said the least I should do was send you flowers after you did my party. But I chose them. I got them with my own birthday money. So, if you did ever want to come back, I wouldn't mind. I mean, I'd like it. We all would.' She looked at me now. 'It's nicer with you there. Dad was happy, and … yeah,' she admitted. 'It was nicer. For us. For all of us.'

The cubicle door flung open, Ethan clattering down the steps, eager to get going.

'And, by the way, my best-friend, Janelle really wants you to do her birthday. I told her you do this professionally.' She gestured around the park like her usual child-woman-in-training self. 'Her mum said she'd pay, but it can't be a thing like mine was, okay?'

Ethan suddenly leapt from between us. 'Dad!'

He dashed off in the direction of Dan, who slowed his pace as he spotted me. Starky lurched forward, panting on the end of his lead. I watched as Dan headed towards us in his blue jeans and the oversized sweat top I used to borrow. Ethan was catching up to him, while I imagined how I'd feel if we ever became strangers.

'FYI? I already know you and Dad had a fight.' Grace kept one eye on her father. 'Dad was playing it down, but it doesn't take a genius to work that one out.' She gave one of her mother's trademark eye-rolls. 'And it's shitty on Starky. Living between two homes like that. I mean, at least kids understand. It's gotta be worse for a dog?'

Dan walked up. He took hold of Grace's chin and gave it a wiggle.

'I thought you said you'd be back in the car ten minutes ago? Ella.' He attempted a smile. Starky was already jumping up at my legs, and stuff Captain Clipboard, because I couldn't resist a quick scrumple of his ear. 'I only came to pick up the kids.'

'Ethe was messing around. Then we saw Ella,' Grace explained. 'There was a big queue, Dad.'

'You've got to behave for your sister.' Dan squatted down, Ethan-sized. 'You have to stick together in a crowd. I told you. It's easy to get lost.'

'Ella's working here,' Grace said.

'Selling cheese,' Ethan explained. 'She has to wear this net thing on her head.'

'I do,' I said. Dan stood up, grinning broadly, knowing how much I'd hate anything like that. 'I've been roped into manning a Deli stall. I have to get back, actually.' I realised, without a hair net, there was a good chance Audrey might've been air-lifted into solitary confinement by now. 'It was a nice surprise, seeing you both.'

'Likewise!' Grace spoke with the assurance of the newly bilingual, practicing speaking Grown Up. 'Thanks for putting up with Ethan.'

'I never have to put up with you, do I, Ethan?' I couldn't resist combing my hand across the top of his head, as he gazed at a trailing kite.

'Love the boots, Grace.'

'Mum brought them back from Australia.'

'Anyway,' I gave Starky a final stroke and took a few steps back. 'Enjoy the festival.'

'Hey,' Dan said. 'Thanks for watching these two.'

'You don't have to thank me.' I shielded my eyes from the sun.

'Remember what I said?' Grace called, looking hopeful.

'I will. I promise. Better get back to work,' I shouted. 'I've got people lining up to sample my cheese cubes...'

'I bet you have…' Dan smirked.

'Oh, by the way.' I turned back, a few metres away. 'Dan? It was good to see you too.'

'Yeah? Well, it was great seeing you.' Starky sat at his feet, looking over. 'Just wish I'd caught a look at you in that hair net…'

I carried on walking, hoping he'd still be standing there as I turned back.

'Aren't you going to go?' I grinned. 'I'm working.'

'I might just stay here. Hoping you'll turn around, come back…'

I carried on towards the stalls, smiling to myself. Before I got back on cheese duty, the three of them, four if you included Starky, ran over and ground to a sudden halt.

'Go on!' Grace gave her dad's hand a squeeze.

'Grace said I should go after you…'

'Uh.' She shook her head. 'Don't *tell her* that! Right.' She sighed. 'You still like her, don't you, Dad?' Dan laughed. 'And Ella still likes *you*,' she announced. 'So, go on!' She pulled at his sleeve. 'Can't you ever be just a little bit romantic? Tell her! Kiss her or something!'

Ethan laughed, grinning up at us, as Dan tightened his grip on Starky's lead.

'Well, Grace's right. We can't leave here without you, can we? The girl I love, selling cheese? C'mon,' Dan offered me his hand. 'Let's make a run for it.'

A NOTE TO THE READER

Dear Reader,

Thank you so much for reading GIRLFRIEND, INTERRUPTED! I hope you enjoyed spending time with Ella as much as I enjoyed navigating her world.

I often get asked how much of my storylines or characters are based on real-life situations. I can say for the first time, while I'm relieved no specific incidents influenced the story, the stepfamily-theme was inspired by personal experience.

In my mid-twenties, while my friends were still casually dating guys whose biggest commitment was gym membership, I became a fledgling step-girlfriend. I knew, one day, I'd love to share those dynamics in fiction, and do my bit to take the 'wicked' away from step-parent. They say it takes a village to raise a child, and as our perceptions of family continue to be redefined by all of us, I hope I've respectfully represented everyone who ever loved a new bud on their family tree.

And I hope I made you smile, because that's the real joy of being a Romantic-Comedy novelist, though, I'm much more comfortable thinking of my books as Com-Roms, than Rom-Coms. Hearing from my readers is a real honour. It's fascinating and incredibly motivating when you share the ways my books have entertained you. The fact I get to share my stories continues to put a smile on my face, so the least I can do is return the favour.

If you'd like to join the GIRLFRIEND, INTERRUPTED discussion, please share a review on my **Amazon** or **Goodreads** pages. You can also find me on **Facebook**, or follow me on **Twitter**. To fully delve into the Caliskaniverse, make your way over to **www.patriciacaliskanauthor.com**.

You'll find me there, working on my next book. I'm always grateful for a happy distraction, so make yourself at home, take a look around, and most of all, thank you. It's always lovely to hear from you, and as long as you keep reading, I get to keep on writing. Until next time…

Muchos Gracias,

Patricia X

Sapere Books is an exciting new publisher of brilliant fiction and popular history.

To find out more about our latest releases and our monthly bargain books visit our website: **saperebooks.com**

www.ingramcontent.com/pod-product-compliance
Lightning Source LLC
Chambersburg PA
CBHW021231060726
47590CB00005B/1726